THE OTHER SIDE OF GREED

THE SEVEN SINS, #5

LILY ZANTE

AUTHOR'S NOTE

The Other Side of Greed is the fifth book in **The Seven Sins,** a contemporary romance series of steamy, angsty and emotional stories featuring characters who are loosely connected.

All books in this series are STANDALONE but loosely connected.

Other books in the series:

Underdog (prequel)
The Wrath of Eli
The Problem with Lust
The Lies of Pride
The Price of Inertia
The Other Side of Greed

Sign up for my newsletter and get a FREE book:
https://www.lilyzante.com/news

PROLOGUE

Twenty years ago ...

BRANDON

"Take me with you," Kane begs.

"I can't. The lady said it's just me for now." I'm crying inside because I have to show him I'm strong. I'm his older brother and I've got this. Kane hugs me, throwing his skinny little hands around me, like a wretched rat hanging on to a sinking ship.

"Come on, now, Brandon." The lady from the home walks over to take my hand, but I'm not ready to go. I will never be ready to go, not like this.

Kane wails. "Don't go! Don't leave me."

"Kane," she says harshly. "Move away. Your brother has to go."

"I don't want him to go." His sobs shoot a round of bullets

through me. I can't listen to this and walk away. I've never walked away. He is all I've got, and I am all he's got.

I hug him tightly. "I'll come back for you, okay? I promise."

"Brandon." The woman's voice is stern. "You need to come with me NOW."

I give Kane the biggest hug of my life. Life is cruel. It's never been fair for the likes of us. "I'll come back for you, little buddy." I kiss his head, he tilts his face upwards, looking at me with wet, soppy, sad eyes. My heart breaks into a million pieces.

"Step away before I—" The woman tries to pry Kane's hands off my body, but he doesn't give an inch. Instead, he kicks her. Hard. The sound of his boot smacking her shin is loud enough to make me wince. I felt that. She wails, reaching down to rub her leg. "You little—"

Two others grab my little brother. He's so small and skinny, powerless to fight them off. They grab him like he's a convict. "Come here you little shit. Don't even think of trying anything."

"Brandon! Brandon!" he cries, as they drag him away, a tiny nine year old.

"I'll come back for you. I'll find you, I promise," I yell. My insides fracture as he is taken, kicking and screaming, away. It's the last vision I have of him.

When he disappears, I fall apart. My body shuddering as I howl, my sorrow twisting and tearing me to pieces.

"Wipe your face." The woman shoves a tissue in my face. "You can't meet your new family looking like that."

CHAPTER ONE

BRANDON

"The scent of money is intoxicating." I hang up the phone and mimic a chef's kiss. "Another deal done." I savor the glow of warmth that spreads through me. There is nothing more satisfying than sealing another deal.

It's better than sex.

"We should celebrate." Neville, my lawyer, shuts his briefcase and looks hopeful. Because this deal has put another couple of million dollars into my coffers, he expects that I will celebrate with an expensive meal in one of Chicago's finest restaurants.

Ordinarily, I would, but I have other plans. "Jessica is expecting me at the art gallery. I should show my face."

Neville raises an eyebrow. "Are you dating yet, or are you still keeping this purely platonic?"

I pull at my shirt cuffs. "We're good friends, for now."

"Still just good friends? You disappoint me, Brandon. You've been sniffing around her long enough."

"I don't sniff, Neville." And certainly not around someone like Jessica Montrose. A socialite and an art gallery owner, she is smart, polished, rich and powerful, all thanks to her father who once operated a hedge fund in the city.

I have recently taken over Hawks Enterprises, a conglomerate which my father founded many decades ago. He has recently retired due to ailing health—heart surgery has taken its toll—and he has passed the mantle to me. While I have enjoyed not being in the limelight—and I still prefer to fly under the radar—the idea of having this much power and wealth is overwhelming.

I have my eye on Jessica because she is perfect wife material. It's one reason why I haven't jumped into bed with her yet. I want to take things slowly. I'm taking them so slowly that I haven't even made it to first base yet. I'm not inspired to. There's no chemistry, *yet*. She's ... polished. Good for me and my brand. The perfect trophy wife.

"We'll celebrate another time, then. A five-million-dollar deal is nothing to be taken lightly, even for someone like you."

"Some other time," I tell him, glancing at my watch. I want to go home and shower before I go to the art gallery.

Neville rises slowly, as if his portly and round body is too heavy for his knees. His jowls hang around his neck, giving him a St. Bernard Dog air. His love of red wine, blue cheese and rich foods have no doubt helped.

He gets rich off of people like me but he lacks the killer instinct that I have, which is why he's a lawyer charging me by the hour, and why I'm where I am. Making deals, and obscene amounts of money, being driven by the urge and greed to possess, these things run in my blood.

Strange, because that wasn't how my life started.

While I also like the finer things in life like fine dining, thousand dollar bottles of wine and whiskey, and watching sunsets from my private jet, making money is what truly makes me happy. Amassing *things,* possessions, properties.

Emma, my PA, who is smarter and sharper than I give her credit for, notices that my newfound interest in Jessica has a similar trait to my desire to own things. "She's not a building or a commodity, Brandon," she said to me when Jessica first came on the scene, "she's not a 'thing' that you can own or possess; she's a person." I beg to differ. People, like things, can be bought, and owned and possessed. I believe that after much wining and dining, and whisking away on exotic holidays, after gifting her expensive trinkets, and clothes, and accessories, there will come such a time.

My lawyer grabs his briefcase by the handle and swings it off the table, then pauses.

"Greenways. Have you given it some thought?" His greedy little eyes settle on me awaiting orders for my next project. A fun project, I think, before I step into the limelight as Philip Hawks' successor.

"I have."

Neville cocks his head expectantly. "Care to share your plans with me?"

Greenways is a plot of land I am interested in acquiring. It's a prime piece of real estate even if, to the unknowing eye, it looks like an eyesore. Once ignored and forgotten, the area is slowly becoming gentrified—due to money being pumped into the infrastructure in the surrounding areas.

It will be worth a hell of a lot in years to come. Naturally, I want it. My contact, Charlie Stagg, in the city's planning and development department, is available to help as and when needed. The land presently houses a few factories and stores and it's just a matter of getting business owners to move. The problem is, getting them to move isn't easy; they're stubborn, but Stagg can help us.

Reaching out to them in the hopes of coming to some sort of financial agreement isn't going to work. I've seen other companies fail. I've come up with another strategy—which Charlie will help to facilitate by designating Greenways to be a redevelopment project area due to blight. Then the city can rehabilitate it later.

'Later' is when Hawks Enterprises will be given the contracts to build new condos. We'll make a shitload of money in the process.

"I told you, I want to try another way," I tell Neville.

When Neville's thick caterpillar brows meet angrily in the middle, I try to assure him. "Don't look so worried, Neville. I've got this."

"That's what I'm worried about." Neville's brain has short-circuited, and he seems to have forgotten who I am. When I broached this idea with him before, albeit briefly, he didn't sound so eager.

"You are crazy to think you can change Kyra Lewis's mind."

"Shhhh." I hold my finger to my lips. I scratch my chin, bored by this talk of worrying what the peasants at Greenways may or may not like. "Let's not talk about her right now." I've read up about this feisty little upstart. This poor girl do-gooder. Someone needs to warn her that I eat people like her for breakfast. "I want to have some fun with this." I put on my jacket and adjust the cuffs of my shirt.

I'm also eager to be on my way. Working late is the norm for me, but tonight is a rare social evening. Art galleries are not my forte. I find them boring, but if my future wife-to-be is involved in that world, it's something I'm going to have to get to like.

Though the door to my office is open, Emma still knocks

on it and hovers, not coming in. "I have some paperwork for you to sign. It's urgent."

"Don't you worry about Lewis," I tell Neville. "I'll update you in due time." I motion for Emma to come in, then survey the sheaf of papers she hands me.

Neville doesn't look amused. "You underestimate people sometimes, Brandon. The Greenways store owners are a different breed."

Emma chortles. "You can say that again."

I give her a not-you-too look before flicking through the pages. She has thoughtfully put bright blue and green stickers on the pages I need to look at. I continue signing as if I don't have a care in the world.

Because I don't.

Worrying is Neville's problem. Not mine.

I've learned from my father, and he is the best. All business deals, all the projects, deals and proposals he was involved in, he's always managed to come out on top. It has benefited him in some way. That's how he operates, and that's what he's taught me. He created opportunities and made boatloads of cash by taking buildings, then breaking them up, and selling them for parts. I watched and learned from him as he took land, bulldozed the crap out of it, and built something better and more upmarket in its place.

Newer and better. Upscale buildings, exclusive enclaves. That's what we build and we've never *not* been able to do as we please.

"I've told him," I hear Emma say to Neville as I skimmed the fine print. "He doesn't take her seriously."

"You don't need to worry," I tell Emma.

"Share it with me, your proposed plan, and then we'll see how much we need to worry." Neville is about to set his briefcase on the floor when I shake my head.

"I don't have time."

"He has an appointment." I can't figure out if Emma's tone is sarcastic or if she's being serious.

I tilt my head and look from one to the other. These people should know me better than that. I always get what I want, and I always win. "If my plan doesn't work, burning the place down will ensure Lewis and her crew leave."

Neville nods his head as if he approves. "That's something we could revert to as a last resort."

"I was joking, Neville." I may be a lot of things, but criminal isn't one of them. Though, technically, what I'm about to do to Kyra Lewis might be deemed as such to some.

Emma snorts loud enough for me to hear as Neville disappears. "I shouldn't have to listen to this," she mutters, giving me a disapproving glare. "I swear, it's like working for the mafia sometimes."

"Surely I'm more palatable?" I suggest, winking at her.

"Did you sign them all?" She ignores my remark and shuffles through the pile of papers I've left on my desk.

"I signed everywhere you indicated."

She nods appreciatively, clutching the papers to her chest. "Date night with Jessica?"

My jaw tightens. "Not quite." Looking at paintings that make no sense, sipping champagne and picking at canapes isn't what I would call date night. I'm not the type of guy who wastes time and money chasing skirt, but Jessica Montrose is a worthy endeavour. These things take time and there is no rush.

Emma clutches the sheaf of papers to her chest. "*Just* an appointment, then." There is a glint of amusement in her eyes. For a PA, she's upfront, and takes risks in the way she addresses me. She says things that many wouldn't dare. She would be my social conscience if I possessed such a thing.

An appointment.

I open my mouth to put her in her place but I raise my eyebrow instead. She's only a couple of years older than me, but behaves as if she's thirty-four going on seventy.

But she's not far from wrong. These sterile-as-a-science-lab encounters I have with Jessica are closer to an appointment than anything else. The pursuit of this socialite is slow, and not exactly fun. It often seems like work.

Kyra Lewis and Greenways? Now, *that* to me seems like fun. Emma moves towards the door. "Have you had a chance to read the notes I collated for you on Kyra Lewis?"

"I skimmed through them." I know enough about the woman to go ahead with my plans.

"If anyone is going to stand in your way, it's her, and, to be clear, I disapprove of your plan."

"You don't know my plan."

"I know *you*, Brandon. Enjoy your evening." She saunters away before I can say a word. I replay her cautionary advice to me. No one stands in my way. Because I'm fucking invincible.

CHAPTER TWO

KYRA

"We have more pasta. Just give me a moment, okay?" The woman smiles at me. There is embarrassment in those eyes. I see this same look every time I hand out hot food, drinks and napkins to the people standing quietly and politely in line. We've run out of pasta, but Fredrich quickly empties out a big pan into the serving platter.

We do this every Wednesday night; provide food for the homeless and hungry. It's something that Redhill, the company I run, decided to do when the factory was up and running, and started to become successful. We make blankets, sleeping bags and clothes for homeless people. They're made from lightweight insulated waterproof material and are easy to roll up and put into a bag without taking up a lot of space.

They are made by homeless people and victims of domestic abuse which I hire from homeless shelters. The food program was born out of Redhill's mission that every person deserves to live a good life; has enough to eat, has a place to live and has some type of employment.

Simona says I'm not content until I've fixed the world's problems, and then she tells me I can't. But I can try.

The evening goes on without drama. Everyone is obedient and grateful. They thank us for everything we give them as they go down the line. I put a couple of scoopfuls of pasta into polystyrene boxes and Simona adds a few slices of bread. The other servers add in fruit, crackers, bags of chips and cereal bars. Fredrich takes care of the drinks. There are plenty of water bottles to be handed out and there are also urns for tea and coffee.

On another table, we have other necessary items. Sometimes it's women's sanitary products or warm items for the winter. As it's summer here, those aren't needed as much, but we have sleeping bags and tents, and a few items of clothing. It depends on what our funds can buy.

"We've got two more pots of pasta left," Fredrich informs me.

I eye the line which is about one hundred deep. "It should be enough."

He nods. Gargantuan, with hair as wild as Hagrid's, he's a tattooed sweetie pie and the best IT person I could have ever asked for. He joined the company and was one of my first employees, along with Simona, my second mother.

Redhill has quickly become one of Chicago's fastest growing nonprofit organizations. My brainchild, that's what the media refers to it as when they want to butter me up in an attempt to interview me or to get me on their shows. I don't have time for such things, and I don't trust organizations, per se, but I'm aware that I need publicity to help spread the word. Though I am secretly pleased that we've done amazingly well without going out and courting attention.

Over the next hour, we manage to feed everyone. They tend not to hang around for too long. Some eat quickly, hovering around the serving table, and sometimes they come back for a second helping, which we always give them. Others take the food away. They return back to the streets. Some stay overnight at the homeless shelter, but at least we know they've had a hot meal.

They come here every week to the makeshift area we've set up. It's a stone's throw from the factory, in the wide-open square at the back. This also makes it easier for us to keep a list of the food items in our store room.

Everything is laid out and cleared away with military precision. There's a small core team of about ten helpers, and everyone brings something. Tables, food, cleaning supplies and disposable food service gloves which we use to serve the food.

Doing this grounds me. It makes me feel humble and grateful for all that I have.

"I hate to think what would happen if we ever had to move," grumbles Simona when we start to pack things away at the end.

"We're never going to move." I heft a box of unopened crackers and start to head towards our rickety old van.

We have a good group of shop and business owners here. Some businesses have folded over time, but we've held strong. The area was on its way down a few years ago—which was how I was able to buy the factory building outright, and then grants and funding helped me to set up the business. The buildings around here might look like eyesores from the outside, but inside they are solid. They might not have state-of-the-art interiors, but they are fully functional.

The area has slowly been changing. Over the years, we've had our fair share of letters from big-ass property development companies wanting us to move. They've offered tempting compensation packages but they haven't managed to persuade us.

I have plans to expand—either by taking over another building close by if and when an existing business owner leaves, or we'll go ahead and build a new factory.

"One day we might get an offer that is too good to ignore," says Fredrich as he lines the empty pots and containers into his pickup truck. With his six-foot-two frame, he has enough ink on his arms to print a book. He's also the muscle of the company. I would be stuck without him especially because he's the one who returns these items to the restaurants which were kind enough to donate food for tonight.

I wave my hand, dismissing his comment.

"But what would you do?" he asks.

With my hands on my hips, I square off with him. "We're not moving." This part of the city is becoming more gentrified. It's up and coming, and Redhill is positioned perfectly in the center of it all. "I'm going nowhere. We're going nowhere. We're staying put."

"And what about the 'eminent domain' issue you were worried about?" he asks.

"Don't worry about that." I try to keep abreast of these things and am aware that the government can take private property and convert it for public use under certain circumstances as long as they offer us what they claim is fair compensation. Yeah, right. Fair compensation is anything but that.

And, as far as I'm concerned, we're already doing things that benefit the public, though they don't see it quite like that.

We also have donors who are rich and famous, like Elias Cardoza, and Callum Sandersby, the Hollywood movie star his sister is dating. High-profile donors will rally to my cause if and when I need them. The eminent domain issue is a worry, but I try not to dwell on these things. Besides, with the business growing so fast, I have numerous other things to think about.

"Have a little faith, Fredrich." Simona brings over a box of napkins.

"Kyra!" I turn at the sound of something calling me. One of the staffers raises his arm at me. A woman, someone I don't recognize, stands next to him. "Do you have a moment?" he hollers and sends the woman over.

I wipe my hands on my jeans in anticipation. The people who come here don't usually ask for anything. They take their food, thank us, and leave.

"Are you the woman who makes those blankets?" Her voice is louder and clearer than I am prepared for.

"Yes." I nod. "What can I do for you?"

She looks bruised and battered, not physically, but in her stance. There's a defeated look in her eyes. Her hunched body and tiny frame give me that tell-tale signal.

"Do you ..." she straightens herself up, growing an inch or two taller before my eyes. "Do you have any work? I need to work. I'll even take less than minimum wage."

"I would never expect you to work for less than that." Minimum wage is a joke as it is. She doesn't look as if she's living on the streets. She looks cleaner, her clothes aren't as dirty or rumpled as they would be. Her hair looks brushed and yet she seems in a bad way. Desperation slips unmasked out of her eyes, even though the tilt of her chin tries so hard to prove otherwise.

"We're hiring all the time. What can you do?"

"I can do anything. I'm a good learner. I can help in the factory. Or in the office. I'll work anywhere you'll have me. I'll even clean if you want me to. I'm good with my hands and I can sew. With a little practice, I'll be able to make those clothes and things you make."

She's done her research. People on the streets or surviving in shelters during the night don't have laptops and phones with which to find out such things. Many come to me with no idea of what we make, even though when we show them the products, many have heard of them. We have given out countless jackets and blankets.

"Why don't you come by tomorrow, and we can talk then?" I don't recall seeing her in the line for people wanting food, and I wonder why she's come to me now. "Did you ... would you like some food to take back?" Wherever 'back' might be. The woman shakes her head. "I ate before I came."

"What's your name?"

"Yvette."

"I'll see you tomorrow, Yvette. Take this." I hand her my business card, just so that she'll have my details, but there are also the numbers of the local shelters and soup kitchens on the back of it.

She nods, and thanks me before slipping away into the night. Unless something goes badly awry tomorrow, I decide that I will take her on. I hope I don't come to regret it.

CHAPTER THREE

KYRA

I quirk an eyebrow at the screen. How is it that my inbox gets so full overnight? I leave the office late most days, making sure we're still on target and have enough inventory. That is my main focus, but making sure I've dealt with my emails is one of the last things I do before I leave.

I love what I do. It's all good, but overwhelming, especially as the company has grown, and I've taken more staff on. I would take on a PA but I don't want to waste money on things like that. Every penny needs to be spent on making other people's lives better. I can live with being overwhelmed and overworked. This isn't a job to me. It's my passion.

Inviting the woman from last night for an interview is a slight deviation from the norm for me. We tend not to take people who approach us directly, rather, we prefer to see people who have been vetted and recommended to us from one of the social services departments. Yet she sought me out.

That tells me she's desperate, but also, perhaps, that she's smart. That she's proactive. That there's more to her than meets the eye.

A knock at the door interrupts my thoughts.

"Come in," I holler.

The door opens and the woman from last night from the homeless food session appears. "Hi." She shuffles in, looking hesitant. "You said for me to come over."

"Hey, Yvette, isn't it?" I rise up.

"Is this a good time? I can come back later if you want." She looks nervous.

"This is perfect timing."

"Uh ... I was just leaving." Fredrich picks up his paper coffee cup and leaves. Simona is on the factory floor, doing the daily rounds and checking the products being made. With the small office now empty, I hold out my hand and Yvette shakes it, her thin, bony hand so fragile in mine. In the cold light of day, she looks frailer than I remember.

"Take a seat." I motion for her to sit down. "Would you like a drink? Something hot? Or cold?"

She shakes her head.

"So, you would like to work here?"

She nods. I'm going to have to coax it out of her. So many of the people we employ have had difficult lives. Some have known hardship their entire life, and for others their lives fell apart after a major event. Getting laid off, discovering a partner was unfaithful, having a child or a partner die, has hit like a juggernaut, making them spiral and crash. Some turn to alcohol, some to drugs, some gamble, but all of them fall apart.

I don't know this woman's story, but I can see that she is desperate.

"I have two children." She stops and swallows. Her chest

rises and dips, as if it takes a great deal of effort to try to keep it together. I force myself to remain quiet and listen. "I need to be able to take care of my children."

I nod. "Your husband ...?"

She blinks more than is normal, at that. "He's not here. He won't be able to ... he can't ..."

"He can't what?" My voice is low, almost like a coaxing whisper.

"He can't touch us now." She lifts her head. I see scars that I didn't notice before. I thought they were lines, but there is a scar above her eyebrow, and one below her lip. I try not to stare, knowing that she might feel self-conscious, but already I have a picture of this woman's life and struggle.

It's not advisable to hire people that I know nothing about, and this is a risk, because some vulnerable people can be paranoid, psychotic and a risk to others, as well as to themselves. Still, I cannot bring myself to turn her away.

"Do you have experience? Have you worked anywhere before?"

"I used to work in an office, but it was a long time ago. A long time ..." Her voice trails away.

She scratches her neck, and I notice more scars. She goes on to tell me that she lives in a women's shelter, but now that her husband poses no danger, she has been given a small room in an apartment to help people like her.

"Why does your husband pose no danger?" It's a question I have to ask, even though it is obvious that any talk about her husband makes her uneasy.

"He'd dead. Got beaten to death in prison."

Her reply stuns me, even after all the interviews I have conducted, I should be better prepared, but I'm not. Every one of these people have a story to tell, and each story is hard to comprehend. "I'm ... I'm so sorry." Though I suspect that she's not. I ask her about the duties she used to perform, and the answers she gives me tell me that she is way more qualified than I first thought. That she is not who I thought she was. This woman, who was qualified to work in an office, now wants to work.

By the end of our talk, I am suitably impressed enough to take her on. She says she can't start today, but that she will be here first thing tomorrow morning. This will give me time to process her paperwork.

Simona comes in just as Yvette leaves, and I introduce them both.

"Are you sure this is wise?" Simona looks worried. "She didn't come from the agency."

"She's legit. She's okay. She needs help." I understand her concerns. I've broken my rule of not hiring directly, but my instinct tells me that Yvette is a desperate woman in need of help. I like to think we can give her that help.

My mom was one of these women—not quite as desperate, there was no husband in prison, or dying. Just a cheating husband who walked out one day after his lover turned up on our doorstep in tears, and very visibly pregnant. My mom was a single mom who raised two daughters. She worked three jobs just to keep a roof over our heads and she could have benefited from something like this. That's why I do it, why I'm driven to the point of being obsessed. Why I devote all my time and energy to Redhill, much to Simona's annoyance.

She thinks I should be spending time going out, having fun and meeting Mr. Right. At the age of twenty-eight, I'm not looking for Mr. Right because he doesn't exist. My last boyfriend was a testament to that.

I have people to help. My younger sister, Penny, is in college and that's one thing taken care of.

Between keeping her in college and running Redhill, there is no time for anything else.

CHAPTER FOUR

BRANDON

Billionaire undercover. That's how I'll do it. A Trojan horse into Kyra Lewis' company. I'll convince her, gently nudge her towards a decision, do what it takes to get her to see that relocating would be in her best interests.

The idea is brilliant. So much so that I couldn't even hold my attention at the art gallery yesterday. Luckily, Jessica was too busy showing art collectors around, and I was left to stare at paintings that a three-year-old chimpanzee would have created if he'd been given a bucket of paint.

At least the champagne was flowing.

When Emma walks in, I steeple my fingers together and stare at her, deep in contemplation.

"What now?" She puts down the pile of daily newspapers.

"Brad Hartley," I state.

She frowns. "Who's he?"

"My new alter ego."

Emma raises an eyebrow and I pick up one of the papers, pretending to glance at the headlines so that I can give Emma time to absorb this news. "What?" she cries.

"You must have seen those reality TV shows?" I prompt. She stares back with a blank expression.

"I'm going undercover like that, working for Kyra Lewis."

A tangle of lines forms on her otherwise smooth forehead. "But not to help her."

I smile, because she understands. "Of course not."

"I should leave," she mumbles, her wrinkles deepening.

"Hear me out." If anyone will find holes in my idea, it will be Emma.

"You're obviously not going on a TV show." Her dry response and the disapproval wedged into her lips tells me not only that she knows what I plan to do, but that she doesn't approve.

"Never." I guard my privacy and am hardly ever seen in the press. "This is how I'll get Kyra Lewis and her people, and all the other Greenways business owners to leave. I think it's perfect."

She scoffs. "Only you would think of that."

"Persuading her to move is the easier option. This way I avoid the circus of a public hearing with all its hoops and legal tape to jump through."

"But it's wrong," she replies, her voice flat with weariness. Enamored she is not.

"Do you have any idea how much money this deal will bring in? We'll make millions. A heck of a lot more than Kyra Lewis and her outfit."

"She's doing good work. She employs vulnerable people from homeless shelters, victims of domestic abuse. She gives them a chance to rebuild their lives. The work that woman does has meaning." And though she doesn't say it, her death stare indicates that mine doesn't.

I press my lips together. I didn't expect her to clap, but I expected her to be impressed. I'm going out on a limb here. Stepping out of my usual business-like domain. This is different for me. I'm thinking outside the box, but she doesn't see any of that.

"You putting that report together for me has turned you into her biggest fan."

"I can't help but admire her," Emma states. "Did you read any of it?"

I cock my head and grimace. "I flicked through it."

She shakes her head. "How do you propose to go about this, given that you don't fully understand her or her business?" she asks.

"I don't need to understand her. I just need to infiltrate her workplace. I'll pretend I need a job. I'll work for free, naturally, and then I'll win her over with my charm."

Emma rolls her eyes. "It's a crazy idea."

"But it will work."

"She's smart. She won't fall for your lines as easily as you think."

"I'll tell her I have ideas. There will be holes I'll have to fill. Things I haven't thought of. I'll make it up as I go."

"People aren't stupid, Brandon. Even the ones you call 'peasants.'" Her voice is almost a sneer. Sometimes I wonder if Emma hates me and is simply tolerating this job because the perks and salary are good. I've only used that term a few times. While I don't consider someone like Kyra Lewis to be a peasant, everything I've read about her tells me she's not Jessica Montrose, although I knew that already.

Who the hell starts a business for the betterment of society instead of for the sole reason of making money? I will never understand people like her, but I don't need to understand Lewis in order to get her to do the things that need to be done; the things that will benefit me.

"You're not going to tell her who you are?"

"Do you think she'd want to listen to anything I have to say if she knew who I was? This way is better. She won't know me, or why I'm there."

"Won't she hate you when she finds out? When they all do?"

"Do I care? I'll have secured the land by then. I don't care what happens to any of them after that."

"Why not leave it to Neville and your usual sleazy tricks?"

"Those things take time. He's on it. That's the back-up plan in case this doesn't work."

"I don't see Kyra Lewis falling for your charms."

"I'm not planning on seducing her, Emma. She's not my type. Besides, she's young and not fully experienced when it comes to business matters. I'll convince her that it's a bad idea to stay where she is. I'll make suggestions to relocate. Who cares?" I stand up, feeling rather proud of myself and adjust my cufflinks.

"You have no soul."

"And I consider myself very lucky."

I've done my due diligence, and I plan to build condos and luxury apartments, and have an upscale shopping mall filled only with designer boutiques. The area will abound with restaurants and bars. I'm looking at insanely, filthy profits from this development, and nothing or no one will stand in my way.

Not even Kyra Lewis.

"What if she recognizes you?"

"Who, aside from the people who work here, know what I

look like? I don't do the celebrity, paparazzi circuit. I don't court publicity." I've avoided the limelight for years. Many in my position wouldn't, but I have more to hide than most.

"This will get you only so much publicity, and when you're found out, it won't be good for the company."

"No one's going to find out. I'm not going to force her out. I'm going to gently persuade her. The choice to leave will be hers." My persuasive skills are legendary, as Kyra Lewis is about to find out.

Emma heaves out a sigh. "You're making a mistake."

"This is a business proposition for me. Not a date."

"Then send someone else to do your dirty work. There's no reason for you to go. You've got far more important things to do here."

I sit back and examine my clean fingernails. "Because if I find some dirt on her, I'll soon knock that Florence Nightingale crown from her head."

Emma's school-teacherly look is highly condescending. The firm press of her mouth tells me she's holding back from giving me her true opinion but I'm intrigued. She's my compass. She lets me know when I've strayed too far from levelheadedness. "Say it, Emma. Don't hold back."

"What you're doing is pure evil."

"I'm not a saint."

She folds her arms together, her body posture spelling defiance. "You won't find any dirt on her, because she doesn't have any. Have you read about the things she's done?"

I flick my hand in an air of defiance. It's wearing on my nerves, how everyone blows this woman's horn. Talking about her as if she's the best thing to happen to the city. "No one can be that good."

I should know.

Emma eyes me in surprise. "Yes, they can."

I shake my head, refusing to believe such bullshit. "It will give me extreme satisfaction to prove to the world that Saint Kyra doesn't exist. No one is that selfless. She's up to something."

"She has lots of corporate donors clamoring to donate to her cause."

I disagree. "She's a media darling, but she's not an angel. People aren't squeaky clean," I tell her. I can find dirt on Kyra Lewis, if I put my mind to it.

And then, it won't look too bad, when the truth comes out that I, and Hawks Enterprises, developed the land for our own gain. More than that, taking her down will give me a sense of satisfaction.

Emma eyes me with more contempt than a school principal would show to kids smoking weed in school.

"You're going to lie and cheat your way into their lives, and steal their land from beneath them?"

I open my mouth to protest, but my PA's appraisal of the situation is accurate. I can't fault it. "Correct."

"I don't know how you can face yourself in the mirror each morning."

"I can, and quite easily, too, I might add."

She blows out an exaggerated huff as she walks away, everything about her screaming scorn for my idea. She can't fully see or appreciate the brilliance of it.

"You have to help me."

She turns around. "I will do no such thing. I'm your PA. I won't be a party to your evil crimes."

I stand up and slide my hands into the pockets of my slacks. "Emma. I pay you to do as I say. And for the record, I pay you very, very well."

She mumbles something under her breath as her hand grips the door handle. It amuses me to watch this battle of conscience playing out before my very eyes. She glares at me. "Help with what?"

"I don't know how to do 'poor'. What to wear, what to drive. I have no idea."

"'Poor'? You want to know how to do 'poor'?" Her tone scalds like hot water. "These people aren't 'poor'. They have heart and history, they've worked in those businesses for decades, and all they're trying to do is earn a living."

"They can earn a living, just not on my real estate."

"What do you need my help with?"

"Advice. A resumé, a new wardrobe of clothes. A car."

She scoffs. "Yes, you won't be able to cruise over in your Tesla."

"I'll need something old. Something with a stick shift." I rub my hands with glee. "This is going to be a lot of fun."

CHAPTER FIVE

KYRA

Yvette is a fast learner and its clear to me that she wants to do well. My experience has been that every person who comes to us, who has made that decision to get off the streets, or to walk away out of an abusive relationship and go into a women's shelter, all of these people have a reason to live; they want to prove themselves.

They want a better life. They aren't homeless because they're lazy—which believe it or not, some skeptics have said to me—but because of life's circumstances. Either they were by life's cruel twists and circumstances, or lost their jobs, or lived paycheck to paycheck and a huge calamity blindsided them. Or women fell in love with men who became monsters, beating them to within an inch of their lives, until they found the courage to flee.

"Nice work." I stop by one of the workers and examine the jacket that she has just finished making on the industrial sewing machine.

"Thank you."

"How are you finding it?" I stare into the eyes of a relatively new worker who joined a little over a month ago. She looks happy, pleased with herself, and so she should be.

"I like it here. I like it a lot. It takes a bit of getting used to, using these big sewing machines, but I reckon I've got the hang of it now." I return the jacket to her now that I've finished taking a good look at all the seams. "I'd say you've definitely got the hang of it. Keep up the good work."

I walk around the factory floor, something I do a couple of times during the day, just to see how everyone is getting along, and to find out if there's anything that's not working.

Simona waves at me from the other side of the floor, beckoning me over. A man is by her side, someone I don't recognize. My face tightens. I didn't have a meeting planned, and I'm not expecting anyone.

I hope it's not someone wanting to do a cover story. Recently, Redhill has attracted a slew of donors as well as interest from the media.

"Hey." I nod at Simona first, then the stranger. His blue-gray eyes lock onto mine.

"This is Brad Hartley." Simona's eyes bubble with excitement.

"Hi." He confidently holds out his hand.

"From?" I look at the guy then back at Simona, unable to figure out why she's so excited. "I'm not expecting anyone today."

"Brad's looking for work—"

"That's right. I'm looking for work." With his hand still held out, I have no option but to shake it.

"We're not hiring." I notice that he's dressed way too neatly, even in his ripped jeans and shirt, and the jacket he's got on, his clothes don't have that weathered, beaten, years' old hand-me-down look about it which I've become accustomed to. Something doesn't feel right. I wonder if he's from a newspaper and is snooping around for information.

"Will you at least give him a chance?" Simona insists. "We took on someone last week who didn't come through our usual channels."

He slides a finger inside his shirt collar, as if it's too tight and uncomfortable, and I note that he's not wearing a tie. "I've got experience. I was involved in a couple of start-ups in San Jose, before I got burnt out."

The lever on my bullshit-o-meter turns to max. San Jose? Start-ups? Tech? "What are you doing here?" I ask him.

"I didn't like where I was so I took a break and I went traveling around the world."

I glance at my watch. I don't have any meetings, but I have a lot to do. I don't really want to hire this guy, and I find my interest waning.

"I have lots to offer," he says eagerly.

"Shall we step somewhere where we can talk?" I lead the way upstairs to our shared office. Fredrich is inside. Simona introduces them both, but she introduces the new guy as 'someone looking to work here and help us out.' She's already made her mind up about this man. She already likes him.

"Do you want me to leave?" Fredrich gets up as if he's ready to go.

"No, stay put. This won't take long." I sit at my desk, and Fredrich gives the guy his chair, and I could be wrong, but I'm sure the guy made a face, as if he wasn't sure he wanted to sit down on it. It's plastic and has splotches of paint all over it. Updating the office furniture isn't a huge priority of mine yet.

This isn't the cleanest of offices, nor the most comfortable, because the paint is peeling off the walls, and our tables, chairs and the computers are second-hand. We don't need

Macbooks or designer furniture to do our jobs. The business is doing well, and everything we make goes back into it, so that we can help more people. I have an eye on my five-year plan and so far, things are progressing accordingly.

The new guy catches me looking at him, then mumbles a 'thanks' to Fredrich before sitting down. It's like he's sitting on a cushion of pins, pointy ends upwards. Fredrich disappears, presumably to get another chair for himself.

"Is this where you all sit? Together? In *here*?"

"Is it not to your San Jose start-up standard?" I make no effort to hide the barb in my voice. He smiles uneasily. "What sort of start-ups?" I cut to the chase. I don't have the time or patience to put up with his patronizing attitude.

"Software mostly, but I got bored. I wanted more, so I went traveling."

I notice that he didn't elaborate.

"Traveling?" Simona rubs her hands together. "Anywhere nice?"

"All over Central America. I saw how local communities banded together and worked and had success in their endeavors."

"And what do you want with Redhill?" I ask. He talks a good talk, but the cynic in me finds him too smooth, too practiced. More than that, it doesn't make sense that someone who's worked where he claims he has now wants to work here with us because he suddenly became enlightened on a trip.

He clears his throat, then sits up, straightening his back, his interlaced fingers resting on his stomach. He looks very business-like, even though he's in casual clothes. He has an air about him which I can't pinpoint.

"I only got back a few months ago—"

"To where?"

"Excuse me?"

"Got back to where?" I play with a paperclip, straightening it out so that it is a straight wire.

"Here, to Chicago."

"I thought you said you worked in San Jose."

He laughs uncomfortably. "I relocated to there from here. I'm from Chicago, through and through." He eyes me for a second longer, as if he's appraising me, as if he doesn't trust me. "I didn't want to get back into tech, and I'm looking at ways of helping the community. I liked the way people came together in poorer countries and I want to see if I can help in any way here. I read about your company."

"Kyra's everywhere lately," Simona announces proudly. "She seems to get requests for interviews almost every week."

"Not every week," I say, dismissively. New guy laughs, revealing a row of perfect teeth. "I can see why. It's impressive, what you've done here."

"What is it that you want from us, Mr... Mr?"

"Hartley. Brad Hartley, but please, call me Brad." He tilts his head. We hold gazes, before I find myself staring at the dusting of stubble across his face.

A rogue thought strays into my mind. He could be an undercover journalist wanting a story, but there is no story. This is nothing interesting, in regards to gossip for magazines. There is also nothing for me to distrust him about. Maybe the fact that he's easy on the eye has put me on guard. Maybe Simona being smitten about him has furthered my reluctance to hire him.

"Thanks for your time, Mr. Hartley, but we don't need anyone and we're not looking for anyone at the moment."

"Even working for free?"

That there, working for free, for a tech guy who used to work for start-ups, that doesn't make sense. "Why would you want to work for free?" I can see Simona in my periphery, and I can feel the heat of her stare.

"If he's offering," Simona says. "We need all the help we can get."

"I can bring you experience. I've run start-ups before. I know how to make a profit, and turn a business from failing to—"

I put him in his place. "This business isn't failing."

"I'm not talking about yours." He holds his hand up by way of trying to placate me. I'm riled up, and I don't get riled up. I usually have the patience of a Grandma but my gut instinct tells me not to take everything he says at face value.

"I can see that you're obviously annoyed about something—"

"I'm not annoyed about anything."

His tone turns a tad harsh. "I don't understand why you would turn down a perfectly good offer. You could do wonders with this business."

"We already are, believe me."

He looks over at Simona. "I sense that this is a bad time, how about I leave my ..." He gets up and slides his hand into the back pocket of his jeans. "My, uh ..." He pulls out a cell phone. For a moment there, I thought he was going to pull out a business card.

"If you want to give me your contact number," he says to Simona. That makes sense because he must know by now that I'm not so easily pleased. He seems to think he'll have better luck appealing to Simona than to me. He's right. "Or I could give you mine. You never know when you might need my help."

He and Simona exchange numbers, then he bids us goodbye and leaves. I turn my attention straight to my computer, but Simona stands in front of me, her arms folded as she gazes down at me with her disapproval in her eyes.

"You weren't very nice to him."

"He's arrogant."

"Arrogant?" She gives a mirthless laugh. "Were we both at the same interview?"

"It wasn't an interview."

"No?" There is a shedload of questioning behind that simple question.

"I don't trust him, Simona."

"Pffffft. You haven't trusted anyone since that man cheated on you."

I bend the paperclip back into shape, my insides tightening as she talks about my ex.

"Good riddance to bad rubbish," she continues.

I don't share much about my private life, not even with Simona who is as close to a mother figure as I'll ever have, but my ex cheating on me for most of the time we were together broke me more than I want to admit.

"Don't turn away a perfectly good candidate, Kyra. Don't let the other stuff cloud your judgment."

"We don't take people off the street," I protest.

"He didn't look like someone off the street. You took Yvette on." Simona's brow creases. "You don't like him because he's too much like you."

I laugh at that absurd accusation.

"He wants to do good in the world, like you," she continues. "He doesn't need to be homeless or in difficulty to work here."

"We don't need anyone else. We have our team and we're doing well."

"He offered to work for free."

I scrub a hand against my cheek. This is my point exactly. I look up at her. "Doesn't that raise alarm bells?"

"He sounds exactly like someone we need."

"Not really."

I start to type away on my keyboard.

"He's young, and good-looking, and wants to help, and you're doing your damndest to push him away."

I have to laugh. "And *that's* why you wanted him to work here?"

"Here." She taps away on her cell phone. "I've sent you his number."

I can't pinpoint what it is that grates on me about this man. I barely know him, but I sense trouble. Working for a start-up, then traveling around and helping out in less advantaged countries means he would be perfect for Redhill.

He also sounds too good to be true.

CHAPTER SIX

BRANDON

"What happened?" Emma asks as I enter my office.

"With what?" The weekend has flown by and I have no idea what she is referring to.

"I want to know how your 'undercover' visit to Redhill went." She air quotes 'undercover'.

"She didn't hire me." I walk into my office wishing to be left alone. But, of course Emma isn't one to let this slide without wanting further elaboration.

"She didn't hire you?" she strides into the office. I take off my jacket and fold up the cuffs to my sleeves. To my chagrin, she's sitting in the chair opposite mine, waiting for the cliffhanger.

"Don't you have work to do?" I ask her.

I loosen my tie before sitting down. I feel constricted. The collar feels tight around my neck, and most of all I'm just really pissed off that I seemed to fail at the first hurdle. "She said she didn't need anyone."

"Even though you told her you would work for free?" She sounds surprised. "She doesn't trust you."

I rock back on my chair. This is what I sensed. Kyra Lewis is paranoid and doesn't trust a soul. She's going to be harder to get through than I first anticipated, but I will rise to the challenge. There's nothing I like more. "She will." I need to find another avenue for reaching through to her. It won't be through her, but maybe the older woman can help. She seemed friendlier.

"She will." I'm confident of that.

Emma stands up. "I told you she was smart."

"And I told you I'll find a way in." That's what Trojan horses do. I'll need to find another way to break into Redhill.

"These are divine," Jessica says. The selection of amuse-bouches—courtesy of the head chef and prepared solely for us—looks mouth-watering.

"Not bad," I say, staring at a cup holding a crab filled pea pod straddled across the top of it. I don't know whether to eat it or admire it.

"This looks heavenly." Jessica's deep-red talons shine as her fork stabs a shrimp nestled in a martini glass filled with crushed ice. Only in places like this does food become art.

We're sitting in one of Chicago's most expensive French restaurants. My slow and subtle pursuit of her continues. She's playing hard to get, too. Which helps. The chase is exhilarating. At some point, I'll find her sexually attractive, which is important given that she ticks the right boxes for so many other things.

"You are a man of exemplary taste and refinement, Brandon. It's one of the things I like about you."

"Just one?" I take a sip of water from the sparkling thin-stemmed glass.

"Stop fishing for compliments." She gives me a provocative smile. Those shiny, glossy, red lips are inviting, and yet I don't feel the rush of adrenaline that I should. Could it be because we haven't yet jumped into bed yet?

"I'm not fishing." I sober up, not that I'm drunk, not the slightest, but the more I meet with her and get to know her, the more I keep wondering and waiting for a flash of desire to scorch my already cold heart.

It hasn't so far, and I tell myself it's because Jessica is composed and self-assured, that she's elegant and refined, and that tearing-one-another's-clothes-off sex isn't how this relationship will go.

I found her on a list of the most eligible and successful women in Chicago. What struck me was her quiet beauty; perfectly coiffed chestnut brown hair, swept back '50s style. She's more polished than voluptuous. Physically and otherwise, she is perfect and she ticks all the boxes for the type of woman I envision my future with; a future which will involve society parties, gala evenings, fundraiser events. I need to be with someone like Jessica.

I tell myself that the desire and lust will come later. She has made it perfectly clear that she doesn't want to rush into anything either, having come out of a relationship that 'trampled her heart to shreds'. That sounds brutal, and she's had a hard knock, which means she must have loved hard and fiercely. I can't remember loving anyone like that. I don't let go of my emotions or give up my feelings. Being vulnerable is not a state I allow myself to be in.

"You're successful, powerful and rich, of course you're going to have impeccable taste." Jessica leans across slightly, so that her lips are harder for me to ignore. I dip my head, analyzing the order of her words. Women want a man who is rich and powerful. She and I are looking for the same things and we couldn't be more right for one another.

"I don't want to rush anything," she says as an afterthought, and the fact that she has mentioned this before makes me wonder if she also doesn't feel that bolt of desire shooting through her.

For all our fancy dinners, and polite and refined conversations, often taking place while we admire various works of art in her gallery, there is the niggling feeling that the chemistry is lackluster. My father had a string of mistresses, and perhaps that is how things will be for me later on.

The server brings over the champagne and starts to pour.

"To the good things in life," I say, when both our glasses are filled.

Jessica raises her glass to mine. "To all the good things."

I chuckle to myself, thinking about my interview with Kyra Lewis. Now *that* is one woman I wouldn't touch with a ten-foot pole, even if she were the last woman left on Earth. There is nothing sleek or polished about her. No admirable qualities that I can discern and, given her desire to make life better for the losers of our society, I struggle to understand her.

"What's so funny?" A questioning twinkle in Jessica's eyes loosens my guard. I have told her about my next ambitious project, of my desire to turn Greenways, that dumpster fire of real estate, into something that will make money, instead of bleed money for useless causes, but she doesn't know of my ploy, or the pathetic attempt I made to infiltrate Lewis's outfit.

"I'm not sure what to do about Greenways. One of the business people there, a woman, runs a nonprofit organization and she's going to be a thorn in my side."

"You must be referring to Kyra Lewis."

"You know her?" This surprises me because the two women might as well be from different galaxies for all that they have in common.

Jessica looks visibly disgusted. "People like *that?* God, no. She feeds homeless people, and I … don't."

I sit upright. "How do you know?" This catches my attention like a bolt of lightning. I casually skimmed over the file that Emma had prepared for me on her. I didn't take her seriously before, but maybe I should. The fact that Jessica knows of her is a testament to Lewis's draw.

"She's the city's newest icon, aside from Elias Cardoza." Jessica's voice drops an octave. I don't like that she's talking about that boxer guy as if she's in awe of him. Cardoza is the toast of the town. The King of Chicago. He used to be Chicago's New Hope when he first came on the scene. The city loves him. Even when he lost the fight to defend his title, the people didn't give up on him. There's a rematch slated for next month and everyone is rooting for Cardoza to win.

He and I have something in common. We both stayed at the same children's home, but I didn't suffer the abuse that he did. I was rescued by a wonderful couple who gave me a new life.

"What do you know of her?" I ask.

"That she looks like a mutt. Short-haired and skinny. It's a national disgrace that there seems to be so much interest in her."

While Lewis is not my ideal woman, I wouldn't describe her the way Jessica has. Short shoulder-length hair, green defiant eyes, and attitude, that's how I saw her.

"Don't you read any magazines?" Jessica asks.

I only read the financial papers, and the business news, and I'm certain that the likes of Kyra Lewis don't appear in them. Jessica runs her hand down her chocolate brown hair. Her manicured hands and her perfectly painted nails indicate that this woman has time to run a business and take good care of herself.

She goes on to tell me how Lewis has become a rising star in the last few years on account of her business.

It's a shame that Lewis didn't hire me for free. Now I have to come up with Plan B.

CHAPTER SEVEN

KYRA

"What happened to you?" I rise from my chair in shock. Fredrich stands at the door with his arm in a sling.

"I tripped and fell down the stairs."

"Fredrich," I murmur, feeling sorry for him.

He only went home a few hours ago. We've got another homeless food night tonight. We start getting things ready for it around six o'clock in the evening and given that I'm often still in the office then, it always ends up being a long, long day for me.

Simona says that I live in this factory and she often wonders out loud why I don't set up a bed in here. That's a great idea, and I would, were it not for the fact that it's so cold. I don't mind the spiders and insects, or the dirt. We try to keep it clean but I don't pay anyone to clean it. I guess I ought to. The employees take care of things, and I've been known to go around with a broom now and then.

This factory came at a good price, and I like the idea of not having any landlords to deal with, of owning something outright, but I just wish we had a bigger place. Redhill is doing well, much better than I ever thought and we are expanding fast. Every year, we help more people and change more lives, and it's exhilarating, running a company which helps people. Sometimes I wonder if we should stay here or go elsewhere. It makes sense to find somewhere else with more space rather than staying put and building another factory on the side, but I have a good feeling about Greenways and my instinct tells me that we're onto something good here.

"What are you doing here?" I ask him angrily. "You must be in so much pain."

"It's food night." He saunters in and perches slightly on his desk, as if he needs to rest. He doesn't look anything like his usual strapping self.

"You can't go to that." He's the one who does the bulk of the lifting. He can easily swing the pallets of water bottles and food and he's also the one who goes to the various restaurants around Chicago who have signed up to donate food on these nights. They supply us with warm pasta, some rice and bread rolls. We wouldn't be able to do what we do without the spirit and help of these people who donate weekly to our cause. This is the community helping the community; it is much appreciated and vital to our success.

I suddenly realize that Fredrich being out of service is going to cause me a huge problem. "You need to take a couple of weeks off," giving him my sternest look.

"I've only fractured my arm, Kyra. It hasn't fallen off."

"It might as well have."

"I'm sorry! I tripped and fell." He touches the cast gingerly, as if he's getting used to it.

"I didn't mean to gripe. It's just... busy." What with

tonight, and everything else going on at the factory, there is just too much to do, and right now I don't see how we can function at the same level as we need to with my strongest man out.

"It's a shame you turned away our only chance at free labor, from someone who sounded pretty smart." Fredrich, like Simona, seems irritated that I didn't take on that Brad guy who came here last week. I throw my hands up and tsk. Both he and Simona have been telling me at every chance what a great opportunity I threw away.

"Hiring more people at our level is not our number one priority." We don't need a new guy. Especially not in the office. We have enough people in the management team with three of us. We're not managers sitting at our desks watching everyone do the grunt work; we get on with things.

We are *doers*.

I'm not sure that this guy they both seem to like so much is a doer. He seems to me like someone who can talk a good talk. He looked too slick. Too salesman-y, even in his ripped jeans.

But, Fredrich being out of commission is going to set me back a lot. "How will you manage?" he asks.

"We'll manage."

"You could use that guy now," Fredrich insists, before pushing off with a grimace.

I ignore that comment. "You should go home and get some rest."

"I need to go load up the truck."

I'm about to sit and reply to my emails, but I can't. Fredrich is stupid enough to think he still has his Herculean powers and that he can continue one-armed with his duties. "No, you don't." I march towards him. "I'll do that." I gasp. "Did you *drive* here?"

"I didn't fly."

I tilt my head and flash my disapproving look at him. "You're in pain, and you're grumpy. Go home, Fredrich."

"Who's going to get the food?"

"I will."

"It's not going to fit into your car," he points out. He's right. It won't.

"I'll just have to use the old van," I mutter to myself. I've been meaning to buy a better van for our factory but as usual, it's not our top priority. I've relied on Fredrich to drive his pickup truck to get the food from the restaurants. We have most of the other supplies in the storage room here in the factory—cans of soup, water bottles, crackers, sanitary products and so on. "Go home, Fredrich. You're no good to me injured."

"And let you do this alone?" He raises himself to his full height, his face and body posture indicating that he is in pain.

"I'm not doing it alone. There are plenty of us here to help out."

"Let me help a little," he insists.

"No. Go home. Please." I can't have him be even more injured than he is. He's the one who moves things around and lift things, not just for the food night but whenever a heavy hand is needed, it's Fredrich I turn to.

Yvette is here and the employees on the schedule for tonight are all here. I refuse to let the lack of Fredrich's muscle power be our weakness, even though it has highlighted something to me; if anything should happen to me or Fredrich, or Simona, this business is on shaky ground, and I can't afford for that to happen. Many already vulnerable people are depending on us and we can't let them down.

There's no time to waste. I pick up the keys to the van and decide to make the restaurant run myself. "I'm going to get the food." I mumble some instructions to the others letting them know what's happened and that they need to band together and make sure Fredrich doesn't make his injury worse.

Rubbing my aching lower back, I climb into the rumbling old van. My back has been acting up lately, because, like Fredrich, I also think I have superhuman strength and can do everything. I cross my arms on the steering wheel, then lean forward and rest my head. I could fall asleep here, and the thought of the next four hours makes me want to go to sleep. I am so bone-tired. It's a good thing Simona isn't here to see me like this. She already hates that I work so hard and play so little, and she would have something to say if she saw me like this.

I turn the ignition and the van splutters to life on the first try. Phew. I've known for months that we need something more reliable, but as with most things, and me, I squeeze every last gasp of usage out of it.

Tonight will be hard work. I'm going to have to return the pots and containers to the restaurants, and then make sure everything is put back in the storeroom.

It's a shame you turned him away. Fredrich's words float back to me.

I could call that guy. The slimy one who's traveled around the world and found his calling, or so he thinks.

Use him.

I don't use people. That's not me. Yet there would be something satisfying to be gained from watching him at the food night. This is my chance to see if he can rally to the cause and help me on demand.

It's just as well that Simona sent me his number. Now I can find out how serious he was about wanting to help out.

CHAPTER EIGHT

BRANDON

I'm about to cut into my nice, juicy steak when my cell phone goes off. It's on vibrate mode, but I can feel it jiggling around in my jacket pocket.

I ignore it but a few seconds later it goes off again. I give Jessica an apologetic grin and reach for my cell phone to quickly see who it is and to turn the damn thing off, but the darn thing stops buzzing.

I stare at the number. It's one I don't recognize. Just as I go to switch it off, it starts to vibrate again.

It could be a prospective investor. A client. A chance to make another deal. I can't ignore these things. "Excuse me. I have to take this." Jessica shrugs and plays around with her salad.

"Hi, is this Brad? Brad Hartley?" It's a voice I vaguely recognize but can't place.

"Who?" My jaw clenches during the few seconds it takes for the penny to drop.

"This is Kyra Lewis. You came for an interview at Redhill last week."

The corners of my lips turn upwards in a wry smile as I wipe my mouth with a napkin. Well, well, well. She wants me after all. "How can I help you, Kyra?"

Jessica's interest rockets. She sets down her fork, her eyes widening.

"Are you still interested in doing some volunteer work?"

Of all the times she could have called, she picks now. "Can we discuss this another time?" The quiet ambiance of the restaurant and the sight of my tantalizing steak divert my attention. I wish I hadn't taken this call.

"I don't have another time. You either want to help or you don't, and right now we could do with some help."

I cough lightly. It's late in the evening. What the hell could she possibly want right now? "Now? As in, right *now?*" It's after hours. I never signed up to work after hours.

"You said you were free. You said you were eager to help."

"I am, but, I'm kinda busy."

"You don't seem to be interested. Don't worry about it."

She hangs up.

My eyebrow lifts. No one hangs up on me. Jessica eyes me coolly. "Did I hear correctly? Was that ... Kyra Lewis?"

I hold up a finger, indicating to Jessica that I need to deal with this. Then I call Kyra Lewis back. She doesn't pick up until about the fifth ring, and this infuriates me even more.

"What?" Her irritation crawls down the phone.

"You hung up," I state, breathing in slowly, in order to ground myself.

"Look, Bradley. I don't have time to talk. Either you can help right now, or you can't."

This could be my chance to get into Redhill. "Where do you need me to be?"

"At Redhill."

"I'm making my way over." I hang up and stare at my barely touched steak, my mood plummeting at the meal I'm going to have to give up. Lewis had better make it worth my while. "I'm sorry. I have to go," I tell Jessica.

Shock animates her face. "Was that Kyra Lewis?" she asks, again, trying to read my expression. "It has to be. Such an unusual name. Such an unusual woman."

"It's business." I hesitate on whether to tell her.

Jessica wipes her mouth as her cool expression slips into confusion, wondering what I am up to. She doesn't need to know. "But you've barely touched your food," she cries."

"You've barely touched yours." I nod at her plate. She's had maybe a tiny flake of tuna, and a couple of salad leaves.

"I'm done." She presses a dainty, manicured hand against her super flat stomach.

I chortle. "You've hardly eaten a thing."

"What are you up to, Brandon? Level with me here. Why are you leaving me to see Kyra Lewis?" Is that a hint of disappointment I detect behind that cool mask, that flawless porcelain skin. I sense unease behind her cool blue eyes and perfectly painted glossy lips. Dare I think that she might even be jealous? "I'll explain later."

"Explain now."

"I have to go, Jessica."

"To see Kyra Lewis?" she snarls. This surprises me. Jessica is usually emotionless.

"What are you up to, Brandon?"

The muscles in my neck tighten. "I need to take care of something."

"At this time of the evening?" She's going to pry it out of me unless I tell her.

I huff out an irritated breath. "It's … you know I have my sights on Greenways?"

Jessica's eyebrows lift ever so slightly north. "Go on," she says, a wicked grin spreading on her face.

"I've offered her my services."

"What services?"

"My business acumen."

"What for?"

I'm tempted to quickly wolf down my steak, because I don't know what Kyra wants me to do or how long it could take. While this is a useful turn of events, it's not ideal, her interrupting my evening like this.

"To convince her that moving somewhere else would be better for her company. She doesn't know who I am. She has no idea. She thinks I'm a hippie-cum-redeemed-capitalist who has returned from a sabbatical visiting Third World countries and now I want to do good here."

Jessica claps her hands together. "That is brilliant! Absolutely brilliant!"

"Thank you." But I am still completely bummed about having to give up my steak. I need the deal, and this woman has summoned me. I should go because I have no choice. "Sorry to leave you."

"Don't be. I'm intrigued. This is fabulous; this idea of you going undercover. I want you to keep me up-to-date with your progress."

"You can't tell anyone, Jessica. It will ruin things."

"I won't tell anyone. I'm impressed at the lengths you're going to."

"The situation demands it." I get up and leave a wad of bills on the table. "Are you staying?"

"I'm all dressed up with nowhere to go."

"I can drop you back."

"You run along. Keep me posted."

"Sorry."

"Stop saying you're sorry. Why does she even want you at this ridiculous hour? Doesn't she have a life?"

"Evidently not."

She gives a stiff laugh. "What a crazy world, you leaving our dinner and seeing Kyra Lewis instead."

"*Seeing* her? I don't think so. I'd rather rot in Alcatraz."

"You owe me another evening, Brandon."

"We'll have dinner again soon, I promise." I take her hand and kiss it.

"I'll hold you to that." The smile she gives me has more sizzle than ever. She wants me. Odd that it's taken the mention of Kyra Lewis for her to express her feelings so pointedly.

I rush away, remembering that I have to get into character. That I'm not a billionaire any more, but a down-on-his-luck, broke loser.

Kyra hasn't told me a single thing, she hasn't given me a clue as to what she needs me for. I suspect she's calling my bluff. I got the impression she doesn't like me much, and for that very reason, I'm determined to rise to the challenge.

I rush home to change into my casual clothes, then drive the battered old Toyota Corolla. The fucking stick shift takes some getting used to. It's a cart. A real pain in the butt to drive. Every time I have to get into this, I cry for my Tesla.

I reach her factory and walk around the side to the back. What I see is like a punch to my gut. The huge expanse of land is now teeming with life. Lowlifes, by the looks of it. I suddenly feel as if I'm in the middle of Hell.

The place is a hive of activity, filled with people. A shiver rolls over me as I glance around. This assortment of people makes me want to retch. I suddenly fear for my life.

A long row of tables is on one side. People are setting them up, and others are bringing things over. I see the big guy, and then I notice that his arm is in a sling. He catches my eye and waves at me. I walk over to him, grateful to see a familiar face.

"Hey, glad you could make it. Kyra said she called you."

"Yeah, I came as soon as I could."

At least he seems happy to see me. When I ask him about his arm, he says he tripped and fell. I catch sight of the older woman setting up the tables with a bunch of others.

Still none the wiser, I ask him what's going on.

"It's our weekly food night for the homeless. Didn't Kyra tell you?"

Food night? We're feeding homeless people?

I gave up steak and Jessica for this? I look around with a sinking heart. This isn't what I signed up for. I fight the urge to gag.

We're feeding people who don't shower? Or clean? People who could be crawling with all sorts of lice and fleas? And then I remember what Jessica told me. Fredrich starts to pick up a box with his one good arm but I tell him I'll do it.

Holy crap.

It's heavy.

I follow Fredrich over to a table. Just as I set the box down I catch sight of Kyra who is carrying a box that looks way too big and, given the way she's struggling to carry it, seems too heavy for her.

"Will you stop it?" she cries as Fredrich tries to take the box from her. Then she sees me as she sets the box down.

"I see you made it," she states in a voice that drips more with disappointment than relief.

"You asked me to, and here I am."

"How about you help me get the rest of the stuff out?"

I swear under my breath as I follow her.

"I hope I didn't ruin your evening," she says.

"I was free, like I said." My voice is tight, like hers. We eye one another like pit bulls about to fight. She opens the double doors of a large van, fumbles around inside it and then hands me over another heavy box. She tells me to take it back to the tables and then to come back for more.

This is shit I'm not prepared for. Feeding people? I've left a perfectly fine, ridiculously expensive meal at a Michelin-starred restaurant, for *this*?

A quick glance at the crowd of people all standing quietly, patiently, waiting for something, unnerves me.

I have never been in a situation like this. Not in this life. I have spent the last twenty years trying to forget. I wipe my hand across my face and turn away, wondering how I am going to get through this evening. I see now that the people at the tables must be Kyra's staff and workers, and the group of misfits over in the distance are the ones needing to be fed.

"You can admire the scenery another time." Kyra's voice ricochets off my back. I turn around. "Jump in, make yourself useful."

"I carried a box." The words sound pathetic out loud.

"Get used to it. There are a lot of boxes to carry."

"I can manage." I sound like a teen trying to convince his parents he can handle booze.

Kyra stops. "Do you have any questions? I know it must seem like I've thrown you in at the deep end."

"You don't say."

"You told me you'd be willing to do anything. If you can't handle it, just let me know."

This woman is taunting me. I quirk an eyebrow. "I'm up for this."

She folds her arms as her expression turns jubilant. "You look as if you're going to throw up."

I force a laugh. And then my stomach rumbles, reminding me of what I gave up for this.

"You're mistaken." I head towards the tables, towards Simona where I expect a better reception and I get it.

"Brad!" She greets me with a smile. "How lovely to see you."

CHAPTER NINE

KYRA

The new guy looks lost. Like a fish out of water.

It struck me that his speech about him wanting to do this type of work, was too good to be true. And now I know that for a fact. He had no idea what he was letting himself in for.

He has stationed himself next to Simona which means I've been able to observe him from a distance.

He seems hesitant. As if he doesn't want to touch anyone lest he catches something. While I am aware that this is a hard situation to be thrust into without knowing the full details, I was determined to give him the benefit of doubt. His reaction tells me that he can't have worked in those poor communities doing what he claims he did, if he looks so uncomfortable now.

I expect someone like him to be more at ease in the financial district than here.

"He's getting along with it." Fredrich catches me ogling Brad. "Why do you keep looking at him?"

"He doesn't seem to be handling it well."

"He came, didn't he?"

Because Fredrich won't stay away, I've put him on napkin duty. It's not really a duty, but he doesn't seem to want to go home, so I've given him something that won't damage his arm even more.

I'm going to have to force him to stay at home for a week or two, otherwise he will make his arm worse and I can't afford for that to happen.

We've got Mr. Hartley now.

At the end of the evening, I tally up how many plates we've used, which gives me an idea of how many people we've fed. It's good to know, so that we can adjust the amount of food and supplies we need to bring for the next week. "One hundred and four people," I announce proudly as we start to clean up. Brad blinks at me. "We fed that many people this evening."

He looks unimpressed, and Simona hands him the empty containers and tells him to start loading up the van.

So now, I have to take him on even though I can see he's not cut out for this type of work. Still, he might be of some use at the factory. I'll try him out for a few weeks, by which time I expect him to fold and leave of his own accord.

I sent Fredrich home a while ago, citing that we had Brad now, and if he didn't go home, I wouldn't hire Brad.

"How did you find that?" I ask Brad.

"Great fun." His voice is flat. Unenthusiastic. Dry.

"He loved it." Simona gushes, even though I see no indication of this on Brad's face.

"I can see that he did," I reply enthusiastically, giving him a rare full smile.

"Can't wait for next week." His stony look is a treasure I adore looking at.

"You're on board then?"

"Wouldn't miss it for the world."

His sarcasm irks me. "It's not a show."

"No, right. Right." He scratches his brow as if he's unsure about something.

"If you can't deal with this, it's better you say so now," I tell him.

"It's not compulsory for our employees to do this," Simona points out. "If Brad is busy in the evenings, it's understandable."

I'm beginning to wonder if she sees Brad as an extension of her large extended family, as if he's one of her grandsons that she wants to take under her wing.

"It's not compulsory," I state calmly, "but no one has ever complained about giving some of their time for a cause such as this."

"He has business skills which I'm sure he can put to good use here," Simona says.

"Ladies, I'm here. You don't have to talk about me like a third party."

Simona apologizes.

"I'm fine. I can do this. I don't have a problem," he says. "You just caught me off guard."

"Did it ruin your date night?" I suggest, glancing at Simona and watching as she waits with bated breath.

"No. Just, uh, dinner ... with friends. But this is ... uh, this is ... yeah, it's cool. I can do this. I'm sorry if I seemed a little off at the start. I didn't know what to expect, and you can't hold that against me."

I stare at him defiantly, if he's looking for words of

encouragement, he won't get them from me. "Welcome aboard," I say, and even those words didn't come easily.

Simona claps excitedly. For some reason, she's ecstatic about the idea of Brad joining us. "Where's Fredrich?" She looks around for him.

"I sent him home. He's going to make his arm worse if he's not careful."

"Who's going to return the restaurant containers and things?"

I huff out a breath. "I am."

"I can take some containers in my car," Simona offers.

"I've got this, Simona. I've got the van." I shake my head. It's been a long day for all of us, but I won't have Simona, who is in her sixties and who works tirelessly, do too much. "I can take care of this. I'll ask a few of the others."

"You can't possibly carry everything yourself, you're not built like Fredrich. Would you mind giving Kyra a hand?" she asks Brad, much to my annoyance.

I observe his reaction; his unease is palpable. "We've already ruined his plans for the evening," I say, hoping to prevent this. "I don't think we can ask him to do any more." The guy looks as if he'd rather chew razor blades.

"Kyra already has a bad back, which is not a good thing at her young age," Simona counters. I glare at her. I've hefted too many things, and done my back no favors, but this isn't something I want her to tell Brad of all people.

"I don't mind helping." The tightness in his voice is apparently something that only I can detect because Simona looks incredibly happy, as if Brad has walked on fire for me.

"You're such a godsend." Her face lights up like a firecracker. And then something niggles in my brain. I might be wrong, but I think she has other reasons for wanting this man to work here.

"What needs to be done?" he asks, but his expression and body language indicate that he'd rather be anywhere but here. I flash him an over-the-top smile and lead the way.

Unease zigzags through me at the idea of just the two of us in the van.

CHAPTER TEN

BRANDON

She surprised me, and that's a rare thing. People rarely surprise me, but Kyra Lewis did. For someone as tiny as she is, she has the power of an ox. Those boxes and restaurant containers were heavy, as I found out later when I had no choice but to help her.

She drove, and I sat in that filthy, broken-down, rackety van with everything clattering in the back. It took so long. My whole evening wasted on some goddamn cause I find to be a waste of time and money.

Who knew such a thing even existed? Kyra said many good people and businesses in the city donated the food on those nights. I had no idea.

I hauled as much as I could, and we returned items to the restaurants. After that I was ready to leave. I'd had enough, but then I felt bad for letting her clean up in the storeroom by herself. So I offered to help her with that.

She observed my every move. I sense that she doesn't trust me or my motivations.

Wise woman.

She's smart. I have to give her that.

By the time we checked everything and locked the factory, ready to go home, it was almost midnight.

Midnight.

Apparently, she does this every week.

And she doesn't earn a cent out of it.

It's insane.

A complete waste of time and effort.

For nothing.

This is not how successful businesses are run. I don't understand these people, but I can already see that it's going to be eye-opening working here.

No wonder her business is a nonprofit—which is exactly as it sounds—*nonprofit*, because she's making squat. She'll never get rich, no matter how clever or smart or determined or hard-working she is.

She doesn't deserve to have Greenways. The value of that piece of real estate is lost on people like that. Far better for someone like me to move in and take care of things.

The next morning, I update Emma.

"You fed the homeless?" she asks, as if I've announced that I've got the nuclear codes.

I scratch my wrist. The thought of last night mixing with *those* people sends shivers down my spine. I stood under the shower for a good while after I got back, dousing myself with shower gel to make sure I had gotten rid of all the grime from that place.

"I did. You would have been proud of me."

"This won't end well, Brandon. I hope you know that."

"I'm only interested in securing that piece of land."

"Remind me again as to how exactly this is going to help you?" Emma's folded arms and stern expression indicates her continued disapproval. I'm sure she was secretly pleased when Kyra didn't hire me that first time. But this latest turn of events has really helped me.

"I'll earn Lewis's trust. I'll give her lots of great business advice. I'll convince her to believe in me. She influences many. The Greenways business owners listen to her. She's active on the committee over there. Through her, I'll earn their trust and along the way I'll advise her to move someplace else. Then I'll swoop in and take what I need without the headache of dealing with eminent domain."

"You don't think she will find out at some point?"

"Who cares? Nobody knows which company is behind a development. Nobody. Not the average layperson, that's for sure." I run my hand over my stubble and decide not to shave for a few days so that I will fit right in at Redhill. "It might not be such a bad idea for her to move. She wants to expand and she has a crazy idea about building another place next to her factory. It's going to be easier and will make more financial sense for her if she moved somewhere that had everything she wanted."

"It's wrong, it's so wrong, on so many different levels." Emma's shoulders sink. I wouldn't be too surprised if one day she walks in and tenders her resignation. There are limits, and I seem to be pushing hers all the time.

"Let me be the judge of that."

"If she's agreed to let you work for her," Emma air quotes the 'work' part, "who's going to take care of your business interests here?"

"I've taken care of that." I explain to her how, when Kyra

and I were unloading things into the storeroom, I casually mentioned that I'd found another job helping another company for a couple of days a week. She didn't seem to care. If anything, she seemed relieved to hear that I wouldn't be at Redhill today and that I'd come in the day after. I only offered to work there for two to three days a week, and that's two days too many. This whole charade is costing me a shit load of money, and it hurts.

"The things you do," Emma says quietly.

"Don't go leaving me. I rely on you. Also, I'm not hurting anyone."

Her eyebrow raises. She annoys me when she goes all Zen-like on me.

"I'm not *physically* hurting anyone," I clarify.

"Lies, lies. So many lies. One day, they will all catch up with you."

"I'm not going to get caught." I straighten my tie and sit up, ready to get to work. I have a lot of things to do in my office today, especially if I'm going to be splitting my time between here and Redhill. My businesses can't go unattended. There is too much money, and there are too many investments for me to take my eyes off Hawks Enterprises for too long.

"I'm pleased to hear that you fed the homeless. It might do something to reset your karma."

I look up and loosen my tie. "It's not easy feeding the homeless. I could have caught something bad; fleas, pneumonia, bronchitis or even TB."

"How worrisome for you."

I blink at the lack of Emma's sympathy. "You don't know what it was like, dishing out the food, then refilling the containers. Then having to take everything back to the restaurants. Then we had to go back to the factory and finish off there. I was ready to drop when I got home."

"My heart bleeds for you."

"It should, because on top of that, I had to give up a really good steak."

CHAPTER ELEVEN

KYRA

It's quiet as I sit in the office, sipping my cup of coffee. I didn't sleep well. Not only was it really late by the time I got back, but a thunderstorm rumbled and roared most of the night. I now appreciate more than ever just how quick and efficient Fredrich is at getting things returned after the food events, both to the restaurants and back at the office.

Not only did I not sleep, but my back is worse than before. I have to go easy on myself, but there's too much to do, too many things to lift and move, and the food nights are always hard.

I don't know what to make of the new guy. Sometimes he seems to want to help, and other times it feels that he's begrudgingly doing something he would rather not be doing. I am grateful for his help but he's no Fredrich. I've threatened Fredrich with no pay if he comes back and is less than one hundred percent. I need that man to be back to his normal fit and healthy state.

Brad isn't coming into the office today, for which I'm thankful. I consider myself to be a good judge of character but I'm not one hundred percent sure of him and I can't figure out why. I need more time.

"Good morning." Simona breezes in and eyes the buckets in the corner with disdain. "It was heavy this time, wasn't it?"

"It caught me unaware," I say. We're used to violent thunderstorms in the summer in the Midwest. It's just a shame that they wreak havoc with the roof.

Simona takes off her coat. "No Fredrich?"

"I told him to take a week or two off. I need him to heal completely and you and I both know that he can't sit still."

She looks around. "Where's Brad? Didn't you hire him?"

"He's coming in tomorrow, but he's going to try to do three days at the start of each week. He's got another job he needs to be at for the other two days and he's going to see how he can juggle the two."

"We should have taken him on the first day we saw him, maybe we could have had him for the whole week then." By 'we' she means 'me.' She sits down and switches her computer on.

"That might have been too much. You'll have him for a few days a week."

"At least that's something." She pushes her silver-rimmed reading glasses up.

"I'm not sure we have much work for him."

She coughs in exasperation. "You're always drowning in work. Surely you can offload some things to him?"

Simona seems to have fallen for his words. Me, I'd rather be more wary. I'm a control freak, too, which doesn't help. But there is no way I'm giving him too much top-level work to do. "We'll see. I'm not sure."

Simona looks displeased. "Not sure about what?"

"About him. You've spoken to him more than I have. What sort of vibe do you get from him?"

"I like him. What's not to like? He's young and good-looking—"

I roll my eyes.

"He wants to help us, he's happy to work for nothing. He has experience, and he wants to see what he can do for us and with us. Why can't you accept a good thing for what it is, Kyra?"

"Because when things seem too good, they often are."

Simona sighs loudly, then pulls out something from her bag. "They got engaged. He proposed!"

I lift my head because she sounds so excited. "Who?"

She opens up a magazine and holds it up so that I can see. I squint. I don't take any notice of celebrities. They're not on my radar. Shaking her head, she walks over to me and shoves the magazine in front of my face.

"Elias. He proposed to his girlfriend."

"Oh." I take the magazine and examine the photo, which looks like a paparazzi shot of Eli and his girlfriend, Harper. It's a casual photo, probably taken without them knowing. They're walking hand in hand along the street. I can't help but smile. These two make a lovely couple. I'm really pleased for them. I like them both but if Simona hadn't brought this piece of gossip explicitly to my attention, it would have escaped me. "That's great news." I hand the magazine back.

"You might get invited to the wedding."

"Why would I?"

"You will get an invite. Eli loves you and what you do here."

"That doesn't automatically get me an invite to the wedding."

It wouldn't surprise me if she's already planning their

wedding in her head. It's true though. Eli has shown great interest in Redhill. He reached out to us soon after he won the first fight and he came to the factory to meet everyone. It was a pleasant surprise to hear from Chicago's favorite guy. That visit didn't even make it into the papers. That's why I know he's a decent guy, and he didn't do this for the publicity. He's also become our biggest donor. This unknown boxer beat the heavyweight champion of the world against all odds and stole our hearts. He then lost the rematch and sent the city and everyone in it into shock. Now he's staging a comeback; another rematch next month, and we have plans for that night.

I pray this man wins. We all do, because Eli is so good and so humble.

I go through the pile of letters on my desk, opening them one by one, and become fully engrossed in them.

"There you go, working too hard all the time. You're so focused on helping everyone else, you're in danger of forgetting what's important to you."

"*This* is important." I see children in the food line sometimes. It's rare for parents to bring children along but when they have no childcare, what are they supposed to do? I see the haunted look in their mothers' eyes as they struggle to feed the family. The kids are too young to know any different, most haven't known anything but the daily struggle to survive, but maybe some of these mothers have seen better days.

We were never so broke that we needed this type of help. My mom worked all the shifts she could get to make sure that didn't happen. But she also taught us that despite how difficult things were for us, others had it so much harder.

I want to give hope back to these women and men, and teach them how to stand on their own two feet. I want them to have what I have, what I never take for granted—food and a roof over my head. Basic human needs.

***

The new guy comes in the next day, bright-eyed, and reeking of enthusiasm. I ask Simona to give him a quick tour of the factory and show him around.

"Are you sure you don't want to do that?" she asks, a hint of hope in her voice. "I've got a lot of paperwork to wade through".

She's up to something. She's always on top of her work. I had assumed she'd relish the idea of giving Mr. Hartley a tour. "I'm sure. You go. Brad will appreciate you giving him a tour. I'll have the pleasure of his company after, when I go through the ground rules."

"Ground rules? In this place?" He flashes me a smile which I'm sure many have found endearing.

I take offense at that dig. "We run a tight ship here. Don't think that because these people are more vulnerable than most that we don't treat them like employees. We have more checks and balances in place, more stringent rules and regulations because of the nature of the business."

"I didn't mean to offend you." He puts his hands up in a placating gesture but that cocky smirk on his face offends me even more. He's laughing at me. It's not only on his lips, but there's a twinkling of mischief in his eyes. Something I can't pinpoint.

"Let's go for that tour around the factory floor," Simona says, ushering Brad out of the door. She gives me a scowl over her shoulder, which Brad obviously doesn't see.

I call Fredrich, only because I need someone to talk to. Someone who can calm me down.

"What?" He sounds as if he's half asleep.

"Sorry. Didn't mean to wake you." I put the phone down, feeling bad that I'd woken him. Fredrich calls back immediately. "Do you need me to come in?"

"What? No. I didn't check the time before I called you." I drop my head, running my fingers along my brow. Fredrich is always ready and willing to work, even when he isn't one hundred percent fit enough. He was a great hire. He's not a vulnerable person, not from the streets or anything like that. He used to go for a run around the block and one day, out of curiosity, he walked in and asked what we were doing. When I explained to him the business idea, he was so enthused, he wouldn't stop bugging me to take him on. Like Brad, he also offered to work for free. He's grown with the company. "Go back to sleep." I insist, but he tells me that he's up now, and asks if I need him to do anything from home.

"Absolutely not. Don't lift a finger. We have help now."

"You hired Brad?"

"Yes. Simona's giving him a tour of the factory floor."

"Cool. I hope he's not going to replace me."

I snort. "Not a chance." No one could ever replace Fredrich. "I won't be surprised if he bails on us real quick."

"Why do you say that?"

"It's only a hunch." I don't say anything more, because if Brad is working here, I need team unity, and it's not fair for me to put ideas in his head about the new guy. But I saw his face at the food night. I could see behind his shock and dismay. Not everyone can do this work, and Brad is probably one of those people.

I hang up and get back to work, but the morning has been different with Fredrich gone and the new guy here.

Simona returns with our new hire a short while later. He goes and takes his place at Fredrich's desk, a move I find slightly presumptuous, given that I haven't told him where to sit. Though Fredrich's chair is the only one that's empty.

"Make yourself at home," I say dryly as he sits down and shifts around in it, trying to make himself comfortable. I laugh inwardly. This must be such a disappointment if he was expecting something made of expensive leather and soft padding.

"Fredrich's off for a week, maybe more, so you can sit where he usually does." I have no idea where to put this guy when Fredrich comes back. This room is too small to accommodate another desk, but maybe by then Brad will be long gone.

"I have an employee contract for you to sign," I say. "Just to be clear, this is a volunteer non-paying position."

"I'm absolutely fine with that. I don't expect to be paid."

"Good, because you won't be."

He laughs as he scratches his nose. "You're the one who headhunted me, so you obviously need me around."

"You have Fredrich to thank." I glare at him, and try not to get too carried away by a myriad of images flooding my mind about how I could wipe that condescending smile off his face. The nerve of the man. Already. "If he hadn't injured his arm, I wouldn't have called you."

"I'll have to thank Fredrich," he says, making himself at home in Fredrich's chair.

"I'm making a cup of tea," Simona announces, purely for Brad's benefit. I shift uneasily in my chair because there isn't much to discuss with this guy.

I've taken him on, but I haven't seen any of his resumes or asked for any references. I never expected to give him a position, and yet I was the one who called him, not really expecting him to show up, and he did.

And now he's here.

"I'll need to see a resumé." I clasp my hands together.

"Not a problem. I'll get one to you."

We glance at one another. Distrust hangs heavy in the air, mingling with the cloud of silence. The atmosphere is prickly, sharp and painful. This is going to affect my ability to concentrate.

"Is that a ...*bucket?*" He stands up then walks over to my desk, standing almost behind me and making me uneasy. "What's a bucket doing here?"

I swivel around on my chair.

"Oh, Jesus. There are two more." He eyes the corners diagonally opposite. I scratch the back of my hand, seeing this place through someone else's eyes is sobering. I've been able to overlook it, but this stranger sees all the flaws, the holes, the problems.

"That storm a few nights ago, it caused water to pool on the roof. It's not a big deal."

"Not a big deal?" The shock in his voice makes me want to cringe. Why is it that this man has barely been here long and already I'm embarrassed about this factory in a way I have never been before.

"This building is sound and safe. Don't worry your head about it."

"How can I not worry about this?" He looks up at the ceiling and he's still positioned behind my chair and I feel hemmed in. Trapped.

"It's not your problem," I say tightly. He's put me on the defensive with his views and his critical appraisal of the building. I find his proximity too much, so I scowl at him, hoping he'll realize he's overstepped his boundary and leave me alone. As I glance over my shoulder and up at him, I am horrified to find him peering at my computer screen.

"Shopping on company time," he tsks, and that *really*

annoys me. Heat pinches my cheeks and I quickly close my browser. I was looking for a pair of sneakers. He has a cavalier attitude, as if he's in charge, as if he's forgotten that I'm giving him a chance to work for us. I've done him a favor instead of it being the other way around. He has delusions of grandeur I don't like.

"Can you go back to your desk?" I make no effort to tamp down the resentment in my voice. I have never wasted company time. Instead, I give this company my all. I spend a lot of my weekends here clearing up storerooms, doing an inventory check of the food and supplies for the business as well as for the food events, and then I shop for these things.

I am entitled to taking a little work time for my personal reasons. This upstart catching me on one of my rare occasions really pisses me off.

"Do I make you nervous?" he asks.

"I'm not nervous."

His eyes twinkle. "You seem a little frazzled."

"I'm. Not. Frazzled." From where did he develop this sense of familiarity? Fredrich has been here for years and he's never spoken to me like that.

"You shouldn't be working in such conditions." He taps one of Fredrich's pens on the table. "That roof could be dangerous."

"It's not. As you can imagine, we have lots of rules and regulations which we have to abide by, and we do."

"Still, it's a safety concern." He stares up at the ceiling.

"It's fine." My teeth snap together. I don't see why he's making such a big deal about it. "The roof isn't going to collapse. Are you scared of getting your hair wet?"

Simona walks in just as I say that, and stands in the doorway, looking from me to Brad, with her dainty teacup and saucer in her hand. "I'll come back if you haven't finished."

I take a few deep, steadying breaths. "You can stay. There's nothing we can't discuss in front of you."

"No, no," she insists and disappears again.

"What type of work did you say you did abroad?" I am more curious than ever to get the lowdown on this guy.

"I didn't. I mean," he coughs lightly, "I helped out on some community projects in … uh … in El Salvador."

"In El Salvador?" I'm aware that many community projects take place in less developed countries, and that there are many tour agencies that facilitate such things. "Who was that with?"

"Excuse me?" He looks confused.

"Which agency did you go with?"

"I didn't use an agency. I'm not a wuss and I'm okay with traveling alone."

I stare at him. "You said you worked for some start-ups in Silicon Valley. I'll need a reference from a former employer."

"Is that necessary, now that I've started?" He stands up. For a moment, it looked like he was about to pull at his shirt sleeves, but he's wearing a t-shirt.

I sense resistance. "It's necessary. I need a resumé, too."

"Do you want to hear about what I can offer to your company?"

"Sure. Just don't forget about the paperwork I need from you." I remind him.

"I won't." He looks around. "I need a whiteboard. Do you have one?"

"Nope."

"How do you brainstorm ideas?" He looks at the walls, dirty and peeling. I suddenly feel more self-conscious than ever.

"We talk."

He shakes his head in disbelief. "Your setup doesn't help."

"With what?" I sit back and fold my arms defensively.

"I suppose you don't even have a conference room?"

"We don't need a conference room."

He swipes a hand over his forehead, as if this place, this setup, me and my management team, are a farce. I don't like his attitude one bit. I stand up slowly. "I don't think this is going to work."

His shoulders slump. "Because I'm telling you some hard facts?"

"Because your tone is insulting."

"I'm making observations."

"So far you've observed that we have buckets to catch the water, and that I've been surfing online on company time. You're complaining about the setup, and the building, and what you perceive to be a shortage of good resources." I cock my head. "Are you a journalist, looking for a story on me? I don't like to do interviews, but believe me, if this is why you're here, this isn't going to get you anything."

He throws his head back. "I don't need a story. You're the story. You're the one everyone talks about."

Simona walks in with her cup and saucer still in her hand. "I can't stand up for too long. I need to sit down."

"I never told you to leave," I say to her. This isn't the type of morning I had in mind. I put a hand to my back. I think I pulled something while I was lifting the boxes and shifting things the other night.

"Have you injured your back again?" chides Simona.

"I'll be fine. It always gets worse after food night." I decide to leave and walk around the factory floor. Or maybe I should check the storeroom. Anything to get away from here. Or maybe I can send Brad out to check for me.

"Will you run Brad through the inventory check in the storeroom when you can?" I ask Simona.

"Don't you want to do it?" There she goes again, trying to offload him onto me.

"No. It's fine. You go ahead. You can get started on things now." An idea comes to me. Why not get him to do the menial tasks I usually end up doing? "Can you show Brad the inventory list and have him go through and write down how much we have of everything?" I ask her, eyeing Brad with a sense of jubilation. "You can make yourself useful from the get-go." The corner of my lips curl up into a satisfied smile.

"Lucky me," he mumbles, loud enough for me to hear. Instantly, my elation freezes. That hint of insubordination puts me on alert.

"You're the one who came to me, looking for work," I remind him. "You're free to leave at any time."

The plastic smile he slaps on his face makes me sit up. He can't even be bothered to hide his displeasure with the task I've set him. "I'm happy to be here," he tells me, as he saunters out after Simona.

I'm left wondering what I've let myself get into.

CHAPTER TWELVE

BRANDON

I follow Simona to the storeroom, anger seeping out of my pores at the thought of the menial task before me.

"This is where we keep everything. My goodness," Simona's hand flies to her chest. "This is all very neat and tidy. It will make your task much easier."

"I helped her with that," I point out. "Last night. We were here until late."

"That's Kyra for you. She has no life outside of work."

I snort. I can tell. As CEO of this business, Lewis needs to work on the business, not waste her time cleaning up storerooms and doing the inventory.

"You don't look happy," Simona comments.

I'm not used to doing menial tasks. I have people to do that for me. But I'm also not impressed by the menial jobs that Kyra does. "She's wasting her time cleaning out the storeroom and rearranging the shelves. She should be focused on more important things."

"She works too hard, that girl. Fredrich does a lot, but she still puts in all the hours. Kyra has no airs and graces. If she sees that something needs doing, she'll do it."

"You can't beat commitment like that," I say, "But she could still make better use of her time." I gaze around the room, seeing it properly this time and not wanting to get my clothes dirty, but I have no option. I've put myself into this disgusting situation, and now I have to see it through. Which means I have to check the inventory against the items that are here. It is craziness of the highest order.

"Is this important?" I jerk my head at the shelves. "Feeding the homeless? Why does she do that when it has nothing to do with the core business. That's where she should be spending all her time and effort."

"Kyra wants to do her part in getting rid of poverty and homelessness."

"Why? Was she homeless?"

"She wasn't homeless, but she's known hard times. Her mother, bless her dear soul, encouraged her daughters from an early age to help out in soup kitchens. Kyra tells me how she and her sister, Penny, used to help out on Christmas day."

"Help out?" My eyes widen as I choke it back, keeping it suppressed, the past that threatens to rise up from my belly and into my throat. "On Christmas day?"

"That's what she told me."

I wonder if she and I have more in common than not.

"Here's the list of things we need for the food nights." Simona hands me a notebook. "Just note down how many of each item we have." I take the notepad and pen and force a smile. Simona turns to leave. "We're grateful that you've joined us."

"You might be. I'm not so sure about Kyra."

"She might not seem very warm, and you might think

she's not grateful, but she needs the help. She has grand plans."

"Grand plans?" My ears prick up. My smile widens as I slide my hand into my pocket. "I'm sure she does, a smart and resourceful woman like her. What is she hoping to do?"

"Build out. For a start, expand the size of this factory. Our demand is fast outstripping our supply. News about what we do here seems to have caught the mood, and word is spreading fast. We're also seeing an uptick in people wanting to work here, and soon we're going to run out of room. She doesn't like to turn people away."

"She turned me away."

"You're not a vulnerable person, someone coming off the streets and striving to make a better life."

"Is that the bar for entry?" What a goddamn low bar.

"We also take on women fleeing from domestic abuse."

What a great line-up of people. I can't imagine what their resumes look like. I also can't get my head around hiring losers. I only hire the best. "She sounds like a saint."

"She's not, nor does she see herself in that vein. She, like everyone here at Redhill, wants to provide an environment where people who have been knocked down have a helping hand. We don't give benefits or welfare checks. We give them hope and a strategy."

"I guess you do." A tiny part of me understands what she's trying to do. Simona examines my face carefully.

"If Kyra isn't being as gracious as she could, it's because you don't strike her as someone who needs that type of help."

"I'm not interested in working on the factory floor. I'm interested in doing my bit and helping her with the business. I had assumed she'd be grateful for my help."

"She will be, she is. Just give her some time to warm up to you."

"Thanks for showing me the ropes, Simona. This place will look transformed when you next see it."

I work methodically, taking note of the supplies. If Emma could see me now, she'd be roaring with laughter. She would think I deserved it.

Kyra walks in sometime later. "Haven't you finished yet?"

"I was double checking everything."

She looks around the room. "Still, it shouldn't have taken you all morning. I had put some time aside to go through some of our marketing ideas."

I rub my hands together, recoiling in disgust at the idea of the filth that has seeped through my pores. "We can do that now."

"There's more. Follow me." She walks away, leaving me no choice but to follow her. She shows me to another larger storeroom off the hallway. I am starving. I need my lunch. Suddenly I'm craving a pastrami sandwich.

"If you could clean up in here. With Fredrich away, I'm not going to get a chance to sort this out until the weekend. This is where we store the deliveries for our product line."

"You want..." I choke internally. My stomach goes into lockdown at the thought of no food. "You want me to clean this now?"

"Do you have a problem with that?"

I do. I'm about to die of hunger. "No."

"Good, because we have a delivery of supplies coming in this afternoon. We get it every few weeks and I'm going to need your help bringing things in here."

"I was about to have my lunch," I announce, my brain furiously looking for ways to get out of doing this. "Do you suffer from OCD?" I lean against the doorframe and rub my hands together as if I'm getting rid of the imaginary dust.

"My mom was convinced I was."

"And now? Does she think you're over it?"

She moves her lips but no words come out, then. "She died a while ago ..."

Oh, shit.

She walks over to a shelf and lines up a box that is already neatly lined up. I follow her.

"I'm sorry." I place a hand on her shoulder but she shrugs it away. That's when I notice it; a small tattoo on the rounded part of her shoulder. It's in the shape of a sun, and I'm suddenly curious about it. But before I can comment on it, she hurls an order at me.

"This room is messy. If you can manage to hold off your hunger, do you think you could tidy this before the deliveries arrive?"

"Sure. I mean, I was going to go to lunch but, whatever."

She hangs her head as if she's having problems coming to terms with what I've said. "You need to eat. Of course you do. Go ahead."

She turns her back to me again and starts to move things around on the shelf. The urge to walk away and get the hell out of this place is strong, but I have a reason I've put myself through this. I can't wimp out now.

"I'll do it. You don't have to. I'm hungry, that's all." She's doing this to test me. I'm sure she would allow Fredrich to have a break, or god forbid, eat, if he was about to die from starvation. Kyra Lewis doesn't bring out the best in me; I turn into a monster when I haven't eaten for a while.

"I've got this, Hartley. You go and eat something before you faint."

Two strikes. She says my name as if it's snake poison, deadly and vitriolic.

If she only knew who I am. What I have. What I own.

"There's no need to get so riled up." I start moving things

around. "Do you want everything lined up neatly along the walls?"

"Yes, and make room there," she points to another wall, "for the delivery that's coming this afternoon." She slaps her hands along her slacks. "Can you handle it?"

"I can handle it, Lewis. Don't you worry about a thing." Satisfaction warms my insides to see the hard set of her jaw. She's the boss, but I don't treat her like one, and she hates me for it.

That's what I call a result.

CHAPTER THIRTEEN

KYRA

Simona thinks I'm being cruel and she could be right.

She says I'm being hard on Brad just because I've had him working in the storerooms for most of the day. He had barely finished in the factory storeroom when our new deliveries arrived. Now I've asked him to move everything and to make it all neat and tidy.

"You don't know how to be around someone who is young and good-looking and of the opposite sex!"

I almost choked on the bite of my sandwich when she said that. "I'm cool around Fredrich, and I'd say he ticks all those boxes."

She scowls. "Fredrich is like a brother."

I make a face. "To me or to you?"

"Don't try to change the subject, Kyra."

"Please don't play matchmaker." Simona likes to meddle in these matters. As much as I love her, Simona has been trying to push me into getting back onto the dating scene. I haven't been in a relationship for over eighteen months, ever since I split up with my boyfriend. He said I was more interested in Redhill than I was in our relationship. He blamed our continuing distance on me spending so much time on the business. Later, I found out that he had been seeing someone else for most of the time we were together.

I give my all to Redhill, and I don't have time for a relationship. The hurt still bruises inside. Simona thinks I'm working too hard, and she's worried that I'm lonely and bored. She thinks I'll die an old spinster. There are worse ways to die.

"I don't know if Brad is single or not. I haven't yet gotten around to asking him," she says.

I'm just about to ask her why she needs to know this, when I hear his voice.

"I am, as it happens. Why? Who needs to know?"

That same old wry grin, irritating as anything, is the first thing I see. Simona's face lights up. "We were just wondering."

"I wasn't," I grumble, feeling the heat on my cheeks.

"I don't have a girlfriend at the moment, if you must know."

Because I need to look busy and not as if I'm embarrassed by this conversation, I keep my eyes on the screen and start typing random words that make no sense.

"I've finished organizing the new delivery. Do you want to see what I've done?" This is leveled at me, but I can't bring myself to look at him.

"Ky-ra?" His tone is deliberate, as if the slight elongation of my name is an attempt to annoy me.

"What?" I snap back. I can sense a telepathic link between us, as if he can read my thoughts and is doing his best to irritate me.

"You're looking flustered," he notes, inflaming me even more. I glance at him standing in the doorway, his broad shoulders filling out his t-shirt, as he crosses one foot over the other, displaying a sense of ease and nonchalance that is the exact opposite of my mood right now.

"I'm not."

Simona laughs in the background. "You bring a much-needed dose of humor to this place, Brad."

I want to glare at Simona, because I don't like her putting down our workplace, but I manage to remain calm. I smooth my hands over my thighs, then rise from my chair. "Let's see what's taken you all afternoon."

"I'm not as fast as Fredrich, and I'm not built like a tank."

"That's obvious." I try not to stomp down the stairs.

"Are you annoyed because I overheard you both of you talking about me?"

"Can you get it through that skull of yours, *we* weren't." I throw him a stony look, a dangerous thing to do given that we're walking down the stairs.

"Didn't sound like that to me. I'm curious to know how the pair of you ended up discussing my relationship status."

We reach the bottom and I head towards the storage room, ignoring him. Everything is neat and clean. The boxes are all lined up perfectly, and there is a whole side of the room that's empty.

"Not bad. Almost as good as Fredrich." I smile smugly at him.

"Like I said, I'm not built like him. I can only try."

"I don't suppose you're used to getting your hands dirty."

"What makes you say that?"

I stare at his hands. "You have soft hands that look like they haven't done a day's work of hard labor."

"Lewis, are you hitting on me?"

"No, Hartley. In which alternate universe would you think I was?"

He hooks his thumbs into the belt loops of his jeans and flashes me a cheesy grin as if he's enjoying this immensely and at my expense.

"You're admiring my hands, you and Simona are talking about whether I have a girlfriend or not—"

"Don't flatter yourself." He's driving the conversation into uncharted waters. Worse, he seems to enjoy making me feel uncomfortable, and even worse than that, he thinks I'm crushing on him. "What brings you here?" I ask. "Someone like you could go work in the city. You could get a job as a banker or something, because you look the part."

"Look the part?" He guffaws, then appears to stumble back, holding his hand to his chest. "Of all the lines I've ever heard, Lewis, this is the most unexpected."

He has steamrolled this conversation into something that it never was. "It's not a line. It's definitely not a line. Hear me say it again, it's not a line. It's not even a compliment. It's merely an observation."

"I'm going to take it as a compliment whether you intended it as such or not."

"You do that," I tell him, feeling worn down by this volleying back and forth. A conversation with him drains me, and I suddenly wish Fredrich was back.

CHAPTER FOURTEEN

BRANDON

It's going to be jarring, splitting my time between Redhill and Hawks Enterprises. I can already tell as I rush back to my office later that day to check in on things. Emma follows me to my desk, wearing her tell-me-more face.

"Well?" she asks.

I examine my hands, trying to look at them with Kyra's eyes. "She has a crush on me."

"Oh, for goodness' sake!"

My PA's reaction takes me by surprise. I am a catch, so her reaction is unwarranted. "Trust me on this."

"Kyra Lewis has a crush on you? I find that somewhat hard to believe."

"Careful, Emma." Still, I find her reaction amusing. "It's the end of the day, shouldn't you be going home?"

"I can't, not until you tell me how this saga is unfurling."

"It's hardly a saga." I quickly look through the various folders that are lying on my desk, marked for my attention.

"It's beginning to sound like one." Emma perches on the armrest of the executive chair opposite my desk eagerly awaiting my update.

"Oh, I need a reference."

"A reference?"

"And a resumé. I'll type something up, but she needs a reference from people I told her I worked for. She wanted a couple, but I guess one will have to do. I'm going to give her your email."

"What am I supposed to say?" Emma looks horrified.

"That I worked with you in San Jose. Just make it sound like I was a great worker, a team player."

"I won't lie for you, Brandon."

I suck in a breath. "Fine then. I'll type up something and can you at least use it to reply? You're not technically lying then."

"I'm an accessory."

"I'm not committing murder." Though sometimes Kyra makes me mad enough to feel like I could kill someone. "I spent most of today cleaning up the storerooms at the factory."

Emma's hands fly to her face in shock. "Cleaning up? Storerooms? *You?*"

We spend the next few minutes, Emma in shock, and me trying to convince her that I got my hands dirty, picking up huge crates and boxes and moving them around. "I don't believe you."

"I know, crazy isn't it? But it's true."

"This. Isn't. You."

"I know." It's a miracle that I didn't walk out and turn my back on this sorry situation.

"I'm shocked that you're still there."

"I'm on a mission. Trojan horse and all that. Undercover—"

"For all the wrong reasons."

"For the right reasons." I point my thumb at me. "The right reasons for me."

"You're going to break this girl's heart."

"I don't care about this girl."

Emma's expression hardens. "This isn't fair."

"All's fair in love and war."

"You're better than this," she insists, before muttering, loud enough for me to hear, "Not much better, but *better*."

"I'm going to convince her to relocate to another place, and who knows, it might work out better for her in the long-term. It might turn out that I've done her a favor."

"That's a lie you're telling yourself, Brandon."

"It will work out in the end, you'll see."

Emma won't understand, but I do. Sometimes, things work out for the better, even though at the time it doesn't seem like that.

I happened to have struck gold and I got lucky early on in my life, when the odds were stacked against me. I was adopted by a man who was filthy rich. Unfortunately for me, he only wanted to adopt one child.

That lucky break meant I had a lucky start in life, when the real circumstances couldn't have been more different. That's how I ended up being the son of a billionaire. It meant that I could reinvent myself and forget my past and everything in it.

I can't force Kyra to move, not yet, but I do intend to persuade her to move. And if she does, that's on her. The ultimate decision will be hers.

"I don't like it," Emma says, pushing off the armrest. "Good night."

I wait for her to close the door behind her, and then I rub my eyes. It's going to be a long night by the time I've checked all of this paperwork. I open a folder and look inside, but my mind isn't on the work. It's on my day at Redhill, and the work I did, something I never could have anticipated for myself.

And Kyra.

Lewis.

There's something about her that grates on me. I don't hit on women, especially on women like her, but there is something about us being together that rubs off on me and winds me up the wrong way. It brings out a side of me that enjoys riling her up.

I don't even have this with Jessica. Jessica is all ice and water. Kyra is fire and sizzle. It confounds me more because it is so unexpected. Her short hair, slim frame don't appeal to me. There is no height, no long legs, no ample bosom, no long hair, or twinkling eyes. No full mouth. No finesse. Nothing.

And yet, I enjoy pissing her off.

But I also see another side to her. She works hard. I can see it now that I've had to step into her shoes and do some work. And while from the outside, the factory looks like it's going to fall apart, I am mildly surprised that inside it looks much better—aside from the buckets to catch the rain.

But my eyes are firmly on that coveted piece of land which I will turn into an acre of diamonds. A slice of paradise in the urban oasis. Not an urban jungle.

All I have to do is take down Kyra Lewis and the people of Greenways will follow her like a pied piper to a place far away from here.

By the time she finds out my part in all this, it won't matter. It won't matter because I'll have amassed more wealth, more buildings, more real estate. All the things that really matter.

CHAPTER FIFTEEN

KYRA

I'm not usually so hard on people and Simona's reminder that I am with Brad makes me consider why I'm being like this. Maybe she has a point. The breakup with my ex has hardened me.

Brad isn't going to be here for that many days in the week, so maybe I should make an effort to be civil to him and not jump to any conclusions.

Perhaps I am guilty of some bias, and that's why on an unconscious level, I find myself unable to trust him. He comes across as someone who hasn't had it hard. I shouldn't hate people who haven't suffered hardship.

I don't.

Simona hasn't suffered, and neither has Fredrich. So, that can't be it. Maybe I'm wasting too much time thinking about our interactions, and the best way to overcome the analysis, and to get Simona off my back, is to make a conscious effort to be nice to him.

"How about we go through a few things, and I share with you our plans for the future?" I say when he comes in the following week.

For a moment, he looks surprised, but he quickly covers it. "Sure."

"Grab a chair." Simona looks up from her desk at this looking very pleased. I narrow my eyes at her while waiting. This is Brad's small reward for spending all day cleaning up the storerooms. Him doing that saved me from coming in over the weekend and for that I'm grateful. "This is what I envision." On a large sheet of paper, I draw the layout of Greenways with the factories, and the row of stores, and large expanse of land at the back.

A whiteboard would help, because it would mean that Brad wouldn't have to sit beside me at my desk, and that way I wouldn't be able to catch a hint of his shower gel or cologne.

It's distracting. I never notice this about Simona or Fredrich. I don't waste countless minutes of my brain time obsessed about their shower gel.

"That's a lot of land," he remarks.

"Here is where we're thinking of setting up another factory or warehouse." I indicate the area to the side of our factory.

"But that's not empty land," Brad points out. "There are still buildings on either side of you."

"I'm hoping that they might sell soon, and then we can either rebuild or take them over."

He scratches his jaw as if he's unsure. "Are you sure you want to stay here?"

"I'm absolutely sure. Why?"

"Look around you. This building has holes in the roof. The area is becoming more downmarket—"

"Who told you that?" I ask him. He blinks but says

nothing. "This area is up and coming, especially with all of the new roads and infrastructure that they've been building around here. Soon enough, it's going to have an impact and we will see the benefit."

"I don't know." He doesn't look convinced.

"Who told you that this area was diminishing in value?"

He shrugs and slaps a hand across the back of his neck. "Maybe I got it wrong."

"You've been out of the loop too long. How long were you away for?"

"Away?"

"You said you worked abroad on community projects."

"A couple of years."

"A couple of years? I had no idea it was that long. I got the impression that you were there for a few months, less than a year, if that."

"I guess that's what it felt like. That whole time is a blur to me because I moved around a lot and worked on a few different projects."

"You must have been gone a while because this part of Chicago is up and coming. It would be silly of me to leave now when things are picking up around here. I know this from the city officials."

"The city officials?"

"We have access to people who are informed about these things. It's nice getting noticed for the work we do. We've had lots of people reach out to us with donations of money."

"Excuse me, Kyra ..." Simona interrupts to announce that Elias is on the line now.

"I need to take this. Elias Cardoza is our biggest benefactor. Put him through, Simona."

BRANDON

Holy crap.

I move back to my desk and absorb what Kyra has just told me. She has officials that are on her side, and Elias Cardoza has called her.

How is it that Lewis has people like him on her side? The fucker didn't get in touch when my people reached out to him. Knowing that he is Chicago's favorite son, and the city's biggest draw, and that he's suddenly accumulated vast wealth which someone of that caliber won't have a clue what to do with, I told my people that we needed to meet with him. Having him endorse a few of our projects, or even invest in some, wouldn't be such a bad thing.

But he never returned a single call, and now he's calling Saint Kyra Lewis.

I'm also not sure she bought my story about going abroad and helping out in community projects. That was a near miss. It's not easy keeping my story straight, and Kyra has an annoying habit of quizzing me on details when I least expect.

She's smart and that's something else I wasn't prepared for, as well as her letting me in on her plans. This is a turnaround from yesterday. I woke up aching all over. It wasn't the gym type of ache, where only the muscles that I've worked out hurt, but a dull whole-body ache. Lifting and shifting those pallets around wasn't easy work and I came in today dreading that Kyra would find something else just as hard for me to do.

I have nothing to do now, except eavesdrop on her conversation with the boxer. She's laughing, and her voice is softer. They're talking as if they're friends.

This is news to my ears.

I had all these preconceived ideas about this woman and they are all coming apart one by one.

"You're on her good side today." Simona's whisper sounds positively jubilant.

I hold up my hand and cross my fingers. Kyra—still on the phone—lets out a hoot of laughter which pinches my sides. "Are they best buddies?" I ask Simona, because I find it strange, the idea that Lewis and Cardoza are friends.

She opens a tube of hand cream and rubs it over her leathery hands. "Elias supports Redhill. He got in touch with us a while back, and he's a very generous donor."

He got in touch with *them?*

The fucker.

"We're doing a special food night event when he has his big fight." She's still massaging the cream into her hands. "But I'll let Kyra tell you all about it when she gets off the phone." She stands and picks up a notebook and pencil. "I'm going down to the factory floor. Would you please let Kyra know, in case she needs me?"

"Sure."

"You can come visit any time, Elias. You're always welcome here," Kyra smiles into the phone. My belly hardens. I swear she's doing that on purpose, wanting to show me how friendly she is with Chicago's biggest draw.

I'm not used to playing second.

Not in business.

Not in conversations.

Not ever.

Kyra has managed to get results where my team and I have failed. When the phone calls ends, I walk towards her, with my chair in one hand, strategizing and plotting in my head. "You guys seem to know Elias Cardoza well." Kyra was talking to the guy as if they were best buddies.

"We all do. He's a cool guy," Kyra replies.

"Yeah?" I've tried to get the guy to commit to a few special projects I've had on the go but he's been impossible to pin down. His management team isn't forthcoming either.

"He's one of our biggest donors." Is that a smugness I sense around Kyra as she delivers this news? She seems to enjoy pointing out this fact. "He's been here quite a few times."

"Really?" This is incredible and it pisses me off. I've got it all wrong. I used to think the doors opened if you were filthy rich, but it seems that Hollywood and sports types want to help the poor.

It's an interesting angle and one I hadn't considered or appreciated before. I listen as she tells me about the times Elias Cardoza has come here, how he was given a tour of the factory floor, and how he seemed particularly interested in Kyra and how she set the entire operation up.

"He's empathetic, he wants to do good, he doesn't take things for granted. He isn't a—" She stops. She was reeling off a list and I am sure she was making a point about me.

"He isn't a?"

"He's just a really great guy." She blinks at me, and I suddenly find myself marveling at the length of her long lashes. They're naturally long, because she's not wearing any mascara, at least, not that I can tell. "What were we talking about before?" she asks, suddenly.

"You were telling me about the city officials."

"And I was also telling you that we're not moving from Greenways."

"But expanding and building a new factory or warehouse might not be efficient," I counter. "What if you could find exactly what you need, more space, a larger factory, and all you had to do was move in? No rebuilding, no nothing."

"Greenways is perfect for what I have in mind. I'm not just talking about having a larger factory, I'm talking about developing the land."

"I hear you wanting to stay here. This is your baby. You've created this magnificent company and you want to see it grow tall and strong, but you need to have a strong foundation." I pause for effect and point to the buckets behind her. "Those things do not indicate that."

"We had a thunderstorm and because the roof's flat, it causes the water to pool," she explains matter-of-factly. "There's nothing wrong with this building. In fact, we have plans about developing the land."

"You? Developing the land? For what?" I sit up taller, straining my ears because she's beginning to sound like me with all this talk.

"For future projects." Her guarded voice tells me she's not so willing to share that dream with me.

"What future projects?" I lean forward, and the tiny flinch her body gives—the slight, imperceptible jerk of her moving a quarter-inch away from me—tells me I'm invading her space in a way that makes her uneasy. Or excited. I look directly into her eyes. She has freckles along her nose and cheeks that I never noticed before. Just like I never noticed the little embers of yellow in the green of her eyes.

She clears her throat, the way someone does when they want to buy time to figure a way out. Only, I'm not about to let her out of this. She's the fly in my sparkling, glittering web, and I can smell her unease.

"Are you not willing to share because they're not solid plans?" I ask, now that I have her full attention.

"They're solid. They're definitely solid."

She didn't like what I said. Kyra doesn't like to be seen as weak, or lacking a spine. She's also the type of woman who doesn't soften with flattery.

"We may not have the best building, but in time, we can build anew." She gets up and walks over to the window. "You see the almost derelict row of buildings across from us?" She indicates with her finger. "I want to create small units for people to rent out and base their own small businesses in."

"Small units? What do you mean? What people?" A ball of disbelief, as flimsy as the fabric on which her new dreams are drawn, catches in my throat and holds.

"People who want to start their own business but don't have the infrastructure in place. We're talking little mom-and-pop units."

"Wait, wait, ..." I have to hold it together. If I understand this correctly, the idea is plain batshit crazy. "You want people who have no business experience to set up a small business at absolutely no cost to them?"

This is in complete contrast to my own plan to build luxury condos. The idea that she wants this for people who have no business knowledge sets my guts on fire.

This is crazy. It shouldn't be allowed because it makes no financial sense. My plan for what I will do with this area is solid, and it will make money. Hers is a straitjacket of insanity.

"It depends on what people want, what their passion is."

"Most people go through life not knowing what they want, and they certainly have no clue about passion."

"And some do."

"But you're talking about the down-and-outs of society. Do you really think they would magically know about their passion, and what they want out of life?"

At my lowest, it was food I had to forage for. For both of us. I forget to watch what I'm saying because I am so pissed off. That's the difference between people like her and people like me. Kyra wastes money by investing in losers. I don't.

Her soft and friendly post-Cardoza demeanor hardens in an instant. "Down-and-outs? Is that what you think of them?" She looks more pissed than I've ever seen her; hands on hips even though she doesn't have the height or body to make a strong stance.

She's trying, though. I have to give her that.

"I want to empower people to take control of their lives and to fend for themselves," she snaps.

"These people are happy for handouts."

"Is that what you think?" The rage inside her combusts and she looks more pissed than I've ever seen her. She looks as if she'd like to take a swing at me with a baseball bat. "These people want a better start for themselves and their families. Like many of us do. I don't understand how you can't see that."

"Because it makes no sense."

"You have no empathy, no compassion," she rages. Her eyes fire up like angry flames in a furnace.

I'm a businessman and I know better. It's not what I say to her, of course. I try to level with her. "You have to be careful because if people don't know the basics of running a business, of knowing their profit and loss, of keeping costs down, and especially if they haven't had to pour their hard-earned money into something, they won't care as much as you do."

Her brows push together. She's not taking the bait. "We're done for now." She dismisses me with a nod of her chin, quickly.

I grab my chair and walk it back to my desk. "This is … this is a great piece of land you have here. It has potential," I concede. "All I'm saying is that not everyone is as smart and as determined as you."

"Don't try to flatter me."

"I wasn't trying to." I bite down on my teeth because she pushes my buttons, and unlike Emma, I can't give her a dismissive nod or tell her to leave because I am not in charge. This is her domain.

CHAPTER SIXTEEN

KYRA

"That man annoys the hell out of me. I can't stand him. He's a ... He's a ... UGH." I stamp my foot like a child having a tantrum. I've come to check on Fredrich. It's also because I need to vent my fury, because I've just finished telling him about my conversation with Brad earlier today.

"Whoa." Fredrich leans back on the couch, his arm still in a sling, resting on his thigh. "He really gets to you."

"I was trying to be nice. I thought I'd let him in on our vision and future plans to see what he thought of it."

Fredrich blows out a loud breath, but he doesn't say anything, and that irritates me even more.

"Don't you agree?" I press him for an answer. "He doesn't see our vision. He thinks that letting vulnerable people open their own businesses is a waste of time and money. This surprises me because I would have expected him to be more understanding given that he helped people when he was on his travels. There's a disconnect between what he *says* and what he *does*."

"Have you been watching him closely the entire time?" Fredrich runs his good hand through his hair. I don't like the way he hesitates, as if he's trying to find an excuse for Brad's behavior, for his point of view, for who he is. "You can be quite scary at times."

"Me? You think I'd make Brad Hartley scared?" This is ridiculous.

"Maybe he hasn't seen first-hand what a difference Redhill has made because he hasn't seen how people have benefitted. We know, because we've seen our employees' lives transform. He hasn't had that vantage point. If he doesn't know what people are capable of, then you can't blame him for being ignorant."

Fredrich has a point. Part of the reason I do what I do is because transforming people's lives brings me such a sense of accomplishment. It gives me immense joy to know that someone who lived in fear of her husband, and could barely look me in the eye when talking to me, is now one of our model employees and a team leader. I've seen this many times over.

"But he was convinced that we'd be wasting our time and money setting up small business units."

"You told him about that?"

"I told him about that. Simona told me to be nice, so I was being nice, or so I thought, by sharing our future vision."

"He's only been with us for a few days, Kyra. Give the guy a chance. Have his references checked out?"

"I only got one. His resume looked good."

"Maybe it's something else then." Fredrich looks at me oddly.

"What?"

"I sense a love-hate thing going on between you both."

"Oh, for the love of all things sparkly. Not you too."

He roars with laughter. "Who else has noticed?"

"Please stop." I place my palms together, prayer-like, and point them at him. "Please."

"Simona?" he guesses.

"Who else?" The woman has come to see it as a personal crusade, trying to get me paired up.

"You have been more uptight than usual," Fredrich comments.

We are not going to have this conversation. "He's bossy. Don't you find him to be bossier than our usual hires?" I say this having observed Brad for a few days. He has an air about him that is not submissive, but more dominant.

Fredrich considers this. "You have to remember that he was in a different industry before, working with start-ups in San Jose. This is probably his first time working for a nonprofit."

"He does have a way about him. Like he wants to be in charge," I challenge. I can't explain it in words. "Maybe it's a man thing."

"A. Man. Thing?" Fredrich rests his plastered arm on his lap. "Which reminds me, I'll be fine and back to work in time for Elias's fight event. Don't you worry about a thing. I've been taking care of everything."

Elias's fight. I haven't thought about it at all. We have an event organized for the night of Elias's next fight against Trent Garrison, the guy Elias first won the title from, and then subsequently lost the rematch to.

It was Fredrich's idea to have some sort of bigger food night on the night of the fight. We're having a big screen put up, and more food, and security. It's our way of making the fight accessible to people who ordinarily might not get a chance to see it, but it's also a way of doing our bit to support Elias after all the support he has given us. All of it has been genuine and under the radar rather than for the benefit of the TV cameras.

This is why I need people like Fredrich in my team. Even when he's not fully able-bodied, he's still pulling his weight.

I get up to leave. "This is why I want you rested and well, so that you can run with this when you get back."

"We'll still need all hands on deck."

"Everyone at the factory is pitching in that night."

"And our newest recruit?" Fredrich asks. "Will he be there?"

I roll my eyes. "I haven't told him yet. I suppose I should."

"Yeah, damn right you should. It's a big event for us." Fredrich gets up and sees me to the door. "I'm definitely getting the love-hate vibe."

"You're delusional." There's definitely a hate vibe effect going on. Brad Hartley has opinions and a way about him that borders on presumptive.

CHAPTER SEVENTEEN

BRANDON

What the fuck am I doing here? This is the question I ask myself as I walk up the stairs a few days later. Going undercover, putting up with this ploy when I could so easily strongarm my way in and get my hands on the land. I could serve my interests better that way. I have the means and the contacts, and the ear of certain city officials.

But as I peruse my cell phone to check for the local news, I'm reminded why I'm going in stealth mode. I find myself staring at a photo of Kyra and the rest of the crew. The write-up is glowing. Kyra is portrayed as an angel. The savior of this city. The Mother Teresa who empowers these people to rise up and fend for themselves.

This is why I'm undercover. Because when it comes down to me—a businessman and the face of capitalism, someone who wants to make more money—versus *her,* I'll be labeled as the greedy capitalist pig. I will lose to the good people of this city who will hate me and what I stand for. Getting into a fight with Kyra, in a blaze of publicity, means I will lose.

I have absolutely no problem with greed, or making lots of money, but going into an open fight with someone like her would damage my reputation in the eyes of the many who live in the city.

It sucks that many people have morals.

After mumbling a 'Good morning' to both women, I stroll over to my desk. Simona tells me she has some things for me to do. Paperwork, light work, she reassures me with a friendly smile, and then she makes small talk, asking me how my evening was, and how I'm settling in.

Kyra sits at her desk, her eyes on her screen, looking extremely focused. Or maybe she's trying damn hard to block me out. I can't even recall if she acknowledged my morning greeting.

For the rest of the day, I don't hear a peep out of her, and she's in and out of the room, checking on things on the factory floor. I've watched her from a distance, and she has good rapport with her staff. She knows them all by name, from what I've seen. I barely know people outside of Neville, Emma and my management team.

"She'll be okay," Simona says, after she catches me eyeing Kyra leaving the room. "You're like bulls in a ring, you two, locking heads over everything."

"I was offering my opinion."

Simona tilts her head. "She has a vision, and she's passionate about what we do here. You didn't need to rip it to shreds."

I'm flabbergasted at this. "I didn't rip it to shreds." I didn't come across that strongly, did I? I recall trying to rein in my response, because no matter which way you look at it, her idea and her vision are nothing short of crazy.

"You did."

I rub my neck. "I didn't mean to." So, *that's* why she's mad at me. That's why I'm getting the silent treatment.

It's food night again and, unfortunately, Fredrich is still away. It's going to be a hard night with more lifting and carrying and back-breaking work. I wish Fredrich would hurry up and get well and return.

Simona leaves at the end of the day and informs me that she will be back later to help set up. Kyra is nowhere to be seen and when I ask, Simona tells me she's gone to a meeting and she'll come back later.

There's no point me going home, or to my office, and then returning later. I sit around, checking business emails on my cell phone and dealing with any urgent concerns relating to Hawks Enterprises.

A short while later, Kyra walks in. "Can you help unload the food from the van?"

"You already got it? Why didn't you tell me? I would have come with you."

"I managed."

Clearly, she has, and she also wants to keep her distance from me. I get up and help her. She's distant the entire night, even when we set up the tables and get everything out.

The food line is longer than last time and even though Kyra seems to be at home in this filthy environment, I shudder to think what Jessica or Neville would say if they could see me now.

I watch her as she moves around quickly from table to table, making sure everything is running smoothly.

At seven o'clock on the dot, we start serving. I look at the bedraggled faces of the people expectantly waiting for food, but I see something I wasn't expecting, something I didn't take notice of the last time. They're happy, grateful when we hand over boxes filled with food. They pass along the line, murmuring their thanks, saying 'God Bless', smiling.

It's alien to me, that they have anything to smile about. The rest of the evening passes in a blur. I rush from the van to the tables, refilling empty serving containers, and getting things out of the store room as and when needed.

I'm about to walk out of the storeroom with a box of plastic cups when Yvette's two kids stare at me. "What are you doing here?"

"Mommy said to get some napkins," the girl answers. The boy looks at me silently.

Jesus. Why is their mother allowing them to help out at something like this? "Take this." I shove the box at them. It's light and they can manage. "I'll get the napkins."

I'm going to have a word with Kyra about this. Kids shouldn't be allowed to help. Isn't it late for them? Don't they have homework or things to do?

I go back outside and hand the napkins over to Yvette. I think better of saying what I had intended, and walk back to see if anything else needs refilling, and when everything seems fine for now, I take a moment and step back, and watch.

I was too young to know if something like this existed when I was a child, but we would have benefitted from this. I wouldn't have had to rummage through trashcans whenever we went hungry. I shake my head, hating that this thought has bubbled up from nowhere.

As the queue of people dwindles to nothing, and the area starts to empty, the cleanup begins. Like everyone else, I get on with it, not needing to be told.

"I can help you take stuff back to the restaurants," I offer when Kyra walks by carrying a large pot.

"Think you can handle it?"

"I can handle it."

We load up and get into the van. The silence swells like a huge balloon as she drives.

"How long are you going to be mad at me for?" I'm assuming that this is due to me 'ripping her idea to shreds,' yesterday, which is what Simona said I did.

She glances at me. "Sorry, what?"

"You haven't said a word to me all day. I'm sorry if my blunt assessment of your plans for Redhill offended you."

"I am mad at you, but your opinion is your opinion. It doesn't affect me. I couldn't care less what you think because I'm still going to do what I had planned."

"As in create those units for people who—"

"Yes. Exactly that," she cuts in.

I look out of the window. This isn't as easy as I thought it would be. Sitting here with Kyra, knowing her future vision, and knowing that I'm going to trample all over it. I feel a pang of an emotion I am not familiar with. Regret, or shame, I'm not sure which. It just feels odd. I'm not supposed to care about the effects of my actions, and yet I find myself thinking about what I'm doing. Getting to know her and Simona, and the rest of these people, and what they do, is having an odd effect on me.

"We have different opinions," she says. "I've met many people who have your views, and equally, I've met many who share my views. We're just different people, you and I."

She's right about that. We are so different.

"The kids. Yvette's kids," I say, finding the silence uncomfortable.

"What about them?"

"They were helping out. Why is that even allowed?"

"Because they want to help out. Do you have a problem with that?" she asks.

I do. I have a big problem with that. It's bad enough

remembering things, without having those kids in my face. "Don't they have things to do?"

"Like what? After school activities? Do you think their mom can afford childcare and have someone keep an eye on them while she comes here?"

I hadn't thought of that, and it's not my fault. I don't know how these people live.

I can feel the fury burning inside Kyra. Even though I'm not even looking at her face, I'm become a sensitive barometer of her moods.

"Sorry I asked," I say, my tone sulkier than I intended.

We return everything to the restaurants and then head back to the factory. The doors are still open and I follow her as she heads into the storeroom. A few employees are clearing up and they soon leave.

It's just me and Kyra.

I am so tired, and I have no idea how this tiny slip of a woman does this and then continues with the day-to-day work as well. I lean against the wall, waiting for her to give the storeroom her final seal of approval. I'm almost tempted to ask her how she does this.

"All done," she says, heading out. She waits for me so that she can lock up.

"How come you do this on top pf the core business that Redhill is known for, sewing jackets and blankets?"

"*This?* You mean the food nights?" She locks up the factory.

"It's extra stuff that you have to do. It's almost like a part-time job on the side."

"You obviously don't approve but my mom worked hard all her life, to keep a roof over our heads."

"Our?"

"My sister and me."

"You have a sister?" This is something new and personal I'm learning about her.

"Penny. She's at college." We stand awkwardly by the door, neither of us moving. She's opening up to me, and even more surprising, I want to know about her. "And this? The food night? Why?"

"My mom used to take us to make sure we helped out when we could, at soup kitchens and at events like these. It's giving back, that's all it is."

"You don't owe anyone anything."

"I don't see it as owing anyone," she replies, testily. "When my mom died, nine years ago, from pneumonia, I didn't stop doing this."

"I'm sorry for your loss."

"It sucks, but..." She shrugs, a sigh making her chest rise and fall. "That's life, right?"

"Yeah."

"And you? Do you have any siblings? What's the deal with you, Hartley?"

I push off from the wall, needing to end this conversation now. Delving into my life is strictly off limits.

"No siblings." I get out my keys and walk towards my car. "Goodnight."

"Goodnight."

CHAPTER EIGHTEEN

KYRA

I take it all back. Employing Brad hasn't worked out to be such a bad thing. Maybe I was just cautious about him, and he was wary of me. He was responding to my coldness. I didn't trust him, and I didn't care to hide it from him, but I've taken note of his level of commitment and how much it has helped having him around. Especially given the fact that Fredrich decided to take another week off and only returned yesterday.

Who knows how much longer Brad will stick around for? We are different in so many ways and disagree on so many things. He seems eager for us to move elsewhere if we get the chance. We clash the most on my ideas for the small business units. Redhill employs people to work in the factory but in talking to some of them, I've come to know of their hopes and dreams too. Take Dayna, our factory manager. She used to run a small home business making cakes, until tragedy hit and her only child was killed in a car accident. Her marriage fell apart, she and her husband divorced, and then she lost her day job. She sank into depression and it spiraled. She lost her home, her marriage, everything.

Dayna does a fantastic job here. She's been so good that I promoted her. I can see her potential, and I see the way her eyes light up when she talks about the joy that baking cakes gave her. She is one of those people I see working in those business units I'm determined to set up. What if I could make that possible for her again?

Unlike me, Brad doesn't seem to understand that people, when given a chance to prove themselves, can and will. He doesn't see their true potential, or how life changing giving people a second chance can be.

I keep trying to find out what he does the other two days of the week, but he's so vague that I wonder if he's growing weed or doing something dodgy because he changes the subject quickly.

Still, I never thought I'd find myself being glad he's on board.

I was wrong about him, and I can see now that having another guy on the team definitely helps. We don't deliberately turn men away, but none have wanted to work here. With the factory being completely staffed by women, and only Fredrich in the office, I've come to rely on him more. I grudgingly admit that having another guy on the team is a definite bonus, even if it's just for the muscle power.

He is willing and able, and helpful, and I should be grateful for his help. I have to learn to put my quiet frustration aside when I'm with people who don't share my ideas.

But there is a plus side to him being here. Having Brad to bounce ideas around with isn't such a bad thing. There is truth to the words that you often need to see things from another perspective, that you can't always assume your point of view is the only one, or that it's the right one.

I'm learning a lot from him being around and he and I seem to be getting on amicably enough, and we've put our previously cold and open hostility behind us.

Fredrich noticed this right away, perhaps because it's cozier with the extra desk and with the four of us all in one room,

We managed to fit another small desk in the office. The space is becoming more cramped here and I did consider moving Brad out to another part of the building and even setting him up a space on the factory floor, but Simona said it wouldn't be fair given that he's not here all the time. She says it makes sense to have us all in the same room and to feel more like a team. So we've joined the new desk to Fredrich's, and the two of them now sit almost side by side.

The talk soon turns to Elias Cardoza. Fredrich holds up his newspaper which shows a photo of Eli. There's not long to go now before his fight. "It's going to be a great night," says Fredrich. "I was thinking we'd go bigger with the screen."

I laugh nervously. "How much bigger do you want to go?" Fredrich rubs his hands together as if he's got a big juicy idea.

"Like drive-in movie size. I spoke to a company specializing in that and they're happy to come and set it all up. They're going to give us a discount, too, on account of what we do and why we're doing it."

"Screen?" Brad echoes.

"Elias' big fight," says Simona. "Haven't you told him about it?" she asks me.

I mumble something about it not being on my radar. I seem to be juggling everything all the time. The fight night is just something extra, and thankfully I haven't had to do much about it, because Fredrich seems content to run with it.

Fredrich soon fills Brad in on our plans for that night.

"You're going to throw a party for homeless people?"

We all look up at him, it's not just the way he says it, there is shock and disbelief and, if I'm not mistaken, a hint of why-the-hell-would-you-do-something-like-that?

"We're going to need more manpower," I say, tapping my pencil on the table. I'm not sure exactly how many people will come, above and beyond our usual numbers. I guess that's something we'll find out on the night."

"How much more?" Simona asks.

"We'll need to know numbers for the food," I add.

Brad folds his arms and I immediately brace myself for opposition. He catches my eye. "Say it," I tell him. I can see that he's itching to say something, and that he also isn't fully on board with this.

"You're hosting a night for homeless people to come and watch Elias fight? And you're giving them food and ..."

"It's just food. Not food and alcohol, in case that's what you were going to say." It seemed to me like it was on the tip of his tongue. "It's not a *party*, Brad, we're aware of that. But whether the usual crowd turns up, or something slightly bigger, it doesn't matter, does it? As long as we have enough food and security just in case we need it. So, what's the problem?"

"There isn't a problem."

But his insistence doesn't win me over and I push back. "Don't be shy. Let's hear it. I can see that you don't think this is a good idea. Tell me what's wrong with it." I brace myself for his answer.

"I mean, it's a good idea." He slowly backtracks.

"But?"

"No buts."

"Oh, really? Because it sounded like you didn't agree."

He opens his mouth but seems to think better of it. "I just... uh ... I mean, ... uh, are you sure they would want that?"

"Why would they not?"

He looks confounded, his glance shifting to Simona and Fredrich, as if he's being careful of what he says, as if he's got to watch his mouth and can't mouth off like he would around his frat buddies. "Because ... it's not important, surely? For them to see a boxing match when they're still fighting for basic survival."

At first this seems like a cruel opinion. But, I see his point. To the uninitiated, it would seem like a waste of time putting on a huge TV screen for 'these people'. But if we can have an extra food night, and tie it into an event that involves our biggest donor, why not? If this would give these people a chance to forget their woes for the night, why would we not do it?

BRANDON

"Will you come?" Simona asks me.

I blink. "Come where?"

"Aren't you paying attention?" She laughs, but also looks at me with concern, as if I've suffered a concussion and have forgotten who I am and where I am.

"To the food night. On Elias's big fight night?"

"Uh ..." I can do that.

"He's probably got better things to do," Kyra says. They're all looking at me oddly, sensing my hesitancy.

"It's just a Saturday night. Bring your girlfriend, dude," says Fredrich.

"Why not? I'll come."

"It's not a night out," Kyra informs me dryly. "And we're going to need the manpower."

"I wasn't expecting it to be a night out," I reply, pointedly.

The next day I pass by the art gallery to check in on Jessica. What with my days at the factory and then catching up at my office, I haven't been able to catch up with her for a while.

"Hey, stranger." She kisses the air on the side of my face and we embrace.

"It's been a while. Sorry. I've been busy."

"Nice of you to come."

"I wouldn't have missed this for the world."

"Where have you been?" She has another event showcasing something or other. More art that a monkey with crayons could create. I can barely hear the low music in the background. Beautiful people in designer clothes hang around the gallery with long-stemmed glasses in their elegant hands. Waitresses, dressed all in black, grace the room with their trays of miniscule canapes too pretty to eat. They're almost as mesmerizing as some of the artwork.

"I haven't been anywhere," I throw back defensively. My days at the factory aren't too hard. They are long days, but not as physical as when I first started. I've cleaned the storerooms and we've taken another delivery of supplies for the products. Between me and Fredrich, we manage.

It's not all manual labor. But the homeless food nights are every Wednesday, without fail, and Fredrich or I go with Kyra to do the restaurant run. I still think these evenings should be scrapped. She's running a business not a soup kitchen. This side gig is going to wear her down.

It's a far cry from my own life. I don't do any of the dirty work. I don't even do my own laundry or wash my own dishes at home. And at the office, I have Emma. My business dealings are conducted over the phone, or over dinner or drinks.

That's my idea of work, and it is yet another difference between me and Kyra. I can't help but admire her strength and stamina.

Jessica slips her arm in mine, surprising me with her touch. She's not usually so tactile or so physically clingy. She's obviously missed me. "Tell me what this Mother Teresa of Chicago is like." She gazes up at me through her mascaraed lashes.

I chuckle and try to move myself away because her scent is strong and overpowering, as if she added too much of her witch's potion to it. She can't even bring herself to call Kyra by her name.

"She's ..." I'm at a loss for words, completely stumped.

"She's?" Jessica fixes me with eyes full of malice. "Has she grown her hair out yet or does she still look like a dyke?"

I choke out a gasp. "Why the maliciousness, Jessica?" Kyra travels in a different orbit, these two women have nothing in common and will never meet, therefore the level of Jessica's hatred surprises me.

"It's the only thing I remember about her. Her hair. She's a skinny, scrawny scrap, isn't she?"

"I haven't noticed. I'm not there to make advances at her. I'm there for a reason." Kyra is everything I don't desire in a woman. Shortish hair resting on her shoulders, small and slight, no sign of voluptuousness. No feminine curves.

"She's got a scrunched-up face."

I wince, disliking Jessica's bitchy comment. "You don't even know her."

"But you do, Brandon. You've been working with her for going on a month. What's she like? Because the city seems to love her as much as they do that boxer."

"Elias? Funny you should say that. He's a great fan of the work she's doing. They've met him a few times."

"Riffraff. People like that flock together."

"Riffraff?" Her jibes make me uneasy. Jessica is in frosty bitch mode tonight. It's unbecoming for someone of her stature, or maybe it's just about right. I've never noticed this before and suddenly, I don't want to hear her gripes and her snipes. Why did I ever suffer them before? "Cardoza is a good fighter. I wouldn't call him riffraff. The guy has more than proved himself."

"I was talking about your new best friend."

Something pinches my belly from the inside and doesn't stop. "Kyra isn't riffraff."

Jessica's eyes narrow the tiniest amount, it's enough for me to see that she doesn't like me defending Kyra. "You've changed, Brandon. What are you doing with these people? Becoming best friends?"

"These people?" It's not until I say it out loud that I realize it's a term I've often used to describe us and them. 'Us' being the top one percent of the wealthy, and 'them' being the rest. A false laugh leaves my throat. "You know what I'm doing there."

I wish I hadn't ever told her. For the first time, I see the danger in letting someone as nasty and as evil as Jessica—someone who hates Kyra with a passion—in on this little secret of mine. I lean in and put my lips to her ear. "I hope I can trust you to keep this to yourself."

"You disappoint me, Brandon. I was hoping for some

gossip on the girl, but you haven't given me any juicy tidbits on her."

"Don't be silly, Jessica. There are no juicy things for me to bring back to you."

"No gossip?"

"None."

"None?"

"It's purely work, and boring work, at that. There is nothing to relay back to you."

CHAPTER NINETEEN

KYRA

"We could write to more corporations," Brad suggests. We're discussing how to get more sponsors, how to get our message out. This is something I consider myself to be good at, and we've done well so far, but I'm interested to hear what Brad has to say, since he claims he's a know-it-all.

"We already do that."

"You should do the small and personal approach. Meet people in person. Cultivate relationships."

"We already do that."

"Then it sounds as if you're doing all the right things. You could go big and take out an ad in the paper."

I laugh, because his idea is so ludicrous. "You want us to pay an exorbitant amount of money for an ad? In the newspaper, or on a billboard, or in a glossy magazine, or maybe a TV ad? Which is it?" I'm shocked that he's suggested a crazy solution.

"It's not so strange. You want to attract the big donors. Get the eyes of the big corporates. This is the way to do it."

"Dude, people would think we're throwing money away. We're not a corporation," Fredrich says.

I scowl at Brad in disbelief because what he's suggesting is so insanely wrong, I can't believe he had the audacity to suggest it. Everything I started to assume about him begins to dismantle. He catches my tight expression.

"Your idea doesn't make sense," I tell him.

I hear a noise, like something scraping, like lots of sand falling, an out-of-place noise that alerts my sixth sense. We all stare upwards, and then WHAM! Brad comes at me like a bull, hurling himself at me. My chair topples over and I scream as we fall to the floor. His hand cushions the floor before my head hits it. Something dull and chunky thuds to the floor directly at the spot where my chair had been.

It happens so fast that I forget to breathe.

"What the—" Fredrich jumps to standing, Simona too. They help us to get up. Miraculously, I'm not hurt despite being bulldozed to the floor in my chair. The armrests saved me from taking the full brunt of Brad's body weight. He stands up slowly, surveys me lying on the floor, and offers me his hand. Then he helps me to stand.

Dazed, I look up at the ceiling, then at the floor. Shock holds me frozen to the spot.

"A chunk of plaster," Fredrich cries, walking over and prodding it gently with his foot. It's a hefty chunk. . "You're lucky it missed your head."

Simona stares at it. "That could have killed you." She looks as worried as if it had happened.

"He saved your life, looks like," Fredrich announces.

"Thank goodness for your quick reflexes," Simona adds in. They are both singing Brad's praises.

"Are you hurt?" I ask him, slowly shaking out of my shock bubble. There is too much to process all at once: Brad's side tackle, the plaster from the ceiling, the fact that I could have been so badly—fatally even—injured.

But also the feel of him against me. The firm yet soft feel of his hand as my head smacked against it. Everything except my heart rate slow-motioned. I caught a whiff of his cologne—clean and fresh with a hint of pine, it took me out of this damp-smelling room and led me to a field of flowers. Even now, my heart flutters just thinking about it.

He saved my life.

I reach for his hand shakily, gratitude washing over me as I turn his palm over in my hands. He lets me. "Does it hurt? Can you move your fingers?" I examine both sides of it carefully. He flexes his fingers.

"It's all working. Can I have it back now?"

Everyone laughs.

I can't, because what happened scared me. If he hadn't moved me out of the way, who knows what injury I might have sustained?

"Thank you." The quiet words tumble from my lips. "The water pooling on the roof must have gone through."

"Your ..." He touches his own lip. I squint at him. "Your lip is bleeding," he says, pointing at it. It's only then that I feel the pain on my lower lip. I run my tongue along it and taste the salty blood. Brad winces. "Looks painful. It could be deep. You might want to get it looked at."

Simona comes over, motherly-like, and tilts my head up so that she can get a better look. "It's not as bad as it looks."

"I think we should split for lunch," Fredrich announces.

"Another man who runs at the first sight of blood." She rolls her eyes. "Get me the first aid kit before you go."

"I'll get it," Brad pipes up. "I know where it is. You showed me when you took me around the factory."

"Now *that* is what I call a hero," says Simona proudly, as he disappears out of view.

———

BRANDON

I don't even want to think about what might have happened had that chunk of plaster fallen on Kyra's head.

When Emma asks me at work the next day how my little experiment is going, I don't know how to answer that.

"It's trickier than I thought, working at the factory." I'm back in my own office, but lately I seem to prefer going to Redhill. I don't even know why. I must be going soft in the head.

"Now there's a surprise." Her voice drips with sarcasm.

"She'll come around. I haven't had a chance to properly work on her yet."

"You mean pull the wool over her eyes?"

I pick up my crystal egg-shaped paperweight. The smooth surface is cold and I roll it around in my hands as I contemplate recent events. The things I do and say, the way I'm trying to manipulate Kyra, these are things I routinely do. This is nothing new to me, but this time I'm not so sure.

"It's impossible to pull the wool over Kyra's eyes," I announce. "She's way too smart for that."

Emma rolls her eyes, "Heavens above. The man has a heart."

"I didn't think it would be this hard to lie to these people."

I wait for Emma's caustic remark, but to my surprise, she is silent. She hands me the paperwork instead.

"This could be the making of you, Brandon," she says, sashaying towards the door and giving me a backward glance.

I stop rolling the paperweight and look up at her.

"Are you playing with her heart, Brandon?"

"No way in hell." The way I say it seems to convince her.

"You have a ten o'clock meeting with Frontier Group, and lunch with the people from Delanque."

I groan. A busy day isn't what I need. Splitting my time between two places is starting to make my head spin. I've managed well so far, but today I have no interest in meeting with the movers and shakers of the corporate world. I don't care about new deals and mergers.

My head isn't in the right place. I'm in danger of turning soft. I feel bad when I say things to Kyra that are deliberately wrong.

Things that aren't in her best interest.

She's adamant that the factory is in a good state, but a falling chunk of plaster could have killed her or someone else. Water pooling on the roof after a storm shouldn't cause such problems. She knows Greenways is up and coming, even though she has no clue of the vast amounts I intend to make from it, but she has a sixth sense about things.

I get through the day, but my head is at Redhill. I'm fighting to contain my feelings for Kyra, and maybe seeing Jessica tonight will remind me of the taste I have in women.

"I'm still going to drive them out." I smile at her, even though the smile doesn't come from the heart. Emma winces as she closes the door and I contemplate the state of events.

My project is going slower than planned. These things take time to get moving. Neville thinks I'm not being very business-like about it. He thinks I should force my way in.

This is also what my father would say, but thankfully I don't need to involve him in the minutiae of such detail. The poor old man needs to recover and not worry about his empire. I'm going to take care of it.

Me.

What a strange twist of fate that someone like me ended up like this. That I rose to such heights when life was so cruelly stacked against me.

Kyra, Simona and Fredrich, the 'supposed' management team, aren't the type of people I would count as my friends. The people working there, the broken people with sad stories about their broken pasts, they would normally be invisible to me. Their world and mine shouldn't intersect.

And yet in a weird way, it does. During my few days there, I am forced to face things I would rather pretend weren't there. It's changing me and making me feel bad about my intentions. Its churning out the very things I've tried so hard to hide and push away.

It's Yvette I need to stay away from the most. That skinny slip of a woman, with the years' old face, she reminds me of too much. Walking around the factory floor, I get talking to these people and against my better judgment, I find myself being reeled into their lives.

I've tried to put my feelings and emotions away. Hell, I didn't have any going in. I didn't care. But now I have started to, and it's messing with my head.

Those goddamn food nights were the first line of my defense to break down. Week upon week of seeing those people—poor and hungry, with defeated looks in their eyes—people grateful to receive a hot meal.

Over time, it's hard to see that and not be affected.

CHAPTER TWENTY

KYRA

As we get closer to the day of Elias's fight and our big night, I start to have some doubts as I head towards the storage room to do another check of the inventory.

"What's up, Lewis?" Brad catches me frowning at my clipboard.

We've reverted back to using our surnames like we used to in our early hate-filled days where we barely tolerated one another. It's not because we're at odds again, but because it feels safer. Something has changed ever since he saved me from that falling chunk of plaster.

I look up and try to remain calm. "This is turning out to be bigger than I thought."

He shrugs and throws his hands in the air. "This was your crazy idea." I ignore his comment, knowing that he always has something negative to say. What we do isn't for everyone. It takes a certain type of person to want to help those less fortunate than ourselves and Brad clearly is missing that part.

I turn my back to him. "What are you doing here?" I ask. It's a Friday, and he doesn't usually come here on Fridays.

"I figured you would need help setting up for tomorrow. Fredrich said you could have double the capacity tomorrow."

"Did your 'other' employer let you have the day off, Hartley?" I clasp the clipboard to my chest and wait for his answer. He's always so coy about his other interests.

He gives me a smile as an answer. "I have permission to be here."

"Are you really not going to tell me what you do on your days off?" His concerted refusal to answer my questions makes me even more determined to get to the bottom of it.

"They're hardly days off."

"Then what are they?" I ask, digging and prying. He walks towards me until there's not much distance between us, and I catch a whiff of his aftershave. Only, I wonder if it is aftershave or too strong shower gel. The sharp and refreshing smell of pine takes me to the outdoors and reminds me of woodland hikes. I step back, until my back hits the wall. He angles his head. "You're very nosy about what I do on my days off."

My insides twist with discomfort. In that life of his I know nothing about, he could have a girlfriend. Or be married. Curiosity swirls around me, an uneasy dance of things I want to know, but also don't want to know.

"Nosy? No," I manage to say, miraculously keeping my voice level.

"No?" He steps closer, his breath is warm and sweet, he's that close to me. His eyes trail a slow, lazy curve over my face, from my lips to my eyes and back down to my lips again and I rub my bare arms, unsure of where these pesky goosebumps have sprung up from. "You're not?" he asks, when I say nothing.

I press my lips together, self-consciously. Nervous. Jittery. Excited. "No," I manage.

"There is nothing to tell." His voice is low, like a hoarse, sexy whisper.

Sexy? What in the world made me think it was sexy? Aside from it sending shivers darting along my skin. I jerk back, trying to force my back to sink into the wall, and of course I fail miserably, but I'm determined to maintain the upper hand. In the foggy recesses of my brain, it comes to me that Brad always has a presence. He can fill a room with his aura, just by walking in. Something tells me that he's been trying to slow things down, and this knowing sixth sense of mine suddenly takes this new hint of an idea and runs with it.

Who is he?

I'm growing accustomed to him invading my space. It has a dizzying effect on me, his continued closeness which is both a drug and a danger. I want him, but I'm also afraid. "Are you a drug dealer? A corporate investor? Something else?"

He guffaws as if this is the funniest thing he's ever heard. "I didn't think it was possible to have those words in the same sentence."

His breath is warm, his aftershave mildly intoxicating. I catch another drift of pine and mint. Or am I overthinking, oversmelling, over imagining? I seem to have become obsessed in such a short space of time. "Can you move back, please? You're invading my personal space."

He steps back. Not enough. Not as much as he could have. Or should have. He's still hovering around the edges of the boundary.

"Better?"

I arch an eyebrow, and give up because I'm none the wiser as to what he does on the days when he's not at Redhill. I should let it go. We have other, bigger things to think about, and we have a big show to get off the ground tomorrow.

I push away from the wall, smooth down my blouse and clutch my clipboard as if it were a lifebuoy I desperately needed. Brad is like a deep, dark well to me, and I'm scared of falling in and drowning.

"Why don't you see if Fredrich needs your help?" I suggest. It's a miracle that I've managed to sound normal-headed, because inside, I feel anything but that.

"I will, seeing that you obviously don't need me." Brad leaves and now I've forgotten what I was looking at before he came by.

BRANDON

I walk away and wonder what the hell just happened. I'm not the kind of guy who makes moves like that but Lewis makes me react. It's one thing I can't control, and I'm used to controlling everything.

I spend the rest of the day helping Fredrich. He talks me through the plan for tomorrow and tells me that the crowd could be much bigger than expected. No shit. Like Kyra, he has no idea how it's going to go. I think they're being very adventurous with this idea.

I guess it's not a bad thing to do. I mean, how else are these people ever going to see a fight like this? But, given that this is Cardoza's hometown, I would have expected the city officials to put on an event for him, something like this—a public party somewhere in the park. Maybe they don't want to put on an event for homeless people.

Only someone like Kyra would ever do something like that. It reminds me of what I am up against and why I'm going through with this crazy charade.

All over the city, people are getting together in bars and restaurants, throwing dinner parties to watch the fight. One of Jessica's friends is throwing a party and she asked if I wanted to come. I should have accepted. She's still trophy-wife material. A socialite with brains and beauty, dressed from head to toe in Chanel.

I told her I was busy working on some bullshit deal I need to take care of. It wasn't a complete lie because I'm going to travel out of state to have a meeting with a prospective investor. I promise her that I'll make it up to her sometime.

On the day of the fight, we start earlier than usual. This time, all the factory employees are helping, not just a small handful from the usual food night roster.

Yvette is there with her kids.

Kyra shows up, and she looks nicer than usual. She's still in her jeans, black skinny ones with boots and a tight-fitting top over which she's wearing a jacket.

If this is her idea of doing something 'wild' on the weekend, that girl obviously hasn't lived enough. I feel sorry for her.

I volunteer to go pick up the food from the restaurants, along with Fredrich. Kyra has insured me on that clapped out heap of metal on wheels, which roughly passes for a van, and Fredrich is taking his pickup because we have a lot of things to pick up from the restaurants. Everywhere we go, it's busy on account of it being a Saturday night.

By the time we get back, I'm feeling the tiredness and the

night hasn't even begun. The huge movie screen is up, and the guys from that company are hovering around talking to Kyra.

She comes over and tells us that the tech guys are staying here the entire time in case we have any problems with the screen. At least that's one less thing to worry about.

"They're probably also making sure you guys don't ruin their equipment," I mutter.

"That too." She gives me a smile. It's the first time we've acknowledged one another today. Up until now either she's been busy, or I have, and we've managed to stay out of one another's way.

"People are starting to come in." Simona's words make us all turn towards the entrance gates.

"Are they going to stand the entire time?" I scratch my head, because I don't know how this will pan out.

"They'll sit on the ground," Kyra informs me. Sure enough, I see people have brought sleeping bags, pieces of cardboard and blankets, which they start to lay out as if they're claiming their territory. "Okay." She claps her hands together. "Let's get to it. I need you two to work the general area. We have security, but you know these people, and they know you. This looks like a pretty big crowd."

I look at the crowd and instinctively know that I don't want to be wandering around and getting too close to these people. "You want us to walk around all evening?"

"Put on the high-vis jackets, and just work the crowd. We have security, so you don't have to do much controlling of the crowd. Just let them know when food will be ready, make them stand in line."

"They already know to stand in line."

Surprise dances in Kyra's eyes. She surveys me carefully. "What are you scared of? You've done this before."

"Yeah, dude." Fredrich claps a hand to my back. "I've got

your back. Don't worry. These people aren't going to bite you."

It's not their bites I'm scared of. It's catching something. TB or ... *something*. Half of these people are probably psychos. It's one thing being on the other side of the table and serving food, watching from a distance, it's another to be walking around surrounded by danger with no barrier between us. And now Kyra wants me to walk around as if I'm a server in a restaurant?

Not happening.

"I just ... I like being on the other side, serving. It's nice, and .... humbling, to give out the food."

She narrows her eyes at my pathetic excuse, before giving a dismissive shake of her head. "Don't you want to keep an eye on the crowd and maybe get a better chance to watch the fight?"

"I'd rather serve the food."

"Do you have a weak immune system or something?" she asks.

"No. I have a robust constitution." And I'd like to keep it that way. If it was only suspicion swimming around in her eyes, I could tolerate it, but there's also a look of disappointment. As if she expected better from me.

"Knock yourself out behind the tables then, Hartley." Then to Fredrich. "I'll go walk around, with you."

I remember that I need to make a call. All of this back and forth between Redhill and my office, juggling the two worlds has been jarring. I have an important deal to take care of, and I forgot to sign some paperwork. I need to call Emma and ask her to pick them up from my office and drop them off at my house. "I need to make a phone call," I say, walking away a I pull my cell phone out.

"Calling your girlfriend, dude?" Fredrich calls out after me.

CHAPTER TWENTY-ONE

BRANDON

I feel like a total wimp when Kyra sticks me on the serving tables and patrols the ground herself. I should be doing that. Me, except that I'm too chickenshit to do so. She has more drive and ambition than a lot of the people I know, and she makes me feel ashamed.

I help Simona and the others to set up. A couple of local journalists are here, too. The more I look around, the more I see that this event is so getting bigger and bigger. It's not just another food night, with a movie screen, it's an event. Kyra and her team are seen as saviors. I see now how and why the city supports the underdog.

Yvette is here with her kids who are both helping. They end up on the table next to me. "Is it okay if they go here?" Yvette asks me timidly, as if I might bite. "They want to help and Kyra said it would be okay."

She always looks so haggard, like a shell of a woman, and I

get scared that if I accidentally brush past her, I'll knock the life out of her.

"There's plenty of room for more helpers." I shift and leave a gap for them. Simona is on my right, and then Yvette and her girl and boy are on the other side. Because the tables are longer, there is a whole line of helpers this time and there is a lot more food.

There's even some music. Music? "Where the heck is that coming from—" And then I see that the screen has come on. A cheer goes out from the crowd.

"I've never seen them so animated." Simona beams as if she's glowing with happiness, as if these are her children getting ready to watch a movie. I do not understand this ... connection ...this empathy.

The people who set up the movie screen also put up a few lights around the place so we're not in complete darkness. I scour the crowd and see Kyra moving through and talking to people standing in line. She's acting as if they are lining up for summer camp, and she's obviously not worried about catching anything.

"She's a natural, isn't she?" Simona catches me staring as I put a dollop of pasta on someone's plate.

"Doesn't she ever get scared?"

"Scared of what?" Her tone suggests that my question is stupid.

"That someone might turn on her? Do something scary, or stupid or both?"

She looks at me aghast. "These aren't people on death row, Brad. These people are hungry."

I lift a hand to the back of my neck, feeling foolish. Kyra seems to have always been aware of the suffering of others, because her mom highlighted it to her. Not because she had to live it. It's admirable. It makes what I am, what I have become, seem all the more lousy in comparison. I'm supposed to know better, but somewhere along the line I lost the ability to empathize.

"We're going to need more crackers," says Simona. "More water bottles too."

"I'll get them."

I busy myself, and everything comes together. Everyone works like one large, well-oiled and efficient machine.

The crowd is growing bigger. It's way bigger than the usual Wednesday night one. I, for one, am relieved that we have security. Tonight's fight is at an earlier time than usual. I wonder if it's because Cardoza has managed to get the networks to show it earlier, because these people wouldn't wait all night for it. Surely he can't wield that much power?

Everything seems to be going according to plan. The line of people slowly worms across the length of the tables. A constant murmur of "Thank you" fills the silence as we serve.

"There you go." Simona's voice is chirpy and cheerful as she doles out food. Yvette disappears to refill a food container. I glance over at her kids. They seem shy and quiet, handing out cereal bars and crackers, but avoiding eye contact with the people they are serving. The boy looks young ... almost like ... I bury the thought, even as guilt ricochets off my chest. For a second, I struggle to breathe.

I look away and stare at the screen in relief. There's a fight going on, but it's not the main one. People take the food and walk away, sitting on pieces of cardboard, on sleeping bags, on bags, watching it.

It's impossible for me to watch anything properly because the line for food keeps growing. Every few seconds, I have to put some food on someone's plate. Or refill the containers, or relieve someone else who wants to take a break. Fredrich comes over later and asks me if I want to trade places. I tell him I'm okay.

Kyra walks past, asking all of us if we need anything, if any of us want to take a break or help out with something else. Everyone seems content.

After an hour has passed, the line of people has dwindled. A cheer goes up and I see that the main fight, Elias's one with Trent Garrison, has started. People here become animated watching their hero walking into the ring. I glance over at Kyra, see her face turned up, her eyes glued to the screen. An arrow of something sharp and painful hits me. She seems completely glued to the screen. Jessica must be salivating over this man too.

Cardoza takes off his robe, his tattooed physique on display. The crowd's roar turns deafening. And still Kyra's face is upturned. She can't look away even if she tried. My teeth clench involuntarily.

I busy myself by looking over at the tables and checking to see if we need anything else. And then I hear more cheering. Cardoza looks fit and strong. He sends a powerful left hook into Garrison's face and the crowd cheers. Kyra is clapping and cheering.

A part of me wishes I'd taken Jessica up on her offer. I could be drinking champagne, eating the best canapes, and mingling with the likes of Jessica and her friends.

"Elias!" the boy cries jubilantly, no longer invisible. His eyes are glued to the screen. He's frozen. The cereal bar remains in his hand while the person he is serving patiently waits. I take it from his hand and give it. "Don't forget why you're here," I remind him.

"Sorry." He chews his lip and gets back to the task, still without giving me any eye contact. His sister watches him, turning all protective, like I used to be once.

"Do you want to watch this?" I ask him. "I can do this if you want to." I feel bad, as if I've ruined his Saturday night for him. Who knows what horrors this kid has suffered? I'm guessing this is a respite for him, and guilt heats my face to think that I've rebuked him.

"Nah, it's okay," he replies, in a somber voice.

"Hey, buddy. Watch the fight. I can do that for you, or your sister can. Watch the fight, okay?"

The boy is about to hand out another cereal bar and I'm about to take it from him, when a memory shoots at me out of nowhere. He's about the same age as Kane was when I left him. I try to suffocate the thought, putting it out as if I'm throwing a wet blanket over a fire. Killing it before the flame blazes out of control.

"It's okay," he says, and continues to hand out cereal bars, and watch the fight. I let him.

Yvette returns briefly to check our containers and refills them accordingly. She asks the girl and boy if they are okay, then disappears again. I ask him who he wants to win tonight.

"Elias," his sister replies, as if I'm asking her a silly question.

"What about you, buddy?"

"Elias." The boy's focus is singular, handing out a cereal bar one at a time, his gaze going only as far as the hand of the person he is serving.

"Elias, huh? Everyone wants Elias." I want Elias too. He's the city's hero, but something about him working with Kyra and Redhill, and ignoring my company, has given me a sour taste in my mouth.

Another shriek from the crowd makes us all look up. Elias staggers backwards as Garrison pummels him to the mat. Gloomy disquiet spreads around the air.

The boy shrieks as if he's in pain. The girl moans with disappointment.

And then a chant breaks out. "Elias, Eli—yus, Eli—yus."

Yvette returns just as the line starts to thin out even more. People are now scattered around the open space, eyes on the screen.

"We might get a bit of a break now," says Simona. I forget she's a good few years older than us.

"Why don't you sit down?" I suggest, knowing that we've all been standing for a long time. "I've got this."

"Are you sure?"

"Yes. Go on, you have a break now."

"Mommy, can we eat something?" The boy asks.

"I don't know... uh..."

I turn to face Yvette and her kids. "Sure, they can eat. Your son wants to watch the fight."

"I wanna watch it too," the girl chimes in.

Yvette remains silent, her gaze trained on my face as if she's waiting for authorization.

"How about you all hop over to the other side and let me serve you?" I suggest.

"But how will you manage?" Yvette asks.

I'll manage because I don't want her kids to go sit by themselves. "I can manage. Look, the line is dying down now."

"Can we watch the fight, Mommy?" The boy. The damned boy. He's smaller than Kane would have been. I turn my head away, desperate to push the sudden rush of unwanted memories back down into the ground where they belong.

"Please go," I beg, needing them to go so that I don't have to look at them. I drop my voice. "Your kids are hungry, Yvette, and you must be too. It's been a long evening. Eat and let them watch the fight."

Her eyes beam with gratitude and she thanks me. She is thanking me for letting her go and eat food with her kids. We're serving at a fucking homeless food station. How the hell is *this* my world all of a sudden?

In no time, they're on the other side and I'm serving them. I make sure to put an extra helping on their plates. Their quiet 'Thank yous' are reward enough that I have done the right thing, here at least.

The crowd shrieks with delight, and I look up to discover that I've completely lost sight of the fight. I have no idea who's winning, but Garrison is drenched in blood.

One of the other helpers comes up to me and asks if she can take a break. She asks me if it's okay for her to eat. I don't know. Is it? We don't eat the food we serve, not on the weekly food night. Seeing my confused expression, she tells me that Kyra said it was okay to. So I tell her to go ahead and then I take charge and coordinate the rest of the servers to take turns having a break.

It's not until now, when the lines have slowed down, that I take a breath and realize how relentless tonight has been.

Kyra is over by the side of the screen talking to a couple of the security guards. Sharing a joke, it looks like. Something sharp and pointed slices through me. She's laughing, and so are they. It look like she's having a great time.

We've run out of all the food in most of the containers and a couple of the helpers are refilling them. Having stood for a few hours, I could do with a hot drink, a hot bath and a bed.

I can't wait for this night to be over.

A huge cheer goes up from the crowd and a few more lights come on, illuminating the parking lot so that I can see everyone clearly.

The fight is over. I glance up at the screen and see Cardoza collapse in a heap on the floor.

He lost?

Shock zooms through my core, but then I see it's a victory pose, of someone who has fallen to his knees with the enormity of what he has done. He jumps up and fist pumps the air. The crowd here erupts, clapping and cheering. It's the most energized I've ever seen them.

Caught up in this moment, in the pride that engulfs us all, I nod as Cardoza walks around the ring jubilant, his fists punching the air. In this moment, it doesn't matter that he's ignored dealings with Hawks Enterprises. This guy has taken back his belt and his title. This man has made the city proud. Blood streams from his face, he looks beat up, but when the camera pans over to his opponent, 'The Tank', the guy looks worse.

I've missed what looked like an amazing fight and I'll have to watch it properly at home again and catch the fight highlights. Kyra is hugging Fredrich, and the two of them—his biggest fans, it looks like—are jumping for joy. I've never seen Kyra look so excited. Never. She's glowing with happiness.

A sliver of anger burrows deep into my chest.

Why can't I do that to her? Why do I *want* to do that? I shake my head, dispelling this thought. I'm hungry and tired and not making sense.

Hope and excitement blanket the air, and I am swept up in the uplifting moment. It's not such a bad place to be. Yvette's kids are doing a happy dance in the crowd. The boy and girl are delirious with joy.

Kane's face hovers in front of my face again. The air turns thick and heavy like tar as I remember a time when we were starving. I remember grabbing his hand and running away. I took him to a park and we hid in a wooden play hut; it had dark green chipped paint. I can see it now as vividly as if it was in front of me. We hid there for hours, but hunger had made Kane so weak, that I got scared. I rummaged through the trash cans desperate to find something. His face lit up when I returned shortly with the crusts of a sandwich and a half-eaten donut. We shared it, but I gave him more, because he was stick thin and I was older, and I was supposed to be the stronger one. I was supposed to take care of him.

The past steamrolls over me making me feel sicker than I have in a long time.

"Is it okay if we leave now?" Yvette asks. She seems to think I'm in charge. "The kids are tired and—"

"Go," I tell her, trying to push away the memories which have bubbled up and lodged in my throat. Breathing becomes harder and heavier.

"Are you sure? I can help you clean up a—"

"Go, please." From my periphery I see her boy and girl standing behind her staring at me. I can't look at them. I want her to take them and go. "You don't need to stick around. There are enough of us to clean up. You go on home."

She bites her lower lip as she hesitates. I understand in that instant and take out a few takeaway boxes, getting ready to fill them up. "Tell me what you'd like. We've got plenty of food here."

She can't bring herself to meet my eyes, and I am now accustomed to that look of embarrassment that I see on so many people's faces who come here for food. I spare her the discomfort and fill the boxes up, then fill up another two extra ones. She tells me that she has enough.

"You have a good night," I tell Yvette, knowing that this will help her get through tomorrow. I can't bear to look at the kids. My heart is in my throat as they walk away.

I head towards the van, then open the doors and look inside, pretending to be busy looking for something. Instead, I rearrange some containers inside.

"There you are!" Kyra's voice cuts through the air like a firecracker, only I'm in no mood to celebrate. I can't hide because she's suddenly by my side. The elation in her voice is hard to ignore. I so don't need this right now. She slaps a hand across my back. "He won! Did you see? It was a knockout!"

"I was, uh ... I was cleaning up..." I say, turning to face her.

Excitement rolls off her in waves until she looks at me. Her face peers closer. "What's wrong?"

"What? Nothing. I, uh ... I was just, uh... I've been standing the whole night and it just got to be too much. The crowd and the ..."

Her quiet stare, her sudden silence. "It can get overwhelming at times." She doesn't ask me or pry, and I like that. She steps back. "I'm going to start cleaning up. The sooner we can leave, the better."

I cough. "Great idea."

CHAPTER TWENTY-TWO

KYRA

"I can take over now. You've been working hard all evening," I say to Brad. He's fiddling around in the van, and I'm not sure exactly what he's doing, but he's been working like a fiend and he hasn't stopped. I pick up on his subdued mood. I can tell that something is wrong, but I don't want to push him to tell me.

We don't have that kind of relationship.

"I've got this." He doesn't even bother to turn around. I wonder if he's annoyed that he was stuck serving behind the tables all evening. It's not as if I didn't give him the chance to walk around and mingle with everyone. Guilt pinches me. Maybe I should have checked in on him more than I did.

I got carried away by the energy and the sheer excitement of the night. It was so potent, so palpable. It was electric. I couldn't pull myself away. "Hey, Brad. It's not okay. Let me do something. I've done nothing but watch the fight and walk around talking to everyone."

"Couldn't take your eyes off the screen, huh?" There is a rough edge to his voice but I can't gauge the expression on his face because he's still got his back to me.

"It was an amazing fight," I counter.

He turns around slowly. "Yeah, I'm sure it was." Just as I'm about to ask him what his problem is, and why he's so testy, he says. "Why don't you supervise getting everyone to clear the tables so that we can get everything back as fast as possible?"

I almost choke with surprise. He's giving orders as if he's in charge, but for now, I'll let this slip. He's on his A-game, and I'm caught up in the giddiness of Elias's victory.

This has been a great night, not just for Elias. It was a great night for these people to be able to watch him fight. For many, this will be the closest that they get to a night of celebration and I'm super thrilled that we made this possible.

Maybe that's why Brad is quiet. He's feeling sheepish that he was so wrong. He thought we were all crazy for putting on something like this, and I, for one, am glad to prove him wrong.

I set about getting the area cleaned up quickly. As soon as the fight was over, people started to make a quick exit. A few had gone back to the serving tables to get some more food to take away—which is fine, because we have plenty. The place empties much faster than I expected.

Over the next hour, the tech guys are still busy dismantling the screen, and our people have almost cleared everything away. I've sent most of the employees home. Simona was one of the first to leave. I appreciate that it's been a long day for her. Yvette and her kids must have gone home, too.

Fredrich takes a few of the employees with him to return

things back to the restaurants. Brad and I, and a few others deal with the storeroom.

When everything has been put away, I send everyone home. It's very late. Brad doesn't heed my advice. I feel bad because he's been here and done the most, which is surprising to see. I don't understand why he won't leave. I like to do a final quick check and make sure that everything is back, because ultimately, this is all my responsibility.

I attempt to make conversation. "You didn't see much of the fight." I saw it all, even wandering around in the midst of the people, making sure everything was okay, but I'm aware that many of the helpers didn't.

"I can watch it again. I'll catch the highlights later."

"It was a great fight." I've come away feeling buoyed up by what we did. Feeding people, getting them together, seeing that we might have made a difference, all of this elevates my soul. I feel light, and bright, and warm. But seeing Brad's somber mood makes my enthusiasm over Elias' victory float to the ground like a lead balloon.

He has been silently putting things away. Everyone has left, and I don't see the need for him to stay. I want to do a quick inventory check, so that I know that we have enough for the next food session. For one thing, I don't want to have to come in again tomorrow. I try to shop during the weekend.

"I'll stay behind and finish off," I say, making another attempt to reach him, but he isn't giving me anything. Not even his usual bout of sarcastic verbal ping-pong. I would love some of that now. A reaction. *Any* reaction would be better than his silence.

"Is something wrong? Are you annoyed that you were stuck behind the tables all night? I did give you the chance to be on the other side, if you remember."

His brows push together as if he doesn't understand. "I'm not annoyed. It's fine."

I nod, but I don't believe him. He doesn't seem like his usual self. "You probably feel like this was a waste of your Saturday night."

I'm sure he has places to go to, and people he would much rather be with. I can't put my finger on who Brad Hartley is, but the scent of his aftershave lingers with me for longer than is comfortable.

"It wasn't a waste."

I roll my lower lip between my teeth, about to say something, but he says something that completely floors me.

"It took me back, seeing everything."

"Took you back?"

He stares at me. "Yvette's kids, more than anything." His voice is far away, his gaze seems to see beyond me. "I felt sorry for them."

"Those people don't want you to feel sorry for them," I remind him.

"I felt sorry anyway."

There is something different about him tonight, as if the cocky guardedness he wears so easily has developed a crack that seems to grow deeper. Any moment soon it will snap completely, and maybe he will unveil himself.

He's not the man he was when he first walked into Redhill. The work we do affects us all in some way, but to my surprise, I didn't expect Brad to feel it the way we did.

CHAPTER TWENTY-THREE

BRANDON

This evening has messed with my head. What I need is to get the normal back into my life. Dinner with Jessica. Sex. But that's out of the question given that we haven't even been to first base.

I'm losing my edge. In my desire to acquire, I'm messing up on an industrial scale.

Pursuing Jessica.

Pursuing Greenways.

The way I'm feeling, I'm not sure I'm going to walk away with either of those things.

By the time I leave, I am so bone-tired, all I can think of is dropping into my bed. I leave my dead phone to charge up in the living room and then I crash onto my bed. I don't even care that I haven't showered or gotten out of these dirty clothes.

It's only when I check my phone the next morning that I see a heap of messages, many from the managers working for me. And then, just as I'm about to dial my voicemail, I see a text that turns my lungs to stone.

Emma was involved in a car accident last night, driving to meet a friend. She's in a critical condition in the hospital.

Emma. My PA.

My friend. My conscience.

The woman who keeps me on the straight and narrow.

Fuck.

How can this be?

Shock propels me into action, and I call up one of the managers to find out where she is.

I rush over to the hospital. Guilt—a familiar emotion that fits me like a second skin—mingles with fear and worry. This woman is my conscience. She tries to keep me from being a complete jerk. She's my right hand, and my left. She's the best PA anyone could have, and I don't know how I'm going to get shit done without her.

They won't let me in to see her because I'm not family. I see an elderly couple crying as they come out of the room I've been told she is in. I assume they are her parents. I don't want to bother them, but I need to know, and no one is giving me answers.

I can see her through the window. Her eyes are closed and tubes are going into her.

Is she sleeping or in a coma?

I put my hand on the door, I'm about to stride into the room.

"Excuse me, sir. Are you part of the family?"

"I'm her boss."

"Only family are allowed to see her, sir."

"I need to know how she is." I twist the door handle, poised to walk in.

The nurse looks annoyed. "Sir—Don't make me call security."

Fury swirls from the depths of my belly. "My family has paid for a wing in this goddamn hospital. The Philip Hawks wing? It's named after my father, so don't you tell me I can't—"

"Is there a problem?" A doctor intervenes. The nurse whispers something into his ear. When he looks at me, I can tell he's trying to gauge if I'm lying or not. I pull out my business card. It's a shitty, fickle thing to do, but money and power can open doors and get you access and information.

"My company, and if you look up my father, you'll find he paid for that wing in this place." The doctor assesses me for one uncomfortable second before opening the door.

I suck in a horrified breath. It almost sounds like I've choked. Emma's eyes are closed and she looks peaceful. At least that's something. I clutch onto that line of hope like it's my safety net.

"Is she in pain?"

"No."

He tells me she has a ruptured spleen, a collapsed lung, a fractured pelvis and head trauma which they are trying to assess the extent of.

Fuck.

"She's lucky to be alive," he informs me.

"What happened?"

The doctor tells me that Emma was involved in a collision with another vehicle. When he tells me where it happened, my body sags with the weight of guilt. She was around the block from Hawks Enterprises.

It happened near my office. Whether she was going there or leaving from there is irrelevant. She was only there because I had asked her to do something for me.

This is my fault.

Seeing her lifeless and silent, I wonder how I'll get through the coming weeks.

Me.

A selfish good-for-nothing piece of shit.

How is it that in this moment, it's me I think of?

Because that's all I've ever done.

"You need to leave now, sir."

"She's going to be all right, isn't she?"

"She can make a full recovery. It's going to take months before she's back to normal, and of course, we still need to see the extent of the head trauma."

My stomach lurches, and I fight the urge to throw up. "The couple who came out of here earlier, are those her parents?" The doctor nods.

Emma didn't have a partner, as far as I know. Although I kept her suitably informed of most things in my life, she didn't reciprocate.

I leave and start to head towards the elevator doors, but just as I press the button to descend, I turn and head back. I spend a few moments talking to her parents, trying to comfort them, watching them cry in front of a stranger who can do nothing to alleviate their pain.

As I walk away, all I can think of is how I was going to tell her how last night went. She wanted to know about it. She believes in Kyra and the work Redhill is doing. I was beginning to think that Emma is Team Kyra rather than my PA. She has never approved of my actions at Redhill, and now I can't even tell her how things are going. She would be interested in knowing what we did tonight.

Shame curdles in my chest when I recall my initial plan. It's bad enough that Yvette's boy and girl have raked up a cauldron of memories.

Now this.

She wouldn't have been in that accident had it not been for me. It's all my fault. My fucking fault. How is it that I've ruined this woman's life? As if a mirror is being held up to my face, I see myself for the monster I am. For what I've done to Emma, and what I have set out to do to Kyra.

I am my father's son. Whichever father you look at.

I don't want to go home. Even if I go and do a high-intensity workout, it won't help.

That's not the solution for the healing I need. I go for a long walk, heading towards Greenways, to remind myself why I have embarked on this crazy-ass journey. I question my motives, because I don't feel right. Maybe taking a look at that piece of land will remind me of what is at stake; the multi-million-dollar development and all that I stand to make from it.

I head in the direction of Redhill. The area is deathly quiet on the weekend. Factories and buildings stand silent. When these become million-dollar condos filled with people who have good money, this place won't be dead. It will be quietly, discreetly buzzing. The row of stores will have the kinds of eating places that people will want to visit.

Even as I try to imagine this, my heart is heavy and I've lost the will to continue with my deception. I close my eyes, trying to get a handle on my life, because right now, I am not feeling this. My world has turned slate gray, hard and dark. I don't want to do this anymore.

"Brad?" My eyelids fly open. "Brad?" Kyra walks towards me, smiling and happy, as if she's pleased to see me. Oh, shit. "What are you doing here?"

My mouth opens, but no words come out because I don't know what to say, I don't know how to start. She seems warmer, and friendlier, staring up at me differently.

"I just, uh... I was in the area." It's a lame answer, but it's true, and it's not like I can really tell her why I'm here.

"In the area?" She lifts her hand to her forehead because the rays of the sun are getting in her eyes. She squints. "Do you live around here?"

"Not so far away."

"I didn't know."

Thank goodness I didn't put my address down on my resume. I nod, wondering how to get out of this mess. I need to go. To walk away. "What are you doing here?"

"I had some cleaning up to do. I left soon after you did last night, but I needed to do a quick check of the inventory. We need to have enough supplies for the upcoming food night."

Another food night?

Doesn't she get tired of this shit? We had a big event last night and here she is, bright-eyed and eager, planning for the regular weekly event.

I feel exhausted just thinking about it.

She's here now, on a Sunday, on her day off, working. As much as I'm trying to resurrect my defenses, they always seem to get weaker when I'm around this woman. I don't have the fight for any of it.

"Are you okay, Brad?" she asks me. What do I tell her? Where do I start? A piece of me longs to open up and let it all out because I am done with carrying all of this baggage around with me.

"Do you want to get something to eat?" she asks suddenly. "It's almost noon, and I've been here since eight."

"Since eight? Don't you have a life, Lewis?"

"Yes, I have a life." She looks taken aback, as if I've hit her with something she wasn't expecting. I didn't mean to upset her. Hell. She's been here since eight in the morning and given the kind of day we had yesterday, my admiration for her just tripled. But I'm feeling contemplative, and not in the mood to talk or go for something to eat. "I can't."

Her expression sobers and the light goes out of her eyes, like a flickering candle gasping for its last breath. "Can't?" I see her brain going into overdrive, maybe she's wondering if I have other plans. She alluded to it last night when she wondered if I had anything better to do on my Saturday night. "Yeah, I ..." I give a gentle kick to a piece of rubble lying on the ground.

"That's okay, you don't need to explain. You have things to do. I get it, I really do—"

"My friend was in a car accident. I've just come from the hospital."

Hurt widens her eyes. "Oh, I'm so sorry. Is he okay?"

I stare at the ground, because seeing Emma the way she was, I don't know. She looked lifeless. Not the Emma I know. "The doctor said it will be a slow recovery. She's hurt really bad. Really bad."

"I'm ... I'm so sorry, Brad." When I look up, there is a knowing in her eyes. She's looking at me a different way. "What happened?"

I tell her what I know, that it was a car accident and that my friend is in a really bad shape. Just talking about it makes me choke up.

This is all my fault.

Mine.

I lower my head. It's not just Emma's news that has me feeling lost. Recalling the past from last night and now this, it's dented my soul. It has crushed me and I no longer feel invincible. I feel less like Brandon Hawks than ever.

"I don't know what to do. I don't know what to say, or how to be," I say.

"Brad." In that moment, she steps forward and places her hands on my arms, as if to console me.

"I can't come into work for a few days. I have ... I have things I need to take care of ..."

"You don't need to explain. Take as much time off as you need."

Emma held everything together. She was the fortress between me and the managers, the teams and all the people who keep Hawks Enterprises going.

She is irreplaceable.

"Thanks. I appreciate it," I mutter. In that moment, I feel so broken, so bereft, all I can do is put my arms around her. She stiffens for a split second, before she gives in, and then her arms come around me strong and firm.

I just need to hold something. I just need to have someone hold me.

CHAPTER TWENTY-FOUR

KYRA

Brad has a girlfriend, and she nearly died. He's upset and distraught. I wish he'd told me before I'd asked him if he wanted to get something to eat. I feel like a fool. He went home, and I returned to the factory and made myself busy here.

I feel silly for asking him out to lunch and drop my head in my hands, feeling the urge to disappear..

The storeroom is clean and neat, and I've made a list of things we need to get for the next food night. I've done everything that needed to be done. What I didn't want to do was go home, where I would have only the four walls and my thoughts.

It's humiliating.

And now he thinks I made a pass at him. Of course he didn't want to get something to eat with me.

He has a girlfriend.

And she has been badly injured.

I try to force myself to focus on work and to deal with correspondence and emails. Because I want to erase every shred of emotion and feeling I have about Brad.

It's been there for a while, creeping up on me like poison ivy. I don't want to find him attractive, but I do. I don't want to hear my heart thumping each time he comes close to me, but it does. I don't want my breath to catch in my throat when our hands brush as he hands me a box, or a pallet, or something. But it does.

And now he's all broken and vulnerable. I've never seen him looking so weak before. He usually wears his cockiness like a badge of pride. There's something vulnerable about him. I can see it, because I'm a sucker for wanting to fix all broken things.

It's what I do. I'm a fixer, and maybe that's what I saw in him today.

Sucker, that I am.

I should have known that a guy like that wouldn't be single. It was obvious. He looked so upset, as if he was close to tears and just about managing to hold himself together.

Even last night, he wasn't the usual caustic, snarky Brad I have come to know.

Stupid.

That's what I am. Stupid. Having feelings for a guy who isn't even available.

I tell Fredrich and Simona about Brad not coming in for a few days, and I mention that he's devastated because one of his close friends, I don't say girlfriend, was badly injured in a car accident.

"He did seem quiet on Saturday night," Simona comments.

"The dude wasn't himself," agrees Fredrich. "I was starting to think he didn't want to be there."

"The accident hadn't yet happened then, I don't think." But he had been somewhat pensive that night.

"It hadn't?" Simona frowns, an unanswered question in the lines on her forehead. Something had him feeling down and we all noticed it.

I can't stop thinking about his girlfriend and my mind goes into overdrive as I slice the letter opener through the envelope.

Maybe Brad and his girlfriend had an argument, maybe that's why she got angry and drove carelessly? Maybe that's what caused the accident. Maybe he blames himself, and that's why he's so upset and feeling so low.

What an idiot I've been, getting high on his aftershave. Thinking about him when running this business should be the only thing on my mind.

I have received a price estimate for the ceiling and the roof. I had a couple of companies come in last week to take a look and give me rough quotes for what it would cost to fix them. I groan loudly, staring at the figures in the letter.

Fredrich walks over to my side. "What?"

"It's the quote for getting the roof fixed." At this price, I will happily put up with having buckets dotted around the office to catch the rain. "What if we moved? What if we found a better building, a bigger building with more land?" I throw the idea out there for Simona and Fredrich to ruminate over because this is painful, paying this much money just to get the roof fixed.

Brad is right. We should at least consider it. We would be better off finding a building that is everything we need.

"Move where?" Simona asks.

"Move why?" Fredrich wants to know as he walks back to his desk.

I run Brad's ideas past them.

"Brad suggested we do that?" Fredrich raises his arms and folds them across the back of his head, looking pensive.

"He's not wrong about the factory. You could have died when that plaster fell on your head." Simona still worries about that. I've caught her staring up at the ceilings more often than not.

"With the amount it's going to cost to fix the roof, I'm not sure it's worth it." I tap my fingers on the letter opener. "Maybe I've been too stubborn by insisting we stay here."

"But the strip mall store owners don't want to move." Fredrich's voice is abrasive and it's clear that he doesn't like this idea.

"*They* don't have to move," I counter. We've all been in this fight together, and we've successfully managed to hold our own and hold off the last few times when there was talk of developers being interested in this area. "But we need to do what's best for us. Redhill is the biggest factory here and we are still growing."

"They won't have a leg to stand on if we move," Simona reminds me. I'm all too well aware of how a lot of the smaller businesses around here look up to us. Redhill has clout because of the publicity we garner, and the recognition for the work we do. This comes from celebrities like Elias backing us. Because of this, we've been able to prevent investors from pushing us out and taking over. If we move, the rest of the businesses will move. They're here because we are.

"We have to do the right thing for us," I maintain.

"Since when did you think moving was the right thing for us?" Fredrich asks, walking over the window. "You've always wanted to stay here. You said this area was up and coming, and we have so much land for potential. You know exactly where your self-funded business units will go. I don't understand it."

My brows push together. "Understand what?"

"Why you're all of sudden talking about moving someplace else."

"We should consider other alternatives. Why have the expense of building when we might find bigger premises?"

"But you always said we should stick to our guns. Land developers have come and gone, but we've never caved in."

Deep down, I know he's right. Why am I even considering it? "It's something to think about," I throw back. "Brad suggested it as an option."

"So now you're taking advice from him?" Fredrich's tone catches me off guard. It startles me. There's a hint of menace in it that I don't like.

"He's got ideas. Isn't that why we hired him?" I try to keep my voice calm. "That chunk of plaster missed my head narrowly but consider how much worse it could have been if it had fallen on an employee. We'd get sued."

"We have insurance."

"But we also have a lot of rebuilding to do," I reply.

"Why have you changed your mind all of a sudden?" he wants to know. "Is Brad giving you ideas?" His tone startles me because until now, I didn't know how against the idea Fredrich was. I was against moving too but it seems that Brad is making me change my mind.

I put the letter away. "Brad has other things to worry about. We don't need to worry about this now. It was only a suggestion."

CHAPTER TWENTY-FIVE

BRANDON

I'm still waiting to hear news of the extent of Emma's head trauma as I head into Hawks Enterprises.

I'm going to be lost without her. She was brilliant at her job. She *is* brilliant at her job. I'm determined that she will be back. She can take as long as she needs to recover—I'll have to find a temp PA worker to take over for now—but Emma will recover and come back to this.

I need her.

She kept everyone at bay, and more than that, she held me accountable, even if it meant stepping outside her PA role. She hates what I'm doing with Kyra and Redhill, and I wish I could tell her that I'm thinking of giving that crazy idea up. I wish I could see the look on her face when I tell her that she was right.

I rest my head back in my softly cushioned leather headrest and prop my arms on the plush armrests. I sink in, needing something to rest my weary body especially after a long morning of meetings with my managers. Someone comments that I'm out of the office more than I've been here.

Did they just notice this now?

This is the kind of shit I haven't had to deal with.

I look over the resumes of temporary PAs and let one of my other managers take a look. I leave it to her to organize and interview the person.

Right now, I don't even want to be here. Reminders of Emma are everywhere. My guilt trickles through the fabric of the day. I consider going to Redhill. But why? What would be the point of that?

I have a lot of things to take care of, and it's better that I stay here and get on it. Being around Kyra will only confuse things further. I get to work. Or try to.

Sometime later, Kyra texts me to ask about Emma. Simona and Fredrich texted me and have expressed their shock and sadness at the news too.

I'm touched. These people don't even know Emma, but they're checking up on me to see if I'm okay.

Later this week, I have a dinner date with Jessica. I'm about to ask Emma to cancel it for me, and then I remember. *She's not here.*

I need to find myself a temporary PA who will do for me the dirty work I'm not prepared to do myself.

KYRA

It's time to serve, but Simona and the other helpers are all crowded around in a circle. The line is starting to form, and the food still needs to be put out. We're one man down and it is noticeable how much we have come to rely on Brad's help.

It's only when I hear Fredrich's loud voice, and then everyone moves away, that I see Brad.

He came?

It's like I've been winded when I see him head towards me. This has to stop, me feeling like this. I rub the back of my neck, trying not to look at him too much, as if he's the only man on the planet.

"Hey, stranger." I attempt a weak, gentle punch into his arm. "I didn't expect to see you here."

"It's better that I'm here."

There he goes, being all cryptic again. I wonder if he's with the FBI or CIA, and I'm tempted to tease him but then I remember about his girlfriend. "How's your friend Emma?"

The friend emphasis isn't needed, and now I wish I'd said girlfriend so that he could deny it or allow it, and that would tell me.

"She opened her eyes today."

"Oh, that's great. That's really good news." This makes me happy. I don't know her, but I sure am glad that she is at least opening her eyes. From what Brad said of her injuries, I was beginning to worry.

"I know. I know. The doctor says it's too early to tell, but it looks good."

"I'm really happy to hear that. You must be relieved."

"I am. I just miss her being around—" He stops, blinks, and hesitates as if he isn't sure what he's going to say.

I swallow my hurt and clench every muscle in my body so

that I can keep it together. I can't trace the time when it happened, when Brad Hartley stopped annoying me and started stealing into my thoughts, but knowing that he is unavailable is wrong. I can't think those thoughts anymore.

It's been so long since I was with someone, and being single has made my hormones go weird whenever Brad is around. I'm sure it would be the same around anyone 'eligible', as Simona would say. I'm not a mess of emotions because of Brad. I'd be the same if it were any other young, good-looking, flirty guy. I just haven't been around people like that for a while and it's wreaking havoc with my thoughts. Not just my ovaries.

I make sure that I stay away from Brad for the rest of the evening. I need to go back to how I used to be before.

Redhill is my focus. The expansion of the company, the new site. The roof. My insides sink as I remember the cost of fixing the roof. I have so many things to think about and I don't need to get wrapped up in this added melodrama.

I'm really pleased for Brad that his girlfriend is okay, but I have to learn to push away.

CHAPTER TWENTY-SIX

BRANDON

The slate gray matte walls of the restaurant are flecked with dots of gold, and yellow glass lamps hang low over the tables, their sultry dimmed lights eavesdropping on secrets of the rich and famous. The clientele and ambiance in this, one of the city's newest restaurants, drip with riches. Jessica made this reservation.

"I have an invitation to city hall to meet with Elias Cardoza," Jessica announces as our food arrives.

"You? Why did you get an invitation?"

"Yes, me. Why do you sound so shocked?"

I'm shocked because Jessica is as far removed from Cardoza and the world of boxing as any two identities could be. It's almost as ridiculous as someone like me helping out on Kyra's food nights. "I don't see the connection. Why would someone like Elias Cardoza reach out to you?"

"I've donated to some causes dear to his heart." She picks at her salad.

"What causes?"

She waves her fingers, as if she's trying to remember. "Some ... some children's charities, I think."

"You think? You don't know?"

"I picked what he was associated with. Things like that aren't hard to find with celebrities. You can look up these things online. I've even donated to that Kyra Lewis' place. I see Elias is a big donor to that." Jessica picks up the napkin with her perfectly manicured nails, sharp as talons and her almost dark purple nail polish. "You're just jealous because you didn't get an invite."

"The people at Redhill did." Fredrich mentioned it to me. Kyra didn't.

"I'm not surprised. Causes like that are very dear to the boxer's heart, I hear." She picks at her salad.

"But you run an art gallery. You're not interested in those causes."

With a flourish of her hand, she jabs a forefinger at me. "Neither are you, Brandon. Not really. Not for the right reasons." Her wily smile reveals her perfect teeth. She has no soul. No empathy. "You and I care nothing for those people or those causes, but at least I'm not actively working against them without their knowing."

I shift in my seat, the lamb on my plate suddenly not so appealing.

"I am a huge benefactor in this city, Brandon. I donate to worthy causes."

"You do?" I don't believe she's doing it for the right reason. She would strike a deal with the devil if it served her.

"Yes, really. Who wouldn't want to be at city hall at Elias Cardoza's celebration party?"

I don't answer. The gleam in her eye is sharp and cutting. Like a laser. "The local news networks will cover it," she continues, with an enthusiasm I haven't seen before. "He's the pride of Chicago. What do they call him?" She clicks her fingers trying to remember.

"Chicago's New Hope." My voice is as dull as my mood.

"That's it. Chicago's New Hope. Me being associated with him—which I intend to be at that event—is great publicity for me."

"You're using him," I point out.

"What's wrong with that?"

I'm still peeved that Kyra and Cardoza are such good friends, but Jessica? Even I have more heart than her.

"He's the champion of the world, Brandon. Do you have any idea what kind of money he got for the fight?"

I shrug. "It wasn't on my list of things to find out." But I bet it's a heck of a lot. My mind drifts away while Jessica oozes over Elias' newfound wealth. She purrs about getting the chance to meet him in person finally.

"He's got a girlfriend," I announce. "Some journalist."

Jessica makes a face. "I know. They got engaged. It was all over the papers like a rash."

"Keep that fact in mind when you're introduced to him."

"I'll try."

"You surprise me, Jessica." I pick up my glass of wine. "You're not such a refined connoisseur after all."

"Connoisseur?"

"An art gallery owner," I state, not understanding her sudden girl crush over the surly, tattooed fighter. I can very much see why women are drawn to him. Cardoza is the epitome of ripped bad boy as well as a world class boxer. Lucky son of a bitch, and yet I've never considered Jessica to be the type to fall for someone like him.

"He has charisma."

"Emma was in a car accident," I announce suddenly, derailing the conversation.

"Emma?"

"My PA. You've spoken to her a few times, surely you should remember?"

She dabs a napkin at the corners of her lips. "How awful. What happened?"

I relay the information, but I notice that I got a more sympathetic reaction from Kyra. I wish I was sitting here with her instead.

Jessica still picks at her food, and at the end, says, "That's tragic," but her voice doesn't echo the gravity of the news I have imparted.

I wait for her to say something more, to offer sympathy for Emma and words of comfort to me. But she doesn't. "She's opened her eyes, and ..." I tell her, but Jessica is busy craning her neck, trying to get the server's attention. I give up. We eat in silence until the server comes over and Jessica asks him for another type of salad dressing.

"What were you saying?" she asks.

"Nothing. It wasn't important." I vow not to speak to her about Emma again.

"So, I'll be meeting the new heavyweight champion of the world at city hall." She suddenly sounds like a groupie, and I can't believe I have to hear her gushing about Cardoza and this event all evening.

"He's only caught your attention because of his fight money."

"Of course. Why else would I notice him?" She lifts a forkful of salad, to her lips. this has to be her fourth or fifth forkful, while I've almost finished my dinner. It occurs to me that Jessica barely eats. She plays with her food, just like she plays with the people in her life. I suddenly realize that the woman who I thought was everything I wanted in a wife no longer holds my interest. She has everything I like—power, wealth, status—but it is no longer enough.

She has no heart.

I also have no heart, but something in my DNA is shifting. I feel things I never did before. Some good, some bad. Some hard to understand.

"He was amazing in the fight," I say. Having seen the highlights, Cardoza was like a ferocious beast in the ring. Garrison stood no chance.

"I didn't watch the fight. I find those matches vulgar." Jessica turns her nose up as if she's sniffed something rancid.

"Good party?" I allude to what she was up to on the night of the fight.

"It was a fabulous party. Great company and food. You should have come."

"I was busy." I don't even want to tell her about what I did on that night.

"You're always busy these days," she counters.

"It's not easy juggling two different worlds."

"First world problems." A smile spreads across her lips. I brace myself. "I'm going to bump into your new boss. I can't wait to give her the once-over."

The complete change in topic jars me. It takes me a moment to make sense of this. Then I realize she's talking about Kyra. "If you mean Kyra, she isn't my boss."

"You work for her, don't you, *Brad?* That woman will want to kill you when she finds out what you've done."

Kyra will hate me. I'll probably be better off dead. I don't even want to think about that moment when she finds out the real reason for me joining her company. I don't want to face seeing the look of disappointment in those sparkling green eyes. "We'll see." I lift my glass and take a sip.

"I hope I'm there to witness it. Come with me," Jessica exclaims, sounding overly excited. "I have an extra invitation for my plus one."

"I'm not your plus one."

A line appears between her eyes as she observes me over the rim of her cocktail glass. We haven't talked about us, or where this is going. I'm aware that this subtle dance we've been doing for months is leading nowhere. It has suited us both, but it has run its course.

I no longer want to pursue this, but I'm not sure what Jessica thinks. I sense her glacial exterior of noninterest is a façade. When I try to walk away, she might try and sink her hooks in further.

"Come anyway," she purrs, thankfully not questioning why I'm not her plus one.

"I can't. Kyra will be there and I can't run the risk of meeting anyone I know."

"That's a shame. What a missed opportunity."

"You'll have to tell me all about it."

"We could have had so much fun." Her voice is flirty, with a girlish tone I've never heard before. She's playful tonight, it's almost as if that granite guard of hers has come down and she's allowing herself to show emotion.

"I can't risk it."

Jessica would love to see me running into Kyra with Jessica's arm hooked into mine.

It's not going to happen. No way in hell.

CHAPTER TWENTY-SEVEN

KYRA

I'm moving things around in the storeroom again. I shopped for some supplies yesterday and left them here in a rush, and now I'm organizing things neatly in place. "I thought you'd be in here." I jump at the sound of Brad's voice.

I turn around, my cheeks blushing as our gazes meet. I hate that my face has such tell-tale signs, and I pray that he'll think it's because I've been working at this.

"Where else would I be?" I give a light laugh and throw my hands up. With all that simmering chemistry between us it has been difficult for me to stop thinking about him. I was almost getting back to my normal self because he's been away from the office, and I stayed away from him at the food night. But this, him, now, *here*. It all comes back. He's been away for a week, taking care of Emma and I need to fight harder to keep my feelings at bay.

"Are you sure you're okay to come back?" He's not being paid, so I don't understand why he is here.

He hunches his shoulders, hand in his pockets as he slowly walks towards me. "I need a distraction."

He must be so badly upset about it. My imagination sparks to life, and I deepen and color in the argument I assume he and his girlfriend must have had before she had the accident. "How's your girlfriend?"

"She's not my girlfriend."

"No?" I hope my voice is strong, and unwavering in the silent moment that passes between us. But I don't think it is. My heart jumps like a jittery fool, and I'm worried that he's going to hear it.

"What make you think she's my girlfriend?"

I turn my back to him, and line up the already lined-up boxes. "Just ... you've been so concerned about her."

"I care about her, but she's not my girlfriend. Whatever gave you that idea, Lewis?" His voice is husky and inviting. I'm convinced he's back to playing games with me. We lock gazes, the way we used to do so many times before. I force myself to look away and fail completely, my eyes drifting back to his face, taking in the curve of his lips and noticing the way they're slightly apart.

Tempting.

He is tempting.

Every little thing about him is suddenly tempting.

I've been love starved. Attention starved. Sex starved. That's why I'm behaving like this.

And now I wonder how his mouth tastes. My beating, crazy, lonely heart demands to know.

I'm convinced he's back to playing games with me.

She's not his girlfriend.

It's supposed to be good news.

Why is that, Kyra?

"Those boxes look pretty well lined up to me. The entire

storeroom is symmetrically in sync. You should be proud of your OCD." His voice is low, and I can feel him standing behind me, not because he's touching any part of me, but because I can sense it. I'm like a barometer, sensitive to the change in temperature which just shot up. Inhaling what I hope is a good dose of calm, I try to keep calm. "I take pride in my work."

"What made you think she was my girlfriend?"

He's not going to let this go. "You seemed really upset," I answer.

"She's a good friend."

"She must be someone special." I stare him right in the eyes, as if I am X-raying him to find the truth.

"She is."

"How is she?"

"She's getting better, but she might suffer from partial amnesia. That will be hard." He bites his lip, stares away, looking pensive and sad. "She'll recover, but it's going to take some time."

"She'll recover. That's the main thing. That's what you have to focus on."

His face crumples. "She doesn't remember the accident. She doesn't even remember that evening or what she did."

My mouth falls open. "That's tragic. That's awful. I mean, maybe it's a blessing that she can't remember the event, but to forget a chunk of her life like that. It's awful."

"Sometimes it's better to erase the things that hurt too much to remember." I'm not even sure that he's talking about his friend now. He seems to have zoned out.

And all of a sudden, I don't even know if I believe him. Even if she's not his girlfriend, he's so cut up that it doesn't make sense. Is he lying to me? My last boyfriend broke my heart so badly that I've not been able to put it back together.

There are cracks in it that will never mend. I don't want to fall for another liar.

BRANDON

Sometimes people want to forget. Sometimes it's better to forget because remembering is too painful. It's something that most people won't understand. Kyra gets too close to the truth without even realizing. I'm scared that she sees inside me and knows every single demon that haunts me.

Seeing Emma's empty desk, and finding myself becoming increasingly irritated by the new PA makes me want to be at Redhill instead of at Hawks Enterprises. At first I found it safe and comforting, being around Kyra but lately, coming here isn't working out so well for me.

It's bad enough that I have to put up with the homeless food nights and seeing Yvette and her children. She brings them with her and it seems to have become a regular thing. I hate that it forces me to face the things I would rather forget.

I have to come clean. Or quietly slip away.

I spend the next hour talking to Fredrich and Simona, and answering their questions about Emma, without giving too much away. Kyra isn't stupid. She knows I'm being vague.

They start talking about the city hall event on Friday.

"Will you come, Brad?" Simona asks me.

"Uh ... I don't think so."

"Come on, dude. It'll be an awesome night." Fredrich seems to be eager for me to come along.

"I'm not up to it, sorry."

"Don't force him," Kyra chimes in, throwing me a sympathetic glance.

At the end of the day when the others have left, she comes over to my desk. "That was nice of you, sending food boxes back with Yvette on the night of Elias's fight. She told me you did that."

I slot my pen into the desk organizer, unable to meet her gaze even though I know she is staring at me. "We had lots of food left over."

"But still, it was nice of you. Her kids are still really traumatized from—"

I hold my hand up, wanting her to stop. I don't want to know. I already can't sleep well and I don't need to know what hell Yvette and her kids have suffered. "It's fine. Really."

"Okay," she mumbles softly. I'm aware that I've been giving her wrong signals all day. Knowing the type of person she is, she'll blame herself for something that is clearly not her fault.

It's mine.

My life was fine and orderly before I came here. Now, memories of my past stare me in my face. I can no longer push them away. This thing with Redhill isn't going according to plan, and I'm falling behind with dealing with matters at Hawks Enterprises. I stress about Emma, and then I stress some more about Kyra.

I could leave. Just disappear for a month, take a vacation. Go out into the wild, and hopefully, by the time I come back, all will be forgotten.

But I can't leave with Emma still in the hospital, especially when the reason she's hurt is because of me. I'm the one who told her to pick up the papers from my office and to drop them at my house.

The accident happened near my office.

This is *my* fault.

"Are you sure we can't convince you to come to City Hall?"

"I can't. I'm busy. Sorry."

"You could have met Elias Cardoza."

If I hear this one more time, I'll explode. "My bad." I force a smile, something I seem to be doing most of the time.

She gives me a weighing, assessing look. Her standard X-ray look, and I involuntarily fold my arms, as if this will be protection enough to prevent her from delving deeper inside me.

CHAPTER TWENTY-EIGHT

KYRA

What's up with that man? It's almost as if he has a split personality. One minute he's fine, and the next he's closed off. I can't work him out.

I keep my head down, and I ask Fredrich to get Brad to work with him. Maybe it's a good thing that he declined the invite to Elias's event. It would be awkward trying to make conversation with him there.

Simona, Fredrich and I are going together, but because Elias supports our organization, we were given a few extra invitations. We held a raffle to make it fair so that everyone from the company had a chance to go. Entry is by ticket only, and I'm supposed to meet Simona and Fredrich there

On the evening of the event, everyone leaves early.

I've been racking my brains on what to wear. A dress? Nice jeans? Dressy slacks? It's going to be a fancy affair, but I'm not sure how fancy.

I finally settle on a pair of dark jeans which don't look like jeans, but they are, and I dress them up with a spaghetti strap top. It shows off more of my tattoos, but I'll have my nice blazer on most of the evening.

I get ready quickly, but Simona calls as I'm about to leave my place. She's forgotten our invitations in her desk drawer. Thank goodness we gave the raffle winners theirs. I pass by work on the way to city hall, and I quickly rush out of my car and head into the factory. I'm surprised to see that the light in our office is on. Dayna, the factory manager, is still here. She whistles when she sees me. "My, girrrrrl. You're lookin' mighty fine."

"Thank you!" I blow her a kiss as I rush up the stairs in my high heels.

BRANDON

The Redhill office is empty and there's only me up here and a couple of the workers on the factory floor. I have nowhere else to go, so I stay on at work a little longer and wonder what's going on at city hall. With Jessica and Kyra at the same place, it seems like I've made the right decision to stay out of it.

Jessica will have plenty to brag about, but I'm not eager to see her anytime soon. Fredrich and Simona will have plenty to say about it. I wonder what Kyra will think, and whether she will drone on about Elias the way Jessica has.

I drum my fingers on the table, wondering what to do with myself. I'm not going to pass by the hospital today. Emma's sisters are over, and they're going to find it odd that I keep visiting. They'll get the wrong idea.

I fucked up. If I hadn't asked her to pick up the paperwork for me, she wouldn't have been in that accident.

I hold my head in my hands, elbows propped on the desk, wanting to clamber out of my pity party. No amount of me feeling bad will transform Emma back to exactly who she was.

That's something I will have to live with.

Like my guilt over Kane.

I stand up and walk around, hoping to shift these gloomy thoughts. I should go home, get something to eat, or head back to my own office to deal with the mounting deluge of emails. I've had a dozen messages from the new PA. She is completely useless. Maybe I should check in at my office and see what a mess she's made of today.

But something else draws my attention. With the office is empty, here's my chance to see if I can find anything of interest on Kyra.

Like the dirt I was so sure I'd find.

The dirt I could expose her with.

Back in the days when I was so sure that no one could be as well-meaning as Kyra.

How wrong I was.

But still, I walk over to Kyra's desk and sit in her chair, gingerly staring up at the ceiling to make sure nothing is about to fall on my head and kill me.

A moment of madness hits me and I snoop through her drawers, rummaging around, looking for something, anything. A clue to her. I want to know more about her. I take a peek but I find nothing significant. Some hand cream, lip balm. A copy of Paulo Coelho's *The Alchemist*. A hairbrush and a whole heap of unopened pastel-colored Post-it notes and other stationery.

I tap my fingers on Kyra's desk. It's not super neat, but it's not a chaotic mess either. I see some letters lying around under a paperweight. One of them has Greenways Committee letterhead.

I shuffle through the pile. I'm about to tug the Greenways Committee letter out from under the paperweight when the door opens.

"Damn!" Kyra stands there, her knee bent as she glances over her shoulder examining the sole of what looks like a high-heeled boot. She looks amazing. "Damn heels," I think she mumbles.

I let go of the letter I was about to pull out and fall back into her chair. The sound of it creaking makes her look up at me.

"Brad ..." It's a breathless whisper, shot through with surprise. "You're here late." Furrows form on her brow. I can't talk, because I'm fixated on her bare arms. The small sun tattoo—the one I've seen many times before—almost winks at me.

"I'm ... I was ..."

"You said you were busy tonight?"

"I was about to leave. Check in on Emma ..."

"That's why you're not coming with us tonight?" she asks. It's a lame excuse and I don't know how to reply because one white lie leads to another and before I know it I'll be caught up in a fishing net of deceit, feeling like a hapless little fish. I stand up, because I've been caught red-handed—not that she seemed to notice—and because she looks so breath-taking.

Stunning, is the word that shoots to my mind. Something else, white hot desire, shoots directly to my cock.

I've never seen her dressed up. She's not red carpet dressed up, but she looks different. Dark jeans hug her hips. High heels, pencil thin, make her legs look longer. A blouse with thin straps caresses her skin. She's the epitome of rock star glam. Rock chick glam. My interest in her just hiked up fifty notches.

The transformation is a complete makeover but not a drastic fix-the-teeth-get-Botox type of makeover. I could have sworn she only went home less than an hour ago so she hasn't had long to get ready but she already takes my breath away.

She sashays into the room, keys in one hand, handbag in the other, and goes straight over to Simona's desk where she fumbles around in her drawers.

Fuck.

She has another tattoo in between her shoulder blades. It looks like a compass, and it has me thinking. Why *that*, and why *there*? Where she can't see it but I can? A hot-blooded man like me who now has no choice but to gawk at it because I sure as hell can't seem to turn away.

My eyes are riveted, and it's like I'm seeing a new side to Kyra for the first time. She is sexy as hell. There was something about her before, which I begrudgingly noticed, but this... this is her sexiness on steroids.

I have to work hard not to let my eyes rake down the length of her as she walks towards me.

"The invitations," she says, holding them up. "Simona forgot them, and now I'm running extra late and—"

"You look like a model."

She laughs, confusion making her brows slant before she looks away. We don't exchange words like this.

"You do," I insist.

As if a blindfold has been untied from around my eyes, I see Kyra in a whole new way. In a possessive way. In an I've-got-to-have-her way.

She ignores my compliment and comes over to my side. When she bends over and pulls open her drawer, my attention falls to her back and her compass tattoo again. I've never been with a woman who has ink on her body. I've never been with a woman like Kyra, and now I want her even more than before.

She has a beauty on the outside that matches what's inside, and she has the biggest heart of anyone I know.

Jessica couldn't hold a candle to her.

My cock twitches. As Kyra rummages around, the throbbing between my legs intensifies. This is awkward.

"What are you looking for?" Not that I should be asking her. She should be asking me what the hell I'm doing sitting in her chair.

She pulls out what look like a couple of lipsticks. "I'm so late," she wails, oblivious to the effect she's having on me. My heart lurches as she opens and swivels the lipsticks one by one, presumably to check the color, but with her back to me, I can see clearly the tattoo on her back, between her shoulder blades. I reach out and touch it, not caring that I've invaded her space. She flinches, as if the shock is electric, then bends over and rummages through her drawer again.

"Your tattoo. It's a ... compass." I try to compose myself. "Why's that, Lewis? Are you lost?" I venture a casual laugh that I don't feel. The moment is hot, sparky and weighted with the boulder of desire which is suddenly too big for me to ignore.

She turns to look at me, her smoldering eyes burning into me, causing a chain reaction that threatens to explode. I'm going to turn into a jabbering wreck, unable to string together a coherent sentence if she stays here any longer.

As if she can sniff out my weakness, she tilts her head, observing my reaction. "Not anymore."

I hold my breath, wanting her to elaborate, wanting to ask her but my tongue seems to have stopped working and my mouth has dried up. It's only my eyes that function, raking down the length of her. My gaze naturally drifts to her sun tattoo, then to her spaghetti straps, then my brain starts to wonder if her bra is strapless or something else. All this in the space of a few seconds. I wish I was going with her.

"Not anymore?" I manage to ask. She's wearing a touch of makeup. Her lashes are thick and long, her lips moist and pouty. Her skin is velvety. I wish I hadn't turned down the invitation tonight. I suddenly don't like the idea of Kyra being at city hall, around Elias Cardoza. I don't see how anyone can resist her looking the way she does, and the chances of Cardoza talking to Kyra this evening are a dead cert.

She turns to leave and it sends my hormones into a tailspin, seeing her back, the silken skin, and those pipe-thin straps.

"I never had you pegged for being into tattoos." This is my pathetic attempt to catch her attention, to need an answer that makes her face me once more.

She stops, turns and tilts her head, as if she's considering whether to tell me or not. My breath hitches in my throat. It feels like a secret, and now I want to be her best friend so that I can hear it.

"I wasn't. My ex was. He had them all over. I was curious, so I got this first." She touches the sun on her shoulder. Involuntarily, I lick my lower lip. "Then he convinced me to get a rosebud tattoo." She rolls her eyes as if she regrets it. The whole time she's talking, I picture tasting those lips.

I fold my arms, as if this will help stem the flow of blood from rushing south. "Convinced you? I didn't think anyone could convince you. You're a woman who knows her own mind."

"Love," she says, with a shrug, as if it was a huge mistake which now means nothing. Her face turns serious. "We were together for four years, and he cheated on me for three of them. I dumped him the day I found out. Three years of my life with a cheat. It knocked me for six. Left me lost and broken, but Redhill gave me direction. This ..." She hooks a thumb over her shoulder, "is to remind me that I'm on a journey, an adventure, even, and that I'm not stuck."

I want to say something to comfort her, but I'm scared of saying the wrong thing because I'm glad that shithead is out of her life. Crazy fucker, cheating on her. He doesn't deserve her. "You're better off without him."

She nods, then stares down at the invitations. I hope she doesn't have her eye on Cardoza.

"He was great at the beginning, when I was starting Redhill, and he helped me a lot. I mistakenly thought we shared the same ideals. What I didn't know was that he shared our bed with someone else."

"His loss." I leave the words floating around in the heavy haze of desire which permeates the air. It surprises me that she is opening up so much. Longing and lust topsy-turvy in my stomach, and I want to suck her lower lip, to elicit a moan from that pretty little mouth of hers. "Where's the rosebud?" I ask, in a voice so hoarse that I barely recognize it.

"Further down, where no one can see."

Further down?

How much further down?

"Yeah?" My voice sounds disgustingly high-pitched. An indecent thought rockets north from the base of my groin. In the push and pull that has been the sum total of our strained relationship, I've tried to hold back from thinking such things. Now it's impossible.

My gaze rakes in her back, sauntering slowly from her spaghetti straps, to the compass tattoo, all the way down to her fuck-me heels.

She throws me a look over her almost-bare shoulder. "You're blushing, Brad. Are you okay?"

She knows exactly what she's doing. I don't answer, for fear of giving my teenage horniness away. I grimace, and hope it resembles something like a passing grin.

Her lingering gaze sets flames licking all over my skin. This is a new side to her. A vampish and unexpected side that I never would have thought someone like her possessed.

I want her.

Watching her stride away, I'm overcome with the thought of grabbing her and pushing her up against the door. I want to claim her mouth and rain kisses down her bare arms and shoulders. I want to make her mine.

"Don't forget to lock up," she tells me, completely oblivious to the tsunami of emotions she's sent sweeping all over my body.

She's so naive, so trusting, she hasn't even asked me what I was doing sitting in her chair.

CHAPTER TWENTY-NINE

KYRA

I made him blush.

My tattoos caught his attention. Brad looked at me in complete shock, as if he never expected little old me to have anything like that. I wish I could tell what shocked him the most, the tattoos or that I unexpectedly showed up. Or what I was wearing.

Who knows?

I can't believe I spilled my guts about my ex. I don't ever talk about him, but it didn't feel so wrong telling Brad.

This isn't me. But Brad makes me react like this. I fan my face as the air hits me. I can't be like this. I've already wasted years on a cheating man, and my precious broken heart won't suffer another setback. Brad is like the night sky, vast in its darkness and unknowingness. It would be better for me and my broken heart to stay away from him.

By the time I get to city hall, I'm not too late but I'm all knotted up inside like a ball of cotton wool that a litter of kittens got a hold of. I tell Simona and Fredrich about my run-in with Brad at the office, making himself at home in my chair.

Fredrich has his hand wrapped around a bottle of beer. "What was he doing there? He said he was too busy to come out with us tonight."

"He's still upset about his friend who was in the car accident," I reply.

"Is she his girlfriend?" Fredrich asks.

"He doesn't have a girlfriend," Simona replies smoothly.

Fredrich takes a swig from his bottle. "I don't understand why he's so upset about it." Simona and I stare at him, shocked.

"She's a good friend," I insist, but he wasn't at the hospital. He was sitting in the office.

"A friend? Yeah, right." Fredrich doesn't look convinced. "She must be some friend for him to be so upset about it even now that he can't come out to this event. Who would give up the chance to meet Elias Cardoza? The guy is a legend. Heavyweight champion of the world. How come Brad is so upset that he's turned down this chance?"

"I'm sure he has his reasons." Simona seems to be Brad's biggest fan and won't have a bad word said against him. But I wonder, all the same, especially since he was sitting at my desk and looking as if he was pretending to be the boss.

We spend the evening enjoying the fine hospitality at city hall. Soft music plays in the background and everyone is dressed up. It's a rare night out for us and the other employees from work whom we eventually locate and hang around with for a while.

Fredrich is working the room. He's good at this. He's confident, and with his huge frame he stands shoulders above everyone. People seem to notice him, and he seems to bask in that sense of acknowledgment.

I'm by myself when a tall woman comes up to me. She's dressed beautifully in a long stylish black and gold dress and a chunky gold necklace with it. Her legs seem to go on forever. It's easy to tower over me, and even in my heels, I feel like a Hobbit standing next to her. "Are you Kyra Lewis?" she asks.

"I am. And you are?"

"Jessica Montrose. I own the Montrose Art Gallery in town. You might have heard of it?" She doesn't offer her hand. I don't offer mine.

"It doesn't ring a bell." I shake my head. I have never heard of the gallery, and I haven't met her before.

"You're the one who runs that ..." She clicks her perfectly manicured fingers together. "That place where you make bags and jackets, and you employ people off the streets."

"We give people a chance to get their lives back on track," I clarify.

"You're always in the papers," she says, as if this annoys her.

"I try not to be." I smile back but don't know what to say. She seems friendly, but I can sense her judging me. It's not her words, but her eyes that give it away.

"You've made such progress, given how young you are, and ... and ... what you do. It's astounding." She rakes her hand through her mane of glossy dark curls.

"Thank you." I should ask her something about her gallery, but I know nothing about it, or her, and I can't make polite conversation. I give her another smile, then look around and pray that Fredrich or Simona, or the others, will rescue me. When my gaze circles back, she's still here. I catch her checking me out, her eyes slowly going over my outfit.

Something is off. Because when people approach me, it's because they know about Redhill and they love what we do. They are interested in finding out more. "What was the name of your art gallery again?" I ask her, and when she tells me, it still doesn't ring a bell. And yet I have the distinct impression that she seems to know of me.

"How is business?" she asks, but her eyes are dead and it seems as if she's just going through the motions of being sociable.

"It's ... good. Business is good Why do you ask?" Someone like her would have no interest in someone like me, or in Redhill, and I know my donors. There are definitely no art gallery owners on that list as far as I can recall.

A sudden cheer bursts in the crowd and the sound of people clapping makes us both turn. Elias walks into the room, hand in hand with Harper. While everyone is staring at Elias, she catches my eye and waves at me. I wave back and silently pray for her to come and rescue me but, to my dismay, she and Elias walk to the front of the room.

There's a short speech by someone, the party organizer, I think, and then the music starts up again and everyone starts talking again. In dismay, I see that the art gallery woman is still stuck to my side. Stuck for conversation I start to talk about the thunderstorms we had a few weeks ago. These are desperate measures, talking about the weather. I have nothing in common with her, not that commonality is the only vital ingredient in two people being able to connect. The woman gives off strange vibes and I feel on edge around her.

"Kyra!" Someone taps me on the shoulder. I'm shocked to find that it's Elias and Harper. Shocked, because they've come directly to me.

Thank the lord.

"Hey," I say, overwhelmed and relieved. "You did awesome!" I bump fists with Elias, because it seems less formal than a polite nod, and as much as I'm super excited, throwing my arms around him doesn't seem to be appropriate either. "Congratulations."

"Thank you." His brown eyes are twinkling. He must be on a high from all the adoration everyone in this room has for him.

I'm so proud of him. We, all the people in the city, are so proud of him and to have him be here, talking to me, when he has a room full of people who are so much more interesting and accomplished than me gets me giddy with excitement. I glance around for my Redhill people, for Fredrich and Simona to come over, but in my excitement, I don't find them.

"We all watched the fight live. We were all rooting for you."

"It was a tough fight, but it ended well." His customary humility endears him to me more than ever. "Congrats on staging your event," he says. "That was an amazing thing you guys put together."

"You saw it?" I ask, wondering how I didn't think to send him any photos from the event.

"It was all over social media," Harper informs me.

I look around the room quickly and wishing that Simona and Fredrich would hurry up and get here so that they could take some of the credit. "It was one heck of a night. You winning made everyone's day."

"Expect to see another donation from me in the coming days."

"Aww, thanks, Eli. We greatly appreciate anything and everything."

His face turns serious quickly. "Glad to help. The work you guys do is important. Harper and I were saying that only someone like you could have put on an event like that with a huge movie screen."

I laugh. "It was Fredrich's idea, actually." I turn to

Harper. "How were you on the night?" I know she hates watching Eli fight.

"A complete wreck." She puts her hands in front of her face as if she's reliving the moment again. Her engagement ring sparkles under the lights and is hard to miss.

"Wow." I take her hand and examine the rock.

"He proposed," she says, all girlie and blushing. The two of them tell me about the proposal and we talk as if we are old friends.

The woman from the art gallery stands by silently. She remains tight-lipped, and it feels awkward having her here. She's like an appendage my body doesn't need. I feel duty bound to introduce her, which isn't so great because I've already forgotten her name and what she does. "This is ... J...J...." My mind blanks out completely.

"Jessica Montrose." She gives Eli a smile that has as much wattage as the necklace she's wearing. Ignoring Harper completely, she offers Elias her hand, something she never offered me, and then she takes over the conversation, talking about the donations she has made to Eli's various charities.

Harper and I exchange knowing looks. "You must be used to this," I whisper so that only she can hear me.

She gives Jessica a sideways glance and rolls her eyes. "You have no idea. I should rescue him," she mumbles. "He looks as if he's in pain."

"Let me make my getaway first," I whisper back. And then I rush away.

____

CHAPTER THIRTY

BRANDON

The weekend seems to last a lifetime. I've been dying to know, from the Redhill people, how the city hall event went. So far, I've only heard Jessica's version of events and she's talked mostly about herself. She also tells me she sought Kyra out and tried to have a conversation with her, but she doesn't elaborate on it except to say that she seemed to be a good friend of Eli's.

"You missed a cool night," Fredrich says when I go to work on Monday. It has killed me going days without seeing Kyra.

"I'm sure I did. My loss."

"We did miss you, Brad. What did you have that was so important?" Simona asks as she goes through the mail. Kyra is quiet as she gets on with her work. I want to see her reaction, but the way I'm sitting will make it too obvious to the others if I keep trying to catch her attention. I need to find a moment to get her alone.

"I had things to do."

"Kyra says you're still upset about your friend, and understandably so," Fredrich adds, "how is she now?"

I tell them what I know. I know from one of Emma's friends at work that her condition is stable, but she's got a long way to recovery. Emma's sisters and parents are still by her bedside.

"That's good, but you should have come, dude. It would have taken your mind off things. You missed the chance to meet Elias Cardoza."

The room falls silent and I'm aware that they are waiting for me to say something. Years of experience with complex negotiations tells me that they aren't convinced of my alibi. I can't tell them about my guilt over Emma, or even my relationship to her without giving away who I am. I understand why they are suspicious of me. "I just wasn't feeling it. Sorry." I turn to Kyra, but her gaze is on her computer screen where it has been for most of this morning. With dogged determination, she's managed to stay out of the conversation and is quietly getting on with her work. Avoiding me, I'd say.

"Were you very late?" I ask her, remembering that night. She looks up at me with a brazen smile. "Not really. I made it in good time, but you did miss a *great* night." Her eyes twinkle more than I like. As if she's fangirling over the boxer. As if he's the one who made it such a fucking great night for her.

"Cardoza made a beeline for her," Fredrich informs me. My heart pinches. Jessica said the same, but not quite like that. I believe Fredrich. Jessica said she'd purposely sought out Kyra because she wanted to get up close and take a good look at her. I wish I had kept my mouth shut, but back then it seemed the natural thing to do, to tell my potential-trophy-wife about my plan to trick Kyra.

"He made a beeline for you?" The words are hard to dress up in a jokey manner, but I somehow manage it.

"She looked like quite the glamor girl," Simona announces proudly.

"I almost didn't recognize you," Fredrich says to Kyra. "If Eli was single, he would have asked you out."

Kyra shakes her head in weary annoyance. "He would not. He and I ... no."

"He's a fine-looking man," Simona remarks.

"What is wrong with you people?" There is a level of anger in Kyra's voice that makes me sit up and take notice. "He's engaged. Did you not see Harper with him? She's the love of his life."

Did I detect a hint of jealousy in her voice? Is there a sinister reason behind Eli being Redhill's biggest donor?

"But he came straight over to you after the intro speech," Fredrich presses.

"Is that right?" A knife twists in my belly as I imagine the scene playing out. Kyra and I aren't even together, so my level of jealousy is excessive. Weeks of simmering tension between us seems to be ratcheting up.

"He came over to talk to me because of the event we had put on and he wanted to thank me in person." She glares at the others. "He would have thanked you two had you been there."

"Didn't you all hang around together?" If only I'd gone. I would have kept Kyra company all night. I picture the worst, that men of all ages and status flocked to her side.

Fredrich rips up another letter and throws it into the bin. "I was mingling." The grin on his face is telling. "Kyra got lumbered with some stuck-up woman before Eli came."

"A stuck-up woman?" I say with a tone of exaggeration.

I've heard all about it from Jessica's point of view and now I'm curious to know their side of events.

But Kyra stands up, as if she's had enough. "Do we have enough water bottles for this week?" she asks. "I forgot to buy some last time I went shopping." She wanders off, presumably to the storeroom. I give it a few moments before I follow her.

She's around the back, crouching on the floor, peering at the crates of water bottles which we hand out on food nights.

"I'm sure I saw some water bottles," I state, pulling out a crate from another shelf.

"Who put them there?"

"Someone must have shifted them there. Not everyone is as obsessed with keeping everything perfectly in line." I attempt a smile, but she doesn't return it.

"If everyone put things back in their original place, we wouldn't have to hunt around the entire room to find what we want."

"What was Fredrich talking about? What stuck-up woman?" I ask, needing to hear her side of the story. More than that, it's her interaction with Cardoza I want to hear the most.

"What?" There's an edge to her voice, of irritation, as she starts looking through the cupboards, noting things down. Is she doing a fucking inventory check when I have so much I want to talk to her about?

I'm sick of these baby steps, of holding back, of Jessica and her whining and complaining, of this little dance that Kyra and I unknowingly have been swaying to.

"What are you doing here, Brad? Why have you followed me in here?"

I can't answer that, because whatever things I've been feeling and thinking about her, she doesn't seem to feel the same about me. Her irritation speaks volumes. "I just ... I ..." I sound like a blubbering, blundering idiot. That's what she has reduced me to.

"What were you doing sitting in my chair the other day?"

"What?" I attempt deflection, sounding more indignant than I should.

"You were at my desk, making yourself quite at home from the looks of it."

My insides churn as those gorgeous eyes—the ones I see each night when I rest my head against my pillow—now look through me.

"Are you looking to take over my role?" she asks, giving me an out which I grab with both arms. A laugh tumbles out of my mouth.

"I was going to write you a note and I was looking for a piece of paper."

"I didn't see any note."

"That's because I didn't write it."

"What were you going to write?" She lifts her eyebrow and looks at me as if she doesn't believe me, and she shouldn't believe me. I'm no good for her. Even though I can't take my eyes off her, I'm trouble for this woman.

She should walk away.

She *should*, but even if she tries, I won't let her.

"I can't remember now," I say, hastily. "It couldn't have been that important."

"No?"

"No."

"It couldn't have been important," she echoes.

"Whatever it was went clean out of my head because you walked in and knocked the wind right out of my lungs." I can't believe what I've said.

Have I overstepped my boundary?

Did I read her signals wrong that night when she showed

me the tattoo on her back? When she told me about the other tattoo further down?

Her frown deepens.

I take my chance and confess. "You all dressed up for city hall, Lewis. You with tattoos and those killer heels. I'm having trouble letting go of that image."

Her eyes widen, in confusion. I wonder if she can sense the sizzling simmering tension between us. Something in the air zings and zaps, and it's too strong, too palpable to not be real.

"I see," she says, smoothly sidestepping my comment and reacting as if I'd told her we needed two boxes of crackers for the next food night. I try to think quickly but it's almost impossible with her this close to me. It's like wading through honey. My brain fogs up. I get a picture of her in my head. I see her tattoos. I can almost feel the velvety texture of her arms and shoulders. Except that she's wearing her customary sweatshirt and sneakers now, and her arms fold together as she waits for my answer.

I suck in a breath, scrambling to find the right words to say next.

Tell her the truth.

This woman has flipped every idea I ever had about her, she's brought me to my knees to the point that I almost don't recognize the man who came here under with evil intent.

I can't push her away. I don't want to. I feel the connection between us so acutely now that her eyes are burning into mine.

My doubts deepen.

What I'm doing isn't right; going undercover like a Trojan horse. Tricking her into leaving Greenways no longer seems easy. I don't feel good about tricking her into doing something that will be so wrong for her, and so right for me.

I need to confess.

"What are you doing here, Brad?" she repeats.

I try to buy more time, because telling the truth doesn't come easy. Lying does. I've lied about who I am. Who Emma is. I've lied about the reason I'm at Redhill.

I've even lied about my name. She will hate me when she finds out, and therein lies my dilemma: I want her to like me, but when she sees me for the devil I am, all hell will break loose. "Here specifically? In the storeroom?"

"Here at Redhill."

Pinpricks needle in my gut. She's onto me. "I told you," I say, putting on my smooth exterior. Hands in pockets, charming her with my smile. Except she doesn't smile back. She's not so easy to charm. "I feel the need to help and do my part."

She opens her mouth, but I put my finger to her lips, making the boldest move ever. "But you want to know why I'm here, in the storeroom with you? It's not because I give a damn about how many bottles of water you have. I followed you, because ever since I saw you that night, —which incidentally is why I didn't write the note—I can't stop thinking about you. I forgot about the note. It couldn't have been anything important, otherwise I would remember. But you, looking the way you did, you blew my brains, Lewis."

She tilts her head, bites her lower lip, making me want to press my lips to hers and kiss her.

I take a step closer. My heart is beating so hard and fast, she can probably hear it. "I wish I'd come to that event with you. You looked like a billion dollars." I lift my hand to her face, a gentle caress more like, and she doesn't flinch. She rolls her lips together, which only makes the air between us even more charged. I want her. I want to kiss every single part of her. I dip my head, almost making my next move. This is

Lewis, and I'm aware that if she doesn't want this, I'll be rewarded with a swift kick to my already enlarged balls.

She doesn't squirm or tell me to get lost; she wants this too. I drop a kiss to the side of her mouth, then brush my lips across her skin, scattering kisses around her mouth but expertly missing her lips. She moans softly, in disappointment, it sounds like. And then my lips press against hers. She is warm and sweet, and the first touch, the first taste, is everything I expected. Heat charges through my veins as we deepen our kissing. My fingers slide and she leans into me, her chest pressing against mine as her hands flank my shoulders.

And then the tempo changes. Urgency replaces calm, wet heat replaces sweetness. We're like two hungry people who have held back for far too long.

Sparks ignite. She moans against my mouth. Her sexy little sigh ignites all the feelings I've held in check, every image I've had of her at that event with Cardoza, except she's here with me. It's my hands around her slim waist. It's my lips on hers. When she looks up at me with hooded eyes, her lips moist, looking at me as if she wants me, I throw caution to the wind. We tongue fuck. This is rough, and carnal. Willfully wild abandonment. No restraint, no shyness. No more furtive glances.

We kiss as if this might be our first and last chance. Soon enough, she'll feel my excitement. My desire for her mushrooms, making it almost impossible for me to pull myself away.

We finally pull apart, come up for air. I press my forehead against her, feel her breath against mine. "Do you know how long I've been wanting to do that?" I ask.

"How long?" She puts me on the spot. How long has it been? There definitely wasn't any attraction when we first met. It built up over time. I could never see myself with someone like her, and knowing her as I do, she would never want to be with someone like me.

We are so ill-suited, so different, and yet we are the same. Did my heart open, because the wound has opened, turning me soft? Or has she changed me?

"How long?" she asks again, her eyes burning into mine. I trace my finger over her wet mouth. "Maybe from the first time I helped you with the homeless food night, when Fredrich was away."

She smiles. It's a soft, gentle, playful smile. Being this close to her, having tasted her lips, I see all too clearly how she and Jessica are so far apart. Jessica has done nothing but whine and bitch about Kyra. But Kyra hasn't even mentioned her once, which is a shame because I want to get her take on that night, on Jessica and see what she has to say about her.

I brush my lips against hers, wondering what it would be like to take this further.

"Your friend, how is she?" There's a questioning tone to her voice.

I shift back a little, trying to buy some more time. "Getting better slowly."

"She must be very special for you to miss out on the chance of meeting Eli." She suspects something.

"Did the others say something?" I ask her, because Fredrich didn't seem to believe me.

"No. We just assumed you were busy."

I put my hands firmly around her waist and marvel at her slender frame. I like my women with more flesh. Ample and voluptuous. I like the lusciousness of their bodies. Kyra is nothing like that, but what I feel for her goes beyond mere aesthetics. She is slight, and slim, and so neatly proportioned; it's not her body that caught my interest, it was her smartness and guts. "She's not my girlfriend. She's not." And then I say something that surprises even me. "You can come and see her at the hospital if you want."

She blinks.

The moment is weighted with anticipation. And then I'm left wondering why I made that insane suggestion. Kyra looks startled, even seconds later, as my request sinks in. "That's not necessary. I understand you're worried about her. She's lucky to have such a good friend as you."

I breathe out a sigh of relief. I hate to think what I would have done if Kyra had agreed. It would have been selfish and inconsiderate of me to put Emma through something like that.

Take, take, take. That's all I seem to do. Always in it for me.

She leans towards me and kisses me. It's soft, and sweet, and seductive, which, I realize, is exactly what Kyra is, now that I've come to know her better. I claim her mouth again, and we kiss, reveling in the taste and touch of one another.

"We should get back," she says.

"Why? You're doing an inventory check," I say, rubbing my lips against hers.

"The others," she hisses. I sense her guilt at being caught. My hand slides down over her buttock, and I squeeze gently. "Careful, Hartley. You'll have some explaining to do with that steel-hard boner of yours."

I lick her lower lip, and her tongue slides out and plays with mine. My insides are roiling. I wish we weren't at work. I have the desire to do things to her that will make her mewl in ecstasy. "I want to see you again,"

"I don't sleep with people I work with."

"Me neither." We exchange a flurry of tiny, playful kisses. Her hand slides down and squeezes my butt. I suppress a groan. I want her naked, stripped down so that I can worship every inch of her body.

I see it in her eyes. She wants what I want. I'm in this, and I can't back out. This doesn't have anything to do with the deal. Me wanting her is because I want her. I try not to think about how this will complicate things. Or what the consequences will be.

I can only live for now.

Her eyes widen, and she moves her head to the side when I move in for another kiss.

"Are you really not seeing anyone?" she asks.

Her words make me jolt. "No, I'm not." But then I remember what she told me about her last relationship and I understand her fear and hesitation. "I wouldn't be standing here with a boner, kissing you like this if I was."

It seems to reassure her, because when I move in for another long, take-me-to-bed-and-fuck-me kiss, she mewls and grinds against me. We need a bed, not this goddamn storeroom.

"You should go," she tells me, her hot breath on my face making me want to do nothing but stay. I could kiss her for hours. Our foreheads are touching, her hands around my waist make me pull her closer. I need to be in bed with her, or somewhere private where we can't be interrupted. I need to find that tattoo she teasingly dropped a hint to.

"I want to see you, Kyra. Outside of the storeroom."

She pushes me away playfully. "You will see me. In the office." Her gaze drops to my middle. She coughs lightly. "You're going to need to take care of that."

CHAPTER THIRTY-ONE

KYRA

I put a hand against the wall and take a deep breath, trying to still my heart when he leaves the storeroom.

I kissed Brad.

Or rather, he kissed me.

There have been many days when I've imagined what it would be like; days when I have fought against my fantasies, thinking that me and Brad could never be together. And yet the reality is even better than I dreamt it would be.

I don't go back to the office right away, because the shame of making out is written all over me. I won't be able to keep a straight face once I'm at my desk. I'm no good at hiding things or lying.

Instead, chicken that I am, I walk around the factory floor, checking in on the employees.

I feel like an oversexed schoolgirl. Fluttery heart, shaky knees. It takes a heroic effort for me to focus on my work when I finally make it back to my desk almost an hour later.

During the next few weeks, Brad and I leave the room within moments of one another. It's not always to make out. We make a hot drink, or go to the water cooler, or walk around the factory floor together.

Small, simple things. A reason to be close to one another. I don't want to get caught and be seen by the employees, and I would die if Simona or Fredrich ever caught us kissing.

I don't know what will happen next. How this will work out. He hasn't said anything about meeting outside work, but it's clear we can't continue like this, sneaking around like schoolkids.

On food nights we have more time. It's a long evening, and at the end of it, when he and I return to the storeroom to put the supplies back, we wait until the others leave, and when they do, we make out again. Our pent-up frustration heats up the walls. It becomes more than kissing. In the dimly lit room, in the cold, against the walls and cupboards, we find warmth as we kiss and touch, mouths and bodies pressed together.

He hasn't mentioned anything about us going back to his place, and I'm careful and tread slowly, unsure about suggesting that he comes back to my place. It has all been slow and sneaky, our being together, as if an air of illicitness taints us.

"We shouldn't be doing this in here, Brad." My boss alter ego tries to rationalize, as I lift my face towards him but he responds by giving me a long, hard kiss—the type of kiss which leaves me undone and begging for more.

"I know," he whispers, as my head rolls back against the wall. I'm soft and boneless, needing to catch a breath. He won't stop. He's as desperate as me, but he feasts on me, now that we are alone, hitching up my t-shirt and sucking hungrily at my breasts through the fabric of my bra.

"We need privacy. A bed would be nice." My voice is raspy with need. Why doesn't he ever suggest it? He never talks about going to his place and even though my brain is fogged by lust, his refusal to bring it up makes me hesitate offering him an invitation to my place.

When we are apart, I need him and can't stop thinking about him, but I also have the presence of mind to view this situation with some level of objectivity. What am I doing? A twenty-eight-year-old woman behaving like this? This is what I did when I was a teen. This isn't the behavior of a grown woman, or a grown man. And the doubts creep in again and I wonder why my brain cells vanish whenever he's around.

And then I see him again, the next day or the day after. His days are all changed up ever since his friend had her accident, and he doesn't come in on fixed days. It leaves me hanging because I don't know when I'll see him next. It's torture. And then I wonder what he does on the days he isn't here.

What is he doing?

And still, who is Emma to him?

His explanations don't convince me.

But then I see him again, or get another text or email from him, all of these thoughts get pushed to the back.

In no time at all, I don't recognize the woman I have become. Like now, up against the wall in the storeroom, trying to catch my breath from the kiss he's just given me.

Simona would be shocked.

Fredrich would look at me as if he didn't recognize me.

Tonight, Brad goes a step further. He unzips my jeans and snakes his fingers into my panties. We stare at one another through the haze of our desire. I moan as his finger slips inside me, and I suck in a breath, forcing myself to face reality, confronting the gritty cold, hard facts—we're in the storeroom, he has me pressed against the wall, and his fingers are doing the most delicious things to my clit. I can't move my legs. My jeans bind me like handcuffs around my ankles. I am his for the taking.

His lips half-kiss, half-talk against my mouth. "We can get a room, but don't you like the risk and the sleaziness of it?"

His wet lips, his scent, his warm breath are like an aphrodisiac. I can only comply and, like a drug addict, want more of him without contemplating the consequences. "This isn't me, doing things like this in secret."

"But you're enjoying it, no?" He slips in another finger, making my breath hiss out. Before he had stroked only the wet fabric, and now his fingers slide down, slipping in between my private places. I jerk at his electric touch, my hands tugging his hair as his fingers pleasure me. He hooks his finger in deeper, and I come apart, biting my lip in an effort not to cry out.

If he can bring me this much pleasure with his fingers, I can only wonder what he can do with the rest of him. He won't let me unzip him, or stroke him, or pleasure him. He seems to take the utmost pleasure in making me come like this.

"Why don't we get a room? Or you invite me back to your place?" There, I said it. He thumbs my clit in answer, and I collapse a little against the wall, my body sagging as he tries to support me.

"I will invite you back to my place," he says, smoothing the hair away from my face. "But before that, I want to take you out on a proper date." My heart is almost ready to explode with happiness.

CHAPTER THIRTY-TWO

BRANDON

"Where are we with this, Brandon?"

I wish I hadn't taken this call. Neville's been calling me a lot lately, busting my balls about Greenways. He doesn't have to spell it out. I know what he's referring to. "I'm still taking care of things."

"You've got a lot going on, with Emma in the hospital. You don't need to do this. Your time would be better served here. The company needs you, Brandon."

"I'm doing my best."

"You don't need to continue with this farce," he insists. "We're still working on the eminent domain. We can still seize the land through other means."

I grit my teeth. "I told you to hold off."

"You were all pumped up at the start. What's the holdup?"

"There is no holdup."

"Doesn't seem to me that you've made any progress," Neville growls back.

Things have become complicated. It's no longer just a black and white matter. Not now when feelings are involved. Try as I do, I can't let them go. Kyra has a hold on me that is hard to shake. "Give me time. Didn't you say that if you have to use eminent domain to take the land then you'd have to explain what the new project is?"

"Well, yes."

"Wouldn't that expose me? Wouldn't I have to take part in the public hearings? Why the fuck would I want that? I want to avoid there being a big public hearing so that Kyra doesn't figure out who I am."

A grunt of displeasure comes across the line. "Okay, we'll do it your way, but Stagg can only wait on us a little while longer."

"Like I told you, we might not need Stagg or any government intervention. No eminent domain bullshit. That's purely a backup. I've got this, Neville. I'm working on her." He doesn't need to hear the truth, I just want him off the phone, and off my back.

"Did you find anything on her?" he asks.

"What?"

"Dirt? Did you find any?"

I coach myself not to curse. "No."

"I know her accountant. I can fix her books. Embezzlement from a nonprofit is a major felony offense."

"You stay the hell away from her."

I hang up.

CHAPTER THIRTY-THREE

BRANDON

"We can't do this," Kyra says a few days later, on the weekend. I volunteered to help her get the supplies. I've replaced Fredrich in that sense, and whether he or Simona suspect anything between us, I can't tell.

We've finished returning everything to the storeroom and I'm sitting in her car with mine parked next to hers. I don't want to leave her. I want to spend the day with her. I want all night.

If anything, Fredrich seems to be relieved that I've stepped in to do some extra work.

And W-O-R-K it is.

A lot of it is physical, lifting and carrying. We give away huge amounts of food on these nights and the supplies need to be constantly replenished. That Kyra has been doing this by herself, and during her free time, leaves me in even more awe than ever before.

"Is this how every evening's going to end?" she asks, when

we have put all the food away and cleaned up the storeroom to her OCD standards. I have her pressed up against the wall. "This isn't me, sneaking around like a teen."

It's not me either.

This isn't the first time she's mentioned it. I press my forehead against hers. She's right. I don't do stuff like this.

Between the cold ice maiden that is Jessica, and Kyra, the unexpected temptress, it's a wonder I can keep it together.

No sex in months has left me a starving, desperate wreck.

"We should get out of here," I murmur against her lips. She's sitting straddling me. This is taboo, and that's why I'm addicted to her. That's what I tell myself when I can't reason or explain my actions.

I like being with her. I cherish our moments alone. I want more of her, and I am torn, because the man I was when she first met me is not the man I am now.

We have been meeting in secret, mostly in the storeroom, for the past few weeks. Like delinquents, making out, and stealing kisses when we can.

This can't go on for much longer. I am the CEO of many companies, I own homes all over the world and have business interests in more industries than I can count. Snatching moments like this in a storeroom, or in the car, are beneath me.

But being with Kyra has the effect of changing my DNA. If I'm not careful, I'm in danger of losing who I am.

You don't care, a tiny voice inside me whispers.

We can't spend our lives making out in places and snatching any sliver of opportunity we get. I have wined and dined women on my private jet, in homes all over the world.

If I showed her who I am, she wouldn't want to be with me. But she deserves better than to be creeping around, hiding from colleagues and snatching stolen moments of time. I want to be with her without worrying about getting caught.

I can't invite her to my place without it ruining my cover. I am biding my time, waiting for the right time, because when it comes, when I tell her, she will hate me. Each moment I'm with her, I forget, and when we're apart, I worry and know I should stop.

"I've been thinking about what you said," she says, her hand in mine, our fingers entwining. I bring her hand to my lips and kiss her fingers. "About relocating somewhere else."

The muscle in my jaw flexes. "Move? To where?" I rest our entwined hands on my lap. A niggling, uneasy feeling is worming its way through my intestines. After what her ex did to her, I'm no better.

Maybe this is the moment when I come clean.

"Someplace else. Somewhere that has everything we need."

I drop another kiss on her hand and it elicits a tiny laugh from her. It's sweet and flowery, pure and clean, a far cry from Jessica's cackle.

"Yeah?" At times like this I forget the reason why I am here. This is going to get complicated. I will end up hurting her, and that's not something I want to do willingly anymore.

"I worry about the building. I can't afford to get the roof fixed, but I also can't afford for anyone to get hurt or killed."

"But you love this area, and your building isn't falling apart."

"Maybe relocating would be better. Maybe that chunk of plaster falling was a sign."

An uncomfortable laugh leaves my lips. "A sign? What is this? Looking to the universe for answers?"

"Meeting you, that's a sign." Her eyes shimmer with happiness. "I hated you on first sight."

"Don't I know it."

Her car isn't the roomiest of places, but she fits snugly against me. My hands instinctively lift to her waist, then under her t-shirt and against her bare skin. This is a new move for us and it excites me. Any moment now, she's going to feel my erection against her.

We smile at one another, and suddenly I don't want her sitting on my lap, I want to be naked in bed, inside her. The thought makes me harden. As if she can read my mind, she leans forward and kisses me, her tongue sliding between the seam of my lips, teasing and seducing and torturing me. My hand slips up and cups her breast. I slide it under her bra, feel her nipple pebble against my thumb, standing up like a rosebud.

Her kiss deepens, her moan signaling her appreciation.

When she pulls away, her eyes are dark and shiny, her lips moist. I tweak her nipples, my hands greedy and possessive under her strained clothing.

She looks around, then moves her hand on top of mine, halting it. "People can see."

"You're helping me to see the business in another way, Brad. Moving to bigger premises means I won't have to build another factory."

I should be ecstatic because this is what I wanted. My mission will be accomplished. She's considering my advice and all I have to do is make sure she follows through. If Kyra moves, then so will most of the others. The rest, the ones who stubbornly refuse to move, I'll get rid of by condemning the land. It was only Kyra Lewis I needed to convince, and now, it seems, I have.

And yet, it doesn't feel like a victory. I don't feel like a winner.

I let out a shaky exhale. My hard-on is making it hard for

me to think, and with this woman looking at me as if I'm the best thing to happen to her and her business, I suddenly feel unsure. "Are you sure you want to do this?"

"You're the one who suggested it."

"I know, but, you need to really think it through, Kyra."

"I have been. It makes sense. Everything started to make sense once I saw things from another angle, and it's all thanks to you." She kisses me on the nose, dismissing my serious words easily.

I blink at her, not knowing what to say. "You even came at the right time, when Fredrich injured his arm. It was perfect timing. I needed you and you showed up." She laughs in pure ignorance. Heat burns across my lying face.

"You weren't so happy to have me around," I remind her. "Simona made me feel welcome."

"Simona thought you were eye candy."

I raise an eyebrow. "Eye candy?"

"For me," she clarified.

"I feel objectified."

"She thought it would be good for ..." She clears her throat, looks away. "After my ex and all that drama ... I kept you at a distance."

I understand it now. I cup the side of her face and attempt to make her laugh. "Afraid you might have fallen for my charms, otherwise?"

"Taking care of my invisible bruises. When someone cheats on you, it's almost impossible to be able to trust again." I press my lips gently against hers, to silence those fears and thoughts. To create new ones for her. But even as our lips touch and I inhale her scent, soak in her familiarity which is now almost like my second skin, a warning bell goes off in my head.

I am sliding across thin ice. I might not be cheating on her the way her ex did, but my initial intentions were just as bad.

"Anyway, I was thinking, why don't we go looking at some places I could move to? You said you had some ideas." She pulls me out of my thoughts and stares at me as if I can solve all her problems.

She's just solved mine, but it doesn't feel like a victory. "I ... uh... sure."

"I've got nothing better to do now." She shrugs. "How about we go now?" She must have seen my expression because she hurriedly says, "Unless you've got plans."

I can hear it in her voice. The hint of nervousness. The doubt. The suspicion. There is a lot about me that must give rise to questions that are unanswered. She never pushes me, but I can tell that she needs more answers than I am able to give her.

I've done enough damage, and even though she doesn't know about it, she soon will. I'll break her. At the very least, I'll ruin her trust in me.

"I have a better plan," I offer.

"I'm listening."

I've been hiding her. I've been hiding what we have, what I feel, and all because everything about me, about us, is based on lies. "Why don't we get some lunch?"

"Lunch?" Her eyes light up, as if I've announced that I'm taking her on a luxury vacation. How easily some people are pleased. A flash of happiness crosses her face; something new, something I like to see, especially when she's looking at me. My heart floats in my ribcage, in a way that is alien to me. "You want to?"

Her words break me. They imply so many things that must be weighing on her mind. I decide in that moment that when we go to lunch, I will tell her everything.

Since we're in her car, she offers to drive, and we go to lunch, finding a little restaurant tucked a few streets away from Grant Park.

Our conversation is easy and flows naturally. We seem to have come full circle from who we were back on the first day I met her. I've come to admire her because she has balls, a hard work ethic, and truckloads of compassion. Hard not to have that compassion given the kind of people we see on a weekly basis. It has softened even a hardened cynic like me. I once couldn't bring myself to even look at these people, let alone make time for them, but my newfound understanding arises from seeing their lives magnified under the lens of the food nights; of seeing them up close, recognizing their pain and suffering and doing what we can to ease it in some way.

Kane's ghost haunts me. I try not to think about it. I've tried to push it away and as always, the story I've told myself from the beginning is that he is better off without me.

I watch in amusement as Kyra takes a huge bite of her chicken burger then looks at me as if she wants to say something. For a small woman, she has the biggest appetite I've seen. Not once have I heard her groan at the menu in dismay or count calories. She hasn't ordered salad. She happily chomps away at her fries, dipping them into the hot, fiery dip, oblivious of my scrutiny.

Mentally, I compare her to Jessica. It's impossible not to. Why I now find everything about Kyra endearing confuses me. I have a checklist of things for a suitable wife and she doesn't tick any of those boxes.

Jessica can take an entire evening working her way through a plate of salad. Kyra eats with gusto. It's refreshing to see. She picks up an big fat fry and slowly bites her way through it, then licks her fingers, looking extremely sated.

This is something else I've never seen Jessica do. She doesn't lick her fingers, but she digs her claws in when she sees fit.

"What?" she says, when she sees me observing her.

"Nothing. I just like watching you eat."

Her expression changes from embarrassed to sombre and I can tell that something is playing on her mind. "Are you ever going to tell me what you do on your days off?"

And there it is. What she wants to know. Do I tell her that I spend those days at Hawks Enterprises? That I am the CEO, not just of that company, but of many others.

That I am not the man she thinks I am.

"There he goes again, keeping quiet," she says, loud enough for me to hear. "Is it something illegal?" She lowers her voice and surreptitiously looks around.

I sit forward, moving my face closer towards her, conspiratorial-like. "Illegal?" If only she knew how close she was to the truth. I have corrupt people in my pocket. People who will lie and bend the truth and the law for me so that I can gain. It's what my father has done, and taught me to do.

I am Brandon Hawks. I will always be Brandon Hawks. The other boy never existed. "What type of illegal activity do you think a man like me would get involved in?"

She drinks through her straw again, and my eyes are riveted to the pout of her lips.

"I don't mean *illegal*," she says, naive, good, caring Kyra. She could never envision the depths of my deception. "But ... are you a male stripper or an escort on the side?"

Her question makes me roar. "You think I could be in that industry? With this body?"

She sits back, breaking the bubble of our tiny, sexy spell. "You're just fishing for compliments."

"Oh?" I like this. "You think I could? Are you saying I would make a good stripper?"

"Stop fishing, Hartley. You're not skinny or obese." She leans in, further than before, making it impossible for me to look anywhere else but into her eyes. I find myself tumbling into them faster than I can pull back. This won't end well. I'm in too deep. I can stop the speed with which we're hurtling head first into the abyss. I can stop it now by telling her.

I should tell her.

I should tell her *now*.

But the urge to suck her lower lip, to kiss her long, and slow, and hard, and dirty, that thought consumes me. Blood rushes south between my legs. Reason vaults out of the window.

And just like that, Kyra Lewis, a woman who ordinarily, in another lifetime, would never had even registered on my radar, gives me the start of another boner that threatens to build and go unsated.

"Can I get you some more drinks?" An annoying server interrupts at the most inopportune time.

"Could I have another refill of this, please?" Kyra hands the server her glass. I nod my head. The server disappears, having ruined the moment. Kyra sits back, resting her hands on her lap. She smiles at me, and I wish she wouldn't. The ground shifts beneath me because my whole reason for being here, the goal I set out to achieve, crumbles a little every day before me. "Are you never going to tell me?" she asks, even though she manages a smile, it's not one that lights up her eyes. It hurts her, not knowing what I'm up to, and yet whatever she might think I do, it's never going to be anywhere near the truth.

"My days off ..." I drum my fingers on the table, trying to buy more time. She sits forward eagerly, as if she's hanging on my every word. The server returns with her drink. Kyra's slipped her sweatshirt off, and my eyes fall to the little sun tattoo on her shoulder.

Arousal shoots to my crotch, confusion mingling with desire, making unlikely bedfellows. Kyra is not my type, I remind myself. But this isn't even true anymore. With every passing day, with every kiss, every touch, every moment spent with her has proven this wrong. She's everything I want.

"Your tattoos ..." I press my lips together without thinking. Breathe slowly as I remember the compass between her shoulder blades. "Will I ever get to see the third one?"

"The rosebud?"

"The rosebud."

"Do you want to see it?"

Is the sky blue? I inhale a deep breath. A server walks past, hovers then asks if everything is okay. It's a welcome interruption, because I can't answer Kyra's question yet. Not in words, but the answer is probably written all over my face, because she bites her lip, and I catch her smiling as I tell the server that everything is just perfect.

She said it was lower down. My mind naturally comes up with images that scorch and torture me. How do I answer her? Crude, vulgar words come to mind. But I want to make love to this woman. She means something to me, and that is something I never considered going into this entire sorry mess.

CHAPTER THIRTY-FOUR

KYRA

"I'll drop you back to the factory so you can get your car."

He smiles as he gets in the car. A start-up, that's what he revealed to me over lunch. He opened up and told me that he and a few friends are heavily into online gaming and they're creating a new game. At last I now know what he does on his days off.

And I already know that he's single.

We're good.

He didn't answer my question about the tattoo, but I could tell by his expression, by how things are between us, that he wants to be with me. But still I tread carefully, having been hurt so much before. Though Brad is a good stepping stone. A chapter of fun. It makes sense for me to see his part in my life as an installment, because I've learned my lesson, to take it one day at a time. To not plan ahead.

I gave my all to my ex, and he broke me. Just as I'm about to start up the engine, he leans forward. "Thank you."

"For what?"

"For lunch."

And before I can ask him why he wants to thank me, he takes my hand and kisses it. That's all it takes for our bodies to twist towards one another. Soon our mouths are meshed together and we're a tangle of kisses. It is a luxury to be alone with him like this, away from work and out of the storeroom, in our own private space, even if it is in my tiny car, again. His lips press against mine and an electric charge zings through my body.

The windows steam up. It's not comfortable making out with the handbrake in the middle, and our bodies twisted awkwardly.

As much as it thrills me to be around him, in the moments when I come up for air, a sliver of commonsense cracks through my skull. What am I doing? But when he plants another kiss on my lips, it's gone, that niggling feeling about why he never asks me to go to his place. Goosebumps trail along my arms and settle in my stomach. My pulse races.

"I should go," he says against my lips.

"I should drive you back," I reply against his. This long, drawn-out phase of kissing and heavy petting without the grand prize is intoxicating. He is all I think about now, he is all I will think about long after he has left me.

His breath is warm and sweet, and I fall, heart first, into another long, soft, sloppy kiss. I ache for his touch, but his hand is on my arm, and as our tongues tangle and duel, the throbbing between my legs deepens. I sigh against his lips. Desire rolls over me. His eyes are lidded, his lips wet, and when we kiss again, it's not a gentle peck, but a longer prelude to wanting more.

"This is getting uncomfortable," I murmur, my lips brushing over him.

He stops, moves his head back, examines my face carefully, as if he might forget me.

"Why are you looking at me like that?" I ask, tracing my finger over his moist lower lip.

"What do you want, Kyra?"

I want for him to want me, the way I want him. I want for him to suggest that we go back to his place. "You."

To my disappointment, this doesn't seem to bolster his spirits. "Don't you want me?" I ask, because he's slow to reply.

"I don't want to mess things up for you. You being the boss and all." These aren't the words I was expecting. He raises his hand to my face again, strokes my cheek, and then my lips.

"We could go back to my place," I suggest. My clammy legs, my beating heart, my desire for this man are all getting to be too much.

"We should take this slow." That's another reply I wasn't expecting. We have been taking it slow. But then he leans towards me and we fall into another long, sensual kiss that makes my toes curl. His actions don't mirror his words, and slow isn't what I have on my mind.

I untangle myself from him, needing to know. "What do *you* want, Brad?" He's answered my previous questions and I should be satisfied.

"I want to kiss you like this all over."

His words paint a picture that my body can't ignore. "Impossible in here," I say, sounding grumpier than I intended to.

"How about we head back to your place?"

A bolt of disappointment shoots through my heated skin. I'm not imagining this, his reluctance to invite me over. Something isn't right, but ... I want him. I start up the car and drive to my place.

Less than fifteen minutes later, we're at my door and I'm fumbling for my door keys. I open the door to my tiny apartment and no sooner has the door shut than he pushes me against it and presses his mouth against mine. With his body tight against mine. The hardness of his erection presses into me, a sharp promise of things to come.

Something feral seems to have unleashed in us now that we're not in the storeroom at work, or in the car with its display-all windows. His mouth devours me. He rains hot, hard kisses against my jaw, sliding down to my neck, before lifting up my t-shirt and trailing his lips over my breasts and then lower down my stomach.

I shiver. His touch is electric. His lips brush over my skin, and my nerve endings sizzle wherever he touches.

A delicious shiver rolls over me because I know where this is heading. This is the longest time we've spent together. Lust pools and spreads between my legs. I bend down, lifting his head up, desperate for his kiss again. We groan against each other's lips, hands feeling, stroking, kneading. He stands up slowly, his tongue sweeping into my mouth, claiming me, making me forget to breathe. I take his hand and lead him to my bedroom where we fall onto the bed. At first it's him on top of me, before I win and get on top of him.

It's heat and sizzle, playful domination, lips pressed together. When he's on top again, he pulls off his t-shirt. My mouth hangs open because he has a physique that he hides well. I reach out, touching the corded outlines of his muscles. My breath stills as I gawk at him in awe filled with need and longing in one sweaty, desperate aphrodisiac. Before I can trail my hand along his six-pack, he switches us, masterfully turning the tables so that I'm on top, straddling him.

"Your turn," he says, his eyes looking darker than I remember them. Everything I am vanishes in a fog of sexual need as he sits up and peels off my t-shirt before burying his face in my breasts. I can't help but giggle because his lips tickle and tease but just as I'm about to arch my back, he rolls me off him, jumps up off the bed and strips off my jeans. My insides quiver as his roving eyes slowly take in every inch of my body. He strips off too, and we grin at one another before tumbling back onto the bed. We melt into another kiss, hands tugging each other's undergarments off. It's a tricky, logistical, balancing act, with lips and tongues meshed, as we try to undress one another through the haze of our sexual urgency.

He grunts, then falls to his knees, completely naked, his face level with my lower stomach. And then his fingers skate over to my hipbone.

"Found it." He glances up at me, and I jolt as he kisses the rosebud tattoo just above my hip bone. He licks it teasingly, then sucks the skin, giving me a hickey to the side of it. Just as the shock of us both naked and my realization that he is almost level with my most intimate parts sinks in, his fingers slide between my folds, teasing, electrifying, each stroke amplifying the riot of emotions which threaten to send me over the edge.

When his tongue slides in, I babble incoherently as waves of euphoria splash over me, drowning me in a whirlpool of pleasure. Biting back a moan, the breath hitches in my throat as he undoes me from the inside out.

He doesn't let up, the expert that he is, worshipping me in a way I haven't been touched for so long.

And, damn. He's good.

I moan, and curse, and say his name, rocking against him, spinning out of control. Time slows to a stop, my heart pounds, and I ride the crescendo. I'm going to come crashing down any moment, but I want him inside. I jolt back, managing to pull myself away, then fall onto the bed. Before I have a second to catch my breath, he joins me, and then, in another fast and unexpected move, I'm on top of him again, straddling him as his steel-hard cock stabs me.

I grasp my fingers around him. I am soaked and all I want is to slide onto him. We eye one another, eyes hooded, intoxicated by the lust that has been pooling between us for so long.

I bite my lower lip, the anticipation, the need for him to slide inside me and fill me to the hilt, becoming almost unbearable.

His eyes narrow and he hangs his head. "I don't have a condom."

My insides still. Every cell freezes in shock. I stopped taking the pill, and now I'm in danger of letting lust blind me, of letting myself go further than I should. He lifts up on his elbows. I shuffle back a little, watch his throbbing manhood tempt me. I almost salivate at the sight of it.

"Hey," he sits up and touches my arm. My attention is on his hard-on and the possibility that nothing further might happen. My brain is still warring with my desire.

"We can't do this," he says, rolling me onto the bed so that I'm lying beside him, his exposed hardness teasing me.

"I don't have any birth control either," I state flatly.

His lips caress my neck. With my panties off and wearing only my bra, my body is primed for all of him. His mouth dips lower, his lips on the front-fastening clasp of my bra. "Don't worry," he says, sliding lower and lower, leaving a trail of wet kisses along my stomach before his tongue skims my bikini line. I arch my back in anticipation. "I'll still make you come."

I clamp my legs together. It's not his tongue I want there right now. That won't satisfy the big aching gap between my legs. I reach down, sliding my fingers around him. "There's a drugstore around the block."

He sits up. "A drugstore?" The meaning slowly dawns on him. I'm lying on the bed, desperate for him. The way his erection juts out tell me he feels the same. I chew my lip.

"You want me to go?" he asks.

"Don't you want to?"

His eyes take in all of me, his heated gaze searing every inch of my skin, before settling on the apex between my legs. I close them tightly.

He nods, once. "Yes."

"Then hurry."

He jumps up and throws on his clothes. In the blink of an eye, he's by the door. "I'll be back."

"Be quick."

The door slams, and I fall back onto the bed, wet, hot and frustrated.

CHAPTER THIRTY-FIVE

BRANDON

F uck.

I'm a jangled-up mess. My dick wants one thing, but my head is telling me something else.

And my heart. I can't look at Kyra and not feel something. That's why we're in this hot, sticky mess. I want her. But everything we have, everything she thinks I am, is a lie. An intricate web of deception. I couldn't even bring myself to tell her the truth about what I do on my days off. I could have started there. I should have started there. I should have told her who I am, what I do and why I walked into Redhill.

Only now I'm in her bed, and all I want to do is fuck her. But it is wrong. Wrong, wrong, wrong, and this makes it difficult. It holds me back, because I can do this and not care. I *have* done this and not cared. Not this—I've never become romantically involved in order to secure a deal. Never. This is a first. But I have run roughshod over people.

With Kyra, this is something else. I have come to care for

her more than I thought was possible for someone like me. But everything about me is a lie. That I've always been Brandon Hawks. That I was born on the day I was adopted by the billionaire Philip Hawks.

That Brandon Clements, the unwanted boy, doesn't exist.

Kyra would like the real me, the boy I used to be. After all, she saves children like this. But telling her the truth over all the lies will be impossible. She will never give me a chance.

I slow down my steps and wonder what the hell I'm doing. This is wrong on so many levels, and yet I can't help the way I feel about this woman.

I will hurt her so badly.

Each lie is built on another lie which is built on another lie.

But she's waiting and my dick will explode unless I bury myself inside her right now. I buy the condoms and rush back. My cell phone rings just as I reach her place and I rush to answer it, my breath ragged from me almost running, but also because my hard-on isn't helping.

"Brandon?"

It's a voice I don't recognize.

"Who's this?"

"It's Emma's father."

The blood in my veins freezes. "What's wrong? Is she okay?" I'm prepared for the worst, because he wouldn't call me unless it was the worst.

"She's better. She's much better." I hear the laugh in his voice. "She asked for you."

"She did?"

"Could you come by? It's not urgent or –"

"I'll be there." Emma asked for me. She wouldn't ask for me unless it was something urgent. I have to go.

I knock on Kyra's door, my hopes deflate, just like my steel hardness. The surge of adrenaline whooshes clean out of my body. She opens the door wearing nothing but a bedsheet, and her smile slips when she sees my face. She can read me in an instant, and I can't hide anything from her.

She steps back as I walk in, closing the door behind me. We stare at each other. "You've changed your mind?" she asks, her head cocked because this sudden turn doesn't make sense.

"Emma's dad called me."

"Is everything okay?"

I nod. "I think so, but I'm not sure. At first I thought it must be bad news if he's calling me."

"You should go."

"I don't want to leave like this. I need to exp—"

"No, you don't. You just need to go, Brad."

Knowing Kyra, I completely get how she must feel. I'm giving up sex with her to go visit a friend. I see her mind going through mental hoops and jumps because something about me—everything about me—isn't adding up. She should tell me to get the hell lost. She should yell and scream at me that she never wants to see me again. But she blinks and listens patiently, drawing the sheet around her really tightly.

"Let me explain." I move towards her, but she moves back. It's guilt which makes me run to Emma. Feeling personally responsible for her accident, I have no choice but to go to her if she asked for me.

"Emma's waiting, Brad. You should go."

Maybe this is a sign, one of those signs that Kyra was talking about. I'm on the verge of making a huge mistake, and leaving here is the best thing to do.

CHAPTER THIRTY-SIX

KYRA

Lies. He is lying to me. That's all I can think of as I quickly get dressed. His scent hangs in the air long after he's gone, and I fall back onto the rumpled bed, breathing it all in.

I am a naïve fool. Too trusting and wanting to believe the good in everyone. But the thoughts I had about Brad from the start now come back and haunt me because what he says and what he does don't align.

He never suggests that we go back to his place. It's odd that a grown man chooses to make out in a storeroom or inside a car. We only ended up in my bed because I initiated the move.

Emma is more than a friend he is concerned about. He told me she was getting better. How is it that she holds so much sway over him unless she is someone important to him? Like a lover.

What is he hiding? A wife? A girlfriend? I should have

learned my lesson from my ex. My damaged heart can't go through this again. This man is a walking mystery. All I know is his name, and not much else.

He has called and texted, probably while he's in the waiting room waiting to see his darling Emma, but I've declined his calls and I've read the texts which don't say much except that he will explain.

I've given him plenty of opportunities to explain. I need to trust my initial gut instinct which warned me not to trust this man.

BRANDON

I messed up, again. She hates me, and she has every reason to hate me.

This is nothing less than I deserve. Kyra will know something isn't quite right. I've been forced to show my hand, and I will. I'll put things right. Kyra and I, we can still be together. She'll hate me at first, but hopefully, over time, she'll learn to hate me less.

I reach the hospital in no time, and as I walk into Emma's hospital room, she's not lying in bed, but walking around on crutches.

The sight of her, still bruised and injured, stops me, but there is hope. She is moving. She's up and about.

She stops and looks up at me, her lips spreading into a slow, careful smile. It instantly erases my worries. Her parents acknowledge me, her dad thanks me for coming.

"Hey, stranger." I walk over and kiss her gently on the cheek. "So good to see you again. Are you in pain?"

"I'm always in pain." She winces as she slowly makes her way over to the armchair. I help her to sit, hovering around, ready to take her crutches or aid her in any way, but I seem to be getting more in her way than not.

"Can I get you something?" I'm ready to go get her whatever she needs, food, drink, a nurse, painkillers. Watching someone who used to be such a powerhouse, now reduced to a tenth of the person she used to be, breaks my heart.

"I'll be okay once I sit down and take a breath."

"I'm ... I'm ... sorry." The words strangle my throat. I've been keeping it all inside, my part in this awful accident and the blame I carry.

"Sorry for what?" She eases back into her seat.

I did this to her. "It's my fault ... the accident. You being in that car."

"How is it your fault?" Her defiance eases my anguish.

"Because you were only there to fetch something for me from the office—"

Her face turns white. "I don't remember. I don't remember going there. I don't remember if I went to the office —" She's getting agitated at not being able to recall it. I take her hand and press it gently between mine.

"Don't. Don't force it."

"Was it something important? It must have been if you asked me to—"

"Hey, Emma. It's not important." Nothing is important anymore. What is all this wheeling and dealing for, when people's lives can change in the flash of a moment?

She opens her mouth, but I shake my head.

"Don't." I attempt a smile, which is difficult, because now that she is sitting up, I can see she has lost so much weight. This woman who was once dressed in sharp suits and high heels, who ran my life for me, organized my days, questioned my motives and plans, told me off without holding back, admonishing me when I was doing something that wasn't right, this woman is now a ghostlike wraith.

"You wanted to see me." I suddenly remember there was a reason for me being here. I'm prepared to pay anything, give her anything she needs, to ease herself back to normal. I need her. And now, more than ever, with my life beginning to fall apart, it seems I really could do with a spoonful of her no-nonsense medicine.

"It wasn't too important. I didn't need for you to rush over to me."

"Hey." My eyes are soft as I look at her. "It's not a problem. I wasn't doing anything. I just want to see how you are."

"I can't come back."

"Can't come back?" I echo, my heart sinking because I think I know what's coming.

"To work for you."

My shoulders sag. "Not now, of course not, but in time you'll be fine. There's no rush. You can come back whenever you feel ready to."

"I can't, Brandon. I don't want to."

I stare back in disbelief. How can this be a life-defining moment for her? "Is it money?" I pay her handsomely, way above the market rate, because what she does for me is priceless. "You're due a raise and a bonus." I flash her a hopeful smile, and I'm stupid enough to think that this might get her to change her mind.

"It's not the money. I've been thinking a lot about things while I've been here, and I don't want to come back. The corporate world isn't for me anymore."

"Travel? Is that what you want to do? Because I'll hold your place for you. Maybe you just need some time off." She sinks further into the seat, rings of tiredness frame her eyes. "Don't say anything," I tell her. "Don't make a decision yet." She'll change her mind. She'll get out of here and be a hundred percent back to normal, and she'll want to come back.

"My doctor said he doesn't know how bad my partial amnesia will be. It might be long-term but it's difficult to predict right now."

"That's fine. That's okay," I say, gently. "We'll deal with that. We don't need to talk about it now. We can discuss it later." Anything she needs, I'll agree to.

"I wanted to tell you now, Brandon, so that you can start looking for someone to replace me."

"I can't replace you, Emma." My voice turns hoarse. "You're irreplaceable, don't you know that? I have a temporary PA and she is useless." I get up and pace the room, my insides tying into knots as I recall all the stupid mistakes of this week that the new temp has made. "She's not you."

Emma smiles. "Don't be so harsh on her. There is a lot to juggle in that role."

I want her to come back but I can't force her to do something she doesn't want. I can't continue to be that selfish bastard I have always been.

"What's going on over at Redhill?"

She wants to know about Kyra. Where do I start? My plan has changed, and I have fallen in love with the type of woman I would never even give a second glance to.

I place a hand at the back of my neck. "It's okay."

"Just okay?"

"Yeah."

"What are you not telling me, Brandon?"

"What do you mean?"

"You're not looking me in the eye."

I glance at her. This is why I need this woman to still be my PA. She knows, just by looking at me, and she hasn't even seen me in a while, but she can tell there is something.

This is why she cannot be replaced. I shrug, because it seems better not to open my mouth and say something that she can latch onto and derive the entire truth from. "I've got it under control," I say quietly.

"Got what under control?"

I can't lift my face and look at her, because she will know.

"Brandon?"

"I'm going to tell her."

"Oh, Brandon. Did you do something to hurt that poor girl?"

I lift my head. It's written all over my face, and the cloud of disappointment on Emma's face is reflected back at me. "Tell me you didn't ...tell me you didn't try to seduce her."

I shake my head. Technically, we didn't.

I'm not a playboy. I don't seduce women, but she knows of my orchestrated plan to woo Jessica, and it's not such a gigantic leap of the imagination to think I'd do something underhanded with Kyra. After all, I'm the man who gets anything he wants. I stare at her, wondering how she knows that anything passed between us. "How do you know?"

"There's something different about you. Something softer. You're not talking about business or making money."

"That's because I'm here to see how you are."

She gives me a knowing look.

"She thinks you and I ..." I move my hand between us. "She thinks you're my girlfriend or something."

"Does she now?" Emma's eyes fill with amusement. "If you need to prove it to her, bring her here."

I laugh at the absurdity of her words. "No. It's nothing like that. We're barely ... nothing's ... happened." My voice trails off. I'm lying to myself and with such spectacular ease that it takes me a moment to recover from the shock of it.

"Speaking of girlfriends, how is Jessica?"

"Let's not talk about Jessica."

"Oh." Her forehead creases as if she's discovered a secret. "It's serious, then? You and Kyra Lewis?"

"No. There's nothing going on. You'd be the first to know if there was."

I stare at the floor, lying easily again, but also because I'm not sure where anything stands with Kyra. Nothing can happen within this soup of deceit in which my morals float.

I've become aware of how much a life can change in just one second. Moments shape us. It was a moment that shaped Emma's path forward, just as it has shaped mine.

CHAPTER THIRTY-SEVEN

KYRA

We barely talk when we're back at work. Brad isn't the type of guy to chase and beg, but I deserve the truth, and he can't give it to me.

I can't think or function, not in the full and complete way I used to before this man walked into my life. I hate the rollercoaster of who we are and what I have become.

Luckily, I have plenty to keep me busy, but our tiny office feels suffocating. I avoid going into the storeroom especially after the food nights.

I can't trust myself to be alone with him. We will be all hands and mouths. One thing will lead to another. I'm back to not trusting him again, back to being wary because there is a side to him which he keeps hidden.

Most times, I don't know what to think. This isn't me. Obsessing over a guy who isn't right for me. I should have learned my lesson from the last time.

Clearly I'm not cut out for romance and relationships. I'm

responsible for a lot of people. I have a business to run. I'm doing my best to make life better for these people, and that's what I need to focus on.

<hr>

BRANDON

I try to make it up to her but it's not easy.

It's hard enough sitting in a stuffy little office with Simona and Fredrich, but starting a conversation with her is almost impossible. What I want is to explain to Kyra about what happened, but she doesn't want to be alone with me. Why would she if she thinks I walked out on her to tend to someone she believes I care about more.

How can I tell her who Emma is without giving anything away? And yet, another part of me knows I have to tell her the truth, but I don't want to take the risk.

She has every right to be suspicious of me. She won't catch my eye and she won't return my texts.

I decide to stay behind and wait until the others have left for the day, but when it gets to that time, Fredrich and Simona stay put. I'm determined to wait it out, and I do. A short while later, Simona asks, "When are we leaving?"

Leaving for what? And why do I know nothing about this?

"In about ten minutes." Kyra types away, her fingers flying on her keyboard.

"I'd better rush to the washroom." Simona disappears.

"What's going on?" I ask. "Where's everyone going?"

"We've got a committee meeting tonight," Fredrich informs me.

"What for?"

"They're monthly meetings, unless something urgent comes up which all the Greenways people need to deal with."

"Yeah?" I act surprised. "Like what?"

"Take your pick. We've had all sorts of things to deal with over the years."

"I'm hoping it's a quick one tonight," says Kyra, stopping her typing. "I've got accounts to reconcile."

"I can help you with that," I offer, genuinely wanting to help her, but also needing to have time with just her.

"I don't need your help with the accounts." The tilt of her chin, with her hand on her hip, her entire posture is one of defiance. "But why don't you come to the meeting?"

"Why don't you, dude?" Fredrich chimes in.

"You can come and meet everyone." Kyra doesn't smile, but there is mischief in her eyes. I shift uneasily.

Does she know about me?

I can't go. I dare not show my face there. Neville is getting antsy about me not moving forward but I'm now facing a problem I thought I'd never have: Kyra is thinking about moving, only now I don't want her to.

She should stay, prosper here, and carry out her vision. I won't get in her way.

"I can't." I press my lips, trying to read her expression and figure out how much she hates me.

"Of course you can't." Her tone is mocking. "You couldn't attend Eli's city hall event, and you can't come to this. Who are you hiding from, Brad?"

I clench down on my teeth, wondering if she is testing me, wondering if she knows who I am and what I'm up to. "I have things to do."

"You always have things to do," Kyra throws back.

"I need to visit the men's room," Fredrich mutters before making a hasty exit.

"I can explain—" She's angry about me leaving her when we were about to get intimate. That's unforgiveable, and I should be grateful that she's at least talking to me, even if she's furious.

"Was Emma okay?" Her tone switches in an instant.

I nod. "She's fine."

"What was the urgency?"

How do I tell her that my PA doesn't want to come back to work for me? Answering that question means I'll have to answer all the others; questions that Kyra probably doesn't even have yet.

"She ... uh ..." I'm flummoxed as to what to say. Kyra's cold fury doesn't help.

"Where was it that you worked?" she asks, completely throwing me off course.

"Excuse me?"

"Where was it that you worked?"

Shit. Shit. Shit.

My brows lift. My heart splutters. "When?" I'm trying to buy myself some time.

She suspects.

"When you went abroad, to work on the community project. Where was that?"

I stare at her in complete confusion. Why is she asking me this? Before I can reply, she asks, "Or did you not work anywhere at all?" Her cold, hard words land on me like icepicks.

I manage to retrieve the information I think she wants. "Ecuador."

She smiles. "Ecuador. Is that your final answer? Or do you want to call someone to verify that?"

Simona steps inside just then, and Kyra stands up and starts to get her things together. Fredrich returns, eyeing the two of us as if we're rabid dogs.

"Are you coming to the meeting with us?" Simona asks me.

"He's busy and he has other plans," Kyra replies before I can say a word.

CHAPTER THIRTY-EIGHT

KYRA

We bundle inside a small civic hall. Loud indignant chatter fills the already heated atmosphere. The meeting is loud and noisy.

I'm sitting at the front with the a few elected committee members and the chairperson, a scrawny older woman with angular bones and reading glasses that keep slipping down her oily nose. I wasn't eager about doing this role, because I am already busy enough, but I was hounded into it, partly by Simona and then seconded by Fredrich, since so many of the business owners kept asking me to speak up for them on their behalf.

But since my passion is Redhill, and I became aware early on that there were attempts to get us to relocate, I agreed to be a voice for this group. It's still something I'm passionate about.

The chairwoman brings up the most recent complaint from the city about the food nights turning Greenways into a place which encourages homeless people. "They seem to be going for you," she says, passing me a letter. "I expect you'll be getting one soon."

I scan it quickly. The city officials are claiming that we—as in Redhill—are encouraging homeless people to sleep in nearby streets due to our weekly food nights. The chairwoman reads out from a copy in her hands for the benefit of everyone else. "While the work that Redhill does is commendable, the food night program is making it a haven for homeless people. The buildings are attracting crime and drug addicts, and this does not bode well for the reputation of the area."

I slam the letter down in shock. This isn't a new complaint. Every so often we get letters like this. Maybe we did receive this. I need to check because I seem to be getting more careless with things that need my attention.

"I disagree," I say and a chorus of agreement erupts. Some of the people might linger around while they eat, but everyone leaves by the end of the evening. When we head back to the factory having returned the food and supplies to the restaurants, I have never seen anyone loitering around.

"Sounds to me like they're getting desperate and need us gone from here," someone shouts out.

"The city people don't want us here. They're always trying to get us to move." This was way in the back row.

Agitation spreads like wildfire around the hall. We're accustomed to these requests and we've managed to thwart them successfully up until now. A middle-aged man in the middle row stands up. "I've been here since I was a kid, ever since my mom and dad started their business. I ain't going nowhere."

The commotion amplifies as people become indignant and bitter at the idea that there are underhanded reasons behind this complaint.

"They can't physically remove us," the woman in the front row shouts. I give her a smile which is anything but convincing. I'm sure they can. I wouldn't put anything past these government officials, and I have a sneaky suspicion about this most recent complaint. I try to reassure the crowd. "Why don't we keep our heads down and just carry on as we're doing?" I suggest. "I don't see any of the problems they're complaining about. Y'all know about our weekly food nights, and you also know that there is not a scrap of litter to be found in that space the next day." I survey them all, looking at me with hope, as if I am their fearless leader.

They cry out in agreement. "As long as you're speaking for us, Kyra. As long as you've got our back."

I muster a smile, even though there is nothing to feel happy about.

"Moving swiftly along. What's next on the agenda?"

I groan inwardly. The rest of the evening will be painstakingly dull. There are so many work-related things I could be doing. Between this and the weekly food nights, the time I have to spend on my business is significantly reduced.

And, after spending time with Brad, I have come to see that there are other things to do. Pleasures to be had.

I don't have the hour to spend here.

I chose to be on the committee because I don't want to be pushed around, and because very few people speak up for what they believe in. But my stance has recently changed. I am torn about what to do. A part of me wants to relocate. Another proud and stubborn part of me wants to stay. I have to fix the roof, and then there are a few other parts of the factory that could do with fixing up. And I'm still waiting on one of the factory owners on either side of me to sell and leave so that I can expand out.

It seems like an awful lot of wishful thinking and maybes. Brad is right. I should cut my losses and go.

As we walk out, it's just me and Fredrich because Simona left earlier, slipping out from the first few rows where she and Fredrich were sitting. I'm grateful that he stayed, but now I am eager to get home.

"What was all that about? You and Brad, as we were getting ready to leave?"

I stare straight ahead because I can't bring myself to look Fredrich in the eye. "Nothing."

"Doesn't seem like nothing to me."

We're in such a small office and even though I've tried to focus on my work, Simona and Fredrich have obviously noticed how cold Brad and I have been, especially because we've been getting on so well lately. We've shared an easy familiarity and now that it has turned stone cold, it's no wonder that my colleagues have noticed.

He left me when we were about to have sex. He turned me down. It wasn't quite like that. I get it, but still, it's an embarrassment I can't erase from memory. The idea that we have seen each other naked, that he has probed my most private of places, that we came so close to having sex.

"Has he done something?" Fredrich asks.

My head spins so fast as I turn to look at him. "What? No." My rebuke is too loud. The denial a little too forced.

"I thought the two of you were getting on really well, especially after how you were with him in the start."

"I don't trust him," I mumble. Even now, days later, the imprint of his lips is all over my body. I can't wash it off. I lie in bed thinking of his mouth on mine and his fingers ...

"What? That doesn't make sense. He's been such a great help."

"He's hiding something, but I don't know what." I'm determined to push those images away.

He stops in the middle of the street, holding my arm, so that I too, have to stop. "Kyra, that's insane. Why do you think he's hiding something?"

"I don't know."

"Have you two had a lover's tiff?"

He's hit so close to the truth, that the bullseye hits my heart. "Don't be so silly. I've tolerated that man because he's free to hire. I can't stand him at the best of times." I storm off in a huff, hoping that Fredrich believes me.

CHAPTER THIRTY-NINE

BRANDON

The more desperate I become to talk to her, the more she seems to avoid me.

The next day at work, I put my head down and get on with things. I'm curious to know how the committee meeting went, but I'm also fearful that something I say might give me away. So, I don't ask anything.

Simona is away for a week, because she is celebrating a big birthday and she and her family have gone away.

Needing to resolve the divide between us, I consider booking dinner for us, somewhere nice, not too swanky, but somewhere funky and cool, which I think she might appreciate. Somewhere that I'm not likely to run into any business associates. But, as much as I'd love to take her to dinner, I have a feeling that she won't agree. The chance of getting Kyra to come anywhere with me, let alone give me the time of day, is an impossibility.

I need to get through to her, and I am determined that it is today. This can't fester any longer.

The clock ticks, tension ratcheting up by the second. When Fredrich leaves, I snatch my chance. Kyra hasn't looked my way once. She hasn't spoken properly to me in days. I clear my throat.

"Long day, huh?"

She glances at me for one second, before tapping on her keyboard, her eyes fixated on her screen.

I take my cue, and my courage, wondering how the tables have turned and our roles have switched. How is it that I'm the one being anxious around her? I never used to care whether I had upset someone before.

"I've booked dinner."

Her brows push together, the first indication I have that she's not as calm as she's making out.

"For us," I add.

This earns me an icy stare. "You booked dinner? For us?" she spits out, as if I've presented her with a search warrant.

"I want to make it up to you, after the last time ... I have things I need to tell you."

"You want to take me out to dinner to make up for it?"

"You know I do. Give me a chance to explain."

"Ecuador," she volleys at me.

I quirk a brow. "What about it?"

"You told me that you helped out on some community projects in El Salvador when I first interviewed you, and when I asked you yesterday, you said it was Ecuador."

I scoff, then shrug for added nonchalance. I had a feeling I might have messed up. That was sneaky of her to ask me again, but I would have done the same thing if I had been in her shoes and some slimy son of a bitch had turned up at my company. I would have had a private detective shadowing her by now.

She's gone easy on me. "So?" I feign indignance. "It's an easy enough mistake to make."

"They're two different places more than a thousand miles apart."

"My friend is in the hospital, these last few weeks haven't been easy, you and I have been on a rollercoaster journey, and you're picking on me because I said the wrong country name?"

She blinks, clearly not expecting this reply from me. Emboldened, I spew more of my pity.

"Do you know how hard it's been for me?"

She's about to frown again, but I've done the Jedi mind trick and turned it around. She's now questioning her logic and it takes the attention off me, but I feel wretched for being such a snake.

"Are you married?" she throws back.

The absurdity of this makes me chuckle. "Married? No. Is that what you think?"

"I don't have anything else to go on, given your scheming and lying. You're not who you claim you are."

"I know you have questions, Kyra. I want to give you answers. That's why I booked dinner. It's not to wine and dine you, it's to get out of here and have somewhere to talk, someplace civil where you can't shout and scream at me."

"You think I'd just happily trot off to have dinner with you? After what you did?" Her face flushes, as her voice and temper rise.

She scans the door, catching herself. "I don't want to go anywhere with you. The last thing I want to do is to sit down and have dinner with you. I would rather choke."

I walk over to her desk. "I'm not married, and I'm not

seeing anyone. I haven't been married before and I have no exes lurking in the background."

The lines on her forehead relax, but her narrowed eyes still regard me with the suspicion I deserve. My intentions are always to tell her. But when she looks at me, through me, inside me, the way she does now, delving deeper and deeper into my psyche, I balk. Because when she knows, she will never want to talk to me again.

"Then why do you jump every time Emma needs you?"

I can't answer that question, but maybe I can get rid of her suspicions. I grab her hand. "Come with me." I hold out my hand.

"I don't want to go to dinner with you."

"It's not dinner. I need you to meet someone." What I'm doing is bold, and wrong, for Emma, but it's time I did the right thing by Kyra. "I want you to meet Emma." I hate to throw this on her, and the only reason I'm pushing for it is because Emma suggested it. It should at least convince Kyra that I am not a love cheat.

I expect her to say no, but when she says, "Okay," I have no choice but to keep my word.

KYRA

It's not right, him asking me to go to the hospital with him to meet this 'Emma', so that he can prove that she is not his girlfriend. I feel as if I almost know this woman, because we've talked about her more than a few times and I know a lot about her. She probably knows nothing about me.

I should have declined his invitation, but I'm not sure I know who Brad is, and going along with his suggestion is the only way that I will come to know the truth.

He drives us to the hospital. The car ride is fraught with tension as thick and as heavy as the steam in a sauna turned up too high.

We have been on a rollercoaster ride. Embarrassment and shame have blanketed these last few times I've had to face him at work. This evening will put an end to my suspicions.

I hope.

As we make our way up in the elevator, my breath hitches in my throat. This is wrong. So very wrong. This woman has been in a really bad car accident. A near-fatal accident, and Brad is taking me, a complete stranger, to meet her.

We've come this far, and I'm tempted to say 'Stop!' This is enough. I believe him already. It must be true. She's here and recovering, and she's not his lover. He is single, and he isn't the monster I've made him out to be.

I'm about to tell him that we don't have to do this, when the elevator doors open and he strides out with me in tow.

I follow him, then take a step back when he talks to the nurses at the reception desk. They seem to know him, which fills me with confidence. This isn't a trick. He isn't lying. He's not hiding anything. This is enough.

"Come on," he says when I stand there, debating on this insane turn of events. I hesitate, but only for a few seconds, then follow him. He stops by a door, looks through the window and knocks. My anxiety soars, and my heartbeat spikes.

"Are you... are you sure about this?" I manage to say. My mouth is dry, and I'm left wondering about the stupidity of this.

"You think I'm with her. This is the only way I can prove to you I'm not."

The way he says it places the blame on me. Like I'm the one who is demanding this. He opens the door, and I see a woman sitting in bed. She looks as surprised as I feel.

"Hello, Emma. I'm really sorry to show up like this, but this is Kyra."

BRANDON

Shame curls in my gut. This situation is absurd—like something out of a Tarantino movie. It's almost funny. I smother the guilt which rises like a phoenix from the pit of my stomach.

Emma looks shocked, but her eyes soon go to Kyra, who is standing timidly by my side. "Oh," she says.

"We won't stay for long. Sorry." I make an apologetic face. I will explain everything to her properly later, but her searching look sees through me. I introduce the two women, being extra careful to tell Kyra that Emma is a dear friend.

Surely Kyra won't have any questions after this. Surely this will suffice? Kyra looks uneasy. I can see it in the way she is standing, hovering by Emma's bed. It's surreal to watch and I feel awkward as I ask Emma how she's feeling, then ask about her family. We make small talk about Emma's recovery, and she tells us that she'll be able to leave the hospital soon, then tells us about the physical therapy she has to undergo.

She looks a lot better lately, and tells me that she is walking around more, and the pain of her injuries is lessening.

When Kyra steps out to take a phone call, Emma gives me a look that makes my insides shrivel.

"I'm a shitbag, I know." I exhale, because I don't know where to begin, and I don't have time, and Kyra is just outside. "I'm sorry. I wouldn't ask this if—"

"You're sleeping with her." Her voice is thick with disappointment. It's not even a question, but stated like a fact.

"No." I meet her gaze.

"Something is obviously going on."

"I'm not ... sleeping with her."

She doesn't seem to believe me. Wise woman. "You set out to deceive this woman. Even you should know when to stop," she hisses.

"About that ... I'm going to set things right."

She struggles to sit up, and I help her, adjusting the pillow slightly. "Is this setting things right?"

"She thought I was married, or that you and I were ... you did say I could bring her here."

The silence is deafening.

"Obviously, you didn't think it would come to that," I say, realizing now how misguided my actions are.

"Sorry about that." Kyra returns, looking sheepish. She smiles at Emma. "I'm so sorry about showing up here like this. It's my fault."

"It's perfectly fine." Emma is all smiles. The two women seem genuinely friendly towards one another and I feel like an extra on a show.

"We should go. I'm sorry that this happened at all, but Brad and I were talking and ..." Kyra looks to me to help her out, as if she doesn't know how to explain her sudden appearance here.

"It's not a problem. I like having visitors. Being on my own isn't much fun."

"It's great that you'll be able to go home soon," says Kyra. "Good luck with the physio."

I raise my hand at Emma, steering clear of words. She's furious with me, and rightly so. Once more, this was all about me. My desire to prove that I am not a cheat or involved with Emma. That's all I thought about, and wanting to set the record straight with Kyra, but if I were brave enough, I could have set the record straight by telling her the whole goddamn truth.

But to do that, I will have to go back to the beginning, to tell her who I really am, and that's something I'm not ready to do.

CHAPTER FORTY

KYRA

We walk back to his car silently. After a while, he asks, "Do you believe me now?"

He was obviously desperate to prove it to me. I don't know this woman from the next stranger, and here I am, intruding in her personal space, at the hospital of all places. And this after her traumatic car crash.

The cynic in me rises to the fore. I can't trust anyone enough to get close to them, and maybe this is what it takes. I should give the guy a break. I should let this go and allow myself to open up to someone again.

"Thank you for doing that. I shouldn't have asked you to go this far."

"This far?" He quirks an eyebrow. "You have doubts about me, Kyra, and I don't blame you. There are many things unexplained; things you probably wonder about. The last thing I wanted was for you to think I was a cheat."

He leans against the car, arms folded as if he's not ready to get in until we've sorted this out. I let out a shaky breath. I'm lucky to have someone like Brad, someone who went to such lengths to prove to me that he isn't a cheat.

He seems like the type of man who would move mountains for me, and maybe, for once, I should let myself enjoy the moment. Taking his hand, I tiptoe up and kiss him, missing his lips intentionally and placing a kiss just to the right of his mouth.

"Is that all I get?" He tugs my hand and pulls me towards him. This time, he lowers his head and plants a kiss on my lips. It's chaste by comparison to the way he's kissed me before —all hot and heavy and needy. My insides still heat at the memories of the last time we'd kissed and, as if they remember, the cells in my body jump to attention. I kiss him back, sliding my tongue between his lips, putting my arms around his neck. Just as we begin to deepen the kiss, he slowly moves my arms away, then slides his hands down to hold mine. He breaks our kiss. "Does this mean we're back?"

"Back to what? I don't want to sneak around anymore."

"Me neither." He strokes my face, and my skin tingles at his touch, a reminder of where we had last left things. "I want to do something nice for you."

"Something nice?" Surprise makes me smile. "*This* is nice."

"This?" His eyes grow round. "Being nice to you, kissing you, is nice?"

"Yes."

"He must have really hurt you," he says, quiet as a mouse.

I muster a brave smile. I have tried to hold back and keep my distance from this man, but it seems as if Brad Hartley and I can't keep apart. I lean my face towards his stroking finger.

"It rips you up, tears you down. Makes you think you're worthless. That's why I'm just extra cautious now."

He nods, understanding heavy in his eyes as he pulls me into him and holds me. We have gone from zero to one hundred. He wants me, but he seems to be in a contemplative mood again. I can't read the expression on his face, and I can't gauge his thoughts. But he holds me tight, and I lean against him because, after a long time of putting up my walls, I've finally find the courage to trust again.

BRANDON

We go our separate ways. She might think I have cooled off and wonder why we're not continuing on from where we left off, but I can't go into this being Brad Hartley, the guy who has lied to her about everything.

I want to show her the real me, but who is the real me?

Am I Brandon Hawks, the man who wants Greenways? Or am I Brandon Clements—a poor neglected and unwanted child?

I still want Kyra, but I want to also do things properly. It means I'll have to reveal everything slowly. Bit by bit, and only the parts I am comfortable for her to know about.

CHAPTER FORTY-ONE

KYRA

We revert back to normal at work, but we no longer sneak around in the storeroom like before. There is a more steadied attraction between us. It is evenly keeled. I trust Brad, and even though he still remains a mostly closed book to me, he has hinted that he will tell me in his own time. I will wait.

On the next food night, we work as usual, and then clear up at the end. As we're finishing up in the storeroom, Brad is pensive again and I find myself worrying about him.

He catches me staring. "You always seem on a downer after these nights," I say. He doesn't say anything. I reach forward and put my hands on his chest. "You're not supposed to feel sorry for anyone. You're supposed to feel *good*. Remember, the work we do here helps people like these to get back onto their feet."

"You're doing all the good things."

"It's what I love, and that's why I am so eager to expand.

Redhill is thriving and we need more people, which is why I need more premises."

"How was the committee meeting the other day?"

"We had the usual complaints from the city officials."

"What complaints?"

I tell him. "But now I'm starting to think that your advice is the right advice," I say. "Maybe we should move elsewhere, to bigger premises, instead of trying to make this higgledy-piggledy plot of land work."

His face twists. "Don't listen to me."

"Why not? You have a good business head on your shoulders and being around you has made me see things from another perspective."

"You should go with your gut, Kyra. You told me you wanted to stay here. You said this area was starting to turn around and you got this factory at a good price."

"This factory which now needs a roof to be fixed as well as a long list of items, and that's just in this building. How will I expand? Buy one of the other buildings?"

"Wasn't that your plan?" he asks, confusing me further. "To stay here and fix everything."

"But you told me to think about—"

"You shouldn't listen to me."

I squint in confusion. "But I do. I've been thinking about what you said and it makes sense."

He frames my face with his hands then brings his head lower so that we are touching foreheads. "Don't let me sway you. Do what you feel is the right thing." Then he kisses me, so-so-slowly that it feels as if my feet have lifted from the floor. "I want to take you out." His hands slide around my waist, then lower to my bottom which he squeezes gently. Past reminders coil and twist in my gut. If I'm not careful, he'll have his fingers inside me again. I press against him.

"Take me out, where?"

"Somewhere nice. It's about time we went on a proper date," he replies. His hands keep sliding around my hips then lower, then back up again as if he's caught in a battle of the wills between the Sweet Saint and the Dirty Devil.

"We skipped all the dating niceties," I whisper, tugging at his earlobe gently. Breathing in his cologne sends the blood pumping through me. "Come back to my place ..." I plead.

"Tempting," he murmurs, his voice low, his lips teasing my neck. I grind my hips into him, wanting more, more, more. This teasing and flirting has gone on for too long.

We kiss again, and I groan against his mouth as the force of his hardness presses into me reminding me of what he denied me the last time.

He pulls away quickly, then takes a step away, as if he needs to get away from me because he can't trust himself.

"Keep the weekend free for me."

"What?"

"The weekend, keep it free."

* * *

BRANDON

"You want to do *what?*" Neville grinds out.

"I want no part of Greenways. We're walking away."

"Are you sick, Brandon? What are you talking about?"

"I'm not sick. I just don't want it. The people there are already doing great work. They should be allowed to continue it without the likes of me moving in for pure greed."

Neville roars, and when I stand silently, eyeing him like a mental asylum's new intake, he suddenly stops. "You've gone all soft. Do you have any idea how much money we're going to make on this deal?"

"I don't want the money."

"You don't want ... you *don't want* the money? Why would you say something like that?"

"I'm being deadly serious. I don't want the land. I'm not going after it."

"And the government project? The eminent domain proposition? What the hell do you want me to do with Charlie Stagg?"

"Nothing."

"But think of the money—"

"Your job is to do what I say. You leave the thinking to me." Neville's horrified expression at hearing my instruction borders on comical. "It's only money, Neville. There'll be another deal, another opportunity."

"I don't know what's gotten over you, Brandon. You're ... different. Working for that woman has turned you into a loser."

"Shut the fuck up."

To my amusement, he does. It's almost instant. He coughs lightly before going through the folder on the desk. "McGovern Holdings, they never received the signed paperwork from you."

McGovern Holdings. I rack my brains to remember. "I don't remember signing them." And then I recall. "Fuck." Those were the contracts I'd asked Emma to pick up from the office and deliver to my house on the night of Cardoza's fight. I hadn't signed them because, after the accident, it had been the last thing on my mind.

Neville observes me quietly. "It's messing you up, this

little game you're playing. This undercover billionaire bullshit."

My head snaps up at his curse. The guy is angry because my decision to walk away from Greenways means that he also loses out on a lucrative cut. Government officials aren't easy to find and corrupt. It takes money.

"Emma was supposed to pick that paperwork up from the office and leave it at my house. Obviously, that never happened and that's the reason why I never signed anything. Do you have a copy I can sign now?"

"It's not that simple," Neville cautions. "They have other interested parties."

Typical. "They're having a hissy fit because I didn't sign the contract on time?"

"You haven't called them or said a word. It's been complete silence from you. What do you want them to think?"

"They need to know the truth. My PA was involved in a serious car accident. Not that they will care," I mutter under my breath. I want the deal. I need to fix this. I swipe a hand over my brow. "I'll fly out there. I'll meet them in person." That's what it will take. An in-person meeting. The friendly touch. Face to face.

"Do you want me to come along?" Neville offers. A rare request, because he tends to want to do the bare minimum. I cock my head at him, assessing the motivation behind this. He's afraid I'll mess up. He already thinks I'm losing it. He can't afford for me to lose my head over too many deals, otherwise this lazy slug of a man will lose out on his fat checks.

I shake my head. "I can handle this alone."

The intercom buzzes. "Jessica is on line one," my new PA announces. I hiss out an aggravated breath. Emma would have known to hold all my calls especially when I'm in a meeting. "Stall her."

"I've tried. This is the third time she's called this morning."

I know how forceful Jessica can be, and I'm thankful, in a way, for her interruption. At least it will help me to get rid of Neville. "I'll meet with the people from McGovern next week," I tell Neville. "You'll have to excuse me."

"But what about Greenways?"

"I told you about Greenways. I don't want it."

"You need to think very carefully, Brandon—"

"I have a call to take. Please excuse me."

I wait for him to heave his big body out of the chair and slowly make his way to the door. When he leaves, I slump back in relief and take the call from Jessica. This is timely. Killing two birds with one stone. She's another problem I no longer want to deal with.

"I barely see you these days, Brandon."

I pinch the bridge of my nose. "I've been busy."

"You've always made time for me."

"You know how it is."

"Is that little do-gooder keeping you busy?"

The malice in her tone makes me wonder if she suspects something. I effect a dismissive laugh. "I have a new PA, and it's been challenging, to say the least, getting things done around here."

She pauses, making me wonder what I have given away. "That's an evasive answer if ever I heard one."

"I'm busy, Jessica. Did you call for a reason?" I don't even care if that is too blunt. I have a lot of things to resolve and Jessica sucking up my time is the last thing I need.

"You don't have time for me anymore," she laments, like the spoiled brat that she is. To think that I once considered her as wife material when I used to acquire things because I needed to confirm the man I now was. Because I was so desperate to push the past away.

The problem with my experiment with Kyra and Redhill is that it has put the past firmly in my present. I see it every Wednesday night because Yvette insists on bringing her kids to the food nights.

"I'm hosting a special arts night at the gallery next week. I want you there."

Next week I have plans to fly to Boston to meet with McGovern Holdings. "I'll see. I'm busy and I'll probably be out of state for a few days."

She scoffs. "You can't even give me one night?"

"We didn't have *any* nights, Jessica."

"We hadn't yet, no."

"And we won't," I state, a chill icing my words.

"You have other interests," she remarks. Cool and offhanded.

"I have *many* business interests to take care of."

"Then come to the gallery for one last time. At least give me that," she begs. The airwaves fall silent as I consider this final request. "It's going to be pretty amazing. I've worked really hard to put it together."

She leaves me no choice. It's the least I can do. "When?" She gives me the date and time, and I hastily scribble it down in my diary. I tell her I'll do my best to be there.

Then I stare at the dates on my calendar. Not only do I need to spend a day or two at most in Boston, I also owe Kyra. I want to make it up to her. She deserves to see a part of the real me while I try to figure out a way to get myself out of this mess.

CHAPTER FORTY-TWO

KYRA

"Are you ready?" he asks. We've driven over to the Loop. He's told me nothing so far, and I was surprised when he said he'd pick me up at eight. The evening has already turned dusky.

I'd expected that we'd spend most of the day together, but as I'm quickly finding out, I should never underestimate things when it comes to Brad. He'd also told me to wear long slacks and a fitted jacket. That should have alerted me to the fact that it wasn't a movie and dinner—or that he's psychotic and controlling and that I should stay away.

I'm even more confused when he heads away from the buzzing area filled with bars and restaurants and I see signs for a heliport. I'm glad I had an apple and a small cup of yogurt before I left, otherwise I would be starving. "Where are we going?"

"You'll see."

He quirks a smile at me, almost tugging at my hand as I

slow down. We soon turn the corner and I see a heliport directly in front of me, and a bright red helicopter with a big white H on the side.

"We're going on a helicopter ride?" I suck in a breath. This man doesn't do things by half.

Movie, dinner and a walk; these were the things I had in mind. Not a helicopter ride. This is all so different and exciting.

"Are you afraid of flying?" he asks, when I fall silent. Luckily, I'm not.

"What would you do if I was?" I ask, just to test the waters.

"I'd blindfold you and throw you into the helicopter. No point in wasting a good ride."

My eyes pop. He sees the fear on my face, then puts his arm around my shoulder, hugging me to his side. He laughs. "Of course I wouldn't. I'd ask you what you wanted to do."

I let out an exaggerated sigh. "That's good to know, and by the way, I'm not afraid of flying."

"Then we're good."

He greets a couple of people who seem to be waiting for us, while I stare at the helicopter and look for signs for damage and wear and tear. Under the lights, it looks pretty good.

"Shall we?" Brad holds out his hand.

"All ready?" I assumed we'd have to wait, even though this is a night-time ride. I've heard from others that these things are popular and I was expecting more people.

"Yes. All ready."

Brad introduces me to the pilot who seems very familiar and easy-going; it's as if they know one another. I'm amazed at how good Brad is with people, and as I watch him talking, I realize that I've only known him in a very limited capacity. Here, with others, away from the factory and the food nights, he seems like a different person, in charge and in command. He takes my hand and leads me towards the helicopter.

"Aren't we supposed to have safety instructions or something?" I imagined that we would have something like we do in an airline flight.

"I've been on a couple of these things before. Trust me. You'll be okay."

There it is again. The self-assured attitude. It's almost as if he and the guy are friends.

"Do you do this often?" I ask, my heart thumping with fear.

"Not often, no. You look scared. Don't be. I've got you." He helps me in, and after a few reassuring words from the pilot, we're in the air.

"Hey, Kyra, you okay?" It's only when he asks me that I realize I'm gripping Brad's hand extra tight. I nod.

Sitting beside him, with the world at our feet, I try not to get too intoxicated by the moment. The helicopter lifts up and away. Goosebumps shimmy across my arms, and my heart glides in my ribcage, soaring with the headiness of this moment.

Brad is doing something special for me. I'm a lucky gal.

"Would you like me to give a commentary?" the pilot asks. I stare at Brad, who raises an eyebrow at me. Once again, I'm unsure what's going on. And then I start to get nervous. What if this is his friend? What if he's not a qualified pilot? What if this is Brad's way of trying to impress me? What if there isn't proper insurance in place?

"Sure, why not?"

Why not? Aren't they supposed to give a running commentary of the sights on these trips?

My doubts amplify. "Is this safe?" I whisper to Brad.

He must sense the unmistakable fear in my voice because

he puts his arm around me and kisses me on the top of my head. "This is safe. I would never put you in danger. Mark, would you mind telling Kyra how long you've been doing this for?"

"Sixteen years. You're in good hands, ma'am."

"Hear that? Sixteen years." He drops a kiss on my neck. The scent of his aftershave lingers in the air, and as I bury my face in his arm, it's all I can smell.

Safely snuggled up against him, I start to feel better. Looking out, the skyline resembles a jeweled spider's web cast all over the city which is ablaze with tall buildings all lit up.

The pilot mentions Willis Tower and Millennium Park as we fly over them. The aerial views of Navy Pier and Centennial Wheel are resplendent in the dark black velvet sky.

Every view is breath-taking.

I imagine in the daytime we'd get a better feel for each landmark and building, but Brad picked the right time, because at night, the city is magical. I feel as if I'm gliding around on a carpet flying above a sea of jewels. It is beautiful and rare, seeing the city from this angle, and in a way that very few people are able to.

Sitting close to Brad, the fear slowly leaves my body, and I crane my neck, eagerly looking out and around at the sights from this high up. "How long do we have?" I ask him after a while. This is as perfect a night as any, and for a first date, it's unforgettable. I don't want it to end.

"As long as you want."

His cryptic answer confuses me. "How long did you book for?" I glance at my watch. We've been up here for about twenty minutes.

"How long did you want?" I'm convinced that he's in cahoots with the pilot. They're friends, and that's why he's able to do this. It makes sense, the friendliness between the two men, the slacking off of rules and regulations. All of it.

"You're sure this is safe?"

"It's safe." He traces a finger along my lip. "You're worrying, and it's the last thing I wanted for our first time out. This is my small way to trying to make it up to you, Kyra."

I swallow and decide to get over my niggling worries. Brad wouldn't put my life in danger. He cares for me. He's gone out of his way for me to meet Emma, and now he's dazzling me with this beautiful night. I should learn to relax and enjoy this.

"Let's stay a little bit longer," I murmur, watching Wrigley Field below us, the green shimmering and floodlit.

The pilot soon stops talking, and I sit back and take in everything, but most of all, I marvel at the thought of me being up so high in the sky, with Brad, the new man in my life.

It feels as if I've turned a corner. I have never felt as cherished as this before. The first thing I do when we set back down on the ground, and we've thanked the pilot and walked away, is kiss him, long and deep, and with all the feeling in my heart. "Thank you for the best night of my life."

BRANDON

She looks as if I've given her the world. I've never seen anyone look so happy, and all this just after a helicopter ride. Keeping my real life separate from the life Kyra thinks I lead is tricky. Pretending that Mark is someone new, and that the helicopter doesn't belong to me is tricky.

How will I ever explain to her?

We walk up a few stairs which lead to one of the best restaurants in the city. I'm reverting back to my Brandon Hawks playbook; not because I need to impress Kyra but because she deserves the best, and she expects so little. She does so much for others, and she doesn't get all that love and attention back.

I wanted this night to be special for her.

"Do you come here often?" she asks, after the maître d' has greeted us and shown us to our table. The man talks to me with a familiarity that makes me feel nervous. As much as I'm trying to get ready to tell her some things, I'm aware that the power of observation will plant more questions in her head. The last thing I need is for anyone to run into me and call me by my real name.

Perhaps I have become careless in my attempt to show her some of the real me. If the sleek and chic ambiance of this place hasn't clued her in, the row of expensive cars parked outside should have done.

"I come here for business, mostly," I tell her as we make ourselves comfortable in our plush seats. I've been here twice this month already—in my other life I lead away from Redhill —because this is the place to come to in order to impress people. I picked this place on a busy Saturday night hoping that I won't run into business people.

"You mean for your start-ups?" She looks as if she doesn't know whether to believe me. "I thought when you said start-up you were talking about you and a few guys starting something at the kitchen table."

"Perception is everything. I have ideas and I believe in the project, and coming here signals those things."

"It also signals that you have a lot of money."

We stare at one another. I wonder if she's testing me, if she knows or suspects more. In my desire to want to show her a good time, I might have been a bit too eager and overplayed things.

"It must be a cool project." She looks at me over the menu, her eyes widening as she glances back at it again.

"It is. I think it's one you'd like." She has no idea that the real project I have in mind has to do with her and her dreams and vision for Greenways. After my instructions to Neville the other day, I've decided that instead of walking away, I can invest heavily in Redhill, as well as Greenways. I can give her that dream she has of expanding the factory. I can make that happen for her now. And I can get her goddamn roof fixed ASAP.

"I have no interest in online gaming," she says, perusing the menu.

"I guess not. What would you like?" I ask, nodding at the menu.

"It all looks good." She chews her lip.

"If you don't like anything here we can go someplace else."

"It's not that. The food sounds delicious."

"Then?"

She shakes her head, then closes the menu but still holds onto it. "It's nothing."

"It doesn't look like it's nothing."

She chews her lip again. "I just ... I just can't help feeling lucky for everything I have."

It's guilt. She looks at the menu and now she feels guilty. "You're already doing everything to help people less fortunate than you. Your food nights initiative, it's a fantastic thing. But it doesn't mean that you should feel guilty just because—"

"That's not what I meant. That's not it at all. I'm just really grateful for everything I have. This," she rolls her shoulders and looks around the restaurant, "This place is beautiful. The food smells delicious. I'm just grateful for you. For the helicopter ride, for these hours together."

Now I'm the one who feels like an idiot. "I ... I didn't realize that's what you meant."

"My mom used to tell us to recite five things we were grateful for each night. It made me see how much we have. How lucky we are."

"Your mom sounds like a very special woman."

"She was." She opens the menu up again and examines it slowly. I watch her with interest. She's so unlike Jessica. She's so unlike the high-maintenance ball crushers I tend to date. I like being with this woman.

We place our order, and I raise my glass. "To our first date, at last."

"At last." She clinks her glass with mine. "I'm planning a meal for Simona when she returns. Maybe something like this, though maybe not as upscale. Sometime next week. She would love for you to be there. Will you come?"

I wince. I already have demands on my time. McGovern Holdings., and Jessica, which quickly spring to mind. I could ditch Jessica easily, but then she'll find a way of never letting me forget. And I did promise her that I would try to make this one last time at the gallery. But I've also always turned Kyra down for events and I still regret not going to the city hall event. "What day?"

"I don't know. I need to check with her."

"Give me the date and time, and I'll try to come."

"Try?" Her voice is shaky. "Is it Emma?"

"What? No. No. It's just ... this ... start-up ... it's taking up a lot of my time ..." Guilt reaches into my soul and feels around with pincers. Where are my nerves of steel? My disregard for these people? I feel things now. I *care*. I care about Kyra, and I'm torn. Wearing this new cloak of concern makes me a little uneasy. Because a snake that sheds its skin is still a snake underneath.

Should I tell her? Should I come clean at this very moment and break this little bubble we have? We have a new understanding, but it's still based on lies. It's not the way to start something new.

"Well, that's great. That's really great, Brad."

"Thanks. I have to meet with some people next week and I don't know how long the negotiations will take."

"Negotiations?"

"I prefer not to say too much about it just yet." I chicken out like the coward I am.

"I understand," she says, her voice soft, her eyes shining. "I'm so happy that this is working out for you."

"Me too." But the happier she is for me, the worse I feel. This is the moment when I should tell her that I'm taking the private jet to fly to Boston. I don't know how long it will take for me to sweeten the people at McGovern Holdings. I should tell her that the helicopter we just flew in belongs to the family, and that Mark is our most trusted pilot.

What would she do if I spilled all of the truth now?

"Let's just enjoy our dinner," she says, while I'm still wondering how to broach the subject. "You don't have to explain everything to me, all at once. We're good now."

"We are." I will unravel my life to her slowly. We order and eat, talking about Redhill, and her vision and her plans. No more trying to gently persuade her to up and leave Greenways, I now find myself trying to sway her the other way.

Then we change the subject and talk about easier things, such as our favorite movies and songs and things we like to do.

Afterwards, we go for a walk along the river, talking about

our plans and how awkward things might be when Fredrich and Simona find out we're together.

"I'll be leaving Redhill," I announce suddenly, as soon as the idea comes to me. This is the simplest way to do this. I can't be here. Being here, at Redhill, complicates things. Everything will be simpler if I leave.

She lets go of my hand, staring up at me as she stops walking. "When?"

"I don't know." The thought just came to me and I have no plan. All I know is that working with her, alongside her, juggling my two worlds, is becoming more complicated. Extricating myself from Redhill is the first step towards getting clarity. "It's getting really busy with the other stuff."

"So when were you thinking of leaving Redhill?"

I shrug. "Maybe once I get back from this meeting. If it's okay with you, could I not come in to work this week. I need to prepare."

"Yes, of course. You need to focus on your start-up. Are you saying you'll leave soon?"

"Maybe I can work a week or two at Redhill, and then leave. That way I can tell Fredrich and Simona."

She lets out a heavy breath. "It's all happening so suddenly." She stops at gazes at the water.

I lift her face to me. "It was only ever meant to be a temporary thing, Kyra. You didn't even want to take me on."

"That's because I wasn't sure about you. I had my suspicions. I wasn't sure who you really were." She moves closer, sliding her arms around my waist. "But now, now that I'm getting to know you, I think you could be a great asset to Redhill. You could help me to do so much, Brad."

"You give me too much credit," I tell her, as she looks up at me with admiration and hope in those naïve, trusting eyes. I try to muster my game face, something that is usually second nature for me, but it eludes me right now.

Disappointment sweeps across her features. It guts me, thinking that she was starting to think that I would have stayed. I can help her so much. Hawks Enterprises can go from being who we are to being a company with values and concern for the welfare of others. My father, bless his eighty-six-year-old heart, isn't going to be pleased, but I'm certain I can forge a new way forward without making him completely unhappy.

"I can still give you ideas, I can still give you advice. It might be better for us to have that distance in our working lives."

"But I was just getting used to having you around."

"You can have me around." I drop a kiss on her lips, hoping to reassure her. Hoping that once she knows the truth about me, she'll still want to be with me. Leaving Redhill is the first step and it will make things easier. The distance, both mentally and physically, will allow me to unveil to her who I am and what I had planned to do.

We walk back and I feel as if a heavy load has been lifted from my chest. As we get into the car, she tells me what a beautiful evening she's had, and then she thanks me.

"Don't thank me, Kyra. I wanted us to have a proper date. No more sneaking around." My gaze falls on her lips and I want to kiss her wildly again.

"No more steaming up the windows?" she asks, a naughty glint in her eyes.

I want to steam up the windows not only in the car but in the shower, and the bathroom, and everywhere I have plans to take her. In the extended pause that follows, I can sense what she's thinking, and when I don't say anything, she asks, "Did you want to come back to my place?"

I want her to come back to my place, but after tonight, it might be too much for her to take in all at once.

"I have another date planned for you tomorrow," I announce.

"Tomorrow?"

"Yes."

"Another date?"

"Yes, so if you had plans for going to the factory and checking the supplies for the next food night, it's not going to happen."

She laughs. "I lead a sorry existence, don't I?"

"You make a difference in people's lives, and that is priceless, but you need to have some time to enjoy your life."

"You sound like Simona."

"That woman talks a lot of sense."

"She's also been eager for you and I to get together."

"Has she now?"

"I believe she coaxed me into hiring you because you were young and good-looking."

"We'll have to break the good news to her."

"Not yet," Kyra cries. I understand her reticence at a workplace romance. "Maybe tell them around the time you announce that you're leaving."

"See?" I kiss her on the nose. "Another advantage of me going."

"She'll be upset, so will Fredrich, but not as upset as me."

"I'm not leaving your *life*, Kyra. We're only just starting."

She gives me a smile that I can grow used to; that I want to see before I go to sleep and wake up to. I intend to be in her life still, it just depends on whether she will still want me in hers once I confess.

"Tomorrow," I say, starting the engine. "I'll pick you up around four. Does that work for you?"

"I've been forbidden from checking the storeroom, so I'm going to be free the whole day. You could come earlier ..."

Her sultry tone sends a message straight to my cock. I harden at the suggestions that her words have prompted in my brain. I could so easily take her up on her offer to go back to her place now. It would satisfy this burgeoning need that has been eating me up ever since I saw her naked.

I glance at her. "Or I could pick you up at four, take you out, and bring you back to my place."

"You ... you're going to ask me to come back to your place?"

"Unless you don't want to."

"Well, this is unexpected. I don't know what to say."

"Say 'yes'."

CHAPTER FORTY-THREE

KYRA

Brad drops me back home, and I can't sleep.

I have a spring in my step. A smile permanently etched on my face. At this rate I'm going to need to staple my lips together to stop myself from grinning like a lovesick teen.

I lie in bed thinking of the helicopter ride and the sights of the city which I will forever see with new eyes because Brad showed it to me in a new light.

He's leaving Redhill, but I am not as upset as I thought I'd be. Now that we we're together, I can't see anything pulling us apart.

Not surprisingly, I wake up late the next day, and then, because I have no idea of what he has planned, I panic. And then I panic some more when I remember that he is taking me back to his place and this could be *the night*.

I wonder what prompted that. He seems to be making an effort to rectify things. I look forward to having another insight into the enigma that is Brad Hartley.

I'm not prepped. I start to hunt around for my best underwear. I don't have sexy lace and satin. My undergarments are practical. Decent. Sexy-ish, but not Victoria's Secret worthy.

Brad taking me on that helicopter ride and then that upscale restaurant makes me stress even more. Do I have time to go shopping? At two o'clock on Sunday?

I do.

But then I also need to wash my hair, shave my legs, and put on a face mask.

Listen to me.

I'm changing who I am based on who I think he is.

I stop.

My ex used to moan that I was too tired to have sex with him. And then he got sick of me always being at the factory, and always being in sneakers and jeans.

I didn't change for him and maybe that's why he went and found someone else. I don't want to think that I lost him because of something as fickle as the clothes I wore.

It's what's inside that matters. I am not going to shop for sexy lingerie. Brad knows who I am. He's with me because of who I am. He likes me for *me*. Just like I like him for who he is.

BRANDON

She opens the door and instantly I catch a whiff of exotic fruits. She's wearing a different scent. "Ready?"

"Curious."

My hands slip around her soft, slender frame, and we kiss for a few silent and happy moments.

I don't dare get too comfortable around her, but I have a treat in store for her. Because she's usually working on the weekend, I hope this will help her to relax.

"We're going to be late," I say, hating to pull myself away. She pulls at her lower lip with her teeth, unsure and hesitant. "Can you at least tell me where we're going?"

"No."

"A little hint?"

"No."

"Wait and see."

She giggles as we get into my car. "I feel like a child, excited about a journey. I don't even care where we go, I just want you to know that I've already had a great time."

Gratitude pours out of her, the way malice seeps out of Jessica. Everything Kyra says is the opposite to my interactions with Jessica.

"I'm hoping you'll like it." The ancient baths are a treat. I've been a few times, when I've had hard-hitting negotiations to take care of, and though pampering isn't my style, I was persuaded by Emma to try them. She's seen me at my most stressed and difficult and she booked me a session. I loved it so much, I bought the company.

Emma.

Each time I think of her, I feel bad. She's back home now, and I still have her on full pay for as long as she needs. She can take a year if she needs it. She might be determined not to come back, but I'll create a role for her, even if it is so that she can keep an eye on that new PA.

I need Emma around somewhere. She's too good to let go of, and the guilt consumes me because I'm the reason she's injured.

"Hey." Kyra's hand settles on my thigh, a warm and gentle pull back to the present. "Where did you go?"

"Work stuff. Nothing important."

"You're thinking about work when we're on a date?"

"I was thinking about Emma." It slips out before I think.

"Emma? How is she related to your work?"

My jaw tenses.

"You don't have to answer that," she says quickly. "If you don't want to. Not yet."

She always gives me an out. Always lets me get away with it.

"What's this?" Kyra glances out of the car window as we pull up in front of a building. It's a restored factory and has been converted into an exclusive spa treatment place which offers out-of-this-world multi-sensory bath experiences as well as a whole range of special and exotic treatments, massages and therapies.

A woman's paradise. I hope that Kyra, who probably would never come to something like this, will appreciate it. At least I hope she does.

"This is Fortuna Baths," I tell her. "You must have heard of it?"

"I have." We get out of the car. "Is this where we're going?" she asks, slowly.

"Unless you have something better to do on a Sunday afternoon?"

Because I now own this place, I've instructed that it be closed to the public today, and that only the best staff are here. I've also instructed them to treat me like a guest and not be too familiar.

As soon as we walk inside, I see Kyra's excitement rocket. Her jaw hangs open, then inches open slightly more as she admires the interior. An aura of tranquil calm abounds. The space is scented, the light bright in the lobby, but dim in the individual rooms and spaces which have hot baths, and ice-cold plunges. There are warm pools, jet pools and a saltwater flotarium.

"Wow." The word escapes Kyra's mouth, and her eyes widen with delight. "I don't know what to say." She throws her arms around my neck and kisses me.

"Don't say anything," I tell her. "Just enjoy it."

KYRA

Fortuna Baths is the sort of place only a select few visit. I don't know anyone who's been here, but these places aren't on my radar.

I'm surprised to see that it is empty, but then again, I could be wrong. The place is like a huge cave, with different rooms coming off the hallways.

Within minutes, a stunning modelesque looking woman greets us and tells us that she and her team will take good care of us. She ushers us into a changing room that looks so opulent and plush that I could happily just sit here all day and read a book. Then she tells us to get changed.

"Into what?" I look at Brad because I am completely unprepared for this.

"Relax," he says, taking my hand.

"We have bikinis and swimsuits." She opens the door to a closet, and what look like new items of clothing, hang inside covered with shiny wrap.

"Knock on the door when you're ready," she says, and

discreetly leaves. I gape around the room, content just to stay in here.

"How about this?" says Brad, pulling out a bikini.

My face flushes. I should have prepped. "And what about you?"

"I'm going to put on a fluffy white robe." He winks at me, then hooks a thumb over his shoulder at a door. "I'm next door. Get changed. I'll see you in five." He disappears through the adjoining door, leaving me staring at the clothes rack.

I get changed into the bikini he picked. It happens to be one I like. We both knock on the adjoining door at the same time, both wearing a fluffy white robe.

"Come on," he takes my hand."

"You've been here before."

"A couple of times."

We're in a dimly lit room, inside which is something that resembles a hot tub, only it's taller than a normal hot tub. The therapist tells us about the treatment which involves sinking into a tub filled with antioxidant, rich red grapes.

I'm not sure I like the sound of that.

"Trust me," says Brad, slipping off his robe, to reveal swim shorts. The sight of those finely chiseled abs and that body with its perfectly defined ridges makes my heartbeat soar. Down to his swim shorts, Brad's body is a vision straight out of a Calvin Klein ad.

Hot damn.

My skin prickles. He climbs in and watches me. I take off my robe, and feel suddenly self-conscious, even though he has seen me almost naked before. I rush to get into the tub. I'm slightly wary and dip into it slowly. It's like sinking into a vat of warm honey in a hot tub except that we can't see into it because the liquid is dark, but velvety and comforting.

Brad watches me the entire time.

The therapist places a small metal object on the aquamarine mosaic tiles. "I'll leave this buzzer here. Press it if you need anything."

"You orchestrated all of this just to get me into a bikini?" I ask him when she leaves.

He tilts his head, wearing a sexy grin. "It worked."

It's just as well we were submerged up to our necks in grape juice. I sit back, fighting the urge to step towards him because that would just end up with me kissing him again, and feeling as loose and as relaxed as I am now, I would have no qualms about things turning red hot in here.

"Feels good?" he asks, his dreamy voice making my eyelids fly open.

"You have no idea." I lower my head. "You've given me two perfect days. Such glorious days, I'll never forget them."

"I wanted you to slow down and have a good time."

"I had a good time from the moment you turned up at my door." He steps towards me. One stride is all it takes, before he pulls me up to standing, our bodies warm and wet as our hands tangle around one another, and our mouths sink together.

I feel his boner before his tongue welcomes mine. In the warm, dimly lit room, with our guards down, our bodies relaxed, I press against him, my hands reaching over his shorts, then inside. He's so hard, I have the urge to want him now. He moans against me each time I stroke him, his member engorging in my fingers. Each time I stroke his silky tip, he shudders. The excitement is off-the-chart crazy; a reminder of our storeroom days.

"We could be caught," he husks, his breath catching the harder I stroke him. He thumbs my nipple through the flimsy bikini top fabric. Heat pools between my legs. This feels dirty, and sticky, and forbidden, standing in a tub full of grape juice, doing this.

"I don't care," I moan in between our kisses.

"You don't?" he asks, lifting his head. His hot breath tickles my face. The grape juice seems to have seeped through my skin, intoxicating me.

"You could do anything to me now, Brad, and I wouldn't care."

He unties my halter-neck top bikini and pulls it down. My breasts perk up. They're sticky and wet, like our entire bodies, neck downwards. We're covered in juice, but Brad lowers his mouth and sucks hungrily at my breasts. An electric charge skitters across my skin, making my back arch as I rake my fingers through his hair. He sucks each breast in turn, greedily, thirstily, as if he has been wanting to do this forever. I could come just from this.

And then I start to worry. Reality and common sense prevails.

"She's going to come back," I murmur, lifting my leg and hooking it around his waist. Even as I say the words, my body reacts as if it doesn't care about the therapist. I mewl, shuddering in ecstasy as his fingers slide into my bikini bottoms, then slide inside me. I rock against him, wanting more than just his fingers.

This is messy and unhygienic. These thoughts crop up in my mind, but Brad's fingers and tongue soon push those away.

I fall back, panting and sighing as I float down from my high.

He watches me as I try to put myself together.

"Where is she?" I say finally.

He pulls up my bikini top, then turns me around to tie it at the back. His erection pokes in between my butt cheeks and I reach back in order to grasp him, but he moves away.

"We have more treatments to get through yet." He picks up the buzzer and presses it. A few moments later, the therapist returns and asks us how we are doing.

I'm too ashamed to look her in the eye, but Brad replies and tells her that we've been doing just fine.

My mind is frazzled, and my body feels as if it doesn't belong to me. The scent of orange blossoms permeates through the air. Now, lying on a table on my stomach, I moan in quiet ecstasy as another therapist massages my body from top to bottom.

I'm having an out-of-body experience. It's as if I'm floating above the table and looking down. Brad is on a table next to me and another therapist works on him. I am not only in post-sex haze, but also soft and relaxed from the bath, and now my senses are further loosened with this massage.

Every knot of tension, every crease of worry, is being slowly and gently ironed out of me. I feel myself become lighter, as if I have nothing to fear, nothing to worry about.

Later, we end up in what's called a relaxation room, where we loll about on a heated marble stone surface, sipping mint tea.

I feel rejuvenated. Born again. Refreshed and recharged and made new. I catch Brad watching me, a glint of amusement in his eyes. He made me come in a tub filled with crushed grapes. That's something I never thought I'd end up saying, or doing.

I smile at him, because talking seems like too much effort, because my muscles, all of them, my vocal chords, too, are having an afternoon siesta. It's a miracle that I can sit upright and hold up this glass of mint tea.

"You're glowing," he comments, as we sit there wearing fluffy white terrycloth robes.

"I'm floating on another planet."

The smile he gives me melts my insides like butter. "That's what I wanted for you. Time to relax."

"You need it, too." I lean back against the wall.

"Not as much as you. I couldn't believe it when I saw you hefting those food boxes and cartons when I first joined."

The memory makes me chuckle. "I called you because Fredrich had injured himself, and I wanted to test you."

"Test me?"

"I called you on the spot. Asked you to come and help me. I didn't tell you what the job entailed."

At first, he frowns, then realization dawns and his face lightens. "I was ... I was at dinner with a friend."

"At dinner?" That is funny. "You should have said. I wouldn't have expected you to come then."

"I sensed you were testing me. I dropped everything and came."

We sit in silence. Me revisiting my memories of that day. Him revisiting his. I yawn, suddenly feeling drowsy, even though I have done nothing strenuous. I feel nicely tired and ready for sleep. This has been the most I have ever been pampered, and if I never have another moment of it in my lifetime, this will have been enough.

"Thank you, again, for another awesome day."

"You're welcome."

I yawn again.

"Shall we go?" he asks, as I let out another yawn.

"Yes, we should. How long have we been here?"

"A few hours."

It's only when we get changed and step back into the lobby that I find out. It's late evening.

Late evening.

We have been here for the better part of five hours.

Time slowed, then stopped, then sped up again. Being with Brad is like that. I've had more fun and adventure in one weekend than I've had in years.

I stop and give him a big, wet, sloppy thank you kiss as we reach his car. He stares into my eyes, and we exchange something, thoughts, feelings. Words aren't needed.

I kiss him again, bringing back the memories that we had left abandoned in the tub of grape juice. The fibers in my body come alive and he responds with an urgency that is still new and surprising.

Knowing that it is late, and that we have work tomorrow, I'm about to ask him if he wants to drop me off, but he tells me to get in and then starts to drive. He has that same serious expression on his face again. The switch from light to this is so sudden that I can't help but notice.

He is battling with something, maybe it's something he wants to tell me, and believing this to be the case, I say nothing, but let him lead.

But as he drives and we leave the part of Chicago I'm familiar with, and we head towards the more upscale part of the city, I try not to look around too much or be too surprised. I feel another surprise is looming. Another shock to my system. Another revelation.

When he parks up outside a tower building, I stare at him. "You live here?" I might not know a lot of the upscale places, but who in this city doesn't know about The Water Tower Building on Michigan Avenue?

"My dad owns a condo here."

He's from a rich family?

My knees are like jelly. My insides slowly sliding out of

my stomach. I feel weak. As if this is a surreal dream in a surreal world.

"Your dad?" It's the first time he's mentioned his family. He nods.

The dominoes are falling and it's all starting to make sense. But he is normal, I tell myself as we climb out of his battered old Toyota. Grounded. Normal. A guy who's fighting his rich family's legacy.

"I can't believe you live here," I whisper as we ascend the shiny black marble elevator. It whooshes up, the sound barely discernible. Everything is plush, and fast, and shiny clean.

"I live here."

He swipes a key card to open the door, pushes it open, and all I see is a vast room, blacks and teals, and copper and gold. It reeks—positively drips—of luxury. Money. Wealth.

He closes the door, and I try to close my mouth, but it has fallen open and I am having difficulty getting my jaw to shut.

CHAPTER FORTY-FOUR

BRANDON

I can't tell if she looks enraptured or disappointed—that I live in a place like this. I also can't figure out if the shock is from her seeing me in a new light, or if it's the sheer shock of seeing this place.

The Water Tower Building does that to people.

"You kept this quiet," she says, her guarded eyes assessing me carefully. I don't know where to look, or what to say. What can I say in my defence? I don't have a defence.

She walks in, her eyes darting around the limestone floors and the crisp, contemporary lines of all the decor. She walks around slowly, then glances out of the floor-to-ceiling windows, her jaw slowly sliding open as she takes in the views of the skyline and the navy pier.

For a man who has no problems negotiating or addressing a group of investors, for a man who is full of confidence, I am scared to admit what a nasty excuse of a human being I am.

She stops to admire a million dollar painting on the wall.

Something I bought from Jessica. Crazy really, for a man who has no interest in art. But back then, all I wanted was to acquire things.

"I've always felt that you've held things back from me, but I never expected this."

I swipe a hand across the back of my neck. "It's a lot to take in. You probably hate me."

"I don't know who you are."

I bite my lip, wondering how on earth I will ever reveal my plan to her. It won't matter that I didn't execute it. What will matter were my initial intentions and they were so wrong.

"My birth mom had mental health problems, and my dad was a domestic abuser. They were both drug addicts."

Fuck. I said that out loud. My heart thumps as if a wildebeest is stomping inside my chest. I want to tell her that this is not who I have always been, I want her to see that I came from a completely different place, but letting the truth loose on her, like a boulder dropped from a great height, isn't the best way to go about it either.

Kyra stutters. "Wh-wha-what?"

"I was adopted by a very rich man, a billionaire who had lost his teenage son in a skiing accident." I find myself sinking into an abyss from which there is no return. She will see everything differently about me from this point on. Shock skates across her eyes, the cracks in her understanding of me slowly break, break, breaking like the cracks in a river of ice. Any moment now she'll take me under with her.

But the suspicion and surprise in Kyra's eyes vanish and, in their place now lies concern. She's by my side in an instant. Her face is a question mark, because what I've just told her doesn't tally up with this place.

I'm about to tell her his name, but then realize I can't, because it would mean having to explain why I lied about my name. I brace myself, not wanting to lose her, but knowing I can't hold onto her if she doesn't want me. "His wife couldn't handle it," I continue. "I don't think she ever got over her son's death, and they adopted me because I closely resembled the son they had lost."

She looks horrified and shocked. "Oh, Brad. I'm so sorry." To my surprise she takes my hand and kisses it. I'm a lucky man, to have met a woman so caring. It was luck that enabled me to switch my life and insert myself into Philip Hawks' world. It's luck now that has put Kyra in my life. I would never have met her in the usual circumstances. "It must have been so awful for you."

Was it awful? To be rescued from the life I had, and to end up like this? I've spent decades wrestling with that very question. I walk across the expanse of the room and head towards the window, opening one of the smaller windows on the side because I need to breathe. If I had known what this mission would cost me, the unearthing of buried regrets, I would never have gone to Redhill in the first place. I would have done what Neville suggested, with Charlie Stagg, and done a dirty.

But the Fortuna Baths treatments have lowered my guard, made me flexible, soft and vulnerable. I stare out, not able to look Kyra in the eye. "My parents neglected me and I was taken away."

"I'm sorry."

I sniff. "It turned out well, though. I was adopted by a great couple. They're who I call my mom and dad." I struggle to explain, to keep my voice level, because as great as this life is, it's empty.

"How old were you?"

"Twelve."

"Oh, Brad." She stands in front of me and puts her arms around me. "I'm so sorry about your parents."

We stand like that for the longest time. Looking out, I see lights and the city's skyline, buildings, long and short, fat and thin, sprinkled with lights, some sparkling like burnished gold. "I didn't want to lie to you anymore."

She lifts her head, her eyes darting from one eye to the other, as if she's trying to read the code, desperate for more answers than I have given her. Then she kisses my chest. I need to hear her voice, but I see that she is letting me take my time. She's giving me the space to let it out.

She's a good person. This is why people relate to her. They see the goodness in her, and only a man like me would try to take advantage of that. But things are different now. That lie is dying, shedding like a snake's skin. I care for her and I can't have any harm come to her. I don't want to derail her hopes and dreams. This is the real me, and that's who I want her to know. That's who I want her to see. "We went into foster care."

"We?"

"I did," I say quickly. I can't talk about Kane yet. It's too much. "My mom was committed."

She looks at me like I'm a damaged, no-good thing that she can't wait to fix and put right. "I'm so sorry. This is all so tragic. You never said."

I shrug.

"How long did you go into foster care for?"

"Not long." I don't like to talk about my time at Grampton House. "It was supposed to be temporary, but my dad got worse, and social services knew we ... I ... couldn't go back home. Then my mom died ... and so I got put up for adoption."

"Brad." The tenor of her voice is soft and caring, her

fingers flutter over my chest. Her touch grounds me even as my past flows into my present in waves heavy as tar.

"I'm so sorry." She kisses my chest, then hugs me tightly. Her touch sets me aflame, and as her hand skates over my bare skin, I wonder if she can hear my beating heart.

Falling for Kyra is like being hit by a car, I didn't know until it was too late. My mind was elsewhere, on a goal I thought I wanted, while she rammed into me with her goodness, sexiness and faith. How am I supposed to walk away from this? She is no fickle, shallow, malicious Jessica. "Like I said, my adoptive parents were the best. I never went hungry again."

"Hungry?" Her eyes fill with horror. Now is not the time to tell her that I rummaged through trash cans to feed us.

"Yvette's boy, he reminds me of ..." I can't say his name. Each time I think about him, I think of Kane. I dream about Kane. I have nightmares about Kane. The memories weigh me down, a heavy anchor chaining my soul.

"Of you?" Kyra offers.

"What's his name?" He's been 'The Boy' to me forever. Maybe if I take the time to remember his name, I can erase the parts I want to forget.

"Stefan," Kyra replies. "You didn't know?"

I let the name sink in, repeating it silently in my head. I shake my head. I might have been told but I've forced myself to pay no attention. Details like that do me no good.

She presses a hand into my chest. "I always wondered why you were so subdued on those nights."

"I don't like talking about that time." I really don't. And if I'd known that this pathetic little project of mine would lead me down the path of my past and stir up memories I had long buried, I might not have chosen to pursue it.

But it's too late now. I've met this wonderful woman who

makes everything seem so much better, even when I didn't think my life needed to be better.

I'd come to believe that I had it all, but meeting her showed me how wrong I was.

This experiment hasn't failed—though maybe by Neville's standards it has—because what I've found instead has been priceless. No amount of money could buy what Kyra brings me.

"Do you want to go? Or stay?" I ask her. It's her choice. This is a big deal to me. I've changed her perception of me. In this weekend, I've tried to tell her things slowly, to prepare her, but maybe I've revealed too much, too fast.

I've brought her back to my place, but nothing has to happen unless she wants it.

"I want to stay."

"I want you to know that I was born into the kind of life the people we see every Wednesday were born into."

"It makes sense now," she says, softly.

"What does?" I lead her over to the sofas, feeling loose, and listless, and needing to sit down.

"Why you worked on those community projects. Why you went in search of something else."

My skin tightens, my throat turns dry, the contents of my stomach churn, and I am reminded of what a con artist I am. The type of man someone like Kyra doesn't deserve.

"You have such heart." She perches on my lap, her legs on either sides of my thighs as she presses her lips against mine. My heart bottoms out of my chest cavity. The lies and shame, the reality of the situation heats my skin. I turn hard, and harder still by her sitting on me, kissing me and staring at me with her eyes full of undeserved admiration.

"My heart isn't so good, so clean, so decent," I caution. She has a vision of me that is the complete opposite.

"You were twelve years old, and you'd had such a bad start, Brad." She presses her soft lips on mine, injecting hope and goodness in one fell swoop. "I'm so happy that you got adopted and were given a better life."

"Only because I resembled his dead son," I remind her.

She chews her lip. "Do you hate him?"

I had reason to hate him, right from the start when, a few months after I'd been adopted, I asked him when we could get my brother.

"You don't have a brother," he'd snarled, his voice chilling my blood and turning it to ice. "We have one son, Brandon. You don't have a brother. Do you understand? Never ask me again, or I will send you back."

His face blurred as tears welled in my eyes, threatening to spill over into rivulets of sorrow. I learned then to never show any emotion. I knew in that moment, that I had to forget my past, even if it meant forgetting the brother I loved more than life itself. I had to survive, and this was how I would.

So, to answer Kyra's question. Do I hate him? No. Not really. "People react to things in different ways. They do things which seem cruel and indifferent, and are inexplicable, but there's often a reason for it," I reply. "I love him, and my adoptive mom. They gave me a good life. I can't complain." Even though it came at a cost too heavy to bear.

She rests her forehead against mine, her hands bracketing my shoulders. I take all the goodness that seeps out of her and I absorb it, because I need something good to hold onto.

"We don't have to talk about this if you don't want to."

Talking isn't what I have on my mind right now.

KYRA

. . .

He is the best thing to happen to me. The worst thing he could have told me was that he was with someone. Instead, the truth I learned about Brad and his life, makes my heart ache.

He's showing me who he really is, and the shock I felt walking into this place, the fear of deception and lies which riddled my initial reaction, are gone.

Brad has had such a terrible childhood. The pain in his eyes rips me to shreds. When I think back, to all the unanswered questions, and his vague replies, they all make sense now.

"You're just a little rebel, after all," I say, resting my palm against his face. His brows push together. His member pushes through and I can feel him against my flimsy dress. I wriggle, shifting on his lap, teasing him. "Working on those projects abroad. Was that you wanting to reject your upbringing?"

His mouth twists, he seems unsure. Hesitant to reply. I lean forward and drape my arms around his neck. I take a deep inhale of him, soaking in his essence, and everything he is. He opened his heart to me and told me everything. I want to share myself with him, and tonight there is nothing in the way. We have privacy here. Not a car, or the storeroom, but an entire apartment.

I unbutton his shirt, one button at a time, the heat in my body traverses up from between my legs, through my stomach, to my breasts, making my face flush. I lean forward, like a woman desperate to please, and kiss him for the longest time, as if that might help to make his pain go away,

"There's so much I want to tell you," he murmurs as our wet lips brush and our breaths mingle. My body is slowly catching fire, heat spiraling and tunneling deep in my core.

"Tell me," I whisper. "Tell me all." I'm prepared to listen, even while I'm in a heightened sense of arousal, but then his tongue slips into my mouth and he drops his hand to my breast, massaging it.

In no time at all, he's undone the top buttons of my dress, his deft fingers making easy work of the tiny buttons and loops. He's so fast, the dress falls off my shoulders and in no time at all he's unclasped my bra. It falls to my waist, along with the top part of the dress. He growls as he sucks, taking big, greedy mouthfuls of my breasts.

My nerves tingle with anticipation, causing my heart to dance out of my ribcage. It falls somewhere between my legs, the thumping and throbbing like a drumbeat signalling a mating call.

I cry out in surprise when he stands up with me hanging onto him like a limp doll, my legs hooked around his waist. But he sets me down, then turns me around, so that my back presses into his hardness. Before I can catch a breath, he pulls my dress down, over my hips. I barely register that the soft fabric is around my ankles when his lips trail around my lower back. His fingers make light work of my panties which also end up around my ankles.

I shiver with excitement, my knees in danger of buckling, as wanton heat courses through me. He lifts my leg, planting my foot onto the couch, his hand falling between my legs, and his fingers teasing, playing, stroking. Pleasure pumps through me as he licks the skin between my shoulder blades. His tattoo fetish makes my lips curl, and then he steps away. It's only when his hard as steel erection pokes me from behind, that I realize he's completely naked. He slides, and slips and teases his cock around my back, as his fingers grab my breasts and pinch my nipples. My heart bottoms out when he tells me he loves my body, and that he loves my tattoos, and then he tells me exactly what he wants to do to me. How hard he wants to fuck me.

"Then do it." It's a voice I don't recognize as mine. I am possessed by a need so feral, a desire so base that I can barely control my mouth.

He pokes his hot, hard member between my cheeks, making me instinctively push back, needing him inside me, but he moves it away each time I try.

We are a tangle of roaming hands, soaked desire, greedy lust. Searching, prodding, stroking; all the things we so desperately wanted to do before but never had the privacy or permission to fully do. Desperate, I reach back and grasp him, then gasp as his length and girth shock me.

"Fuck," he groans as I stroke him softly, then he turns me around and guides me onto the couch.

I lie, legs akimbo, watching him fiddle with a condom. I study his wide shoulders, all the more for me to hold onto, then I stare like a two-bit hussy at his engorged cock, all the more to pleasure me with.

"Here?" I express surprise, because I want a whole bed to romp around with him on. I want to fall into bed with him and never leave. His gaze travels south, rests on the wet space between my legs. He bites his lower lip, lust pooling in his eyes as his gaze soaks in every inch of my heated skin. I lift a leg, carelessly, shamelessly resting it against the backrest, opening for him.

"Fuck," he pants.

I can wait no longer, frustration wars with desperation as our greedy eyes lock and hold.

My insides knot up in a tangled ball of frenzy, the longer he stands there, licking his lower lip, eyeing me as if he's unsure, the more I burn for him.

And then a thought, as random as a stray bullet slices

through me. Doesn't he want me? Anxiety slays my chest and, open and vulnerable like this, naked and ready, I start to doubt. But then he leans forward, a smile spreading on his lips, and I close my eyes, waiting, waiting, waiting. Instead he heaves me up by the wrists, lifting me easily. I'm feather light as he carries me, up the stairs. I nestle my face in the crook of his neck inhaling his scent.

He pushes a door open, then uses my body to shut it. I slide down him and over his shoulder see the biggest bed I have ever set my eyes on. He sucks my lower lip, before his tongue sweeps inside my mouth, the promise inherent in the way he claims me. We kiss as if this is the first and last time. I press against him, my hands clawing at his buttocks. I'm wild with need, hungry for him, and irritated by his dogged refusal to do the deed.

He has an effect on me. He always has, and tonight is the culmination of all our wanton lust for one another. I don't think I can last any longer.

My hands cup his face, as our lips refuse to part, and somehow, we move towards the bed. I fall and sink into the downy cover. Softness caresses my back and Brad's hard, tense, corded body rests over mine, his weight shifting to his arms as he props himself up.

Before I can open my mouth to say something, he slams inside me. I cry out, in gratitude, in euphoria. He slams into me again and again. My muscles clenching around him, and my entire body rocking with each thrust.

"Fuck," he grunts, thrusting his tongue deep inside my mouth, connecting to me on every level as he buries his hardness to the fullest. He groans, it sounds like a release, a long, slow, much needed release. "Fuck, Kyra."

My fingers sink into the fabric, butterflies skittering inside my belly like they're on a high. I barely catch my breath as he sets up a rhythm, hard and fast, hard and fast. I curse when his fingers find my nub and tweak and play.

So much lingering, simmering passion seeps out and mixes in the hot musty air. It's the most beautiful feeling, Brad rutting into me like a battering ram. It's too much. Too much feeling, too many nerve endings on fire. Too much, in one small place. I'm about to explode.

Up, up, up I float, rising to a peak, balancing on a precipice, as if I'm at the top of a rollercoaster before it dives down. Just as I'm about to plummet, he flips me over, then pulls me back on my knees. I take the hint and get on all fours, as his hands bracket my hips. It's only a few seconds rest that I get, before he slams into me, the force shoving my face into the bed. Carnal instinct crashes over us. We lose ourselves, become feral, like animals. He rides me hard, hard, hard, before plunging in for the last time and staying there. We come apart at the same time.

We have sex three times that night. Hard, rough, glorious sex. Not just in the bed, but on his chaise lounge, up against the shower, on the bathroom floor.

He falls asleep before me, in the dimly lit room, with only the light from outside barely illuminating the contours of his face, I trace my finger ever so gingerly across his cheek. It barely touches his skin, because I don't want to wake this beautiful, tender, complex man who has hidden so much pain from me. At last I have met a man who cherishes me and treats me well. *Really well.*

A man who is obviously hurt and is beginning to open up to me about his pain. I always gravitate towards people who are in pain. This wasn't supposed to happen, but now that it has, I have no regrets.

I fight the urge to kiss his chest. I want to heal him, and my heart swells with love to think that he has revealed his real self to me at last. He moans something in his sleep. It sounds like 'rain'. I turn to him, holding my breath, waiting for more. But he's quiet then, so I let him sleep.

In the morning, I wake up in his arms, sore, but sated and in no mood to want to go to work. I try to drag myself away from him, but he reels me in and then makes love to me again. This time it's slow, and gentle, our eyes lock together, our souls melded, as we move like one.

CHAPTER FORTY-FIVE

KYRA

Simona has returned to work after her week off, and I tell her and Fredrich that Brad is busy this week and won't be coming in.

"Busy doing what?" Fredrich asks suspiciously.

"You can ask him when he gets back," I reply. It's not my place to tell her about what he does on those days, or to reveal about the new insights I've had into his life.

"How is it that we still don't know what he does on his days off?" Fredrich persists.

He has a point, and I have been wondering why Brad has been so vague about his start-up in the first place. It's not like it's something to be ashamed of. It's strange that even now that I have some answers, I'm still in the dark about other things. Just when I think I know enough about this man, there are always more questions.

But because he is slowly opening up to me, my doubts are

slipping away. What I can't stop thinking about are the unforgettable few days we've just spent together.

I change the conversation back to Simona's vacation and her birthday celebration, and Simona is happy to tell us all about it. She looks all the better for it. I want to take her out for a meal, just a few of us, Fredrich and me, and hopefully Brad can make it. Somewhere nice. "Can we borrow you for one evening? We'd like to take you out for dinner."

She seems genuinely surprised, and tries to dismiss it with a, "You don't have to do that." She doesn't like being made a fuss of, but she is a prized member of my team, and this milestone birthday deserves to be properly celebrated.

"We want to," I insist.

"You *are* sixty-five," Fredrich winks. "That kind of age needs a good amount of recognition."

She raises her eyebrow in consternation. "Stop it, young man."

"Give us a date, Simona. Just one evening." She has a large family and I'm aware that her celebrations are ongoing.

"I'm free all week. Whatever suits you."

I look at the invitation in front of me. Jessica Montrose Art Gallery. That vacuous monster I met at city hall has sent me some complimentary tickets to an exhibition there.

"Can you make it on Thursday?" I ask, fingers crossed.

"Thursday is good."

"Good with me too." Fredrich gives me a thumbs up.

"Thursday then. We'll have dinner at eight."

A visit to the art gallery, which we'll spring on her at the last minute, followed by dinner at a very nice restaurant. I think Simona would appreciate that.

Brad calls me later that night to say he can't make it to the food night because he's tied up in heavy meetings from Tuesday through to Thursday.

"I wasn't expecting you to make the food night."

"I was going to try."

He does make an effort to turn up to those. The transformation has been amazing because I recall how uncomfortable he was the first time he came. "Good luck with your negotiations."

"Thank you."

"We've booked Simona's birthday dinner at eight on Thursday, so hopefully you can make it to that."

"At eight? Uh …" He hesitates. "I'm going to do my best to get out early, but I don't want to make promises I can't keep."

I respect that. "See what you can do. Even if you just pass by later and can only have coffee with us at the end." There's no point in telling him about the art gallery invite if he's not even sure he can make it to dinner. A smile curls on my lips. Even though I left his place only this morning, I'm missing him already and can't wait to see him again.

He suddenly becomes quiet. "I'll be out of state, on business."

"Oh. I didn't realize that." *Out of state?* I was under the impression that his business dealings were all local. Now I discover something else I assumed about him that isn't true. I'm tempted to ask him where, but I can sense he's somewhat uneasy.

"I want to come, Kyra. I'll try, because I really want to see you again. I'd love to be there for Simona's celebration but there's a good chance I won't be able to get away any sooner."

"That's a shame. Never mind. We'll take Simona out another time, just you and me."

"We can definitely do that," he says, and like a soppy romantic fool, I believe him.

CHAPTER FORTY-SIX

KYRA

The cab drops us off at another upscale part of the city. The art gallery is somewhere around here. I've told Fredrich because I know I needed to prepare him. Art galleries are not his thing. They're not mine either, but we're doing this for Simona. She appreciates culture in a way Fredrich and I don't.

I wonder if Brad would have liked to come here. There are so many things I don't know about him. He's like a closed book which I have opened onto the first page and am only just getting to familiarize myself with.

I look at the door numbers as we walk along the street. I'm not familiar with this part of town, but it's exactly the type of place I would expect someone like that woman to have an art gallery.

How does someone like her know someone like Eli?

I shiver and hope she doesn't put her claws into me like she did at the city hall event.

"Isn't it a bit early for us to come here?" Simona asks. "You said the dinner reservation was for eight."

Fredrich and I exchange sly glances.

"We're not going to dinner just yet," I announce.

Simona's stare indicates wariness. "Where are you taking me?" she asks, her face wearing a mask of dread.

"You're going to like this." Fredrich hooks his arm in hers. They look a sight, him the great big giant, and she the slim and slight elderly woman.

We happen to be passing a beautifully made-up shop front just then, and I tell them to stand while I snap a picture. "For memories," I tell her.

They stand, with the shop window behind them and I take a picture. Then I get them to pose with traffic lights in the distance; this will be a timeless image, I think. Just as I finish taking a few shots, I see a man climb out of a car behind them in the distance. He looks so much like Brad that I do a double-take.

"Let's get one of the three of us," Simona says.

"Kyra?" Fredrich touches my arm as I stare into the distance. "A pic of the three of us."

I stand alongside them, and we all huddle together so that we can get into the shot. Fredrich takes the picture because he has the longest arms and can hold it at a distance so that we all get in the shot.

"Nice," he murmurs, taking a good look at the picture he's just taken, but I'm slow to react, and my attention is more on the guy behind them in the distance.

Simona laughs. "That is a nice picture." But my eyes are riveted on the man who has his back turned and is on the phone. It can't be him. He told me he was away on business. We continue walking towards him, and though he is still some distance away, the similarity is there.

Shock jolts my heart out of my chest. He's dressed in a sharp suit. It looks expensive.

It is him.

Given what I know about him, I'm not shocked at what he's wearing, I'm just shocked to see him at all.

Simona hooks her other arm in mine. "Where did we lose you?"

"Huh?" I force myself to glance at her as we get nearer.

"You're miles away," she replies.

"Is that Brad?" Fredrich asks, looking straight ahead at the man who is now walking into one of the buildings.

"Brad? What? Where?" Simona sounds excited.

"Holy shit!" Fredrich circles the car like a hungry wolf, his eyes twinkling with admiration. "A Tesla. Freakin' awesome."

I try to school my breathing. I'm so crazy about him. So swept up in the heat and sweat of our lovemaking that I can't think straight. I see him everywhere because he is imprinted on every inch of my skin, in every part of my mind.

Shock slams into me like a fifty-ton truck. Nausea makes me falter and sway, as if I've had three cocktails too many. I stare at the Tesla, but I can't be sure I saw him walk away from this. Brad drives an old Toyota Corolla but lives in the Water Tower Building. A Tesla is more like the type of car I'd expect him to drive. Why did he turn up on my doorstep driving a banged up old car, and why did he want to work at Redhill?

He told me he was out of state on business. He told me he wasn't sure that he'd be able to meet us for dinner at eight.

These new lies are more than I can handle. I stop to take a breath.

"What's wrong? Are you feeling sick?" Simona asks as I

lean against a wall because my legs are so shaky I feel as if they're going to buckle.

"What's up?" Fredrich is still ogling the Tesla and looks over at us.

I force myself to pull it together. Determined not to ruin this evening for Simona, I push off the wall. "I'm feeling a bit queasy. It must be something I ate. It's fine. I'll be fine." I hook my arm in Simona's and walk on with determination. Fredrich rushes to catch up with us.

"This is it," I say, stopping outside the art gallery.

Dark windows display a couple of abstract paintings and the gold engraved lettering says:

Jessica Montrose Art Gallery

"Jessica Montrose?" Simona wrinkles her nose as if she remembers. Fredrich enlightens her. "It's that woman from Eli's city hall event, the one who clung to Kyra like a barnacle to a boat."

"A barnacle to a boat?" says Simona, with a little giggle. Simona's face lightens up. "I love artwork, and this is so thoughtful of you both."

I shrug. "She sent invitations. Champagne and canapes and art. We thought you might like it."

She touches my cheek, and gives it a little pull, as if I am one of her young grandkids. "I already love it."

"Good, because we're going to indulge ourselves in here and then we'll go to dinner," I tell her.

"You're spoiling me," she says, looking like an excited child as I open the door for her to go in.

The moment we walk inside, we are greeted with glasses of champagne.

"Got any beer?" Fredrich asks.

Simona looks around in delight. "I've never been here."

"No?" I ask, looking around for the Brad lookalike. I want to see him so that I can convince myself that it's someone else. So that I can set my heart to rest.

"This is disgusting stuff." Fredrich makes a face as he sips his beer.

"Try the champagne," Simona says. "It's divine."

Fredrich sidles up to me. "How do we do this? Do we just look around?" But my gaze is pinned on a tall brunette woman. And then I see Brad. At least I think it's Brad.

It's Brad looking...different. Brad with Jessica hanging onto his arm for dear life. Jessica, introducing him to people. Jessica staring up at him as if he's been in bed with her all weekend instead of me.

My heart splinters on its downward spiral, and the cold, hard truth laughs back at me. This is the man I spent the weekend falling in love with.

Fredrich splutters. "That *is* Brad," he roars. "You said he couldn't make it." He looks at me accusingly.

"That's what he told me."

"He must have a twin," Fredrich counters. "For all we know, he could have, because we don't know anything about the guy." For a nano-second, I entertain the idea. Until recently, I knew nothing about Brad. He was a mystery to me, but ever since our weekend, ever since he showed me his condo and opened his heart to me, I've seen the other side to him.

The man I told never to cheat on me because my heart had already been broken by it.

I suddenly waver. The floor beneath me seems to tilt and

my heart hits the ground, a few seconds after my insides empty.

Him and Jessica Montrose. As if a montage flows before my eyes, I recall city hall and that woman sticking by my side wanting to know things.

And yet, it doesn't make sense.

None of it.

We stare across the floor at him with Jessica who holds a group of men, Brad included, captivated.

There is no denying those eyes, that jaw, those lips.

It's him.

As if he can sense us staring and talking about him, he looks up, and his smooth unlined face suddenly drains of color. There can't be more than a few yards between us. I see his features clearly, while my heart hammers and my breath catches in my dry-as-sand throat.

Brad's gaze locks and battles with mine.

"What's he doing with her?" Simona asks, sounding as shocked as I feel broken.

I can't pretend I haven't seen him.

I need to hear it from his mouth.

I need to know.

There's only an arm's length of distance between us. I stare at him in disbelief. In the picosecond of time which flashes and disappears, I realize that so much of my time with this man has been made up of so many moments of disbelief.

"What are you doing?" Simona cries as I walk towards them. Brad stares at me, pain and confusion are etched in his somber eyes.

Jessica holds onto Brad possessively. "Kyra, how lovely of you to come." Her face lights up as if I've given her a check for twenty million dollars. The smile is plastic. "Brandon, you've met Kyra before, haven't you?"

Brandon?

He can't speak and this gives me a sliver of comfort. Time halts and freezes like a bitter chill, icing the blood in my veins. I sense Simona and Fredrich at my side as the other men in the group discreetly disappear.

"Dude, fancy meeting you here," Fredrich says, breaking the icy mood. "I didn't think this was your kinda place. It's not mine either..."

Brad doesn't speak. No one does. Silence slam dunks into my net of despair. The moment is a dystopian nightmare flashing through my head like a torch over a grave of dead bodies.

He prepared me for this, so I shouldn't be surprised as my glance sweeps over his watch, a great big, vulgar gold thing, and cufflinks that glisten under the spotlights.

"This is a surprise. Kyra wasn't sure that you would be able to make it." Simona's voice is the only soft thing in this barbed-wire nightmare.

"I didn't know you all had plans to come here," he says, while acid boils in the vat that is my stomach.

"I bet you didn't," I bite back.

Jessica pipes up. She's obviously enjoying the show. "I sent them tickets. It was the least I could do after meeting you at Elias's party."

Brad tilts his head up and tries to dislodge his arm out of her Ironman grip. His eyes never leave mine. "I didn't want to raise your hopes. I was hoping to surprise you all at the restaurant later," he says, ignoring Jessica.

"You've certainly done that," Simona remarks. She has the same concerns as me—that Jessica and he are an item—although she doesn't know about me and Brad yet.

The lying, cheating snake.

He cheated on me.

Or maybe he cheated on her.

How could he do that to me, and after everything I've told him?

"Is that your car out there, dude?" Fredrich seems immune to the fragility hanging in the air.

"Yes." We're in a staring contest of sorts, and I refuse to look away. "How could you ..." The words fall from my lips before I can stop myself.

Jessica laughs.

What the hell is she laughing about?

Simona's hand on my arm reminds me to stay calm and steady, and from the periphery of my vision, I can see Fredrich staring at me.

"I can explain, Kyra," Brad says.

"This will be good." Jessica has a nasally voice which now grates on my already frayed nerves like a knife on a blackboard.

None of this makes sense. None of it.

"Did she just call you *Brandon*?" Fredrich says. He looks at me as if he's thinking the same thing: that we know nothing about this man who seems to lead a double life.

"Is that your name, Brad?" Simona asks.

I glare at Jessica. "Is that why you clung to me like a leech over at city hall?"

"I was curious to see what you were like," she replies.

"Why?" Before she can reply, Brad positions himself in front of her, so that he's in my face, blocking out everything else. I step back, before the familiar mint and pine scent of him lowers my defenses.

"I can explain," he starts to say, but I take a step back, otherwise my fist might be tempted to punch him in the stomach. A slow wave of dullness floods my senses, deadening those sharp and pointy emotions that sliced through me when

I first saw him with that woman. It takes me back to the moment when I came home early, because I'd forgotten my phone, and I found my then boyfriend with a woman wrapped around him.

Now, like then, a man has upended my entire world. "Why is she calling you Brandon?" I ask. He never told me Brad was short for Brandon. It's not such a big deal in the general scheme of things.

"Because that's my name."

"Brad, Brandon, what's the difference?" Jessica says.

"Brandon who?" A mist is clearing in the deep recesses of my brain, and I am beginning to see things a little more clearly now.

"Brandon Hawks," Jessica offers. "Didn't you know?"

"Stay out of it." He throws her a stare that would have turned a lesser person to stone. Just watching him reacting to her makes me see another side to him. "I can explain," he says to me. "But not here. Somewhere else, just you and me."

"Who's Hartley?" I ask, as shockwave rolls over shockwave. The Tesla, the watch, him here, with Jessica, as if that isn't enough for me to absorb, I am now even more curious about the name change.

"How about a ride in the car, dude?" Fredrich asks, completely enamored by the Tesla and blinded to the thick veil of duplicity I find myself wrapped up in.

"Another time," Brad answers, his eyes still boring into mine. Jessica places a protective, territorial hand on his arm, and he flinches in irritation, shrugging her arm off, as easily as if he had swatted a fly. "Please, Kyra. Let's go someplace and talk." His voice is low, persuasive, almost seductive, and I'm back at the ancient baths again, or sitting in that expensive restaurant, letting him wine and dine me in naïve ignorance.

"I have nothing to say to you," I hiss under my breath. "You cheating, lying, disgusting piece of--"

"I'm not cheating on you."

"You don't need to do this here, Kyra." Simona's is the voice of reason.

Fredrich's silence informs me that he's finally understood the gravity of the situation.

That he's finally understood something that Simona knew way before. About me and Brad. Or Brandon. Whoever he is.

"He's not cheating on you," Jessica says, "he's after your—"

"I swear to you." He turns to Jessica and one look is all it takes to shut her up.

A photographer rushes past snapping pictures, and I become aware that we are the centerpiece in the middle of the room, and people are watching.

"Let's go." Simona takes my arm and gently leads me away. People part as we make our way. My mind is a riot of disarray.

Outside, I can finally breathe. I'm not the same woman who walked in here what seemed like hours ago.

"That was interesting," remarks Simona.

Fredrich looks at me.

I lean against the wall, needing something to hold me up. "He lied to me. He told me he couldn't come to dinner. And here he is with her." Another man cheating on me. For what? Why would he want me when he can have someone like her? That's the thing that doesn't make sense to me.

"Brandon Hawks," says Fredrich, reading from his cell phone, "thirty-two-year-old son of billionaire Philip Hawks, the man who founded Hawks Enterprises back in the '80s."

"Billionaire?" Simona's eyebrows shoot north.

"He lied about everything." Fredrich kicks the wall. He waggles a finger at me. "You were right about him."

"I can see you're upset," Simona says, putting her arm on mine. Understanding shines in her eyes. "But I don't think he's with her."

I let out a shaky breath. "Shall we ... shall we walk around for a while? Or I could call the restaurant and try to bring the reservation forward," I suggest, even though I have lost my appetite.

Simona shakes her head. "We'll do nothing of the sort. This has put a dampener on the evening."

"Not for me," I say, not wanting to ruin her evening even though I want to go home and cry my heart out.

"I'm not hungry," Fredrich announces.

"Can we rebook for another day? Please?" Simona begs, more for me than for herself.

I'm relieved that she has made the suggestion.

BRANDON

"What the hell were you thinking?" I hiss at Jessica. I should have known better. Should have known there was a reason for her wanting me here tonight.

The snide, sly vixen wanted to get her revenge on me.

"Why didn't you tell her?" Jessica squawks as Kyra walks away from me. The hurt in her eyes cut deep into me. The entire time I couldn't look away, I needed to tell her, but there are things I need to explain first. "Why not, Brandon?" This vulture I once trusted has stabbed me in the back with a scythe.

"You're not the one who decides when," I snarl. I was going to tell Kyra in my own time, not here, not now. But I hadn't bargained on just how evil Jessica is. "This is what you wanted, isn't it?" I glance around and people immediately look away, avoiding eye contact.

Now that Kyra has left, the show is over. People return to their conversations. The photographer snaps another photo. "Tell him to get the fuck away, before I take that camera and shove it up his ass."

"No photos." Jessica cackles, no doubt she finds this entire episode highly amusing.

I've crushed Kyra. I took everything we had and put a fire to it. I have to find a way to win her back. Jessica remains glued to my side and I force myself to stay calm. "You are a nasty piece of work. I must have lost my mind to ever be interested in you."

My words, and my tone, have hit home. Her brows contort. The realization dawns. "Are you ..." Her bright red lips turn into the perfect 'O'. "Are you *sleeping* with *her*?"

My jaw tightens. I hate the way this evening turned out. I made it a point to finish up my meetings as soon as I could. I flew back early, determined to do my final part for Jessica, to cut my ties with her clean. Then I had plans to meet Kyra at the restaurant for dinner. It was supposed to be a surprise.

Jessica saw to it that it was something else.

I've messed things up with Kyra, and now I have to put them right. I walk out without saying another word, but I fear the damage has been done. I didn't cheat on her. I didn't do what her ex did. What I did was a million times worse.

CHAPTER FORTY-SEVEN

KYRA

At home I curl up on the couch in tears. Silent tears fall; the tears of someone who has no fight left in her, no fight for a heart that cannot be fixed because it is so irreparably broken.

I hear another ping on my phone, and see that it's another text from him. I turn my phone off.

The evening has been surreal. I no longer know what is real and what are lies.

I don't know where Brad ends and Brandon starts.

He cheated is all I know.

I feel bad that the evening is all messed up and what should have been a great night out for Simona has been turned into the worst night of my life.

We'll have to have a do-over for her birthday at another time because I refuse to let this man's trickery affect us.

As I lie, like a fetus, cocooned in my misery, I try to work out why Brad would lie about his name, and it makes me think about the many other lies he's fed to me, to us, to Redhill, ever since he joined.

Why did he join? Why did the son of a billionaire join my company? To achieve what?

And then I sit up.

Could it have been anything to do with Greenways? After all, he was the one who suggested we relocate.

Until recently. But now he seems to want me to stay. He's been telling me to trust my instinct and to not listen to him.

I lie back down, because my mind can't work around the implausibility of this idea.

I prefer to believe that Brad was the dreamer and idealist who went abroad and helped with the building projects of impoverished communities.

I wish I could erase all thoughts about our weekend. I wish I could rub away the scent and feel of him. I wish it weren't so recent. I wish time would pass fast, fast, fast, and I could fast forward a whole year.

I get up to draw my blinds when I hear a knock at the door. When I look through the keyhole, it's Brad's face I see.

Hate rises from my belly. "Go away," is the only childish comment I come up with.

"We need to talk, Kyra."

"I don't want to talk."

"You need to hear what I have to say."

"I don't need to do anything."

"Jessica did that on purpose." He knocks again.

"She's a hero in my books."

"You don't mean that. The woman's a vicious little—" He refrains from saying what he really thinks. "Please let me in."

"Why?" I ask.

"Do you want me to have this conversation through the door?"

With hate in my heart, I open the door and let him in. I don't ask him to sit down, and we hover around the door.

"I'm sorry about what—"

"I'm not." I interrupt, not wanting to hear more lies. "How much longer were you going to lie to me for?"

"I kept meaning to tell you."

"So, why didn't you?"

He looks the most somber I have ever seen him. "It just never seemed like the right time."

"But you lied to me. You've lied all along, and about so many things, about who you are, about what you do. How do you do something like this and live with yourself?"

"I'm not a cheat. I haven't cheated on you, Kyra."

"You've cheated on her then. I'm surprised she didn't slap you."

"She and I have a ..." He pauses to think and his hesitation puts me on alert.

"A great relationship." I finish the sentence for him. "She's more your type than I am. She's exactly the type of person I see you with."

"She's not. She's a nasty, nasty piece of work."

"You two sound perfect for one another."

His Adam's apple bobs and he seems slightly anxious. "I made a mistake. I didn't know what I know now."

"And what's that?" I shoot back. Each moment he stays here makes me hate him more because all I see is the lies woven through each and every interaction I've ever had with him.

"That I was so wrong, about so many things."

I don't want to hear his sob story. I don't want to hear about the poor little boy who had such a hard life getting adopted by a rich man. Unable to control my rage I jab a finger in his chest. "What I want to know is what you, the son of a supposed billionaire, are doing at Redhill?"

BRANDON

This is my only chance to tell her. Jessica has forced my hand and it might have been the push I needed. Goodness knows I've had many chances, but I've been too scared to reveal to her my real self.

It makes me ashamed to say it out now. It's the same shame that Emma must have felt when I first told her of my crazy idea to infiltrate Redhill.

"Jessica and I have never been romantically involved. Never." I'm grateful things progressed so slowly that we never even made it to first base, but this isn't the time to confess to Kyra that I had my eyes on that evil witch as a potential wife.

How I have changed. The other me couldn't see past the dollar signs. Kyra saved me, and I owe her the truth. I owe her everything. "I lied to you about a lot of things. I stole into your company because I wanted to try something."

Her head tilts, she stills, her eyes widening as she waits. "Try what?"

I have her complete and utter attention. "I wanted Greenways. It's pricey real estate and it's going to be worth a fortune in years to come."

She moves her head to the center as if things are falling into place and the great mystery is getting unraveled.

"We'd watched as property development companies sought to buy the land from you. You and others on

Greenways weren't interested. Our people on the ground told us that some businesses were considering moving, but that a young and impassioned activist, the Katniss Everdeen of Greenways, didn't want to give in. She had seen that this area was beginning to have better infrastructure and it was slowly being transformed. You convinced people to stay. We watched as companies came and went, each offering you good money, but you held firm. The other business owners looked up to you, they listened to you. To make matters worse, the media loved you. You were a rising star in the city, like Cardoza. Wanting to do good. How could any company go up against you and win? I mean, sure we could *win*. God knows corrupt government officials are easy to find and cultivate. But the people of this city love you. You wouldn't go without a fight, and I couldn't afford to have the stain of removing you hanging over my company. We stood to make millions from Greenways, and I didn't want or need the bad publicity which would follow if people found out that we had underhandedly removed you."

"So, you thought you'd seduce me, and charm me, and convince me to move, and you almost did." Her face crumples like paper. "You worked on me." Anger firebombs in her eyes. "You bastard."

"I never meant to seduce you. I fell in love with you, Kyra. That part was real."

Her mouth twists together, she glares at me as if I'm the devil. "You set out to deceive me."

"Maybe—"

"Maybe?" she cries. "Listen to yourself. You're trying to tell me the truth but you still can't confront and accept it."

I clasp my hands, perplexed and frustrated. I've never been in this position before. I've never had to explain my actions, or apologize for them. "My whole aim was to get you to listen to me and to heed my advice. It was selfish and greedy and evil of me, but that's the truth, Kyra. The rest of it, me falling for you, is another truth. It never even occurred to me that anything like that could happen."

"You're reprehensible. A monster. An evil, disgusting, repugnant monster. You preyed on me."

I stride towards her and grab her hands because she needs to know that that part of it wasn't made up. "I didn't think we would end up together. We're so different, or so I thought."

"We're not together. Not now."

I try to plead with her. "You're angry and upset, and you have every right to be. We started off hating one another—"

"I hate you now." Her mouth sets in a hard line. I'm not explaining myself well. She's trying to break my hand-lock but I won't let her because I need her to listen but with a heroic burst of strength, she wrestles her hands away from my hold.

"I fell for it," she snarls. "I started to trust you, and listen to you. Fredrich didn't understand why I was changing my mind and considering moving." She rubs her hands over her face, anguish pouring out of her. "How can you do this and look at yourself in the mirror?"

"You're not listening. I started to fall in love with you, Kyra,"

"Don't use that word. It's not love. What you did was trick me."

She's got it all wrong. If there is a major falsehood, it is this. "I changed my mind. I knew I couldn't go through with it."

Rage stomps through her eyes as she pieces it all together; all the bits that once didn't make any sense. "All this time you were making suggestions and criticizing our food event on the night of the fight, and you made me think I was stupid when I told you about my idea for the small business units. And your gripes and moans about the buckets and the leaky roof."

"I saved your life."

She blinks and mimics a damsel in distress. "Oh, yes, you saved me." Her hands fly to her chest in a theatrical manner.

"I know that what I did was wrong, Kyra. To think that I could infiltrate your company and somehow persuade you to move."

"It was morally wrong and completely stupid. 'The' Brandon Hawks—not Brad Hartley the traveler who worked on community projects—but a billionaire's son infiltrating Redhill." She scoffs in disgust.

Guilt grips my insides with its pincers and squeezes hard. "I was hiding from who I used to be. I wanted the old me gone. I reinvented myself. With a billionaire for a father, it's easy enough to do. So, you see, nobody knew me. Though that might change now with that fucking photographer Jessica hired." I shake my head in disgust. She has left no stone unturned. Her scheming, manipulative mind had it all planned out.

"You used me." She steps forward and stabs me in the chest with a bony finger. "You used me."

I blink, because my vocal chords fail. Her face twists as sure as if I've skewered her with a screwdriver, the pain of my words cutting her deeply. I want to put my arms around her and tell her that I'm sorry. I want to tell her that I made a mistake, that I could see that the work she did was good, and needed, and only a corporate machine would run over her dreams and raze them to the ground. But I have never seen so much anger in her before and I'm scared that any move on my part will make things worse. "Kyra, listen to me—"

"No! I've listened enough. I want you to get out of my life and never come back. You used me for your own selfish gain. For your greed. You stand for everything I despise."

"I'm a changed man."

"You're the same old snake to me." Her body sags with the weight of my deception. A moment passes, she looks away, wrapped in her own personal pain. "Was any of it real?"

I reach out, wanting to touch her face to comfort her, to show her that this is me now. What I feel for her hasn't changed, and yes, it was real. These last few weeks, ever since Eli's fight, they have all been real.

But she moves away, a shiver of revulsion making her shoulders jolt. I step towards her. "The way I feel about you now is real. I'm crazy about you, Kyra. I might not have fallen in love with you right from the start but the more time I spent with you, the more I grew in awe of you. At the start I was too busy pushing back on your ideas because they reminded me of who I was and where I had come from, and I hated that. I've spent twenty years trying to forget that unwanted child and to make my world be one in which I will never be poor, or hungry, or unwanted and forgotten, but you started to show me the world through your eyes, Kyra. You made me start to care."

"Don't ..."

"It's true. I was wrong. I did a shitty thing. I lied and wheedled my way into Redhill for all the wrong reasons, but once there, working with you, going to those food nights, seeing the good work you do, the lives you transform, it made me see how wrong I was."

"When did you have this epiphany?" she bites out. "A few hours ago, when Jessica had the balls to reveal to the rest of the world who you really are?"

"I was going to tell you."

"When? In the helicopter? In the vat of grape juice? On the massage table? When? When did the lying ever stop?"

"What I did was so wrong, and so deceitful. It wasn't easy to just come out and say it."

"That's why you didn't come to city hall." She puts a hand to her brow, as if this is too much information to understand all at once. Where once she had looked at me with such adoring eyes, now she looks as if she wants to stab me.

"I couldn't."

"I understand now why you couldn't, because of Jessica."

"And other business associates I might have run into."

"And then your secret would have been out sooner, wouldn't it, *Brandon?*"

The muscles along my jaw tighten with every passing second. She's looking at me differently, as if the past weekend didn't happen.

"I don't want to hear any more," she says, sounding as if she's given up. "I can't take any more. Not tonight. Not ever."

"I want to explain," I plead, because this could be my only chance.

"And you have explained."

"Not everything."

"There's more?" she asks, her voice mocking.

I want to tell her who I was. I want her to know the real me even if it means peeling back the carefully constructed layers of wealth I have used to craft my new persona. I want this woman to be mine, because she is the only woman who has understood me, and I know now that it's because we are cut from the same cloth. She didn't have to rummage through trash cans to eat, but she has a heart, she has the type of heart and empathy I need to fix myself. To heal the hurt that broke me. I share more in common with her than I do with Philip Hawks.

"Who is Emma?"

"My PA."

"Of course. Your PA. Why didn't I think of that?" Her

words fall out like an enlightened sigh. "That makes sense now."

"And the reason why I rushed to her all the time was because I feel responsible."

She frowns. "For what?"

"She was driving to my office to pick up some contracts I'd asked her to deliver to my house on the night of Eli's fight. If I hadn't asked her, she wouldn't have had that accident."

"You can't know that."

"But it's true."

"No. You can't blame yourself for that." She folds her arms, her face still hard as she tries to make me feel better. I shake my head, because I don't want to have a pity party. I want Kyra to understand why I did what I did, I want her to hate me, and then to forgive me.

"You can blame yourself for this, though," she says. "*This* is the mess you've created and deliberately."

"I know, and I do. I feel awful. Emma hated the idea."

Kyra plops down on the sofa, hanging her head. This was my plan, I knew the pieces, but for someone like Kyra, the unsuspecting victim, I understand that the entire thing is a cold, hard shock.

"I'm falling in love with you, K—"

She stares up at me, her nostrils flaring, her eyes wild with a thousand accusations. "You can't possibly know the meaning of love. You don't have that emotion inside you otherwise you wouldn't have done what you did."

I try to think of something to say, of finding a way to get her to forgive me.

"Will you do something for me?" she asks, her brow creasing, her lower lip wavering.

"Anything." My heart leaps at the request. I will do anything. Anything.

"Leave. Never, ever return to Redhill again."

I open my mouth, because this is not an option.

"That's all I'm asking. Please." The plea in her eyes slices through me like a knife through warm butter.

"But—"

"It's the only thing I'm asking of you." Her eyes turn glassy.

She's asking me to do something I don't want to do.

I can't.

I've never met anyone like her before. I've never been able to open up to anyone before.

I *need* her.

"Can you do that for me?"

CHAPTER FORTY-EIGHT

KYRA

We don't talk about it back at work, and Fredrich and Simona know me well enough not to ask me any questions. I do what I do best. Push it all to the recesses of my brain in an attempt to deal with it later. I get busy. I plan ahead.

Brad telling me about his real intentions for coming to Redhill has forced me to look back on our time together. I've analyzed every little thing he said to me about the business, and it hurts, thinking about every moment with him hurts.

Simona senses that something is up. Fredrich too, judging by the number of times he's lifted his head and looked my way as if he's about to say something, and then looked away again.

"When is the next Greenways Committee meeting?" I ask, while hunting around my desk for my planner.

"They haven't given us a date yet." Simona eyes me over the rim of her teacup. "Why?"

"I'm just curious." I don't have the heart to tell them about what Brad did. Or, should I say, what *Brandon* did. How can I switch from Brad to Brandon? I won't need to. He's out of my life and I won't have to utter his name ever again.

And we will fight back. Whatever he had planned, however it was he wanted to get his dirty little paws on Greenways, it's not going to happen.

Fredrich sits back in his chair, arms crossed over the back of his head. "I was digging up information on Hawks Enterprises."

I type away on my keyboard. These pesky emails won't reply by themselves. "Yeah?" I pretend to busy myself in reading something.

"The guy is loaded. LOADED."

Simona sniffs. "I could see that. The car, the watch. He seemed like a different man. I don't understand why he came here, and why he lied about who he was."

They have the same confused look that I did when things didn't add up. It's been a shock to me, but at least I knew about the rich parents who adopted him. At least I'd seen his condo. I was prepared.

Simona and Fredrich weren't. This must be so confusing for them, as well as a cold hard shock.

"Do you think his was one of the companies which were interested in Greenways?" Fredrich asks.

I stop typing. "I'd put nothing past that man. Nothing." My words shotgun out, dipped in venom. They both stare at me in silence.

"Did I miss something?" Fredrich asks. "Something that happened while I was away nursing my poor little arm?"

Simona's gaze heats my cheeks. She's probably trying to figure out when it began. I couldn't tell her when, because I don't know myself. "We have to make sure we're at the next meeting," I say, before getting back to my typing.

"Why are you so bothered about the next meeting?" Fredrich asks. "Shouldn't we be trying to decide what to do about Simona's birthday dinner? She shouldn't have to suffer."

"Don't worry about me." Simona waves her hand dismissively.

"Fredrich's right. Of course we have to celebrate your birthday. We'll have to pick another date."

"There's no rush. You settle yourself first. Let's get things back to normal," she says.

Speaking of getting back to normal. "He won't be back," I announce. They stare at me dumbfounded. "Brad. He's not coming back."

"You mean Brandon," Fredrich clarifies.

"Whatever." I don't want to spend another moment thinking about that man. Not a second.

"I don't understand why—" Simona starts to speak, but falls silent. As it was with me, I now see the cogs of her brain trying to make sense of everything. Of why a billionaire's son would ever consider joining a company like Redhill, on the pretense of working for free to do some good.

The way she's looking at me, I can tell that she has questions, but thankfully, she won't ask me, which is just as well.

I suck in a deep breath. "I don't want to talk about what happened. I don't want to dwell on it. Brad's gone, and that's the end of it."

BRANDON

"She never wants to see me again."

Emma lets out a slow breath. She's walking around on crutches, listening to me tell my story of woe.

"I told you it wouldn't end well."

Yeah. She did. She never approved of any of this. She warned me, but I blazed on ahead the way I do when I have set my sights on something.

But it's not sympathy I want, or I-told-you-sos. It's the need to let it off my chest and to tell someone, so I'm at Emma's place. Kyra refuses to answer my calls or texts. She asked to be left alone, and as much as it pains me to do that, it will make her hate me even more if I don't comply.

What I did was wrong and dishonest. I didn't cheat on her, but I shouldn't, in all honesty, expect her to forgive and forget.

Without Emma in my professional life, and no Kyra in my life at all, I've reached a low point, someplace I never thought I would be. It's not hunger that is slowly killing me, it's not neglect, it's losing someone I had finally come to care about.

That's what's killing me.

"What will it take to have you come back to work for me? You can pick your hours. You can pick your salary. You can work as few or as many days as you want but I need you back, Emma, whenever you're good and ready."

Her eyes tell me all I need to know. "I don't want to come back, Brandon."

"I'm a changed man," I throw back, in case my morals are the things that are keeping her at bay. "I'm not going to be doing any more of that stuff. No more stepping over people in the name of making more money."

"You've finally realized that you have enough?" She stops

walking around, her hands on her crutches as she waits for my answer.

"I've learned a lot. I have plans going forward."

She groans, before slowly settling herself down into a chair. I rush over, but she shakes her head. "I've got this." When she has sat down, she leans the crutches against the armrest. "Plans? I don't have the stomach to hear your plans, Brandon."

"They're good plans. Things you'll be pleased about."

"I've been making plans, too," she announces.

"Oh?"

I can see it in her eyes. Her mind is made up and I'll never be able to convince her. She's not coming back. She's leaving me to fend for myself. I'll get by. If not with this temporary PA, then with another one, and another one, and another one, until I find someone like Emma.

It wasn't just for her professional skills, but her sense of right and wrong and also her common sense. She grounded me, and that's what I will miss.

Like I miss Kyra. She started to heal the hole in my heart —the one that leaving Kane left behind.

It's not too late.

I can fix things. I can find Kane. And I can win Kyra back.

CHAPTER FORTY-NINE

KYRA

The food night is yet another reminder of Brad. No, Brandon. I don't think I'll ever get used to that name.

It hasn't been easy. To forget him, or to forget what he did. I question everything I said and everything he told me and everything I believed. I question my weekend with him and I'm left wondering if I will ever trust a man completely again.

Trust is a huge issue for me, and Brad has smashed it into a million pieces.

We've missed the extra help, especially on food nights, but it's help we don't want, I tell myself. True to their word, neither Fredrich or Simona have mentioned him. But Stefan did. He asked where 'that guy' was. I told him that he had left.

The evening passes smoothly enough. I see that we are running low on some of the food items. Fredrich is slacking today. Usually, he'd be the first one to make sure everything was replenished. I look around but can't find him.

Walking back to the van to fetch the replacement containers, I see him. Talking to Brad.

Fury rises like a poisonous gas.

Why is he here? I told him to stay away. I asked him to do that one thing for me.

"Hey, look who showed up." Fredrich's tone tells me he's oblivious to everything. He's lacking a woman's instinct to pick up on things.

"We're out of pasta." I open the doors and start to look around for more containers of pasta. Behind me, I hear the two men whispering. Just as I'm about to turn around and glare at them, Fredrich taps me on the shoulder and announces that he will take over. "Brandon wants to talk to you."

The speed with which he's able to use a different name shocks me. "I don't want to talk to him."

"Just give the guy a chance," he pleads and picks up a food container, then leaves. I stare at Brandon defiantly, hating that he came here in a public space, where he knew I wouldn't be able to voice my hatred of him.

"I told you to stay away from me."

"You told me to stay away from Redhill."

Smart-ass. I want to slap that look of smug satisfaction off his face. My teeth clench together so tightly, I'm in danger of locking my jaw. I hate that he is here, in my face, staring at me as if he cares about me. That puppy dog look on his face doesn't fool me. What I see before me is the same cocky, arrogant guy who strolled in here on that first day, asking for a job.

"I've got nothing to say to you. Nothing. Oh, except this: You will never own so much as an inch of Greenways. We'll fight you. You can buy the best attorneys and have as many corrupt officials in your pocket as you see fit, but we'll stand up to you at every turn."

"I don't want it, Kyra. I don't want anything, but you."

A scream from the tables catches both our attention, and I run. But the smell of smoke in the air sends shivers up my spine. I look around frantically. Flames spiral out from the bottom of the factory floor.

"The factory's on fire!" I scream, running towards it.

"Noooooooooooooo!" Fredrich's voice behind me starts a chorus of people screaming and shouting. Cries of "Call the fire department!" chase me all the way to the factory.

Heat rolls up and through the air, making it harder to breathe.

A fire in the factory?

Our products. The supplies.

Our people. The blood in my veins freezes. Surely there's no one in there now? And then I remember Dayna. She usually works late. "Is anyone in there?" I scream, rushing towards the main door, my mind a riot of confusion.

"My kids!" Yvette's piercing scream cuts through the air and sears into my chest.

"What?" I yell. "Your kids are in there?"

She's a blubbering, stuttering mess. Shivering and shaking, she can't even get her words out. People have gathered around, a group of them, poised to go in, but the flames are licking out of the ground floor. "My kids!" Yvette cries, screaming again.

Simona's face wears a haunted look. "Someone said they went to the storeroom to fetch water bottles."

"Both of them?" Brad yells. Incredulity stretches across his features.

"Stefan and Holly, they went in together," someone else confirms.

In the heat and confusion of the moment, people are bringing blankets and pouring water onto the flames, as if that might help. We can't get to the fire extinguishers inside because we can't get into the building. Flames fan and lick around the entrance.

Yvette screams, and people panic and yell. Commotion fills the air with chaos. I throw a blanket around myself and rush towards the door, determined to get to the children. But someone pulls me back hard and pushes me into the crowd. Before I can say anything, Brad disappears in front of me, through the flames.

CHAPTER FIFTY

BRANDON

My arm hurts. I can't lift it. Everything hurts. My back and sides feel numb. But I can move my toes. At least it's something. It must mean that I'm not dead.

"You were injured in the fire. You have first, second and third degrees burns, and you're suffering the effects of smoke inhalation."

Something fell on it, something heavy. I didn't even feel the heat inside that furnace. Smoke, the smell, couldn't breathe, couldn't see, but I knew the kids were in there and I wasn't going to let them down.

I wasn't going to let them die.

They were crouched on the floor, at the far wall. I screamed out to them, realized that fear had paralyzed them. That's when I scooped the boy up in my arms and was trying to put the girl's arm around my waist so that I could somehow drag her out. That's when Fredrich showed up, and grabbed her.

I remember the desperate urge to survive. To make it out with all of us. We forced our way through the thick wall of smoke, coughing, struggling to breathe, my arm on fire. And then I made it out and collapsed onto a heap on the ground.

I now look around the large clinical looking room and see a doctor looking at her clipboard. "I want to go home," I announce.

"You're suffering from the effects of smoke inhalation, and you have third degree burns on your shoulder, sir. You're not going anywhere."

"I'm not staying here." I wince as I try to sit up. A sharp pain shoots through my shoulder. My whole body hurts, but the pain in my shoulder is as if someone has hacked a machete through it. Still, I am not staying here. "No." I pant through the pain, while attempting to turn enough to put my feet on the floor.

"What do you think you're doing?" Kyra stands with a look of displeasure on her face. She has a bottle of water in one hand, and a backpack. "Is he being difficult again, Doctor?"

"I hope you'll have better luck in persuading him. He can't go home. He's at an increased risk of infection and he needs to be under observation."

Kyra lifts the bottle to her lips and takes a gulp before screwing the lid on. "Don't worry. He's not going anywhere."

The energy I've been trying to summon in order to turn my body, dissipates. Kyra's stern gaze has torpedoed that idea out of my head.

That's settled then.

I'm not going anywhere. Kyra sets her backpack down, pulls a chair over from the other side of the room, so that it's facing me, then sits down.

"Leave him to me, Doctor. He'll comply fully."

Kyra sits down.

She's staying?

"What are you doing?" Just to clarify the situation before I raise my hopes Mount Everest high.

"Keeping an eye on you."

My hopes start to rise slowly.

'Oh?' is the question I want to ask. Does this mean something? That she has forgiven me? And then I remember. "The children. How are the children?"

"They're fine. No burns, or injuries, just smoke inhalation. You saved them. You and Fredrich saved their lives."

I sink back against the bed, then cry out in pain because my shoulder touching the pillow hurts like hell. Kyra's up in a flash.

"What is it? Shall I get the doctor?"

I close my eyes and wimp out. I wish I was brave and could face her, but I have never experienced pain like this before. I breathe through it. Maybe the doctor was right. I can't go home tonight.

"Brad." She whispers. My eyelids slowly open. It's the sweetest sound I've heard in a while. Her saying my name like that, without anger. Without snarling. "I suppose I should call you Brandon, but it will take some getting used to."

She can call me what she wants, as long as she talks to me. I want to think that we are back to normal again but I dare not ask for fear of getting shot down.

"It's just my shoulder. It really hurts."

"The doctor thinks you might need skin grafts."

I vaguely remember him explaining something to me, but my mind has been dazed.

"He won't know for a few weeks," she explains.

"I don't care about the skin grafts. I just care that we saved those children."

Her smile is so deep, it leaps out of her eyes. "You did good, Brad, Brandon." She goes to touch my arm, then pulls it away. "I don't even know where I can touch you."

"Do you want to?" I turn my head towards her.

Her throat moves, as if she's swallowing, trying to compose herself. "What you did was heroic."

"Anyone would have done that."

"Not anyone. Not many did. Fredrich went in but only after you did."

My mind pulls out a memory. "You were about to go in there."

"But you pushed me out of the way and dove in."

"I was being selfish. I didn't want you to get hurt or die."

"Stop making it less heroic. You were brave. It takes guts to go into a building on fire."

"Guts, or stupidity." I wince as the pain comes back. My shoulder feels as if its burning, and it pulsates in pain. I need more painkillers but I'm too scared to fall asleep now while I have Kyra here, talking to me, like this.

We look at one another, questions floating in the empty space between us. The answers will come later, but there is a softness in her eyes that wasn't there before.

"I need to tell you something," I say, my heart beginning to thump. Telling the truth is hard but the lies, they come easily—at least they do to a man like me.

"Don't talk now. Just rest."

"But I need to tell you." I want to tell her about Kane, my younger brother, and how we were separated when I was adopted. I want to tell her how the guilt of leaving him, and never looking for him, has haunted me ever since.

I want to tell her that I want to help her company.

But the pain comes again, and I squeeze my eyes shut. When I open them again, a nurse is standing beside Kyra.

"You should try to get some rest," the nurse tells me.

"I'm not going anywhere," Kyra adds, moving her chair away so that the nurse can get better access to me.

"Promise?" I take the pills the nurse offers me.

"I promise."

The nurse leaves us.

"I have so many things I want to—"

"Not now, Brad ... Brandon." She opens up her laptop. "Get some rest. We can talk later."

"I had a brother ...I *have* a brother."

She blinks, her mouth falls open. "Where is he?"

"I don't know."

She blinks again.

"Kane. My brother Kane," I say.

Confusion makes lines criss-cross on her forehead. "But I thought you said ..."

No sibling. That's what I told her. Because the lies, always the lies, they come to me so easily.

"I abandoned him." A pain shoots through me. It's not my shoulder this time, but the recall of the past. "I gave up on him and forgot all about him. That's why I have no idea where he is or what happened to him."

"Brandon." The word falls from her lips like a dying petal from flower.

"I hate myself for it." I wince and inhale a breath. It hurts. Everything hurts. It hurts all over. "I—I ..." The words, the truth of what I have done, that doesn't come as easily.

"Don't talk, rest. We have all the time in the world to talk and you can tell me later, Brandon. I'm not going anywhere, but first you must rest and get better."

She's not going anywhere, and because it's Kyra, I know she's not lying. Her word means something.

I can rest now; now that she is here, but every time I close my eyes the doubt rises like a threatening cobra. I can't help but remember Neville's words, and the off the cuff remark he made about setting the factory on fire. That greedy son of a bitch didn't like what I said about not going ahead with my plans for Greenways. I wouldn't put it past him to do something like that. I stopped him from tampering with Kyra's books. He hates her. I know what desperate men do for money and how greed corrupts. I was one of those men once.

He blames her for me giving up on this. Because he stands to lose a lot of money. Setting fire to the factory would be a way of hurting Kyra, her business, and ultimately me.

Son of a bitch.

CHAPTER FIFTY-ONE

KYRA

"Philip Hawks saved me from one nightmare only to plunge me into another. I never looked for Kane after that." Brandon recounts what his adoptive father said to him when he had dared to ask when they could go and get Kane.

My heart has broken into pieces listening to Brandon's story. He tells me slowly, in little snippets, as if he can only deal with small fragments of it at a time. I don't push him, but listen.

"I let my brother down."

"You didn't. None of it was your fault. Your father is a billionaire, but a cruel one." I don't want to judge, but I don't understand why a rich man couldn't adopt Brandon and his brother.

"He only wanted to replace the son he'd lost."

Philip Hawks isn't just cruel, he sounds almost psychotic. No wonder Brandon grew up the way he did, thinking that money was the answer to everything. I can't find the right words to say.

"I was the older brother," he says, "I'd always protected him, but then I was shown a better life, and I forgot all about him."

Every time Brandon tells me something about his past, it's like he's taken a six inch needle and pierced it through my heart. My suffering is after the fact; he's the one who lived it for real. "You didn't choose to forget him, you did it because you had to survive. It wasn't your fault," I remind him gently.

"But I never even looked for him once." He scrubs his hands across his face in anguish. I take one of his hands and move it away, so that I can look into his eyes.

"Don't do that. Don't beat yourself up about this.".

"I told myself Kane was doing just fine without me, and I convinced myself not to look for him because it would mess things up for him."

"Maybe you were right."

He lowers his head. "Looking him up would mean having to face who I was and what I had done."

"Your father gave you an ultimatum when you were a scared little boy, he prevented you from doing anything about Kane, but there's nothing stopping you looking for him now, Brandon." The name is new to my lips, but I'm getting used to it.

He looks pensive. "I guess there isn't."

We're sitting at the large dining table at his place, with him looking through the newspapers while I check my work emails on my laptop.

The newspapers have blown up and we both find ourselves in unfamiliar situations. Brandon doesn't court publicity and I'm caught up in it for the wrong reasons. He's in the papers for rescuing children from a fire, and because of who he is—the heir to the Hawks empire—there is so much interest in him. I'm his love interest, according to the press. But I don't care about the press. I care about what Brandon tells me and every day he tells me that he loves me.

He'd been told to take it easy for a few weeks, and when he came out of the hospital having stayed there almost a week, I took him home to his apartment in The Water Tower Building.

And that's when I discovered that he had someone to take care of his laundry, chores, cleaning and his cooking.

Of course he does.

Because this is not Brad.

This is Brandon.

He begged me to stay with him, but there was nothing for me to do when he already had someone to take care of his housekeeping. He had a cook, too. But I stayed with him because I had made up my mind to give him a second chance. Someone who puts their life above others, someone selfless like that, deserves it.

For the first few weeks after the fire, we shut ourselves off in his apartment. I left Fredrich and Simona in charge of Redhill, while I stayed by Brandon's side trying to be here for him as he healed from his burn injuries.

It's only now, weeks later, that we are slowly getting back to some sort of normality. Brandon focusses on Hawks Enterprises, and I do my best to take care of Redhill.

Despite all of this, we managed to keep the food nights going without missing a single one. News of the fire spread, and we were quickly inundated with food supplies which was just as well because we had no store room. Local businesses banded together and helped. I knew they would, because people come together and help others in their time of need.

Fredrich suffered from severe smoke inhalation and Brandon had a burning shelf fall against his side. It will likely scar his arm forever, but they saved those children, and that was the most important thing.

While the damage to the factory has been bad, it could have been worse. I try to remember this knowing that our production has taken a big hit. The food storeroom and a couple of rooms on either side have been badly damaged by the fire and will need to be rebuilt again. Fire and safety experts have cordoned off that part of the building, and we are able to get limited production going, but I am worried about how this will impact us going forward.

Brandon has mentioned a warehouse that is slightly further out of the city. He says it has only recently become empty and there is land around it and no other buildings. He's looking into it while I focus on getting Redhill back to full capacity as best as I can.

I had a lucky break happen yesterday when Brandon told me that Emma, his personal assistant, wants to come and work for me. I hired her five minutes into our telephone interview last night. At least that's something positive to have come out of this.

I've stayed with him here the entire time. I was supposed to go back to my place but I don't want to, and he doesn't want me to, either. My sister, Penny came back as soon as she heard about the fire. It's been wonderful to have her back, even though I don't see her as much as if I were living at my place. It's been strange for her to see me with a man like Brandon, but she doesn't know of the complexities which surround him.

It's something I am slowly getting used to, like his name, and his background, and his life—his real life—not the fabricated one he chose to show me.

Being with him is like going on one of those loop de loop

rollercoaster rides. One moment I'm on a high with my breath catching in my throat, the next, my heart jumps out as I find myself plummeting down at breakneck speed. It's new and exciting and different for me, learning to love and trust again, but what I'm feeling is nothing compared to the demons that Brandon has to confront.

I want to believe that this man has changed, because when he told me who he really was and why he had come to Redhill, he destroyed all the trust I had in him.

I've been hurt before. A heart that's broken badly once doesn't heal without any lasting scars. And Brandon doing what he did— tricking me, lying and pretending to be someone else, purely for financial gain—cratered another line in my heart.

But then he walked into the fire, put his life at risk, and saved Stefan and Holly, that's when I knew.

This man might have started off doing everything for the wrong reasons, but he's now come out the other side. It gives me hope. And hearing about Kane made me realize just how much this man has been through. He told me his worst fear was people finding out about the real him, that he was so broken. Being so unloved that even your parents don't want you is the worst rejection, but digging deeper, I can see how much he beats himself up about leaving behind the brother he loved so much.

The damage it must do to a child to be ripped apart from the only family he has can be irreparable. Brandon's past cuts him deep. I feel so much for him; sadness, and hurt, and I am driven by the need to make things better for him as much as I can. Listening to him and letting him talk about the trauma he has kept hidden, seems to help him. It's not going to be easy, helping this man to heal, but I will.

"Penny's going back tomorrow," I tell him, thinking that it might be nice for us to meet up before she leaves.

"Already?"

"She can't miss too much of her studies. Shall we all go out for dinner?"

"That's a great idea."

I'm tempted to ask him if he's considered looking for his brother. It's something I try not to touch upon too much just yet, but I will as time goes on. I want Brandon to have his real blood family back.

Him not knowing what's happened to Kane is the thing that's weighing heavily on his mind and his wound won't heal until he makes contact.

He looks at me, as if he knows what I'm thinking. We seem to connect like this more, as if we know one another's thoughts. "I'm not ready," he says, turning the page of the newspaper.

"I didn't say anything."

"But you thought it."

I place my hand over his, stopping him from turning the page again, pretending to look busy. He's not really reading the paper. "You should stop thinking about it, and just do it. Reach out to your brother."

He breathes out loudly. Talking about his brother helps, but it also leaves him feeling melancholy.

I know how to put a smile on his face. I move my chair out so that I am sitting facing him full on and then I start to undo my blouse.

He glances up, his body sinking as he sees what I'm doing. My clothes slide to the floor and I continue to undress provocatively. He watches in silence. It's a sure way of taking his mind off the things which plague him. I get down on my knees, place myself between his legs and slide my hands into his sweatpants, then into his boxers. Then I take a hold of him, licking my lips and staring up at him before I bend over and take him in my mouth.

CHAPTER FIFTY-TWO

BRANDON

"I would never do anything like that." Neville glowers at me after I ask him if he had something to do with the fire at the factory.

"I wouldn't put it past you." I recall him hinting once that burning down the factory would be a last resort should Kyra not leave Greenways.

"You're the one who suggested burning the place down in the first place," he throws back.

I snort. "I was joking."

"That's rich, coming from you, after the grand plan you were so enthusiastic about."

A muscle in my jawline twitches. I hate being reminded of that. Kyra hasn't told Fredrich or Simona about what I did, and maybe one day I will summon up the courage to tell them myself.

At least I've told *her*. That was the most important thing, to tell the woman I love what my bad intentions were.

"I have new plans for Greenways," I state.

Neville eyes me like a despondent bloodhound, saggy jowls and saggy eyebags. "I don't like the sound of that."

"You won't." I adjust my cuffs as my new PA walks in and leaves me with a wad of paperwork to sign. It's my first day back after a few weeks off. My shoulder is slowly healing, but every now and then a white-hot pain flashes through me. I might have to have skin grafts, or I might choose not to. Having the scars on my shoulder reminds me that I am a 'new' me. That I saved someone and valued their life above mine. "No one is moving from Greenways, so we will never get that land."

"But ... but what about eminent—"

"Did you hear me, Neville? No one is moving from there."

Neville doesn't need to know of all my plans, but I have decided to invest in Kyra's business and to help her. The building next door will soon be vacant. I've made the owners an offer they can't refuse, and soon she will have the space she needs. There's also another warehouse out of the city that I've set my sights on. But, again, he doesn't need to know.

"What about our plans to build the condos?"

"That's not happening."

He looks pissed, his face turning as red as a tomato. It hurts him, I'm sure it hurts him real bad, all that money he stands to lose.

"You have a meeting at two," my PA reminds me, then leaves.

"She seems to be getting on," Neville remarks, amazing me with the speed of his composure. I expected him to have a hissy fit at my announcement.

"She's going to be a permanent fixture."

"You couldn't convince Emma to come back?"

"To me? Hell, no. She's made her mind up. She's going to work for Kyra."

Neville is about to blow his nose but my words cause him to have something akin to a fit. When he manages to get himself together, he stares at me as if he's seen a ghost. "She's *what?*"

"She's going to be Kyra's PA. It's about time that woman had some help."

"And how do you feel about her poaching your PA?"

The corners of my lips curl up. "She's earned it."

I try to put on my serious face but fail. It's hard to do anything but smile when I think of Kyra. We've spent the past few weeks together, making up for lost time, discovering everything there is to know about one another. Making love in every which way, making love all day.

I am in love with this woman. I can't pinpoint when it happened, but she's not only stolen my heart, she's saved me. She's my healer, the keeper of my heart, and because of her, I can finally face my demons.

I am hopeful of a life with her, and maybe even a life with my brother.

EPILOGUE

Three weeks later …

BRANDON

Kyra rolls over on top of me. "That's better," I tell her, my hands go straight to her buttocks. My cock springs to attention, hard not to when her warm body is skin-to-skin against mine. I knead her flesh slowly. We've been trying to get up and leave for the past hour, but I can't. I want to stay with her in this big, warm, cosy bed.

"We need to go," she says, even though her actions indicate nothing of the sort. A wide grin spreads across her mouth as she impales herself on me. I groan. My pleasure intensifying as I watch her sitting on me, naked, starting to ride me slowly.

I can't take my eyes off this woman. She leans over, her

hands grabbing my shoulders as we buck and bump, draining every single ounce of pleasure from one another.

Who would have thought that this is how we would end up?

She falls onto me, our sweaty foreheads touching. The silence of the moment is punctuated only by our breaths, long and slow, as we float down from our high.

"We are going to be late," Kyra mumbles as she climbs off me. "We need to make a move now, Brandon."

I turn my head and glance at the clock. We are late. Damn it. I don't want to leave, but Redhill is celebrating reaching a huge milestone.

Things have changed there, and after the fire the business took a big hit in production but Kyra now has new premises. A warehouse which is where today's celebrations are taking place, but she also has another factory next to the existing one.

Kyra wanted to celebrate things getting back to normal again, to moving on after the fire, and this celebration is for all the employees and their children. She's got entertainment for the kids and bouncy castles, as well as catered food and servers.

She's also invited all of Simona's family, and we're having a surprise birthday cake for her. After the fire she was never able to fit in another birthday celebration for Simona after the other one got spectacularly ruined.

I recall that day when everything imploded. Jessica did me a favor setting the trap the way she did. She thought it would expose me to Kyra and make her hate me, and it almost did.

I climb out of bed, unable to stop myself from putting my arms around Kyra. The skin-to-skin contact of our hot, sweaty bodies isn't helping.

"We should rush." I don't want to ruin Simona's day again either, but neither of us are making a move, standing with our arms wrapped around one another. My condo has become a place where we cocoon ourselves away from the rest of the world.

"We can come back," she suggests, her tone husky, her fingers teasing around my buttocks. "Penny's back. She's come home for Christmas."

My life has changed so much between summer and now. It's hard to believe everything that has happened. "That's great."

"It's nice to have family to share it with," she says, examining my face carefully.

"I can imagine."

"Is it going to be just the three of us? On Christmas day?"

She has touched on this before. She and Penny still help out at the soup kitchens a few times over the holiday season, and I intend to be there with them, even if I have to wear a ridiculous disguise. The press seems to have whipped themselves up into a frenzy with our relationship. I can't imagine what they'd make of me helping out at a soup kitchen over Christmas.

But Kyra isn't alluding to that. Nor is she pressing to meet my parents. I've kept them out of the loop for now.

She wants to know about Kane. Seeing Kyra with her sister reminds me of Kane and I often find myself wondering how things would be between the two of us now.

Kyra often tells me I should try and get in touch with him. I want to, but I'm scared. I let him down. I abandoned him. I broke my promise. Because of my father, I forgot about him. Kyra can tell me a million times that it wasn't my fault, that I did what I did in order to survive, but now I'm too scared to face what might have happened to my little brother.

We manage to get showered and dressed and reach the new warehouse not too late.

"Hey, dude." Fredrich slaps a hand on me and I howl in pain. "Damn, I'm sorry." His face crumples in shock as I try to breathe through the pain.

"I should wear a 'Stay Away' sign or something."

"Totally, dude. You should. You look fine on the outside. It's easy to forget about the burns."

It's always easy to forget when you don't see the scars. "Don't worry about it. I'm tougher than I look."

Kyra and Emma join us. "He is tougher than he looks," Emma vouches.

"My action man hero," gushes Kyra, in a rare display of public affection and admiration. Standing on my good side, the side that didn't burn, her arm slips around my waist, and she squeezes gently.

Kyra has hired Emma and she and Fredrich are working together to get things set up here at the new warehouse. Simona has been taking care of the old Redhill premises while Kyra and I—when I can get away from Hawks Enterprises to help her—are getting the factory next door set up.

Things have sped up insanely.

The new warehouse is empty for now, and there's just a huge open space inside, which is why we're holding the event here. A party atmosphere permeates the air, and it no longer looks like an empty, unused space. It will soon be teeming with life next week when equipment and machinery start to arrive.

Kyra's dreams really have come true.

"I don't believe it." Emma's jaw hangs open as she stares outside. The doors to the warehouse are wide open. "Elias Cardoza."

"Eli!" My girlfriend sounds just as excited.

I stare. "You invited them?" Elias Cardoza and his girlfriend are climbing out of a black SUV.

"I wasn't sure they would come," Kyra mutters under her breath and heads towards them. We all look on as a tall familiar looking guy helps another woman out of the car.

"Who's that?" I ask. Next to me Emma makes another drooling sound. "Callum Sandersby." She fans her face, then catches me observing her with amusement. The name rings a bell.

"Hollywood heart throb," she gushes.

"Neville never had that effect on you," I remark.

"The perks of my new job."

"Go on, then," I urge her. But like me and Fredrich, Emma chooses to stay here and observe things from a distance. Kyra seems to be at home with her famous friends. I'll go over soon, once they've all caught up.

"Would it be too unclassy to ask for their autographs?" Emma asks, searching the pockets of her jeans. Kyra beckons to me, waving at us to come over.

"Here," I pull out a pen from my shirt. "You could get him to sign your arm."

Emma takes the pen. "Him? I want them both." And off she marches.

This has taken some getting used to, Emma in jeans and casual clothes. My polished and efficient PA is now doing a stellar job working for Kyra, but everything about her is different. Her face is softer, she laughs more, she glows.

Kyra said the same about me a few days ago. She told me she'd noticed a change in me. When I tell her that she was responsible for the change, she refuses to take credit for it.

Neville loathes me and my new business ideas, which isn't a problem for me. He says it's just as well that my father has stepped away from the business otherwise he would die of a heart attack.

I don't keep the old man appraised. He's far too frail, and not always with it. My mother looks after him, but he also has private nurses to tend to him. He's not the sharp and astute man he used to be. I don't allow myself to get angry at him for what he did to us, to me and Kane, by keeping us apart.

But what I can do is reach out to Kane and try to make up for the lost years between us. A thought pinches the edges of my brain, leaving a sharp pain to cut through me.

What if Kane isn't here anymore? What if he ...

But that's as far as I'll let myself think.

He is alive. He *has* to be.

I will find him and we'll be together again.

Fredrich swipes a hand over his face before sniffing his armpits.

"They're not going to kiss you all over," I tell him. "They've both got boyfriends." I assume he's salivating over Elias' girlfriend and sister.

"Emma," Fredrich murmurs. "She's single, isn't she?"

My eyes threaten to eject from their sockets. "Emma?"

He nods slowly.

"She's a few years older than you," I tell him, not that age matters. Or social strata.

I glance at the group of people he's staring at, but all he can see is Emma. And all I can see is Kyra, even though there's a heavyweight champion and a Hollywood movie star in that group.

"You were supposed to be getting all set up in the new warehouse, not making eyes at her, or planning your next move." I pat Fredrich on the back.

"I was," he growls back.

"We should go over," I suggest but he shakes his head,

surprising me. This huge hulk of a guy is too shy to be around Emma. I would never have guessed.

People didn't surprise me before. Not even the Jessicas of this world. I had them all figured out; the ones who surprise me are these people I prefer to be around more than anything —the Redhill crew. They surprise me, and always for good reason.

We've also recently learned that the fire started because a gas line connected to the factory ruptured and a tiny spark must have set off an explosion which caused the fire. It was nothing to do with Neville at all.

"One of us needs to go over. It doesn't look good."

Elias glances in my direction as I walk towards him. He reaches out with his hand. "Good to meet you," he says, as Kyra introduces us.

"Great to meet you." His handshake is everything I would expect from a heavyweight champion. I'm about to shake hands with the movie star next when someone tugs at my shirt from behind.

"Brandon." It's Stefan.

"Hey, buddy." I turn around and we high five each other. It's been a while since I've seen the kids because they don't come to the food nights anymore. The outcome of the fire could have been so much worse, and we were lucky they got out alive. They should never have been there that late at night in the first place. After what happened, I insisted on getting Yvette help. Now she has a nanny whenever she needs it. I've also helped the family to move into a bigger place, somewhere nicer and safer.

Kyra tells me that I can't get too involved, and that we're doing all we can to help people, but how can I not get that involved when it comes to children?

The guilt I carry with me is like a chokehold, slowly

taking my breath away. Helping Stefan and his family is my way of doing the things I wasn't able to do for Kane.

Stefan tells me what he's been up to, and how much he likes his new school, and about all the friends he's made. That makes me happy.

I bend down so that my eyes are level with his. "Elias Cardoza is over there." I recall how ecstatic he was on the night Eli won the fight.

"I know. I saw him talking to you, but I wanted to talk to you first."

I swallow. Because when a child looks at you with admiration, and picks you over a heavyweight champion, it's hard not to be moved.

"It's cold out here." I rub my arms. "How about we go inside and get some burgers?"

"Lemme get a selfie with Elias first."

"Meet you inside, buddy."

He runs away, just as Kyra comes up to me. "That boy adores you," she says, taking my hand. We watch as Elias poses with Stefan and Holly who has come out of nowhere. Their faces are all lit up with happiness and they look nothing like the kids I first saw.

I look at Kyra. Her eyes are glassy. "It's never too late, Brandon."

I was supposed to persuade *her,* albeit into doing something that was so wrong for her. But the tables have turned and now she's the one persuading me, except she's coaxing me into doing the right thing.

It's why I love her so much. *So much.* Her love for me is fierce and strong, and I can feel it in every cell of my being. It shines so brightly that I no longer recognize the man I used to be.

The man Neville misses.

The man Emma is proud of.

The man Kyra loves.

"I'm going to reach out," I tell her. "I'm going to find my brother and make amends."

She lifts up on her toes and kisses me. "Oh, Brandon. That's wonderful. Just wonderful."

She's taught me that it's not too late, that every life is precious, and that people can be saved.

I should know, because she saved me.

Thank you for reading THE OTHER SIDE OF GREED! I hope you enjoyed Brandon and Kyra's story as much as I loved writing it.

There's more to come in THE SEVEN SINS series. Even though these books can be read as a standalone, some of the characters interconnect. If you haven't yet read Eli's story, you can do so in **THE WRATH OF ELI**

A boxer who wants the belt, a journalist who wants the story …

Elias Cardoza gets a shot at the world heavyweight title but nobody expects him to win. But this fighter from the mean streets of Chicago is determined to prove everyone wrong. Harper Lindstrom, a journalist from the local paper, has to shadow him for a month.

Elias despises her on sight. He doesn't need this diva prying into the past he is trying to ease.

If you want to read about the Hollywood movie star mentioned in this book you'll want to check out **THE LIES**

OF PRIDE which features Eli's sister, Nina, and the Hollywood heartthrob she saves.

If you want to know when Kane's book will be ready, SIGN UP FOR MY NEWSLETTER: http://www.lilyzante.com/news

Happy reading!

Lily

BOOKLIST

Buy Direct from Lily at https://shop.lilyzante.com

The Seven Sins:(New Series) A series of seven standalone romances based on the seven sins. Steamy, emotional, and angsty romances which are loosely connected.

Underdog (prequel)
The Wrath of Eli
The Problem with Lust
The Lies of Pride
The Price of Inertia
The Other Side of Greed

The Billionaire's Love Story: This is a Cinderella story with a touch of Jerry Maguire. What happens when the billionaire with too much money meets the single mom with too much heart?

The Promise
The Gift, Books 1-3
The Offer, Books 1-3
The Vow, Books 1-3

Indecent Intentions: This is a spin-off from The Billionaire's Love story. This two-book set consists of two standalone stories about the billionaire's playboy brother. The second story is about a wealthy nightclub owner who shuns relationships.

The Bet
The Hookup
Indecent Intentions 2-Book Set

Honeymoon Series: Take a roller-coaster journey of emotional highs and lows in this story of love and loss, family and relationships. When Ava is dumped six weeks before her Valentine's Day wedding, she has no idea of the life that awaits her in Italy.

Honeymoon for One
Honeymoon for Three
Honeymoon Blues
Honeymoon Bliss
Baby Steps

Italian Summer Series: This is a spin-off from the Honeymoon Series. These books tell the stories of the secondary characters who first appeared in the Honeymoon Series. Nico and Ava also appear in these books.

It Takes Two
All That Glitters
Fool's Gold
Roman Encounter
November Sun
New Beginnings

A Perfect Match Series: This is a seven book series in which the first four books feature the same couple. High-flying corporate executive Nadine has no time for romance but her life takes a turn for the better when she meets Ethan, a sexy and struggling metal sculptor five years younger. He works as an escort in order to make the rent. Books 4-6 are standalone romances based on characters from the earlier books. The main couple, Ethan and Nadine, appear in all books:

Lost in Solo (prequel)
The Proposal
Heart Sync
A Leap of Faith
Misplaced Love
Reclaiming Love
Embracing Love

Standalone Books:

Love Among the Ruins
Tomorrow Belongs to Us
Love Inc
An Unexpected Gift

ACKNOWLEDGMENTS

As always, I would like to say a huge 'Thank You' to my amazing group of proofreaders for their patience and support, and for calmly accepting my ever-changing deadlines. These ladies check my manuscript for errors, typos, inconsistencies and strange words and phrases which often find their way into my story.

Without them, I wouldn't have the confidence to release each book and I am eternally grateful for their help and support:

Marcia Chamberlain

April Lowe

Dena Pugh

Charlotte Rebelein

Carole Tunstall

I would also like to thank Tatiana Vila of Vila Design for creating the awesome cover.

Also, a big 'Thank you' to Karn Jones for coming up with the title to this book. It was perfect for this story.

ABOUT THE AUTHOR

Lily Zante lives with her husband and three children somewhere near London, UK.

Connect with Me

I love hearing from you – so please don't be shy! You can email me, message me on Facebook or connect with me on Twitter:

Website **|** Email | Newsletter sign-up